# Maud

A NOVEL

Melanie J. Fishbane

# Maud

A NOVEL

Melanie J. Fishbane

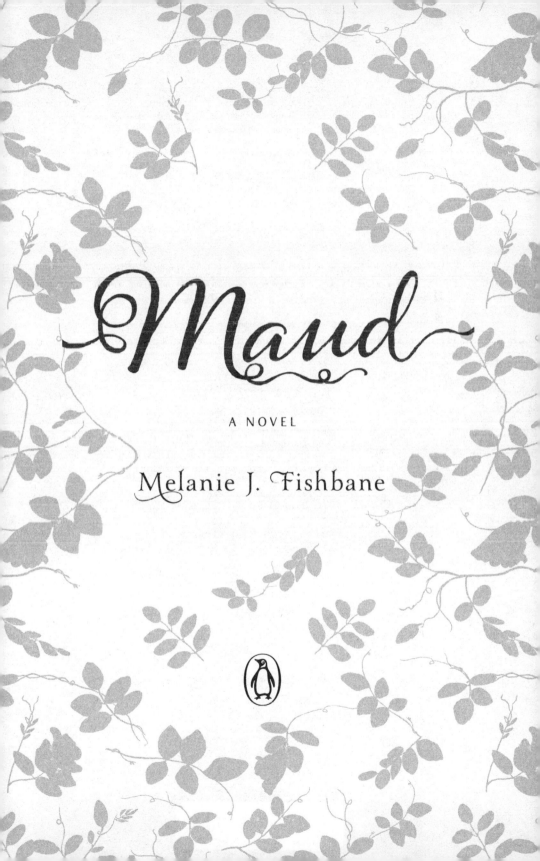

PENGUIN TEEN CANADA

an imprint of Penguin Random House Canada Young Readers,
a Penguin Random House Company

First published 2017

2 3 4 5 6 7 8 9 10  (RRD)

Jacket design by Lisa Jager
Jacket image © Pawaris Pattanoo9 / Shutterstock.com
Manufactured in the U.S.A.

Library and Archives Canada Cataloguing in Publication

Fishbane, Melanie, author
Maud : a novel inspired by the life of L.M. Montgomery / Melanie Fishbane.

Issued in print and electronic formats.
ISBN 978-0-14-319125-4 (hardback). —ISBN 978-0-14-319690-7 (epub)

1. Montgomery, L. M. (Lucy Maud), 1874-1942—Juvenile fiction.
I. Title.

PS8611.I835M38 2017          jC813'.6          C2016-905204-4
                                                C2016-905205-2

Library of Congress Control Number: 2016948322

www.penguinrandomhouse.ca

 Penguin
Random House
PENGUIN TEEN CANADA

In memory of
Zaîda Myer Shaw

I want to do something splendid before I go into my castle, something heroic or wonderful that won't be forgotten after I'm dead. I don't know what, but I'm on the watch for it, and mean to astonish you all some day. I think I shall write books, and get rich and famous, that would suit me, so that is my favorite dream.

–Louisa May Alcott, *Little Women*

But from childhood my one wish and ambition was to write. I never had any other or wished to have.

–L.M. Montgomery

# CAST OF CHARACTERS

*Characters listed here appear in the novel and are not reflective
of the real L.M. Montgomery's complete family tree.*

**LUCY MAUD MONTGOMERY** writer and passionate dreamer; daughter of Hugh John Montgomery and Clara Woolner Macneill

## HER PARENTS

**HUGH JOHN MONTGOMERY** Maud's father, politician, auctioneer; also husband to Mary Ann McRae and son of Senator "Big Donald" Montgomery
**CLARA WOOLNER MACNEILL MONTGOMERY (DECEASED) (1853–1876)** Maud's much-loved mother; daughter of Lucy and Alexander Macneill; died of tuberculosis when Maud was twenty-one months old

## MAUD'S FATHER'S FAMILY: THE MONTGOMERYS
(in order of appearance)

**SENATOR "BIG DONALD" MONTGOMERY** Maud's grandfather; appointed to the Senate of Canada in 1873 when Prince Edward Island joined Confederation
**HUGH JOHN MONTGOMERY** Maud's father
**MARY ANN MCRAE MONTGOMERY** Maud's stepmother
**KATIE MONTGOMERY** Maud's half-sister
**BRUCE MONTGOMERY** Maud's half-brother; born while she was in Prince Albert

## MAUD'S MOTHER'S FAMILY: THE MACNEILLS
(in order of appearance)

**LUCY WOOLNER MACNEILL** Maud's maternal grandmother; postmistress

**ALEXANDER MACNEILL** Maud's maternal grandfather; farmer and postmaster

**UNCLE JOHN FRANKLIN MACNEILL** Maud's uncle; Clara's oldest brother; farmer

**LUCY (LU) MACNEILL** Uncle John Franklin's oldest daughter; Maud's cousin and friend

**MRS. MARY BUNTAIN MACNEILL** Maud's cousin and Pensie's mother

## MAUD'S BOSOM FRIENDS
(in order of appearance)

**MOLLIE (AMANDA) MACNEILL** Maud's third cousin and best friend; one of the Four Musketeers

**PENSIE MACNEILL** Maud's second cousin and best friend

**LAURA PRITCHARD** Will Pritchard's younger sister; Maud's best friend in Prince Albert

## MAUD'S SUITORS
(in order of appearance)

**NATE (SNIP) SPURR LOCKHART** son of Mrs. Nancy Lockhart Spurr and stepson to the Baptist minister, Reverend John Church Spurr; one of the Four Musketeers

**WILL PRITCHARD** older brother to Laura

**JOHN MUSTARD** Prince Albert's high school teacher; friend of Maud's stepmother, Mary Ann McRae from Ontario

# OF THE ISLAND

## THE CAMPBELLS (PARK CORNER)

**AUNT ANNIE LAURA MACNEILL CAMPBELL** Maud's favorite aunt; Clara's older sister

**UNCLE JOHN CAMPBELL** Maud's other favorite uncle; farmer

**ANNIE AND JOHN CAMPBELL'S CHILDREN AND MAUD'S FIRST COUSINS** Clara, Stella, George, Fredericka (Frede)

## THE MACNEILL MONTGOMERYS (MALPEQUE)

**AUNT (MARY) EMILY MACNEILL MONTGOMERY** Maud's aunt; Clara's youngest sister; took care of Maud when Clara died

**UNCLE JOHN MALCOLM MONTGOMERY** Maud's uncle and her father's cousin

## CAVENDISH SCHOOL
(In order of appearance)

**MISS HATTIE GORDON** new school teacher; Maud's first advocate

**MISS "IZZIE" ROBINSON** Maud's old school teacher

**JACK (SNAP) LAIRD** Nate Lockhart's best friend; one of the Four Musketeers

**CLEMMIE MACNEILL** Maud's archnemesis and fair-weather friend

**ANNIE MACNEILL** Clemmie's sometimes best friend; Maud's nemesis

**NELLIE CLARK, MAMIE SIMPSON** followers of Clemmie and Annie (respectively)

**AUSTIN LAIRD** Jack's energetic, exuberant younger brother

## CAVENDISH VILLAGERS

**REVEREND W.P. ARCHIBALD** minister of the Cavendish Presbyterian Church

**MRS. ELVIRA SIMPSON** member of the Presbyterian Church

**MRS. MATILDA CLARK** member of the Presbyterian Church

**MRS. NANCY LOCKHART SPURR** Nate Lockhart's mother; Maud's organ teacher; wife of Baptist minister, Reverend John Church Spurr

## OF PRINCE ALBERT

### THE MCTAGGARTS
(in order of appearance)

**MR. JOHN MCTAGGART** Mary Ann McRae Montgomery's step-father; Hugh John Montgomery's father-in-law; land agent for Prince Albert

**MRS. MARY MCTAGGART** Mary Ann McRae Montgomery's mother

**ANNIE MCTAGGART** Mary Ann McRae Montgomery's younger stepsister

### THE PRITCHARDS/KENNEDYS
(in order of appearance)

**AUNT KENNEDY** Laura and Will's aunt; lives next door to the Montgomery's

**RICHARD PRITCHARD** Will and Laura's father; rancher and businessman

**MRS. CHRISTINE GUNN PRITCHARD** Will and Laura's mother

## THE STOVELS

**MRS. MARY MACKENZIE STOVEL** Mary Ann McTaggart's niece; director of the Prince Albert Presbyterian Church's Christmas concert

**DR. STOVEL** Prince Albert dentist; just married to Mrs. Stovel and interested in Maud's writing

## PRINCE ALBERT HIGH SCHOOL
(in order of appearance)

**TROUBLEMAKERS** Tom Clark, Arthur Jardine, Bertie Jardine, Willie MacBeath, Joe MacDonald, Douglas Maveety

**FRANK ROBERTSON** Will Pritchard's friend

## PRINCE ALBERT TOWN MEMBERS
(in order of appearance)

**EDITH (EDIE) SKELTON** Montgomery family's maid and Maud's friend; from Battleford, Saskatchewan

**LOTTIE STEWART** Maud's friend from church

**ALEXENA MACGREGOR** Maud's friend from church

**ANDREW AGNEW** one of Laura Pritchard's suitors; helps his father manage the local store

**J.D. MAVEETY** editor and publisher of the *Prince Albert Times*

**REVEREND ROCHESTER** takes over the Presbyterian Church after Reverend Jardine leaves; organizes the weekly Bible Study

**MRS. ROCHESTER** wife of the Presbyterian minister; organizes the Sunday School

# BOOK ONE

## *Maud of Cavendish*

CAVENDISH, PRINCE EDWARD ISLAND, 1889–1890

For lands have personalities just as well as human beings; and to know that personality you must live in the land and companion it, and draw sustenance of body and spirit from it; so only can you really know a land and be known of it.

–L.M. Montgomery, "The Alpine Path"

# CHAPTER ONE

S he couldn't breathe. Sweat pooled under the weight of her long hair, soaking her lace collar. The thin gold ring she always wore on her right hand strangled her swelling index finger. She tried twisting it, but it was stuck.

"Stop fidgeting, Maud," her grandmother whispered as she discreetly nudged Maud's grandfather, who was dozing through Reverend Archibald's sermon on the prodigal son. Grandfather grunted awake. "Honestly, I'm surprised at the both of you. This is no way for a Macneill to behave in church." Grandfather sat straighter, and Maud cleared her throat so she wouldn't laugh.

Of course the heat did not fuss Grandma Macneill. Just like the black net that hid her graying hair, she was able to hide her emotions: an ability Grandma was always reminding Maud she sorely lacked. Grandma said Maud was too sensitive, wearing her feelings on the surface like the red sand on the Island shore. And Grandma was most likely right. She was right about everything.

Maud muttered an apology, taking a quick look back at the rest of the congregation at Cavendish's Presbyterian Church from their pew, always second from the front on the left-hand side. The Clarks, Simpsons, and Macneills were all present, as they were every Sunday, to give thanks—and also to take note of who was present, who was absent, and who was caught sleeping during the reverend's sermon. Maud loved to think about how she might describe them if she put them in one of her stories.

They were most definitely watching her—particularly the clan matriarchs, Mrs. Elvira Simpson and Mrs. Matilda Clark. Maud had seen them stare at her when she had followed her grandparents into church that morning.

Maud knew what they were thinking. Hadn't she left Cavendish rather suddenly over some business with that schoolteacher Miss "Izzie" Robinson six months ago? It was certainly no surprise the flighty, overly sensitive (and frankly queer) child of the dearly departed Clara Macneill and her irresponsible husband, Hugh John Montgomery, would act that way. There was no escaping it; it was in her blood.

It was true that Maud had left six months ago to live with her Aunt Emily and Uncle John Malcolm Montgomery in Malpeque and then with her Aunt Annie and Uncle John Campbell in Park Corner. What wasn't true were the particular circumstances people believed—and there was nothing she could do about it.

Now Maud was back with her Grandma and Grandfather Macneill, her mother's parents, on their farm in Cavendish, Prince Edward Island, a small village of about forty families, on the North Shore, where everyone knew everyone's business. She had spent the summer with her merry Campbell cousins, but now was back to Grandma's lectures, uncomfortable dresses, and a new school year with a new teacher.

Maud stared ahead at a straw hat of lush summer flowers sitting on top of a mound of curly blond hair. Underneath it was her best friend, Mollie, who had the privilege of sitting in her parents' pew in the front row with the new teacher. Miss Gordon appeared to be listening attentively to the reverend's sermon. She had just arrived in Cavendish that week, after the last teacher, Miss Robinson, had finally left during the summer. Maud hoped she would get a chance to prove herself to the new teacher. Even though her grandfather had strong feelings about women teachers ("another confounded female teacher," Maud had heard him mutter as they passed Miss Gordon on the way into the church that morning), a teacher still held an important place in the community: people respected your opinion—something Maud had learned the hard way earlier that year.

Mollie turned her head discreetly to catch Maud's eye and, in her typical overdramatic fashion, mimed fanning herself. Maud returned the action with an overly dramatic grin, earning a firm tsk from her grandmother. Maud stifled a giggle and gazed out the window, which overlooked the slope of the western hill, and tried to imagine a cool breeze blowing through the chapel, clearing away the judgment. She longed to run down to the red sandy shore, strip off her stockings—she didn't even want to think about what was happening to her poor black stockings—and jump into the Gulf. The air was as stifling as what awaited her when she got home: an afternoon of reading the Bible in quiet contemplation and the arrival of her mother's brother, Uncle John Franklin, and his family for supper—although at least her cousin Lu would be there.

Maud turned her attention to the front. She had no idea what Reverend Archibald was talking about; her thoughts drifted back to what Mollie had said before church—that she had news. Mollie always had the best news.

Resisting the urge to tap her best friend on the shoulder, Maud quickly looked over at her cousin Pensie, sitting in the pew across the aisle. At sixteen, Pensie could wear her wavy auburn hair in the latest fashion on top of her head, and she sported fringe bangs that accentuated her long chin and big brown eyes. Alas, being only fourteen, Maud wasn't allowed to put her hair up, and she was forced to live under the weight of it. Thankfully, Grandma had allowed her to tie it in two little ribbons clipped behind her head so it was off her face.

At long last, the service came to an end. Had her grandmother not been there, Maud would have pushed through the congregation and raced down the stairs, where there was space to breathe. As it was Sunday—and Grandma was there—Maud walked with what she hoped was graceful civility, as befitted a child of the Macneill clan, to the cemetery in front of the church, managing to find the welcome shade of a tree while she waited for her friends . . . and Mollie's news.

Maud leaned her head against the coarse bark and closed her eyes, trying to shut out the murmurs of people filing their way out of the church, but she couldn't help but overhear the talk around her.

"I heard she had hysterics in the schoolyard," Mrs. Simpson said. "That's what my daughter Mamie told me."

Of course Mamie would tell her mother some falsehood. She was one of the girls that followed Maud's nemesis, Clemmie Macneill.

"I'm not surprised, given . . . everything," Mrs. Clark said. "I hope that new school teacher knows how to handle an emotional child like Maud Montgomery."

"It's the Montgomery side, I'm sure," Mrs. Simpson said.

Maud scraped at the tree. How dare they speak about Father when he wasn't here to defend himself! She was both a Montgomery and a Macneill, which was why she would not lower herself by marching over to those women and telling them to mind their own business. No. She would pretend to ignore them.

"You certainly got out quickly," a familiar voice said.

Maud opened her eyes and sighed. "That heat was unbearable, Pensie. I couldn't stand it any longer."

"That's not a dignified way to behave," Pensie said, in a perfect imitation of Maud's grandmother, right down to the very stern look, but they couldn't keep straight faces for very long and started giggling.

Close cousins who lived only a few minutes' walk from each other, Maud and Pensie had been friends their whole lives, sometimes writing letters more than twice a day, which Maud kept in the small trunk at the foot of her bed. But since Maud had been away, and Pensie was no longer attending school, the letters were becoming less frequent. They rarely quarreled, but Maud wondered if anything was wrong. Just now, though, Pensie was behaving the same as she always had. Everything would go back to normal now that she was back, Maud reassured herself.

"I was beginning to think that the reverend was going to keep us cooped up in that heat all day." Maud looked past her cousin's shoulder to see Mollie smiling at her as she walked up toward them. "Oh, look—there's Mollie," and she smiled back. She and Mollie had been sitting together at school since they were eight years old; right before Maud had been sent to Malpeque, they'd made a solemn vow of friendship. Mollie's real name was Amanda, but they had nicknamed each other last fall when they formed a secret club with Jack Laird and the Baptist minister's stepson, Nate Spurr. Maud was Pollie and Jack and Nate were Snap and Snip.

"Maudie!" Mollie cried out and reached around Pensie to give Maud a hug. Maud hugged her friend back, and tried to suppress a stab of jealousy when she felt the small bustle at the back of Mollie's summer dress. Maud had read in the *Young Ladies' Journal* that the big bustle—a separate piece of clothing that attached to one's waistband from the back, giving it extra flare—had become stylish again. Maud would have loved to have one on her dress, but according to Grandma, bustles were wasteful—"all that material."

"When are you going to give up those juvenile nicknames?" Pensie said, when they had pulled apart.

Mollie puffed under her plush hat.

Ever since Pensie had started wearing a corset the previous year, she had begun to put on airs like she knew everything. It was confusing because sometimes Pensie seemed like the girl Maud grew up with, and then other times it was as if she was entering into that great divide where all she cared about was finding a husband. But it was too hot for quarrels.

"Never!" Maud said. "We love them, don't we, Mollie?" In response, Mollie hugged her again, even more fiercely. Maud couldn't help but wonder if Mollie was doing it more for Pensie's benefit than hers.

"Why don't I have a nickname?" Maud's cousin Lu said, coming up behind Mollie.

"You do, my dear cousin. Your full name is Lucy and I call you Lu," Maud said.

Lu beamed.

"Did you see Jack Laird?" Mollie asked, taking Maud's hand. Pensie frowned down at their hands, and Maud discreetly let go. It was too hot to hold hands anyway. "He looks nice today."

"Amanda Macneill," Pensie said, using Mollie's given name. "You're terrible."

"You're not much better," Maud teased. "Your mother informed Grandma when she last came for tea that Quill Rollings is calling."

Pensie flushed. "He was asking after Mother."

Maud and Mollie exchanged a smile.

"I don't know why you all care," Lu said. Being only almost-twelve, Lu didn't find boys all that interesting.

Mollie tried to smoothly change the subject. "The new teacher is so lovely. She has big plans for our class and is nothing like that stuck-up Miss Robinson. Oh, I'm sorry Maud . . ."

Heat tickled Maud's cheeks—and it wasn't from the weather.

"It will be all right, Maudie," Pensie said, putting her arm around Maud's shoulders. This time Mollie frowned, but Maud didn't move. "I suspect the school board would not have hired her if they didn't think her suitable."

But they had hired the last one too.

"Mother is giving me the signal," Lu said and waved goodbye. "I'll see you this afternoon."

"Good, now I can give you this." Mollie opened her Bible and pulled out a folded piece of paper—a letter! This must have been the "news" she was talking about.

Pensie moved over to Maud's left to block any possible prying eyes. "You need to be careful," she whispered. Maud suppressed the urge to sigh. She wished her old friend could just be curious about the letter's contents, and not so proper.

"That's why I waited for Lu to go," Mollie said.

They all loved Lu, but she was known to accidentally allow things to slip, and then her father would tell Maud's grandparents. Uncle John Franklin was her mother's older brother, but he treated Maud like she was a poor country cousin, dependent upon them for the rest of her life. During family gatherings he either ignored her, or insulted her. Neither was tolerable. But seeing the familiar handwriting of the sender, Maud forgot all about that and was overcome with a fluttery feeling. Thank goodness Mollie had waited.

Maud shoved the letter into her Bible.

More people were beginning to head home for Sunday dinner. Uncle John Franklin, Lu, and the rest of the family would be over at the homestead soon enough and then the long, dull afternoon would begin.

"Maud," Grandma called from the church steps, Grandfather plodding down behind her. "Don't be too long."

"Yes, Grandma," Maud said.

"That's what I'm talking about. I'm just as curious as you are about that letter, but you need to be careful that your grandmother doesn't see it, Maudie," Pensie said. "I already had to be away from you this summer. I would hate for you to be sent away again."

Pensie had missed her! Maud embraced her. "I don't want to be away from you ever again. I promise to be careful," she said.

Pensie took a step back and seemed to be looking around for someone. Maud pushed away the feeling that her dearest cousin didn't want to return her embrace, but then Pensie said, "There's Mother. She'll be expecting me. I'll see you for our walk tomorrow and you can tell me about school." By the way she said "school," Maud knew exactly what (or who) Pensie was talking about—the precious secret of who had authored the letter now in Maud's Bible. Maud expected Pensie to hug her again, but she didn't. Maybe she was just hot.

Mollie and Maud walked through the cemetery's grassy path toward Cavendish's main road. Mollie lived down the hill, near the hollow.

"Thank you for being the messenger," Maud said.

"He gave it to Jack to give to me," Mollie said. "Jack said that he was adamant you receive it before school begins."

"The intrigue," Maud said, making sure the letter was still safely tucked in her Bible.

Mollie giggled. "I tried to get Jack to at least hint, but he was silent as the morning sunrise." Mollie liked to talk in metaphors.

They stopped at the edge of the cemetery.

Maud loved it here at the crossroads, where she could see much of Cavendish. The spot overlooked the red road south to the North Shore and the other one east, connecting her home. Down the hill, facing west past the hollow and Mollie's home, was Laird's Hill, the Cavendish Hall and Baptist church.

"Sadly, it will have to wait," Maud said, her gazing floating upon a particular tombstone.

Mollie held Maud's hand. "Have you visited since you returned?"

Maud nodded. "It was the first thing I did. But you know how I love my little rituals."

"It is why I adore you." They hugged, and then Mollie said, "The first day of school promises to be interesting."

"It certainly does," Maud murmured, watching Mollie walk down the hill.

CHAPTER TWO

Maud tried walking in quiet reverence to her mother's tomb-stone, but her mind kept wandering to the next day at school. While she was thrilled to be back with Mollie and Lu—and, yes, possibly the person who had crafted the letter safely tucked in her Bible—Maud was also quite nervous about how she and the new teacher, Miss Gordon, would get along.

Last year, Maud had been delighted when she heard that the school trustees had chosen Miss Izzie Robinson to be Cavendish's first lady teacher. Of course, back then not everyone in the community had been. There was much talk about women being unable to handle a classroom as well as a man—particularly with the older boys.

And for Grandfather, it was even more than that. He thought that teaching was a man's profession—a profession that was certainly beneath a Macneill. When Maud once revealed that she might want to teach, he had pronounced that "no Macneill would lower herself to be little more than a nanny."

Then, somehow Miss Robinson convinced Grandma to allow her to board with them. It wasn't unusual: teachers often did. Her grandparents made money from the farm, and running the post office out of their kitchen, but the additional boarding income was also helpful. But Miss Robinson's sour disposition and Grandfather's tendency to insult was sure to cause difficulty. And it did.

One evening a month after Miss Robinson had started living with them, Grandfather made some suggestion that Miss Robinson couldn't keep order in the classroom, which was a half-truth, as Miss Robinson could only keep the boys in check if she threatened a whipping.

"If you were one of my students, Mr. Macneill, I might show you how I deal with impertinence," she said.

"The impertinence is your unladylike tone," Grandfather said.

"How about some more peas?" Grandma held the bowl out to her husband.

"I'll take some," Maud said. Grandma gave her the bowl and she took an extra helping. "These are delicious!"

"Thank you, Maud." Grandma nodded over her spectacles approvingly.

"You should come and inspect my class yourself," Miss Robinson went on. "Maybe you would actually learn something, such as how to be hospitable."

Grandfather banged the jug of apple cider he had been pouring on the table and some of the juice spilled onto Grandma's linen tablecloth. Maud flinched.

"Miss Robinson," Grandma said. "I hear your brother will be coming to visit. You know he also stayed with us last year."

This had the desired effect, as Miss Robinson loved talking about her brother, and the quarrel was appeased for the present.

But things between Grandfather and Miss Robinson continued to unravel, which meant things got worse for Maud at school. Miss Robinson would pick on Maud any chance she could and, as much as the young girl tried not to cry in front of everyone, somehow her teacher knew exactly what to say. When Maud told

Grandma, she was advised to stop crying and listen to her elders.

Everything had escalated last March, when Miss Robinson asked the class to memorize and interpret a poem. Maud had spent much of the week practicing so Miss Robinson wouldn't be able to find fault.

After Nate had given his excellent recitation and interpretation of Tennyson's "Sir Lancelot and Queen Guinevere," Clemmie fumbled through her passage so badly Miss Robinson took over and interpreted the poem herself.

Maud was barely listening; her turn was next, and she was quite nervous.

"Do you not agree, Maud?" Miss Robinson said.

Maud recoiled. The class went still. Maud desperately tried to think.

"I suppose you think I'm incorrect," Miss Robinson went on. "You know you have an expressive face that tells us everything you're thinking."

Maud stared at her boots. At least her teacher wouldn't see her face, or the tears.

"Like your grandfather, you think you are all high and mighty and superior. If you know so much, you should be able to do your reading now without any errors."

It was as if a toad had gone to sleep on Maud's tongue. She couldn't remember anything. Miss Robinson smiled triumphantly and told Maud to sit down.

After school, Maud ran upstairs to her room to write the whole ordeal in her journal. Sitting on her bed, Maud wrote as if it burned her to write, but it would scorch her if she didn't. As the words mingled with the anger, the world around her shifted and Maud moved past Miss Robinson, finding herself on the edge of her dream world. Her bones ached, her eyes burned, her shoulders screamed, but she kept writing until she lost herself and found her way back.

After a very awkward dinner, where Maud couldn't swallow her meal from nerves, Grandma called Maud into the parlor. Miss Robinson sat proudly on the green sofa, and the soft lamplight highlighted her grandparents' disappointment. It was considered bad manners to challenge a teacher.

"Did you forget your lessons today?" Grandma said.

"No, ma'am."

"She lies," Miss Robinson said. "You stood there gaping like one of your grandfather's fish."

"That would be your sour disposition," Grandfather said. Maud knew better than to think he was standing up for her; this was one of his insults.

"Alexander, please," Grandma said, and clasped her hands on her lap. "Maud may be flighty and irresponsible, but I've never known her to lie, Miss Robinson."

For a fleeting moment, Maud wondered if maybe Grandma would stand up for her. Reverend Archibald was always talking about God's miracles; perhaps this would be one of them.

"Maud," Grandma said. "Please explain what happened in a calm and rational way."

"I knew my lesson," Maud said, as if each word was sparked with venom. "But Miss Robinson did not give me the opportunity to speak."

"Maud." Grandma peered over her spectacles. "I said calmly and rationally."

"But you don't understand, Grandma!" Maud said, hating the childish whine creeping into her voice. "I did know it, but she had startled me so badly the words completely left my head. I knew it! I knew it!"

"You don't speak to your grandmother that way," Grandfather said, without raising his voice. The sound curdled Maud's stomach, bringing forth the inevitable tears.

"Miss Robinson," Grandma said, standing up. "I'm sorry for my granddaughter's conduct." She glared at Maud. "She knows better than to allow her emotions to get the better of her."

There was no mercy. Her grandparents would always be ashamed of her.

Miss Robinson's pruned mouth twisted into an almost smile. "She's at that age, Mrs. Macneill. Young ladies need to know their place."

Neither grandparent acknowledged Miss Robinson's remark, but Maud's grandmother did ask the teacher to leave the room. Satisfied, Miss Robinson smoothed down her skirt and went upstairs.

Grandma waited until they heard the creaking of Miss Robinson's door shutting before she spoke. "Sit down, Maud," she said, handing her granddaughter a tissue. "You handled that poorly."

"I know," Maud said, blowing her nose. "But I couldn't help it. She treated me so abominably!"

"Shh," Grandma said. "Honestly, the way you talked to her . . ."

Grandfather didn't speak; raising children was woman's work.

"We must protect ourselves, Maud, from gossip," she continued. "That woman is already going around town spreading falsehoods. You're old enough to understand the damage that can happen to a family if people get the wrong idea." Grandma was talking about Father.

"Your grandfather and I will talk it over, and we'll give you our verdict," Grandma said.

Maud stood up. It was as if a gnarled, twisted root was suffocating her when she remembered what had happened in school. And what would happen if she returned. "I can't go back there," she said quietly.

"You can if we make you," Grandfather said.

Maud opened up her mouth to speak, but her grandmother held her hand up as if to silence her. "True, Alexander. But." She patted

Maud's hand and dropped her own back on her lap. "I'm not sure it is the best course of action. Now, go upstairs, and we will discuss it."

Maud listened to her grandmother and went upstairs and waited. She wrote in her journal of how unjustly accused she had felt and how she would never forgive her teacher.

No one said anything for a few days, and for once, her grandparents let Maud stay home from school. Maud helped her grandmother with the chores and at the post office. She took long walks through the cow path she called Lover's Lane, her favorite place, and waited. She wanted to ask what "verdict" her grandparents had rendered, but they were silent.

A few days later a letter arrived from Aunt Emily in Malpeque indicating she would be "willing to take in Maud for a little while."

"It is settled," Grandma said, folding the letter in half. "You are to leave school and we'll make arrangements with Emily. She's had some trouble lately with the children, and I suspect she would love the help. You'll stay there until we decide how to deal with—" she paused—"her."

Of course they hadn't even considered sending Maud to Saskatchewan to live with Father. He couldn't take Maud when he left the Island after her mother died. He had sold his general store in Clifton and went to visit Maud's aunt in Boston. He had come back twice: once when Maud was nine, and then again when she was eleven, but she had not seen him since. He wrote to her, of course, and Maud even had a new baby sister, Katie. While he hadn't said it, Maud knew one day he would come for her.

Now, as Maud stood in front of her mother's grave, she wondered if Father would have even taken her. From his letters, it didn't appear to be a good time. He had originally moved to Prince Albert to run his auctioneering business. But Father had big dreams and went into government too, becoming a forest ranger and homestead investigator. His supervisor had accused

Father of being in a "conflict of interest" for continuing to run his auctioneering business while also performing his other duties, so he and his new wife were living in Battleford, Saskatchewan. In his letters, Father had told Maud that his requests for a transfer back to Prince Albert, where he had purchased his beautiful home, Eglintoune Villa, were consistently denied. It wasn't fair! Father worked so hard. Why couldn't his supervisor see that?

At least she could comfort herself by visiting Mother's grave. Maud stood quietly in front of the white-and-gray-peppered tombstone. Maud loved the graveyard with its old tombstones of Cavendish's founders, ancient clans from the Old World communing together. Everyone in Cavendish was practically related. Her grandparents often murmured one had to be careful if you didn't want to marry your kin—as was the custom with some. By their tone, it was clear they didn't put themselves in that category.

Maud had memorized every deep crevice of her mother's tombstone: the hand with its index finger pointed up to the sky, the "God is Love" inscription, and the often quoted hymn for the dead:

"Yet again we hope to meet thee, / When the day of life is fled," she read out loud.

Even her mother's tombstone showed how much Grandfather and Grandma had disapproved of Father. The hymn was about a dearly departed sister, not a beloved wife and mother. Mother died when she was twenty-three years old, almost eight years older than Maud was now. Father loved Mother, but no one ever talked about how her parents met. No one ever talked about why they married so quickly. No one ever talked about Mother at all. One day, Maud would be reunited with Father and he would tell her about her mother, about their courtship and her life with them before Mother died. One day, she would have a family and a place to call home.

When her mother died, there had been no one else to take care of Maud. Her mother's brother, Uncle John Franklin Macneill (Lu's father), had his family; and Clara's sister, Maud's Aunt Annie Campbell, had hers; so the responsibility fell to Maud's sixteen-year-old aunt, Emily. Maud wondered if that was why Emily now had such a sour disposition; she certainly had picked up her talent for insults from Grandfather. But when Maud was younger, Emily had been kind to her, willing to answer questions about heaven and if Mother was happy where she was.

Standing there with the wind and the low moan of the sea, Maud allowed herself to dwell in memory. No one believed Maud when she told them that she remembered Mother's funeral. It was all Maud had of her mother.

Maud had been just twenty-one months old when it happened, but she could remember every detail. Father crying beside the casket, his dark hair combed neatly, beard trim, his eyes sad and dull. Her mother looked beautiful, pale, like a queen sleeping. Maud had used that exact description in her piece of verse about a queen who had been poisoned by an evil villain. She was calling it "The Queen's Betrayal." It was very dramatic.

The warm wind whistled, and she looked up to see it wasn't the wind at all. Nate Spurr strode toward her from the Haunted Woods—appearing almost as if by magic. Maud felt that flutter again and turned her face to the shore so he couldn't tell she was excited to see him. Being the Baptist minister's stepson, he would have attended the Baptist Church, on the other side of the woods. It must have let out a few minutes ago.

They hadn't spoken since she left last winter, and Maud had wondered if he was still angry with her because she'd refused to tell him why she had to leave. She had given him a message through Mollie in a letter when she was away, telling him where she was, and she'd hoped he would write. They were friends, after all. She never did get a letter back, but the note he'd sent through Mollie showed he had forgiven her. Hands shaking, Maud quickly opened her Bible to read the note before he reached her:

*Dear Polly,*

*A quick message to welcome you back to school. Things were certainly not as interesting with you gone. Now we can get into all sorts of trouble.*

*Snip*

Maud didn't quite know what he meant by "trouble," but the last thing she needed was her grandparents finding another reason to send her away again.

"Polly."

Nate was the smartest boy in school. He'd grown since Maud had last seen him. His ears still stuck out a bit, but his short brown hair curled around them in an appealing way. He had intense gray eyes and a square jaw with a dimple in his chin. He was thin but strong, and looked at you as if he knew your whole story. This always made her nervous.

Maud dropped her gaze and, trying to keep things light, reverted back to an old joke of theirs. "Hello, Snip. Is that *Pollie* with a *y* or *ie*?" Part of the nickname game Maud, Mollie, Jack, and Nate had played involved Nate insisting that her nickname be spelled with a *y* instead of an *ie*, as Maud preferred.

"Why, a *y*, of course!" Nate grinned. "It is the only dignified way of spelling it."

"It is not," she responded on cue. "You know that *ie* is the only way."

Nate cleared his throat. "I see you got my note," he said.

"Yes, but only just." She slipped the letter back into the Bible. "I haven't had time to respond." Maud noticed how Nate hugged a book under his arm. He was dressed in his Sunday best—a fine dark waistcoat—but his brown cap, worn backwards the way she liked it, made him appear more like himself.

"Will I receive an answer tomorrow?" he said.

"Perhaps," Maud said. "If you tell me what you're holding in your hand . . ."

He pulled out the hardcover book he had been carrying and showed it to her. "I must confess, Mollie told Jack you might be here, so I thought I would give it a chance."

"Really," Maud said, getting the courage to look him in the eye.

"Yes. I read this book over the summer and thought you would enjoy it."

"How would you know what I enjoy?"

Nate chuckled. "I know you, Lucy Maud Montgomery." He paused. "More than you know."

Maud's whole body ached to take it, but she only read the title: *Undine* by Fouqué. The title was familiar. It took her a moment to place it. "This is the book Jo is reading at the beginning of *Little Women!*"

He grinned. "I remember last spring you had mentioned being curious about it, so I bought a copy when I went with my stepfather to Charlottetown in early summer. While *Little Women* is a silly girl's book—"

"It is *not* a silly girl book—" Maud said, ready to defend her favorite novel, but then stopped when she realized he was teasing her—as usual.

He held it out to her. The book was made of rich navy blue cloth. On the cover was an elegantly robed mermaid with flowing hair, cradled in seaweed.

Nate Spurr had *thought* of her.

"Take it," he said, stretching the book out to her. "I look forward to hearing your opinion."

She fiddled with her ring. "I don't know."

"I left you some of my thoughts inside." He flipped open the front cover to show his notations. Maud did the same thing to her books, as though she was having a personal conversation with the author.

"You've read it," she said.

"Yes," he said. She twisted her ring.

"I don't think it is proper for me to receive a gift from you."

Nate stepped forward. "Would it help if it was only a loan?" The book lay innocently on the palms of his hands.

A loan. No one—not even Grandma—could say anything about someone lending her a book. Even if it was from the Baptist minister's stepson.

"All right," she said, taking it from him, their fingers lightly brushing over the spine's curved edges. "If it is only a loan."

"Of course," he said. "There's really nothing like starting a new story, is there, Maud?"

# CHAPTER THREE

M aud read over the letter she had just finished writing to Nate and gazed out at her grandfather's apple orchard. It was the morning of the first day of school and she wanted everything to be perfect.

After she and Nate had parted, Maud returned home just in time for Sunday dinner and didn't pay much attention to her cousins, irritating Lu, who finally said in a burst of impatience, "Your head's in the clouds again, Maud." To which her Uncle John Franklin responded, "That's what comes from all of that reading."

But Maud was thinking about what her response would be. She did a lot of thinking about writing before she actually put pencil to paper. Paper was scarce, and Grandma thought it wasteful if Maud wrote something only to throw it away. So, Maud would walk or think, imagining what she might write, and then take some of the letter bills left in the post office to write on. But the letter to Nate was going to be on stationery or writing paper, so she couldn't make any mistakes.

Maud did lose herself in Grandfather's retelling of "Cape LeForce," which he often did during family gatherings. He might be a bit gruff, but Grandfather could spin a story so well that he transported everyone to the old shores of the Island a century ago, when the murderous French pirates brawled over their prized gold. She planned to try her own version of the old Island tale one day.

Maud had written about all of this in her journal during her morning writing ritual, before she started her letter to Nate. Similar to Jo March in *Little Women*, Maud imagined herself writing sweeping epics and articles for newspapers, or traveling to the great cities of the world, and making something of herself. She would be independent, no longer relying upon her family—people such as her Uncle John Franklin—and having to worry about what they thought of her.

Sometimes Maud would write about the weather, practicing the various ways one could describe the wind. Other times she confided certain feelings, feelings she dared not share with anyone. Feelings about being sent away, or how angry she got sometimes at her grandparents.

They didn't understand that she needed to become independent, and that that meant getting a good education. Unless you wanted to be in service, the only respectable option for young women was to teach. While Maud's grandparents believed in education, the only person in the family who was sent to college was her mother's oldest brother, Uncle Leander George, now a minister in New Brunswick. It was clear in her family; higher education was for boys only. Maud was sure there was no expectation she would go to college. Her "scribbling" was barely tolerated.

And, after the Izzie Robinson catastrophe six months ago, it was easier to dream than to convince Grandfather it was worthwhile educating girls. Maybe if she was good in school and showed him what she could do he would change his mind.

"Maud." Grandma opened the old wooden door, wearing her starched, drab-gray dress and crisp white apron. Maud put her pencil down. "You were scribbling again, weren't you?" She sighed. "You're going to be late."

"I was just finishing," Maud said. Grandma shut the door. Closing her journal, Maud stood up and straightened her new green dress, trying to ignore how small the bustle was. When Maud had returned from her Campbell cousins' home last week, Grandma inspected Maud's old calico dress—which had almost reached her knees—and declared there was no way a granddaughter of hers would be wearing a dress that looked like something you wore on dusting day. They had spent the last few days making clothes "practical," meaning only a slight bustle no one could even detect.

Hugging her journal to her chest, Maud walked over to the oak bedside table and safely tucked it underneath a pile of linens in the drawer, locking it shut. Her parents' photos sat on top. Mother was wearing a beautiful lace bodice, her light brown hair piled high in a luscious braid. Maud wondered what her Mother had been thinking then. *She* would have understood Maud's desire for a dress with a grand bustle.

She read over the note she had written that morning:

*Dear Snip,*

*I can only imagine the sort of trouble you mean, but I shall endeavor to stay out of it.*

*Sincerely,*
*Pollie*

As Maud placed it inside her copy of *Little Women* and put the book in her school satchel, she had a daring idea. Maybe she would inspire Nate to read her favorite novel with her note!

Surveying herself in the mirror one last time, she finished by putting on the gold ring Aunt Annie had given to her on her twelfth birthday and went to join her grandmother in the kitchen.

## CHAPTER FOUR

M aud and Lu met Mollie at the bottom of the lane, which was across the road from Maud's grandparents' farm. Maud was sorry Lu was there because she really wanted to tell Mollie about her conversation with Nate at the cemetery, the contents of his letter—and her rather daring response.

"I'm so glad you're home." Mollie wrapped her arms around Maud and gave her a hug so tight she had to keep her hat from falling. "It was like this summer had no sun with you gone."

"There were so many nights where I wished you were with me." Maud sighed.

"I had to sit with Mamie," Mollie said. "And that meant having to contend with Clemmie Macneill. And she and Mamie are tight as ever."

Clemmie and Maud had been friends once. While Maud was cautious of the girl's friendship at first, Clemmie seemed interested in Maud's poems and stories, and Maud appreciated anyone who showed interest in her writing. But after Nate and Maud discovered their mutual love of literature, and Jack and Mollie joined in to make a foursome, Clemmie stopped talking to her.

And when she did talk to Maud, she was cruel. Maud refused to admit the betrayal still smarted.

"How dreadful," Maud said. "I wonder if she is speaking to Annie or if they are having one of their fights." Annie was Clemmie's best friend and—depending upon the weather—her rival.

"They were speaking when I last saw them, but with those two you never know. They're as fickle as my brother, Hammie, when choosing fishing bait." Sometimes Mollie's metaphors made sense, sometimes they didn't.

"It would be easier if you were all friendly," Lu said, stumbling over some red stones while trying to catch up with them.

"Why do you care?" Mollie asked.

Lu sniffed. "I don't want any more trouble. For you, I mean, Maud."

Maud didn't either, but she also didn't need her cousin reminding her of what had happened.

"If we're any later, we're going to miss all of the news," Mollie said.

"And we can't have that." Maud laughed. Mollie prided herself on always knowing the latest gossip. When Maud was away, Mollie had sent her fat letters detailing "all the news" so Maud wouldn't miss a thing.

The new one-room schoolhouse—built within the last five years—stood on the edge of the road, arched by trees. The sun shone through the leaves, giving the school a halo glow and warming Maud's itchy nerves.

"Yes," Mollie said, pointing to three schoolmates all made up with frills and curls. "Those three are as tight as Mother's quilting stitches."

Maud ignored the small pang when she saw Clemmie—whose mother certainly didn't subscribe to Grandma's philosophy of a discreet bustle—Mamie, and a spoiled, puffed, frilly-sleeved thing named Annie.

"Oh, look, there's Snip and Snap!" Mollie said, pointing to Nate and Jack. Finally, the Four Musketeers were reunited.

"I'll see you later, Maud," Lu said, walking on ahead to some girls her own age playing in the clearing.

"What do you think, Pollie?" Mollie whispered. "Do you think Nate will be your nine stars?"

A popular game around school was that if you counted nine stars for nine nights in a row, the first boy who shook your hand would be the one you married. After a number of attempts, the only thing Maud and Mollie had succeeded in was laughing. It was all just as well; if they had succeeded, Maud was sure she would inevitably shake Nate's hand, and that was the last thing she needed: as Grandma had warned her long ago, a good Presbyterian didn't associate with Baptists, and Nate was most certainly a Baptist.

"Good day, Mollie." Nate paused and winked at Maud, who blushed. "Polly."

"How are things, Polly—with a *y*?" Jack said. Maud smiled at him. He was generally a quiet boy, but he had a solid nature, and lovely light brown hair and green eyes.

"It's *ie*," she said. "Happy to be back."

"That's *our* tree," Mollie said, pointing to the birch tree the Four Musketeers always sat under. "Clemmie, Mamie, Nellie, and Annie are standing there on purpose."

"We can go sit somewhere else," Jack said.

"No," Mollie said. "It's the principle. We need to fight for our territory, just like when my brother thinks he can take the last piece of pie."

Maud couldn't quite see how pie represented one's territory, but she understood the sentiment. "Come along, boys, we've got a tree to save."

The boys casually saluted and followed a few steps behind.

"I believe you are lost," Mollie said, approaching the girls lounging on the tree's trunk.

"We wanted to give Maud a nice warm welcome," Clemmie said, in a not-so-welcoming tone. "Welcome back, Maud. Did you have fun? Get some well-deserved rest and relaxation while we toiled away with Miss Robinson?"

The name of last year's teacher made Maud want to pull the curl right out of Clemmie's hair, but instead she took a deep breath. This called for a technique that her Aunt Annie was always recommending: you catch more flies with honey than vinegar.

"Clemmie!" Maud marched right over and hugged the girl, a little too tightly. Clemmie's whole body went rigid. "I didn't know how much you cared!" Maud pulled away and put on her best smile.

Clemmie flushed and looked from Maud to Nate. "Will we be seeing you at choir practice tonight, Nate?"

"It's my stepfather's choir, Clemmie. Of course I'll be there," he said.

Clemmie harrumphed and marched inside with Annie, Mamie, and Nellie in tow.

"Good going, Pollie," Mollie said.

Maud grinned. It felt good to be here, with her friends, showing Clemmie Macneill that what she said couldn't touch her.

Mollie extended her arm. "Come. Let's get our seats by the window."

Taking her friend's arm, Maud started to walk inside, but Nate moved to stop her. "Polly," he whispered. "Do you have something for me?"

"We're going to be late," she said. She was having second thoughts about giving him the note. She had promised Pensie that she would be careful so she wouldn't be sent away again. Still, she and Nate were only friends.

Oblivious, Jack had already entered school. Mollie dropped Maud's arm and whispered, "I'll meet you inside."

"Have you read *Undine* yet?" Nate said, dangling his books loosely in front of him.

"You just gave it to me yesterday," she said, giggling. "As the son "

"Stepson."

"Stepson, then, of a minister. You know one only reads the Bible or sermons on the Lord's Day."

Nate cleared his throat.

Was it possible for someone to have such perfect freckles?

"So."

"So."

"We'd better go inside." She turned to go in, but then paused and spun back around. "I do have something for you."

"Do you?" His ears perked up when he grinned.

Maud reached into her satchel and pulled out her copy of *Little Women*. "It is only fair we exchange books." She held onto it. To lend him her favorite book was almost too intimate. She had underlined moving passages. Perhaps it would reveal too much. But she knew by the way he was looking at her now and the book in her hands that she could trust him. "This is my favorite book," she said out loud, as if to make it clear to both of them what she was doing. "And while you might think it is silly—"

"I only said—"

"I know what you said." She paused. "But I would like to sway your opinion."

Their fingers brushed together as he took it. "I look forward to having it swayed," he said.

# CHAPTER FIVE

As Maud and Nate went inside, she was relieved to find that not much had changed in the new schoolhouse: five rows of desks neatly lined across the room, which smelled like sunshine, polish, and chalk. The younger children sat in the front row, while the older ones sat toward the back.

Mollie waved them over. Maud gladly took the seat beside her, and Nate took his seat beside Jack, behind them. Clemmie's group—Annie, Mamie, and Nellie—sat in front of Maud, while Lu was in the second row with the others in her level.

Maud couldn't believe she had been so bold, lending Nate her favorite book. Would Nate get any silly ideas? Perhaps see himself as her Laurie, the wealthy boy next door who came from away? She certainly couldn't ask for it back now. There would be too many questions. She would put it out of her mind. But Nate joking with Jack behind her was rather distracting.

Miss Gordon turned around and clapped her hands, bringing the class to order. She wore her hair stylishly in a tight bun on top of her head, and was dressed in a long brown skirt with a matching high-necked bodice. She had nothing of Miss Robinson's sourness, and there was a wise mischievousness about her that

Maud found immediately appealing. Yes, Miss Gordon was definitely her style.

As she walked toward them, her skirt brushed the floor. "I'm looking forward to learning how to help you succeed in the future." It felt as if her new teacher was looking directly at her.

Deep down, Maud worried that if she didn't get married, the responsibility of taking care of her grandparents would fall to her. And while it was expected she would marry, the idea wasn't appealing. Not right now anyway. Her Aunt Emily had appeared so tired when Maud had visited her in Malpeque, tending to her children, her husband, and her home. Maud wanted to see things, do things, and write about those things. She wasn't sure yet how, but if Louisa May Alcott, who had fewer opportunities than she did, could do it, maybe, just maybe, Maud could write too.

"Lucy Maud Montgomery."

Maud cleared her throat. "Present." She paused. "But everyone calls me Maud."

"Of course." Miss Gordon penned something in her notebook and continued to call names. "Nathan Spurr."

Maud couldn't help herself; she turned around when Nate's name was called, though she tried to not look at her copy of *Little Women* on his desk.

"Present." His smile showed the completely charming space between his teeth. "But, Miss Gordon, could you please change your record to reflect a recent name change? I had hoped my mother would have spoken to you about it."

Maud and Mollie exchanged a look. Nate's attention was on Miss Gordon, but Maud was certain his gaze was on her. "I've decided to change my last name back to my father's surname, Lockhart."

Mollie grabbed Maud's hand underneath the desk. When he was small, Nate had been adopted by Reverend Spurr when he married Nate's mother. Nate's father, Nathaniel Lockhart, was a ship captain who went missing when the now Mrs. Spurr was pregnant.

*Did you know about this?* Maud scribbled on her slate, letting go of Mollie's hand.

*He must have really kept it a secret.* Mollie wrote back.

*For you not to know, definitely.*

*Definitely.* Mollie elbowed her.

"Ladies, can I help you with something?"

Both girls sat up straight.

"Unless you wish to share your notes with the class?"

Both girls mumbled an apology. Across the room, Lu shook her head, and Clemmie whispered something to Annie, who giggled.

Miss Gordon finished the roll call, then paced the floor, making eye contact with each student. "Now, I want to discuss two exciting endeavors. The first is the annual essay writing competition for the *Montreal Witness*. From Miss Robinson's notes, I know you participated, but no one from this class finished in the finals." Miss Gordon's eyes paused on Maud. "I also understand some of you enjoy writing, so I hope to see yours at the top of the list."

Maud had to stop herself from clapping. Because of what happened last year she had missed the competition. Maybe if she won, her family would take her seriously.

"Those who are interested will have weekly writing assignments so you can practice, and then we'll settle on our topics in a few months. To start, though, we can begin with something you might have already written, or you can think of an important event that interests you," Miss Gordon said. "It could be as recent as the growth of the railroad, or something that happened long ago."

Maud was thrilled. She hadn't had a teacher really interested in writing since Mr. Fraser, who had given her *A Bad Boy's Diry*, by Little George, about a little boy who always got himself into trouble, when she was in the Fourth Level.

It had to be something dramatic—maybe she could look again at her piece, "The Queen's Betrayal." She would return to it and make sure it was perfect, with lots of descriptions.

"The second endeavor will be a Christmas concert in December, where we will also showcase our talents. Everyone must participate."

There was a collective groan from some, but Maud turned to Mollie and winked. They would do whatever was necessary to be the stars of this show, or any other, for they adored playacting.

For the rest of the morning, Miss Gordon held firm control over the classroom (even Jack's brother, Austin, didn't dare put a frog in her desk like he had on Miss Robinson's first day) and then dismissed them for the dinner hour. Maud, Mollie, Nate, and Jack went directly to the old birch tree; Clemmie and Nellie sat under a grove of trees on the other side of the yard in deep consultation with Annie and Mamie.

"That looks like my sisters on sewing day," Mollie said, placing her sandwich on the cloth napkin draped across her lap. "Trouble."

"Miss Robinson certainly spoiled them," Nate said, biting into his sandwich. "I never thought she treated you fairly, Polly." He flicked some crumbs off of his pants. "Is that why you left?"

Maud had a hard time swallowing her sandwich. Why couldn't people leave the past alone?

On the other end of the yard, the four girls had stopped talking and were now staring. Annie whispered something to Mamie, and she giggled.

"I don't really wish to discuss it," Maud said.

"If that's the way you feel about it." Nate sulked.

Maud was reminded again how Nate despised being left out of things, but the last thing she wanted was for him to be angry with her. She had just gotten him back.

"I do trust you," she began, "but there are certain things I prefer not to rehash, particularly when there are other ears about." Maud pointed to the group of girls.

"They're far enough away they won't hear," he said.

"I understand," Jack said. "Some things need to be buried, or burned."

Maud gave Jack a grateful smile.

"Fine!" Nate smiled, showing all was forgiven. "I'll be good and not pressure you, but promise me one day I'll hear the whole story."

"I promise," Maud said.

"I wonder what they're on about," Mollie said, wiping her hands and placing her napkin inside her lunch pail.

"Who cares?" Maud said. Truth be told, she did. Mollie would find out; it was one of the reasons why Maud adored her.

"I hate not knowing what people are up to," Mollie said.

"But what concern is it of yours?" Jack asked.

"It's always hard to explain these matters to boys," Mollie said. "They're like children fidgeting in a pew on a Sunday."

"I believe it is wonderful how Miss Gordon is really preparing us for the *Montreal Witness* contest," Maud said, in an effort to change the subject.

"You would," Mollie said. "Always with your pencil and paper in hand and poring over your journal."

"Do you ever share anything from your journal with other people?" Nate asked.

"Only a select few," Maud said.

"How does one get into this select club?"

"One has to be worthy," she said.

How was it whenever she and Nate got into a conversation, it immediately became about things she didn't want to discuss?

"I hope someday to have that opportunity." He really shouldn't grin that way.

Maud needed to get away from Nate, his grin—and the fluttery feeling. She grabbed Mollie's arm. "I want to talk with Miss Gordon about the writing assignments."

"Yes," Mollie said as if she understood. "Me too."

"We'll see you both later," Nate said, tipping his cap and putting it back on backwards the way Maud liked.

But instead of going inside where Miss Gordon was eating her lunch, Mollie pulled Maud along to where Clemmie, Nellie, Mamie, and Annie appeared to be arguing.

"Mollie, I've had enough drama for one day," Maud said, trying to pull her in another direction.

"C'mon, Pollie," Mollie said. "We need to know the goings-on. And this is quite the fight."

She let Mollie pull her. She was curious, and secretly hoped Annie would finally give Clemmie what was coming to her.

Lu and a few of the younger girls were also curious, gathering on the other side.

"You told Clara and Mamie they shouldn't be friends with me because I lied about why I couldn't meet up with them on Saturday," Annie shouted and pointed dramatically at Clemmie. "You know I had to go home and take care of my little sister because Mamma was ill!"

"I know no such thing," Clemmie said. "You're always using your mother as an excuse. How do we know she is really sick?"

"You wouldn't understand because you are a spoiled little imp," Mamie said.

"Perhaps things haven't changed at all," Maud said.

"Mamie follows Annie as if she's the queen bee. And Nellie is devoted to Clemmie," Mollie said.

"You're the spoiled one, Mamie Simpson," Nellie said. "Always showing off."

Just as Mamie was about to rebut, Miss Gordon rang the school bell and Clemmie and Nellie skirted past her and went inside.

"I'm relieved for once we aren't involved," Maud said, as they went in.

"But you both are," Annie said, grazing past them and blocking the door. "You and Amanda saw the whole thing and can be called upon to defend me if necessary."

"And why would we even help you?" Mollie said.

"Because," Annie said, "Clemmie has said some pretty horrible things about Maud and Nate." She turned to Mollie. "I know you'll defend Maud. Isn't that what the two of you vowed last spring?" Annie and Mamie had been there when Maud and Mollie had made their vows of friendship.

"What did Clemmie say about Nate and me?" Maud asked.

"Oh, you know what it's about." And she went inside.

Maud leaned her head against Mollie's shoulder. "That was uncalled for," Mollie said, "bringing up our friendship vow."

"Do you know what she's talking about?" Maud asked.

"No." Mollie smoothed Maud's hair and kissed the top of her head. "But I suspect she's just trying to cause trouble."

## CHAPTER SIX

M aud lay on her stomach on her bed with Nate's copy of *Undine* propped up in front of her, her feet against her pillow. Dinner had been fairly quiet—Maud had been relieved that her grandparents had only asked how her day went, and then went on to discuss who came by the post office that day, and the goings-on.

Back in her room, she had changed into a more comfortable green skirt and white waist, enjoying the solitude. She was sure Nate was going to ask her about *Undine* tomorrow. Truth was, she wasn't reading—she was thinking about how warm his fingers were when she had given him the book today. She had recorded the entire episode in her journal, which now lay open beside her.

Maud traced the etching of the majestic merwoman on *Undine*'s front cover, her flowing hair caressing the seaweed, her strong arms above her head, ready to take command of her life. Maud loved how the paper caressed her fingers, the curve of the spine, and the musty smell of a well-read and well-loved book. There was also something delicious in sharing a book with Nate. She was enjoying the little breadcrumbs he left in the margins and noting the passages he underlined. It was as if they were having a secret conversation.

As she read, she smiled at how Nate had underlined, "It was in sooth caused by a gallant knight, bravely apparelled, who issued forth from the shadow of the wood and came riding towards the cottage."

Does Nate think himself a true and noble knight?

As she turned the page, a piece of paper slipped out of the book onto the bed. She opened it:

*Dear Polly,*

*I'm looking forward to hearing your thoughts on this book.*
*Perhaps we will find a moment to discuss it after organ lessons one afternoon?*

*Sincerely,*
*Snip*

Maud had started taking organ lessons with Nate's mother, Mrs. Spurr, last spring. Those had obviously stopped when she went to her Aunt Emily and Uncle John Malcolm's in Malpeque. She was hoping to start again, but she had to convince her grandparents she was a worthy investment.

She would have to worry about it later, though, because just then, Pensie knocked on her bedroom door for their nightly walk to the shore, wearing her auburn hair down with a pretty bow to tie it back. Maud leaped up, dropping the book on the floor, and then quickly threw it on the bed beside her journal.

About twenty minutes later, Pensie and Maud were standing on the beach in front of the Gulf of St. Lawrence near their favorite spot, the Hole in the Wall, a carved piece of sandstone that years of erosion had made into a large hole one could walk through. The way the tide was coming in tonight, it was dangerous—it was slippery and one could be carried into the Gulf—but when the tide was out, Maud would walk through it easily, imagining it was a portal to another world.

Maud regaled Pensie with almost everything that had happened at school. A few times she considered telling her about the secret book exchange with Nate, but she wasn't up to Pensie's lectures on propriety between Baptists and Presbyterians, so she focused on the argument between Clemmie and Annie.

Pensie gently squeezed Maud's arm and leaned into her. "It all sounds rather silly." She sighed. "I'm glad I'm through with school. Mother needs me."

"Aren't you bored being home all day?"

"No, I have Fauntleroy and Topsy to keep me entertained," Pensie said, referring to her cats. "Plus, as I said, Mother needs my help around the house, now that my sisters are married."

"If those cats could talk," Maud said, thinking about how only a year ago she and Pensie would play together in the old barn with the kittens sharing their darkest secrets.

After a few moments, Pensie said, "What about Nate Spurr?"

Maud pushed Pensie away and stared out to the Gulf. She didn't want to talk about Nate.

"Oh, come now, Maudie. You promised me you would tell me what was in that letter."

Maud forced a laugh. "Well." She faced her friend. "He goes by 'Lockhart' now."

"Does he?" Pensie's brown eyes widened. "What possessed him to take his father's—may he rest in peace—name?"

Maud shrugged. She honestly didn't know. Maybe he wanted to be closer to him. She could understand that.

The two friends were silent, watching the sun set against the Gulf.

"What did the letter say?" Pensie said after a while.

"He was welcoming me back to school."

"I don't believe it was just that, Maudie." Pensie took hold of both of Maud's hands. "He wants to court you!"

She didn't like what Pensie was suggesting. She and Nate were just friends, so she said, "Like Quill Rolling wants to court you?"

Pensie let go of Maud's hands and turned away. "We aren't talking about me."

Maud immediately regretted her words. She couldn't bear it when Pensie was upset with her. Maud took one of Pensie's hands and kissed it. "Forgive me. It-it is . . . ridiculous, that's all."

Pensie grasped Maud's hand and kissed it back. "My sister Lillie says I should start thinking about such things, and so should you. You must be careful about how you lead boys on because they want one thing." Pensie paused. "Marriage. Men like Nate are looking for a wife."

"Nate is not looking for a wife." Maud guffawed. "He's only fourteen! And even if he were, it wouldn't be me. As I said, he and I are good friends, nothing more. Besides, he's the Baptist minister's stepson. Grandfather wouldn't allow it. Next to marrying a cousin, marrying a Baptist is like going to the devil."

"True," Pensie said.

It was time to change the subject. "When are you coming to sleep over? It's your turn, you know. You haven't been over since I've returned to Cavendish."

Pensie sniffed. "Your place is so dreary."

Maud chortled. She thought the same thing, but would have never dared to actually say it out loud.

"Why don't you ask about coming to stay with me? You know my mother won't mind. She adores you."

"I'll ask Grandma," Maud said.

An hour later, Maud returned to her grandparents' homestead and was about to slip back upstairs to read *Undine* when Grandma called her into the kitchen. She found her grandparents sitting on opposite ends of the kitchen table with two half-finished cups of tea and what appeared to be a red leather book opened up in the middle of the table. It looked much like her journal, which was odd because her journal was locked in a drawer upstairs.

"We are astonished, Maud," Grandfather said.

"Alexander—" Her grandmother's sharp tone made the back of Maud's neck prickle.

"What do you mean?"

"While I believe it is proper for a girl to keep a diary"—her grandmother's hand shook as she picked it up and held it out to Maud—"I never considered you would write about us in such a fashion."

Maud didn't move. If she did, then it would be true. Could her grandparents have actually read her journal?

"If you think I'm going to send you to college after reading this." Grandfather pointed. "A writer and a teacher." He scoffed. "Where did you get such notions?"

"What if someone other than me had discovered it?" Grandma said. She still held the journal out to Maud, and for one desperate moment, Maud wondered if Grandma had read the most recent entries about Nate, but the line of questioning seemed to be going in a different direction.

"You went through my things?" Maud whispered.

Grandma's dark collar accentuated her frown. "I would never go through your things. I was bringing up the linens and saw it open on your bed."

Maud remembered leaving it open on her bed and Pensie coming. This was all her fault. She had forgotten to put it away.

Maud felt as if her grandparents had stepped on her heart. Shaking, tears running down her cheeks, she stood, waiting for one of them to apologize for betraying her. But no apology came. The only sound was the silence of disapproval.

Her hand trembling, she reached out to take the journal. "What are you going to do?"

"We don't know," Grandma said. "But we do think, given this new information and how much trouble you've had this past year, it is clear we aren't equipped to handle you anymore." She paused. "Please! Go to your room."

As if watching herself from above, Maud left the kitchen, her beloved journal a heavy stone in her hands.

A few hours later, Maud stared out into the dark night and then at the picture of her jovial father and her angelic mother. What did Mother think of her now?

The crescent moon had risen past Maud's window. She waited until she heard her grandparents go to sleep downstairs.

It wasn't fair! Why did she have to suffer because Mother had died? Maud had never asked for this. Maybe she was so horrible even her own father didn't want her.

Maud traced the frayed edges of her journal's pages. Since she was nine years old it had been a constant companion on those tear-streaked nights of loneliness.

And now with one careless act, it was stained. Tarnished.

Under the low kerosene-lamp light, Maud crept downstairs to the kitchen and walked over to the wood-burning oven. Turning and lifting the stove's element cover, she was glad to see the low embers of fire were still glowing. She threw in another log, and it caught quickly. The flames crackled and hissed.

The journal contained mostly nonsense anyway, trivial passages about the weather. Sure there were some overly romantic notions of stolen moments with Nate, and the dream of going to college, and the sad story of a girl banished to live with her aunt and uncle for six lonely months while an outsider lived in her home. But if she was ever going to show her grandparents and Father that she could be a proper lady, she was going to have to start a new story, create a new version of herself.

Without looking at the journal again, Maud stuffed the whole thing into the fire. It tumbled into a raging dance, twisting and twirling, pages curling and bending onto themselves. And, as the last page disappeared, burning to black cinders, she whispered, "Now no one will know the true secret of my heart."

In the dawn's light, Maud didn't regret her dramatic action. The only thing she did regret was carelessly leaving the journal on her bed. It was a bitter lesson, but she would never do it again.

She hadn't slept well. Her in-between dreams were haunted by images of her journal, burning. It wasn't just the pages that burned, but a part of her soul too. It was probably wicked to even think of such a notion—burning souls—but for once, she enjoyed the idea that she could be wicked.

Maud slowly slid out of bed and reached for her chemise, but her body grew numb. She wasn't ready to see her grandparents yet. She knew she would have to suffer through their disapproval and silence. But not this morning, maybe not even today.

She felt raw and red, like scraped earth. She couldn't go to school today. Besides, didn't Grandfather say he wouldn't pay for school? If he didn't even care to send her off to college, then he probably wouldn't care if she didn't go to school today.

Maud dropped her chemise to the floor and crawled back into bed, crying until she could push the singed memory far, far down, and fell into sleep.

Later, she shifted awake as she felt someone sit down beside her on the bed. She lay still, hardly daring to breathe. "You are so much like your mother," Grandma whispered.

The weight around her heart threatened to drag Maud into the red clayed earth. What her grandmother said didn't make any sense. Mother was a good woman who died too young. Maud was not good, she always seemed to be getting into trouble. What did Grandma mean?

Maud kept these questions to herself when she returned to school the following day. She also didn't tell her friends what had happened. Still, they could all see she wasn't in good humor. Mollie tried to make her feel better with letters, and even Nate sent her a note during French class asking if she was ill. A part of Maud had burned away with her journal and there was nothing anyone could do to bring her home to herself.

Instead of allowing her to go to Pensie's that weekend, her grandparents decided that Maud should return to her Campbell cousins' home in Park Corner for a few days to "get some distance." Normally, Maud looked forward to visiting her Grandpa "Big Donald" Montgomery—a staunch Tory in the Senate who was home whenever Parliament wasn't in session—her father's brothers; her mother's older sister, Aunt Annie; and the rest of the Campbell cousins. Grandpa Montgomery never made her feel as if she was a burden. She admired the two porcelain dogs, Gog and Magog, who regally sat on the mantel in his dining room; they were the first thing she'd visit when she arrived.

But this time, not even the two dogs could lift her spirits. So Maud decided to visit Aunt Annie, who always made Maud feel comfortable and safe. Aunt Annie encouraged Maud's "scribbling," and her cousins, Stella, Clara, George, and Fredericka (whom everyone called Frede), always made her feel as though she was one of them. It was a place she carried in her heart.

As usual, Aunt Annie knew exactly what Maud needed to do. She believed in keeping busy. "Idle hands is an idle mind," she often said, and suggested starting a crazy quilt to get "her mind off her troubles." Maud didn't know if it would help, but she did enjoy sewing. Focusing on finding the various pieces to sew together did relieve the dull ache for a moment. And while sometimes Maud's mind wandered, it felt good to create something when her heart was so heavy.

But when she returned to Cavendish the following Monday, seeing her grandparents brought that horrid night back. She needed to start over, but how?

After school, Maud acquired some old letter bills from the post office and sewed together a new notebook using some string and a scrap of red leather she found in the barn. Then, she took a long walk through Lover's Lane. The light shimmered along the path, beckoning Maud to keep walking. She came to her favorite tree, with the entwined trunk, resembling two people in love. Maud called it the Tree Lovers, which inspired the path's name. It was a truly romantic spot, with a broken-down fence nearby and a little creek where fireflies danced, whispering secrets to the fir trees and maple groves.

Sitting down underneath the Tree Lovers, Maud waited for the spark of inspiration to come. And when, like a flash of inner light, it came, Maud pulled out the new notebook and began writing about a new kind of diary, one that wouldn't be silly musings about the weather.

*And this one*, she wrote, *I will keep locked up.*

## CHAPTER SEVEN

That Friday evening, Grandma gave Maud permission to stay at Pensie's. Maud was surprised. The whole week, the only time her grandparents spoke to her was to criticize: her table manners were abominable, she slouched, and her stitching wasn't fine enough.

But after school on Friday, Pensie met Maud on the way home from school. "I begged Mother to appeal on our behalf and she did this morning, saying that you hadn't visited overnight in so long and how much I missed you."

"I missed you too!" Maud hugged Pensie, who returned her affection with a tight squeeze. It was probably so her grandparents didn't have to worry themselves about her, Maud reasoned, but she wasn't going to question it. Another weekend without their constant judgment was just what she needed.

Now, sitting in the MacNeills' parlor, Maud, Pensie, and Mrs. MacNeill worked on their sewing. Maud laid her crazy quilt on her lap and gazed out the window. The sun was setting, making the red shore against the Gulf glow violet.

"Mother, isn't Maud's quilt looking quite good?" Pensie said, after a long while.

Maud wasn't convinced her best friend was telling the truth. It was her first big sewing project, and she was sure she was making a mess of it.

When Pensie's mother leaned over, Maud noted how much her best friend looked like her mother. "Yes. Lovely color scheme. That mauve is beautiful. You know"—she stood up—"I have a piece in my scrap bag that would be perfect. I'll go and get it and be right back."

"What's wrong, Maudie?" Pensie asked once her mother had gone.

Maud picked up her quilt and started sewing again. She would rather Pensie focus on something other than her.

"You used to confide in me," Pensie said.

"In letters," Maud said, pulling up a thread.

"I still have all of mine," Pensie said.

Pensie still kept her letters! "I hope they are in a secret place," Maud joked.

"Of course!" Pensie laughed. "We wouldn't want anyone to learn our secrets, would we?" Pensie stood up and peeked around the corner to make sure her mother wasn't coming, and then sat back down. "I think I know what's wrong." She leaned over the chair. "You have quarreled with Nate Lockhart, haven't you?"

Maud felt her cheeks warm. Between her grandparents and her journal, she had practically forgotten about *Undine* and Nate Lockhart. "No," Maud said. "Why?" She put the quilt square on her lap.

"I asked Mother to tell me again about what caused some of the family to break away and join the Baptist church."

"Really?" Maud had to wonder why Pensie was so curious.

"Yes," Pensie said. "You deny it, Maudie, but if Nate Lockhart's intentions are honorable, then you'll have to decide if you'll follow him to that other church."

"Pensie MacNeill, even if I do find Reverend Archibald's sermons a bit long, I'm a devout Presbyterian."

Pensie held her hand up. "I knew you would say that, but perhaps Nate isn't as devout. Perhaps he might be willing to cross over?"

"The Baptist minister's stepson?" Maud guffawed. "Pensie, I think you've drunk too much currant wine."

Pensie laughed. "All right. All right. Shall I tell you what Mother told me?"

Maud was pretty sure she'd heard the story before. Everyone in Cavendish knew it. But she let her friend go on anyway.

"Mother said that the break in the family came when our cousins—oh, I cannot remember their names—one was David, I think—married those two Dockendorff women who were Baptist. Everyone was concerned that these women would force their husbands to become Baptist, but they promised they wouldn't. But Mother said they worked their wiles on our cousins to leave Presbyterianism and create their own church."

"People are always blaming those women for leading the men away, as if they couldn't think about it on their own," Maud said.

"Most men need to be led," Pensie said. "Look at Quill. He wants me to tell him where we're going in the evenings. If it were up to him, we'd just sit in Mother's parlor."

"I don't think Nate wants me to tell him what to do," Maud said.

"All I'm saying, Maudie, is be careful. And, remember, he's also from away, after all."

"Yes, Nate is from Nova Scotia. And that means he has nothing to do with what happened all of those years ago," Maud said. "Neither do we."

"It might as well have happened yesterday," Pensie said. "People have long memories."

"Selective ones," Maud said, picking up her sewing, which she hoped would signal the end of the conversation. Where was

Mrs. MacNeill with that piece of fabric? She needed to change the subject. "How are things with Quill?"

Now it was Pensie's turn to blush. "Well, actually . . . Mary Woodside and I have been talking about it at great length."

Mary Woodside! Since when was Pensie confiding in that girl? She should be "talking about it at great length" with her! But Maud didn't want to ruin her time with Pensie, so she said, in what she hoped was the most natural tone, "What happened?"

"Quill has asked to take me to the monthly lecture at Cavendish Hall. Next month's is Reverend Mr. Carruthers's lecture."

They heard Mrs. MacNeill's skirt rustling and quickly resumed their sewing. "I shall ask Mother while you are here so she is more amicable," Pensie said.

"Of course, darling." Maud didn't tell Pensie that she wasn't keen on Quill. He didn't have any intellect and was dreadfully dull. Not her style at all.

When Mrs. MacNeill returned and gave Maud the piece of pink gingham, it did look perfect against the mauve in the quilt. They sewed for a time, and then Pensie found the right moment to ask her mother, who was open to the idea of discussing the matter with Father. It was all but settled; Pensie would go to the lecture with Quill.

Later, while they were cuddling in bed, Pensie joked that maybe she wouldn't be the only one getting asked to the lecture. And Maud made a secret wish: that Pensie could go to the lecture not with Quill, but with her.

## CHAPTER EIGHT

After her weekend with Pensie, Maud returned to school with renewed determination, inspired to speak with Miss Gordon about her epic piece of verse, "The Queen's Betrayal." But Maud never got the chance. When she arrived, Clemmie and Nellie were sitting on the fallen birch tree, which she had to pass in order to get to the school. Clemmie's hair was tied up in a half bun that accentuated her strong forehead, and she was dressed in a pink floral printed skirt. She appeared to be ready for a Sunday picnic, not school.

The two girls hadn't tried to sit on, in Mollie's words, "their territory" since the first day of school. Perhaps this was their way of getting Maud's attention. Although Maud didn't want to admit it, it was working. Perhaps if she ignored their trespasses, the two girls would leave her alone. Maud would display the behavior Grandma expected of her, but there was only so much a person could do when faced with girls like Clemmie and Nellie.

Maud desperately wished her best friend were there. Mollie was so much better at these things and could come up with the perfect insult, but she had sent word last night she would be late as she was helping her mother with her sick father.

"Aren't you going to say good morning, Lucy?"

Maud stopped. Clemmie knew she hated being called by her first name.

"Yes, aren't you going to say good morning, Lucy?" Nellie parroted.

Maud was comforted by the thought that Nellie Clark would never have an original idea of her own.

"She's so rude, isn't she, Nellie? It's clear that living with her old grandparents and wherever she was this past year—probably some asylum in Charlottetown because she's indeed mad—has corrupted her manners."

Maud turned on her heel and faced them. The girls had stretched their legs out in front of them in a most unladylike fashion.

"Unlike your mother, who has blessed you with her unique talent for pettiness," Maud said, "my grandmother instilled in me the lesson of turning the other cheek. And so while I see you two sitting on what you know is not your place, I've decided to take the higher moral ground and ignore it. And therefore ignore you."

Maud hadn't realized that she was going to say all that, but she also had the sudden realization that she was no longer afraid of them, or the possibility of what they would do to her.

Clemmie pushed herself up off the birch and took two steps toward Maud. She wore a thin-lipped smile that gave Maud a creepy-crawly feeling. Nellie followed—standing an inch behind Clemmie—but her smile didn't have the same effect.

"Lucy," Clemmie said.

"Lucy is my cousin's name," Maud said, already regretting her actions. She and Clemmie were almost the same height, but her nemesis showed no indication of fear, whereas Maud was sure they could hear her heart beating. Just because she was no longer afraid of them didn't mean she enjoyed confrontation.

"Maud." Clemmie extended her hand, and the curled lips transformed into a welcoming smile. "I came here this morning as a token of friendship."

"Really?"

Nellie looked as bewildered as Maud felt.

Maud took a deep breath. "Clemmie, you haven't shown me true friendship of any kind since you had your very quick change of heart last year."

Clemmie dropped her hand. "Fine, I was going to warn you about your new boyfriend, Nathan Spurr—"

"It's Lockhart. My goodness, Clemmie, for such an intelligent girl you really can get it all wrong."

The welcome smile fell. "I forgot. I've known him as Spurr for years. A person shouldn't go and change their name. It isn't proper."

"Nate can do what he wants," Maud said. "He is his own man."

"Maud," Clemmie said, more calmly. "I came here this morning to tell you something about Nate."

Maud felt the creepy-crawly feeling move down the back of her neck.

Nellie fussed with her sleeves. It was clear she was uncomfortable with this odd confession. Clemmie turned around and waved her away.

"Aren't you going to tell me what this is about, Clemmie?" Nellie's tone almost made Maud feel sorry for her.

"I promise, I will. But this needs to be between Maud and me," Clemmie said.

Nellie dragged herself away but stood near the school steps.

"So what is it you wish to warn me about?" Maud said.

"I've missed you, Maudie. I truly have. We always had such fun together, you and I. All of those walks home, making fun of that old witch Miss Robinson."

Maud remembered it rather differently. Maud, Mollie, and

Pensie having a confidential chat and Clemmie appearing sympathetic. Until she wasn't. "I recall you pushing your way in."

"You girls were always laughing." Clemmie paused at the soft chatter of their classmates as they came through the school woods. Maud could see Nate and Jack in the distance.

"You're running out of time, Clemmie. Tell me what you want."

"Well," Clemmie reached out to take Maud's arm, but Maud shook her arm away. "You know Nate and I go to the same church."

Maud nodded.

"We have been friends since he came to Cavendish. We go to Sunday School and sing in the choir together. Mother thinks he would be a good match for me, and that I have the right temperament to be a minister's wife."

Maud watched as Nate and Jack stopped at the clearing to wait for Mollie, who was coming their way. When Mollie saw Clemmie, she started walking toward them, but Maud held up her hand. This was between them.

"His stepfather is a minister, but I don't think Nate has similar aspirations," Maud said.

Clemmie pressed her lips together. "These things could always be managed, if done in a particular fashion."

"So what's the warning? You want to turn him into a minister? Go ahead and try. As I said, Nate is his own man."

Clemmie's mask fell away. "If you and Nate continue with this courtship—"

"We aren't courting, we are just friends!"

Clemmie breathed through her nose. "If you and Nate continue with this courtship, I will make tremendous trouble for you. He is Baptist; you are Presbyterian—God help you—and it isn't right. He's one of us, and we will make sure he isn't led astray by your whims."

Maud guffawed. "You're overestimating my abilities."

"Then how do you explain the name change?"

"I don't know." She truly didn't. "I was as surprised as you when he told Miss Gordon. He had never said anything to me. I think he might want to connect to his father. But why would him changing his name have anything to do with me?"

"We—I—think it has something to do with his uncle the poet in Halifax."

"Pastor Felix?"

"Yes. We—I—think it must have something to do with him."

"While I admire his uncle's poetry, I can't fathom why Nate changing his name has anything to do with him—or me."

"Don't you see? He knows how much you enjoy all that poetry nonsense and wanted to impress you."

Maud laughed again, but it was hollow. Would he do such a silly thing to impress her? No. She didn't believe it.

"You are being ridiculous," she said, and turned to go, but Clemmie grasped her arm. Maud stared at the fingers gripping her sleeve, then slowly lifted her head. It was clear from the sternness in Clemmie's expression, she believed every word.

"You will listen to me. Be careful, Maud, or we'll make trouble for both of you. You will not ruin this for me."

Maud shook Clemmie's hand off. She'd had enough of people telling her what she was supposed to do—and who she could be with. Clemmie could certainly try to get Nate, but Maud would be a dignified Presbyterian and leave this in the hands of Providence. If Clemmie and Nate were meant to be—and she highly doubted this—then God would make it so.

"Clemmie," Maud said, "I will not allow you or anyone in your congregation to dictate who I can be friends with. As I've said to you three times now, Nate Lockhart is his own man and will do as he pleases, whether it be staying friends with me, or ending up with someone of your disposition."

Clemmie scowled.

"Although, if he did end up with you, I would feel sorry for his predicament." She turned and marched toward Mollie, took her hand, and then headed to where Nate and Jack stood in the clearing.

"What was that about?" Mollie said.

"Some nonsense," Maud said. "I'll tell you all the details later."

Mollie frowned. "You promise?"

Maud nodded. "How's your father?"

Mollie tucked her curly hair behind her ear. "He's just tired, I think. Nothing that a little tea and sympathy won't cure." Then she grinned. "Come, let's go meet our young men."

"Yes, let's!" And Maud made sure her laugh was loud enough that Clemmie could hear it.

## CHAPTER NINE

That evening, Maud was sewing her quilt with her grandparents in the front parlor. Her grandmother was working on a piece of embroidery and her grandfather was reading the *Charlottetown Patriot*. Maud had to admit she enjoyed these quiet evenings with her grandparents; there was an ease in the silence of measured, productive work—particularly after the episode with Clemmie.

Since the journal incident, she and her grandparents hadn't spoken very much, keeping their conversation to safe topics, such as the post office and household chores. It had been difficult working side by side when Maud knew how angry her grandmother was over what she had written. Nevertheless, Maud still felt betrayed.

But now, sitting in the front parlor after dinner with the quiet of their work and the fire's light making her feel cozy and safe, she felt peaceful for the first time in a while. Maud looked down at her crazy quilt. She was working on the patch that Pensie's mother had given her.

"Maud," Grandma said. "There's something we'd like to discuss with you."

The stitches Maud had been sewing knotted. She sighed. They would have to be torn out and redone.

"We've been thinking that it is time you returned to your music lessons," Grandma went on.

Maud nearly dropped her square in surprise. If Grandma was suggesting that she renew her lessons, she definitely wasn't concerned about Maud's friendship with Nate—she clearly hadn't read the more recent entries about him in her journal. Maud concentrated on sewing to hide a smile. Despite the fact that her grandparents were still disappointed in her, she felt a heavy weight lift.

"I expect to hear you practice," her grandfather said.

"Of course, Grandfather," Maud said as she picked up her square and started removing the stitches. She couldn't wait to write Nate and tell him.

The Spurrs' gray brick house hid among a clump of trees on top of the hill, across the road from the Baptist Church and the Cavendish Hall.

The organ was proudly placed in the parlor where Mrs. Spurr conducted music lessons, adjacent to a sitting room where Nate would study. Maud's first lesson didn't happen until October, and when she arrived after school, Nate was already sitting in the next room, pretending to read *Little Women*. In her previous lessons, she had liked having him close, but now she was very conscious of his presence, and she lost all coordination.

"Maud, pay attention to your pedal and hand coordination," Mrs. Spurr said. "Let's take another look at 'Abide with Me.' It's such a common hymn that you'll need to know it if you are ever asked to play. You need"—she cleared her throat and looked over at her son, who was studiously keeping his eyes on the book— "to focus."

"Sorry," Maud mumbled. She realized how much she had forgotten. Between relearning how to read music, and having to remember how to coordinate her hands playing the keys and her feet pumping the pedals, she could already feel the strain in her neck. But, as she straightened her back to reposition herself on the bench, her eye caught the lyrics to the hymn and she smiled. "I love these words, Mrs. Spurr. 'Shine through the gloom and point me to the skies.'"

"They are lovely, aren't they?" Her organ teacher smiled. "But do what you can to ignore them for now, and focus on the music."

Maud tried, but ignoring words was like ignoring the color of the sky on a summer's day: impossible.

Nate wasn't helping. She pumped; he flipped a page. She played; he tapped his foot.

"I think we are done today, Maud," Mrs. Spurr said after half an hour of dreadful music. "Try to practice your coordination for next week."

Mrs. Spurr led Maud to the door and wished her good night. As she turned the corner to walk down the hill toward the Haunted Woods, Nate whistled and appeared behind her.

"Shall I carry your sheet music?" he said.

"I'm perfectly capable of handling my music," she said.

"Oh, you are perfectly capable of handling most things." The way he said it made her wonder if she was capable of even looking him in the eye without giggling.

"But what would my mother or the local ladies say about my character if I allowed you to carry your own things?" he said.

Somehow Maud found her footing. "What would the local ladies say about *my* character if they saw us walking together?"

Nate paused at the top of the hill. "Why should we care?" he said. Maud thought about what Clemmie had said, and about how her grandparents were finally relaxing after the journal episode.

And, yet, the way Nate was looking at her now—with a little smile—and their easy banter wore her down: she found herself handing him her sheet music.

It was one of those autumn afternoons when the warmth of the sun teased a person into thinking winter would never come. They walked in silence for a little while, the wind caressing the leaves, causing them to gently fall, one by one. They turned up the path past David Macneill's farm.

"I've been very curious about your thoughts on *Undine*," he said. "I was right, wasn't I? It is a Maud book. Particularly because you still have it."

Maud had kept the novel because she enjoyed it so much— and the notes he had left in the margins. It had helped her after she'd burned the journal. Certain books, including *Little Women*, saved her, giving her permission to forget her troubles. And with Nate borrowing her copy, she found *Undine* a welcome distraction. "I did find it quite delicious. Particularly the predicament Undine has put herself in. Keeping secrets to save yourself, and all for lo—" She stopped herself then and felt the heat of the late afternoon sun strong on her cheeks.

"I think we can all relate to that," he said. His hand grazed hers. She reluctantly moved her hand away.

"I noticed you were reading *Little Women*," Maud said. "Was I right? Not a 'girl's book.'"

Nate chuckled. "Well, there are certainly parts of it that I think only you women would understand, such as when Meg goes to Vanity Fair. But, I must admit I appreciated the *Pickwick Portfolio*. We should see if Miss Gordon would be up to having our own newspaper—"

"Or some kind of club where we write stories," Maud interjected.

"Exactly," he said, and for a little while Maud forgot her nervousness as the two of them talked about the stories they were working on for Miss Gordon and the *Montreal Witness*. She was going to write about the *Marco Polo* shipwreck that had happened when she was little.

When they reached the end of Lover's Lane, Nate stopped and said, "Will you be going to the Reverend Mr. Carruthers's talk?"

"Oh, I don't know," Maud said, remembering how Pensie was now going with Quill.

"It's sure to be quite an interesting evening," he continued. They were standing under one of her favorite trees.

"Pensie and Mollie told me about it, but it depends if my grandparents will allow it." Maybe Grandma would let her go. "I'll try."

Nate grinned. "Perhaps I'll have the opportunity to escort you home?"

He certainly had such lovely freckles.

"Perhaps," she said.

CHAPTER TEN

*You must come and stay with me the night of the lecture*, Mollie
wrote on her slate the following day when Maud told her
about the walk home with Nate. They were supposed to be reading about British history while Miss Gordon was attending to the
second levels, but they were writing notes instead.

*My grandparents might not let me go*, Maud wrote.

*But they must!*

*Would your parents mind?* Maud didn't want to say, but she
wondered if Mollie's father would be well by then. But Mollie
didn't have the same concerns.

*Absolutely not!* She grabbed Maud's hand and whispered, "It
will be as much fun as a moonlight dance on the shore. We'll stay
up and talk all night!"

"Maybe I can convince them." But Maud wasn't convinced
herself.

*Ask your grandparents tonight*, Mollie wrote.

During dinner that evening, Maud waited for the right
moment. Grandfather was in a good mood. The post office had
been very busy, so he had caught up on all of the Island news and
was regaling them with stories. Providence might be on her side.

While Grandma nodded along as Grandfather spoke, Maud could see that she was a bit distracted and had dark circles under her eyes. Maud had heard her pacing last night, and she had wondered whether her grandmother was trying to decide what to do with her—how to get rid of her. But it didn't appear as if a decision had been made, so when Grandfather paused to eat, Maud took a deep breath. "Did you know that the Reverend Mr. Carruthers is giving a lecture at the Cavendish Hall this weekend?"

"Yes," Grandma said. "Why do you ask?"

Gathering her courage, Maud spoke with as much force as she could. "May I go?"

Grandma and Grandfather exchanged a look.

"I don't think so, Maud," Grandma said. "We aren't sure what kind of nonsense this reverend will advocate, and you are quite impressionable."

The fine evening she and Mollie had planned was slipping away. Clemmie and her crowd would be there, since their parents would certainly allow them to attend. She had to find a way to convince her grandparents.

"Grandma, Grandfather," Maud said, nodding at each of them. "Mo-Amanda will be there, and we had planned for me to stay with her." She could hardly tolerate the whine in her own voice. "Pensie is going as well." Maud wisely said nothing about Quill.

"You planned, did you," Grandma said, her mouth creased. "Mrs. Macneill has enough to contend with without you two girls being all silly and under her skin."

"Mollie told me her mother was fine with it." This was mostly true.

"Isn't the reverend one of those Baptists?" Grandfather asked, taking a bite of his chicken.

Maud swallowed the last of hers. She actually wasn't sure. Religion was important to her grandparents—and to people like

Clemmie and her family. She was proud to be Presbyterian, but that didn't mean she couldn't listen to other ministers.

"Many people from the congregation are also planning on attending," she said instead. She had no idea if it was true, but she was sure at least it was mostly true.

"Well," Grandfather said, "I agree with your grandmother. You are quite impressionable, Maud. Who knows what kind of ideas you'll come home with."

"I am not!" Maud practically shouted. Grandfather put down his fork and glared; he didn't approve of girls being loud.

Grandma sighed. "Let's think this over. If Amanda and Pensie are allowed to attend, perhaps it is more educational than religious."

Maud said no more about it, but the waiting was excruciating. She hardly slept all night. But the next morning, Grandma gave Maud the good news.

"Really!" Maud said, clasping her hands in an effort to stop herself from hugging her grandmother.

"There are rules, Maud," Grandma said, wiping her hands with a dishrag. "You must stay on the main road and wait for the carriages to go before you start walking. It will be almost dark, and you don't want to get run over."

"Of course, Grandma," Maud said, thinking of Nate's offer to walk her home.

"And do not, under any circumstances, accept any inappropriate requests from boys," she said.

Maud suppressed a grin. "Of course, Grandma."

## CHAPTER ELEVEN

It was a perfect evening at the Cavendish Hall. To impress the visiting reverend, the Cavendish ladies had baked up a spread of their finest treats and were serving fresh, tart hot apple cider. The hall was decorated with fine white bunting and fall flowers.

The Reverend Mr. Carruthers's lecture was very inspiring. He directed his talk to the "many young people in the crowd," saying that just because they were young didn't mean they couldn't do important things, be part of the community, be an example to others. He was definitely one of the most animated speakers Maud had ever heard. Usually when she listened to Reverend Archibald's sermons on Sundays, she was bored, but Reverend Mr. Carruthers spoke with such great emotion that he made Maud want to ask more questions, think more deeply about what she believed.

Maud sat with Mollie, while Pensie sat with Mary on one side and Quill on the other and spent much of the evening laughing too loudly at his obnoxious jokes. After the lecture, Maud overheard Quill ask Pensie why she spent time with people "half her age," with Mary mimicking his query. Pensie laughed too loudly again, but Maud was not amused.

What was amusing was watching Nate and Jack—well, Nate.

They sat a few rows ahead, joking with one another, and a few times she thought she saw Nate turn to look at her. At one point, Nate was whispering commentary to Jack, which caused the reverend at one point to stop talking while "the young men finished." While Nate didn't seem to mind one bit, Maud felt embarrassed, as if she herself had been caught talking.

Afterwards, Pensie walked home with Quill, and Maud and Mollie waited outside near the entrance of the hall for the villagers to go so they wouldn't accidentally get run over by a buggy, as Grandma had instructed. On their way out, Mrs. Simpson and Mrs. Clark greeted them.

"How's your father, dear?" Mrs. Simpson said to Maud.

Maud stood up straight. She didn't appreciate Mrs. Simpson's tone. "He is getting himself settled out west," Maud said, hoping that she sounded proud of him. And she was, even if he hadn't written since the summer. But her fifteenth birthday would be in a few weeks, she was bound to hear from him then.

"I hear he's remarried," Mrs. Clark said to Mrs. Simpson.

"Yes, another young girl he's pulled the wool over," Mrs. Simpson said as they walked on.

How dare these women pass judgment on Father! Maud took a step forward, but Mollie held her back. "Don't listen to those old crones," she said. "They are like crows cawing in the wind. It will be lost soon enough."

Mollie was right, but it didn't stop Maud from wanting to yank their hats off and throw them into the Gulf.

Mollie put her arm around Maud. "Don't let them spoil this beautiful night."

Maud pushed the thoughts of Father—and what those women had said—out of her mind and looked up. The bright moon would guide their way home.

"Shall we try counting stars while we wait?" Mollie said.

Standing a little to the side, across from Nate's house, they started counting, but after getting to just two or three, Mollie started to giggle, which got Maud going, and then they would have to start all over again.

"We must focus if we're going to do this," Maud said.

"Sorry," her best friend said.

"Maybe if we focus on something, we won't get distracted."

"Such as who we want our nine stars to find?" Mollie said, which got them both laughing again.

When they finally regained control, Maud asked, "Is it Jack?"

Mollie blushed and they both turned back to counting. Upon reaching the ninth star, Maud couldn't help but feel like she was on the precipice of something wonderful.

"We did it!" Mollie said, clutching Maud's hand and jumping up and down. "I thought we never would."

"Some of us don't need to count stars to find husbands," Clemmie said, as she and Nellie passed by.

"That's not what I understand," Mollie said.

Nellie laughed and Clemmie pulled her along the road.

After a few more minutes, Maud and Mollie decided it was safe enough to go down the hill. But as they passed Nate's gate, which was across the street from the hall, the boys leaped out in front of them. Mollie and Maud shrieked.

"Good evening, ladies," Nate said, bowing gallantly. "We didn't mean to frighten you."

Jack bowed his head slightly and grinned.

Mollie laughed. "You fools!" She pretended to be upset with them, but then smiled.

"Didn't you miss your house, Snip?" Maud asked, pointing behind her.

"Did I?" Nate shrugged. "It's such a dark night, we decided it wouldn't be safe for you two to be walking alone."

"These roads are in our blood," Mollie said. "I think we can manage." Although Maud agreed with her best friend, she remembered Grandma's stern warning about walking home with boys—and then promptly dismissed it. This was one of Grandma's old-fashioned notions that had nothing to do with what Maud and Mollie were doing. Nate and Jack weren't courting; they were all good friends.

"I don't need saving, but I am happy for the companionship," Maud said, amazed at her own boldness.

There was something ghostly and gothic about being out at night. They continued to walk down the hill, and Mollie and Jack moved ahead of them. Part of Maud wanted to be with them, while the other part was thrilled by the rebellion of walking alone with Nate.

They were quiet for a moment; Maud searched for something to say. Why was it that at school it seemed so simple, but here, alone in the dark with him, she couldn't think of one interesting thing?

"Are you enjoying Miss Gordon's writing assignments?" Nate asked.

Maud was relieved to be talking about school and writing. "Yes! I've just given her my mystery, 'The Queen's Betrayal.' I'm excited to see what she will say. So far she's given me some interesting notes on how to make my rhymes work. I so love writing verse. It is my true calling."

Nate cleared his throat. "I have a calling too."

For a fleeting second, Maud wondered if that calling had to do with what Clemmie had said. "Sounds like a delicious secret," she said, hoping her tone hid her discomfort.

"I don't know if it is a delicious secret, but not many people know."

"Really? Then you must tell me immediately," she said.

"Good." He paused, knowing she hated to be kept in suspense. "I've been accepted to Acadia and will be leaving for college next year."

"How incredible!" Maud's exuberance hid her overwhelming relief. College she could handle, but she didn't enjoy the prospect of Nate marrying Clemmie. "I'm thrilled for you."

"If I'm going to be a lawyer, it's the next step."

"So you won't be going into the ministry, then?"

Nate gave her a curious look. "Who put that idea into your head?"

She shrugged and realized how worried she had been. She should have known better than to believe Clemmie could make Nate do anything.

"I'll be studying for the teaching certificate and then saving up enough for law school," he said.

"A perfect plan." One she wished she could have.

"You'll write to me, I hope," he said.

"Of course," she said. "I will make you so homesick for Cavendish you'll want to race back at the end of each term."

He grinned. "With you writing to me, I suspect I'll be missing more than just Cavendish."

Maud gazed up at those same stars she had counted earlier that night. She didn't dare look him in the eye, as she was a little afraid of what he might see there. She would miss him, but it wasn't fair. He got to go away to school, and she was stuck here in Cavendish with no one to talk with about books. She would become sour like Grandma, or petty like Mrs. Simpson, or obsessed with finding a boy to marry like Clemmie.

"What are you thinking about?" he asked.

Mollie laughed at something Jack said. Maud wished she could let go and not think about the future or what she would do, or wanted to do. Couldn't she just enjoy this moment, walking with a boy she liked—liked more than any other. The realization gave Maud pause and she stopped walking. She did like him more than anyone else. Did he feel the same way? Clemmie and Pensie said so, but that didn't mean it was true. Nate frowned. "Is everything all right, Polly?"

"I was just admiring this night air," she said.

He extended his hand. "Come."

She took his hand and couldn't think. She had never held a boy's hand before. And after she had just counted her nine stars. The idea was both thrilling and terrifying. They walked along in silence, and Maud desperately tried to think of something to say, but all she could think about was the warmth of Nate's hand in hers. Finally, uncomfortable with the long silence, she dropped her hand and, ignoring how he tried to reach out for it again, said, "Let's catch up to the others."

Nate didn't try to take her hand again, but Jack and Mollie had happily linked arms with each other, and Maud found herself feeling sorry she had let go. She knew Mollie liked Jack, and would want him to take her arm, but Maud wasn't ready for such public displays of affection, where anyone could see them.

When they got to the bottom of the hill near Mollie's place, the two boys pretended to toss an imaginary ball, while Mollie and Maud cheered them on. Jack ran backwards, pretending to catch a long throw from Nate, and bumped right into Clemmie and Nellie, who were standing at the edge of the road in the shadows. Maud moved closer to Mollie.

What were they doing there? Maybe Clemmie was staying true to her threat and was spying on them. Or were they taking their time getting home?

Whatever the reason, the damage was done.

"Good evening, ladies." Nate tipped his cap. "A fine night for it, yes?"

71

Clemmie completely ignored Maud and Mollie.

"It was a fine night, Nate," Clemmie said. "So many stars it is practically impossible to count them."

Nellie giggled.

"I'm surprised she can count to nine," Mollie murmured.

"What do you say, gentlemen?" Clemmie said, ignoring her. "Will you see us home?"

"The nerve," Mollie said in Maud's ear. "Everyone knows a girl should wait to be asked." Maud agreed, but wished she wasn't so impressed by Clemmie's bravery. She would never have the gumption to ask a young man to walk her home.

"I'm sorry, Clemmie," Nate said smoothly. "It would be rude, as Jack and I have already promised ourselves to these ladies."

Clemmie shot a quick look over at Maud before strutting off, taking Nellie with her. When they were out of earshot, Maud whispered to Nate, "What if those two gossips say something?"

"They'll be talking about something anyway." Nate shrugged.

"I wouldn't worry about it," Jack said.

"You don't understand," Maud said, taking hold of Mollie's hand and feeling safer.

Mollie squeezed it. "That girl can make things quite difficult for Maud. For us."

"But I don't care what those girls say," Nate said.

"Neither do I," Jack said.

"And if they cause you trouble, we'll defend you like the gallant knights we are!" Nate said, and he and Jack pretended to ride horses and galloped them the rest of the way home. Maud and Mollie laughed, but a new tension hung over the evening, and Maud was relieved when they said goodbye and walked down Hammie's Lane toward Mollie's house.

## CHAPTER TWELVE

The following Monday, Miss Gordon returned the weekly writing assignments. When Maud saw all the red marks crossing out much of her beloved story, "The Queen's Betrayal," she did everything she could to push down the tears. Didn't her teacher like it at all? On the bottom of the page, Miss Gordon had written, "Write what you know."

Hadn't she done that? She had based the queen's description on her dead mother. No, Maud had never been poisoned, but she had seen what happens when an animal is poisoned; the poor cat she had found one day in the barn had taught her that. Is that what Miss Gordon had meant?

It was hard to concentrate. Maud felt as if she had disappointed her teacher and let herself down. How could she even think about writing like Alcott if she couldn't even manage to write an epic piece of verse? She couldn't look at Miss Gordon for the rest of the day.

Mollie tried to make Maud feel better by writing funny things on her slate, which she appreciated, but it didn't help. It also didn't help that Nate wasn't there, and she didn't know why. He had seemed fine on Saturday night at the lecture. But she wasn't sure if she wanted to tell him about Miss Gordon's remarks, so maybe it was just as well.

The next day, Nate returned. While walking down the aisle to give his assignment to Miss Gordon, he dropped his French text on Maud's desk—with a slip of paper sticking out. Maud pulled it out, tucking it underneath her reader, and then carefully opened her reader, placing the folded note inside.

*Dear Polly,*

*Please forgive my ungentlemanly behavior. Being ill forced me to delay the delivery of this message.*

*I truly enjoyed our walk last Saturday evening, particularly that moment when we stopped and looked up at the stars and I held your hand.*

*Shall we try it again? May Jack and I walk you and Molly home after the literary next week?*

*Your pal,*
*Snip*

Miss Gordon had asked Maud and Mollie if they would perform in November's Literary Society gathering on Saturday. Maud had been very honored, since only a few girls were asked. The literary promised to be a wonderful night of entertainment that included short dialogues (or sketches), dramatic readings, and music. Miss Gordon had suggested that Maud perform "The Child Martyr," one of the poems in her *Royal Reader*, because it was quite dramatic and a favorite with audiences. Maud had spent most of the month practicing, but after getting back Miss Gordon's comments on her writing, she wasn't sure if she could bring herself to do it.

Maud stared at Nate's note. It would be a fun way to end the evening, and if she was a little honest with herself, she wanted to "try it again." And if she had that to look forward to, then she could surely perform in the literary.

On his way back to his seat, Nate casually picked up his book and sat down to read.

Maud showed the note to Mollie, who eagerly agreed. Maud glanced to where the boys were sitting. Nate gave her a big smile, exaggerating his dimples. Maud found herself smiling back, then turned to her desk to write a response.

After thinking about it for some time, she wrote:

*Mollie and I have conferred and agree to try it again.*

As Maud finished her note, she heard Miss Gordon clear her throat. Maud pretended to read, while discreetly tucking her response inside.

The perfect moment came when Miss Gordon paired them into groups to work on their English assignment. Maud slipped him the note. In front of them, Clemmie, Nellie, and Annie were huddled together. "They must be friends again," Mollie muttered.

"I can hardly wait," Nate said after reading Maud's letter.

"Writing love notes," Clemmie said. Nellie and Annie laughed.

"I think you're jealous, Clemmie, because Maud and Nate actually find interesting things to talk about," Mollie said.

"Upper levels, you should be setting an example," Miss Gordon said.

The students quickly went back to work.

Later that day, Miss Gordon, sensing Maud wasn't her normal attentive self, asked her to read a poem, "The Fringed Gentian." Maud stood up and started reading:

*Then whisper, blossom, in thy sleep*
*How I may upward climb*
*The Alpine path, so hard, so steep,*
*That leads to heights sublime;*
*How I may reach that far-off goal*
*Of true and honoured fame,*
*And write upon its shining scroll*
*A woman's humble name.*

As she read the poem, it felt as though she was standing on the Gulf's shore, staring past the Hole in the Wall. There were no mountains on the Island, but she could see it in the distance. Her name upon a shining scroll. That could be her.

"You read very well, Maud," Miss Gordon said as Maud sat down. "I look forward to seeing how you do at the literary next weekend."

"Thank you," Maud said. She thought about Miss Gordon's suggestion to "write what she knew." Maud knew of the Island and the stories her grandfather told. Perhaps she would start there? She would try harder and show Miss Gordon—and herself—that she could climb to great heights and achieve her dream. To be a published author.

Her flirtations with Nate were fun, but this poem—the image of that shining scroll with her name, Lucy Maud Montgomery, scribbled upon it in gold leaf—that was her true calling.

It would have to be a secret for now. She would study and work hard, proving to her family that she could do it.

It wasn't as though her grandparents or anyone in her family could truly know anything about it. Grandfather often boasted that his cousin Hector Macneill was in Lord Byron's *English Bards, and Scotch Reviewers*. Maud knew that if she ever expressed such a desire to Grandfather, he would most probably tell her to concentrate on finding a husband.

After school, Maud stayed behind to talk with Miss Gordon about the assignment. If she was going to be a writer, she needed to courageously take criticism.

"Excuse me, Miss Gordon."

Her teacher lifted her head from the papers she was marking and smiled. "How can I help you, Maud?"

"Can we talk about 'The Queen's Betrayal'?"

Miss Gordon put down her pencil and motioned her over. "I thought you might be upset by it."

"I was," Maud said, sitting down. "You see, a teacher had complimented me on my writing. And I thought"—she took a breath—"I had thought you admired my writing."

"My comments don't preclude that, Maud," her teacher said. "You certainly do have a talent. But the story should have been connected to you, come from you."

"I'm not sure I understand."

Miss Gordon took the paper and pointed to a place she had starred. "See this description of the queen, all pale and beautiful. This seemed to reflect you, how you see the world."

The back of Maud's neck prickled. "It did! It is from the memory of Mother's funeral."

Miss Gordon smiled softly. "Exactly." She handed the paper back. "Is there another piece you have been working on?"

Maud thought for a moment. "I have been experimenting with one of my grandfather's stories about Cape LeForce. It's about some pirates who landed on our shores about a hundred years ago. The pirates conspired to take all of the gold from the crew, but in the final moment one betrays the other." Something stirred within her heart when she thought about writing this story.

Miss Gordon must have recognized this because she said, "Coming from your grandfather, this certainly feels more personal."

Maud began to understand what Miss Gordon was saying. It was more personal because she had heard Grandfather tell it so many times. "Is it similar to Louisa May Alcott?"

"I'm not sure what you mean?"

"I read that *Little Women* was inspired by Alcott's experiences during the Civil War," Maud said. "And living with her sisters."

"Yes, very much like that," Miss Gordon said.

Maud thought, again, of the last two lines of the poem she had just read:

*And write upon its shining scroll*
*A woman's humble name.*

"Was there anything else, Maud?" Miss Gordon said.

"I wondered . . . it isn't possible right now . . . but I was thinking of Prince of Wales College. In Charlottetown."

Miss Gordon smiled. "I think you could do quite well at college. And we are heading into an age where a girl needs a profession."

"Such as being a teacher," Maud said.

"Being a teacher would be a practical option," Miss Gordon said.

The light was fading. It was time to go home.

"You have to decide, Maud, how you want to live your life," Miss Gordon said, standing up and packing away her things. "Not so long ago, women were forbidden to teach. It was believed that we weren't suited to the profession, but slowly we are proving those people wrong. And a woman writer? There are some who don't think women can write." She paused. "You have chosen a difficult path, Maud. But I believe you will persevere. And I will help you any way I can."

It was so rare for anyone to encourage her that Maud asked, "Why?"

Miss Gordon smiled gently. "Each student should have a teacher who sees their potential, and I don't think you have been given that opportunity. You're cleverer than most of the students here. And I'm aware of what happened with my predecessor." Maud stared at her shoes. "Don't worry. I don't allow others to cloud my judgment of people."

"The *Montreal Witness* contest appears to be the perfect opportunity," Maud said, more to herself than to her teacher.

"I agree," Miss Gordon said.

Maud said goodbye to Miss Gordon and took the long way home through Lover's Lane, as there was much to think about, plans to be made. When she got home, Maud burned "The Queen's Betrayal" and started on a new version of "On Cape LeForce." Then, she copied out "The Fringed Gentian" onto a letter bill and glued it into the front of one her workbooks. It would be a constant reminder of a far-off goal: perhaps, one day, if she was vigilant, she would reach those sublime heights.

## CHAPTER THIRTEEN

The following Saturday morning a number of Maud's class-mates—including Nate, Jack, Clemmie, Nellie, and Annie—met to help decorate Cavendish Hall for the evening literary. But as they worked, they were dismayed to hear the sound of heavy rain hitting the windowpanes. Would it keep people away?

Maud and Mollie sat at a table making a bouquet of leaves that echoed the rich colors of a typical Island autumn. Each had tucked one in their hair—Mollie, orange; Maud, red. Maud noted how the orange highlighted the blond in her best friend's curls. They had already worked on some pretty bunting made from leftover cloth Miss Gordon had collected. Even if it was gray and stormy outside, it would be colorful inside.

"I don't know why we're bothering," Clemmie said, pinning some of the bunting Maud and Mollie had worked on to the wall. "People are bound to stay home. I know that's where I would be—if I didn't have to be here."

"What kind of attitude is that?" Miss Gordon said, looking up from her checklist. "People have worked hard, and it is only right that their community should show its support."

Clemmie and Nellie exchanged a look but silently went back to work.

Mollie gave Maud a reassuring smile. Maud was trying not to show it, but she was nervous. Tonight would be the first time she'd ever had to recite something in front of a real audience. The whole village, including her grandparents, was coming. Pensie had stopped by last evening for their nightly walk to give Maud some ribbon for good luck. "Perhaps you can pin it to your hat," she suggested.

The jitters over speaking certainly helped distract Maud from the other thing she was nervous about—walking home with Nate. She just had to be sure to wait until after her grandparents had left, which wouldn't be a problem because they tended to leave right away. Thank goodness Jack and Mollie were going to be there. On the way over, Mollie couldn't stop talking about how she hoped that Jack would hold her hand; he had yet to make that particular move. Maud hadn't told Mollie about holding Nate's hand. It felt too private to tell anyone just yet.

Nate and Jack were setting up the wooden chairs on the other side of the hall. Maud couldn't help but notice how Nate's navy blue shirt fit nicely around his shoulders, and how wide his shoulders were becoming. She fumbled with one of the bouquet leaves, the stem getting stuck in her ring. Avoiding Mollie's questioning look, Maud brought the subject back to Clemmie and Annie.

"Did I see Annie and Clemmie fighting this morning?" Maud said.

Mollie nodded. "Yes, it appears they are at odds . . . again."

"Those girls need to be careful to keep their quarrel to themselves," Maud said. "Miss Gordon is in no mood today."

"She is definitely like my father on planting day."

"I don't blame her," Maud said. "She's new and wants to show the trustees they didn't make a mistake."

"She's infinitely superior to you-know-who," Mollie said.

A chair toppled over and someone screamed. Maud and Mollie jumped up to see Clemmie on the ground, holding her ankle, with Annie triumphantly standing over her.

"Yes, the truce is definitely over," Mollie muttered.

"Miss Gordon!" Clemmie cried. "Annie pushed me off the chair." She sat on a chair, rubbing her ankle. Nellie dutifully stood beside her.

"I did no such thing, Miss Gordon," Annie said. "She had refused to move and I was trying to put up the banner as you requested."

Miss Gordon strode over. "I don't know what is going on between you girls, but I've been watching you and—don't try to deny it, Clemmie and Annie—I had hoped you would solve this yourselves like true ladies, but clearly I was wrong about your characters—"

"But—" Clemmie said.

"Don't interrupt me when I'm speaking." Miss Gordon raised her voice. Maud and Mollie exchanged a look of concern. Their teacher never raised her voice. "Monday afternoon you will be kept after school. We are going to have a ruction—a trial—to determine the cause of all of this and you may call upon witnesses."

Maud dropped the bouquet she was holding. She had heard of other schools having mock trials but she'd never imagined Miss Gordon would do it. Maud remembered how Annie had threatened her in September. Would she dare? Seeing how Annie had pushed Clemmie off the chair, Maud wasn't sure what else the girl was capable of.

After that drama, the classmates quietly concentrated on getting the hall ready. By evening, the rain had stopped and, as Miss Gordon had foreseen, many villagers arrived. Mr. George Simpson told Miss Gordon that the hall looked rather "quaint," while Mrs. Simpson turned to Maud and said, "Don't be too hard on yourself if you make a mistake. Not many young people are practiced in public speaking."

Maud tried to smile back, nervously running her hand over the sleeve of her dress. Grandma had helped Maud make a new outfit based on a pattern she had seen in the *Young Ladies' Journal*. While Grandma still didn't approve of the bustle, she did allow Maud an accordion sleeve, because the *Young Ladies' Journal* had said it was in fashion for girls ages eleven to fifteen. The dress was made from a dark green and blue tartan that even Grandma said was becoming. Maud wouldn't let Mrs. Simpson take anything away from this evening.

She looked out at the chairs, which were starting to fill up, and saw her grandparents sitting at the back.

"Good luck," Nate said to Maud before the program started. He went to sit toward the back with Jack. Maud and Mollie sat in the front row with the rest of the presenters. Pensie and Lu were there—and Quill and Mary. Pensie had come over to give Maud a hug for good luck and beamed at how Maud had incorporated her ribbon onto the hat.

Maud was grateful to at least be sitting beside Mollie, who was going to perform one of Shakespeare's songs from *As You Like It*. Mollie's voice and dramatic flair certainly added to her rendition, but Maud was so nervous that it was difficult to give her friend her full attention.

All too quickly it was her turn. "The next recitation is by Miss Maud Montgomery," Mr. Simpson said and sat down.

Maud closed her eyes and focused on steadying her legs. As she was making her way to the front, Clemmie said, a little too loudly, "There she goes!"

Maud stopped. First Mrs. Simpson and now Clemmie! She would *not* allow that girl to shake her foundation. She stood straight and rolled her shoulders back, somehow making it to the platform as the audience clapped politely.

Staring out into the crowd, she felt as though all of Cavendish was there waiting to see if she would fail. Maud looked for her grandparents and her cousins. Her gaze then fell upon Nate, who had the audacity to wink!

Trying not to giggle, Maud breathed in deeply. Trembling, she was sure she was going to forget a word or miss a line. She began. And, as she spoke, each line fell upon the next with ease.

*A child, with tender, wistful eyes*
*Tripped softly through the shade*
*Of whispering trees, nor sought the spots*

When Maud reached the last line and lifted her hand up in a dramatic fashion, it was as though her voice was coming from someone else, filling the room.

And then it was over. It went so quickly she hardly remembered anything. It was quiet for a few moments, and then Nate stood up, whistled, and lead a standing ovation. Even her grandparents clapped politely.

After the performance, Maud and Mollie stayed together while people congratulated them. One of Mollie's admirers, an awkward fellow from Mayfield, George Robertson, tripped over himself to tell her "How she did that poetry well." Mollie smiled sweetly (as she was always polite) and then pulled Maud toward someone who didn't make "her stomach feel as if she'd drunk cod liver oil." They bumped into Pensie, who had been fighting her way through the crowd to get to them.

"That was well done, Maudie!" She embraced her. "Quill and Mary were quite impressed." She looked over at Mollie, as if she had just noticed she was there. "You were good too, Amanda."

Mollie murmured thanks and looked away.

Maud didn't want them to fight. "I'm so glad you came," she said. "With your guest." She nodded to where Quill was standing off to the side, talking with Jack and Nate.

"Of course I'd come," Pensie said, ignoring Maud's teasing. "Your big night. We'll celebrate the next time you stay over."

Maud felt a bit guilty that she hadn't spent as much time with Pensie lately as she had with Mollie. They still walked together in the evenings when the weather cooperated, but she hadn't slept over since that weekend after the journal incident.

"Someone gave you quite the standing ovation," Pensie said, a little too loudly, pointing to the back of the hall. The warm feeling evaporated, and Maud looked quickly around to see if anyone had heard. Why would Pensie embarrass her? She was usually so careful.

"Well, Quill is waiting for me," Pensie said. "I'll see you tomorrow evening." And she kissed Maud on the cheek and left.

Her grandparents came over next and said that Miss Gordon had organized a "very nice affair." Maud knew it wasn't in their nature to compliment her directly—or she might get airs—but she had hoped that just once (on an occasion such as this) they would have. Still, they had come and that was something.

After the students helped Miss Gordon take down the decorations, Maud lingered longer than was probably necessary. Now that she was supposed to meet Nate, she wasn't sure it was such a good idea. What if Grandma had overheard Pensie? But it was too late: she and Mollie had already accepted the invitation and, despite all of her reservations, Maud had been looking forward to another walk home.

The Four Musketeers had decided that they would meet in front of Nate's house, and as Maud and Mollie approached, the boys emerged.

"As promised, we have kept our solemn vow to take you home once again." Nate bowed.

"In plain English, we are here to walk you home," Jack said, following his friend's gesture.

Maud and Mollie giggled.

Again they paired up, and Maud took in the late autumn stars and the full moon as she and Nate talked of books and the lecture and her plans to go to school and write. He made her promise to write him everything that happened at the trial at school. "If I'm going to be a lawyer, I should know the goings-on," he said.

When they got to the top of the hill near the cemetery where Maud had read Nate's note all those weeks ago, he took Maud's hand and said, "You know, someone might think I was your future husband for taking your hand."

Maud tried to pull her hand away, but he held firm and kissed it. His hand was warm—and the kiss! Maud was sure anyone who had ever written about a hand being kissed couldn't encapsulate the tenderness and joy she felt at that moment. He continued to hold her hand as they turned toward the school woods. Her cheeks felt warm, and she was sure she was all flushed, so she focused her attention on the red earth so he wouldn't see, hoping she was holding her end of the conversation—although she had no idea what she was saying.

A part of her knew she should let go of his hand. They were daringly close to her grandparents' house, and who knew what would happen if they were caught or seen. It would only end in heartbreak.

He was Baptist, she Presbyterian.

She remembered her conversation with Pensie about those Dockendorff brides causing a big rift in the family tree. But as Maud walked with Nate's hand around hers, feeling each fingertip against her skin, all of those concerns were carried away by the stars lighting their way home.

## CHAPTER FOURTEEN

B ut by Monday afternoon all of those concerns had returned. Maud arrived home after school so furious at Clemmie and Annie—and what they said about her and Nate—that even after she had written out the entire ordeal in her journal, she was still shaking in anger.

Maud had promised Nate that she would write him a letter telling him exactly what happened, so it would be as if he'd been there himself. Whatever she decided, she had to make sure that Nate would be so upset that he would never speak to Clemmie again! Clemmie had said that she was going to make trouble for Maud, and she had. Maud wasn't sure what she was more distressed about: her favorite teacher being involved, or that somehow the business between Annie and Clemmie had to do with Maud and Nate.

After pacing her room for almost an hour, Maud was finally calm enough to tell him the truth of how she saw it. Sitting down at the table in front of the window, watching the bare branches of Grandfather's apple tree lash against the wind, she took a deep breath and began:

*Dear Snip,*

*As promised, I'm faithfully recording the events that occurred after school this afternoon.*

    *First, I am impressed with how Mollie got herself out of this mess by telling Miss Gordon that she knew nothing!*

    *Can you believe it? It hadn't even dawned on me to lie to Miss Gordon.*

The tree snapped against the wind.

Maud stopped. Could she tell Nate what Clemmie had said? Perhaps if she built up to it . . .

    *Nate, it was as if we were in a real court of law—or as I have imagined it when I hear Grandpa Montgomery talk about it. Miss Gordon even rapped the drubbing ruler, like it was a gavel. She really could have been a lawyer.*

    *"Annie, Clemmie, and Nellie," she said. "Your behavior has been deplorable. It is time for you to tell me the truth."*

    *"Clemmie started it." Annie pointed at her nemeses. "I was only defending myself."*

    *And then she had the nerve to point to me! Me!! "Maud saw the whole episode."*

    *I was mortified, but I stood up when Miss Gordon asked me to and proudly faced her.*

    *"What do you know?"*

    *"I don't know what Annie thinks I saw."*

    *"That isn't true!" Annie said.*

    *Miss Gordon sighed and clicked the ruler against her desk.*

    *"Maud, did you see Annie and Clemmie argue?"*

    *"Yes." I relented.*

    *"And what was the nature of this fight?"*

*I wished to wipe that smug expression off Annie's face with a dirty rag, but I took a deep breath and told the truth about what I saw the first day of school between Annie and Clemmie.*

*I kept wondering how I got there. I didn't want to get involved with these girls, avoided them, ignored them, and, yet, they snared me into their trap!! I didn't even want to consider what Miss Gordon was thinking about me.*

*Finally, Miss Gordon told me to sit down and then asked Mamie to stand up. "Now, why do you side with Annie?" Miss Gordon asked.*

*Mamie didn't speak for a long while.*

*"There must be a reason why you chose to be friends with Annie and not Clemmie," Miss Gordon said.*

*"There is," Mamie finally said. "Clemmie is a gossip and a tattletale."*

*"I am not!" Clemmie pounced.*

*"Clemmie!" Miss Gordon snapped the drubbing ruler against her desk. "You'll have your chance to speak. It is now Mamie's turn."*

*Clemmie mumbled an apology.*

*Turning back to Mamie, Miss Gordon said, "Please continue."*

The tree clashed against the house again. Maud paused. Could she actually write the words? What would Nate say if she did? But if she didn't and Clemmie told him, it would be worse . . .

*"A few weeks ago Clemmie said something mean about Maud and Nate Lockhart to me," Mamie said.*

*Miss Gordon's eyes were now upon me, but I didn't look away.*

*"And what did Clemmie say?" Miss Gordon asked.*

*Mamie cleared her throat. "Clemmie said, 'Isn't it absurd, the way Maud and Nate go on?'"*

Maud reread the sentence. There it was. The truth as people saw it. Saw her. Maud remembered how she couldn't even look Miss Gordon in the eye, but she wouldn't tell Nate that! No, she had to divert his attention onto Clemmie, show how this was all her fault!

*The sheer nerve of it. But after Miss Gordon told Mamie to sit down, she told Clemmie to stand.*

*Clemmie stood, her hands behind her back, breathing heavily through her mouth so she sounded like a fish caught in one of my grandfather's nets.*

*"How exactly do Maud and Nate 'go on'?" Miss Gordon asked.*

*Clemmie gulped. "Well . . ."*

*"Yes?"*

*"They are always passing notes to each other and talking together. And he's always walking her home. It isn't civilized."*

*The way she was behaving wasn't civilized!*

*I finally looked Miss Gordon in the eye and prayed I didn't show any indication that anything Clemmie had said was true—which as you know it isn't. It is clear to anyone that Clemmie is jealous of our friendship.*

*When Miss Gordon finally spoke, she appeared to be choosing her words very carefully. "I have never believed Maud or Nate required much direction." She paused. "Nor do I think so now."*

*Clemmie flashed me such a poisonous look, and Miss Gordon told her to sit down. Her ruling: both girls got a few slaps on their hands with her ruler, warning that if they continued this behavior they would be expelled.*

   *So now you know everything and I want you to promise me that as punishment you will follow my example and never speak to Clemmie Macneill again!*

*Sincerely,*
*Pollie*

When Maud gave Nate the letter the next day, he was so furious that he vowed he would never speak to Clemmie Macneill again. Victory was indeed sweet.

## CHAPTER FIFTEEN

After the trial, Clemmie kept her distance from Maud and Mollie. Even Annie had taken Miss Gordon's warning seriously, focusing instead on trying to get Austin's attention.

Maud and Mollie were on their way to school one morning when Clemmie approached them. Clemmie's curly hair was tucked under a grayish-blue wool hat and she had her hands in a warm muff.

"What do you want, Clemmie?" Mollie said, when they got closer.

Clemmie tucked her muff close to her chest. "I had hoped to speak with Maud in private."

"Did you?" Maud said.

"Anything you can say to Maud, you can say in front of me," Mollie said.

Maud was grateful for Mollie's devotion, but this was between her and Clemmie. "Mollie," Maud said. "I'll be fine."

"Are you sure?"

Maud hugged her and, reluctantly, Mollie walked away. "I'll be by the school woods if you need me."

When she had gone, Maud turned back to Clemmie. "What did you want to say to me?"

Clemmie took her hands out of her muff, letting it fall to her side. "I wanted to apologize for my behavior." She frowned. "And for what I said."

"That is nice of you to say," Maud said, as politely as she could. But she couldn't help noticing that Clemmie's gaze lingered on the boys who were now coming down the path.

"I never meant for it to go this far."

Maud suddenly felt tired. She really had had enough of Clemmie, and whatever it was that made her apologize, Maud suspected that it probably had to do with Nate ignoring her. But, perhaps by accepting it they could all move forward. "I accept your apology, Clemmie," she said.

"I am so relieved we can put this dreadful business behind us." As she over-enthusiastically embraced her, Clemmie's muff grazed Maud's cheek.

"Me too," Maud said. And as Clemmie walked over to where Nellie had been dutifully waiting for her, and Maud returned to Mollie, she truly was relieved.

On November 30, Maud celebrated her fifteenth birthday with Pensie, Mollie, and Lu, who came over to celebrate with cake and to stay overnight.

Maud hadn't heard from Father in months and was beginning to get worried; he had never forgotten her birthday. As a forest ranger and homestead investigator, he was busy doing important work for the government. Perhaps that was why?

Aunt Annie and Uncle John Campbell sent Maud some scraps for the crazy quilt, and the cousins gave Maud a scrapbook to put her special mementoes in.

The Four Musketeers had also given her a bit of a party at school. Jack brought his mother's shortbread, and Mollie gave her a beautiful piece of lace. Nate presented Maud with a book of verse by his uncle, Pastor Felix, and had signed the front:

*To Polly,*

*Happy Birthday!*

*Your pal,*
*Snip*

Maud adored it and started reading the poetry right away.

The day after her birthday, she received a genuine surprise when Grandpa Montgomery dropped by just when the tea was ready.

"He has impeccable timing, that man," Grandma said to Maud, placing a plate of cold meats on the table.

Grandpa Montgomery was tall and broad with bushy whiskers, an intelligent smile, and Father's eyes, and, even at eighty years old, he stood in sharp contrast to the quiet and demure Macneills. After her grandpa had given Maud his gift of store-bought candies and a wide-brimmed hat with a long blue ribbon, he showed her a letter. Maud immediately identified the crisp penmanship as her father's. She could almost reach out and take it from him, but it wasn't hers to read.

Grandpa Montgomery cleared his throat. "Your father wrote that he is still trying to make arrangements to return to Prince Albert, and so this isn't a good time for Maud to come." He turned to her grandparents. "I know you had discussed the possibility of her joining me next year, but I don't think it will be possible." He lightly tapped her shoulder. "I'm sorry, Maudie."

Maud was surprised. Is that why she hadn't heard from him? Is this what they had been planning after they had read her journal?

She couldn't believe it. Why was this the first she had heard of this? And why wouldn't her father take her in?

"Your son has never taken responsibility for Maud," Grandfather said.

"That is not true," Grandpa Montgomery said, but there was no force behind his defense. Maud knew that Grandpa had arranged for Father's current job and had disapproved of his son's side ventures, which always seemed to lead to him losing money. When she was visiting her grandpa's house in Park Corner last summer, she had overheard her uncles discussing how her father had asked for more money "for some scheme," and hadn't their father "done enough by securing him that post out West."

Maud had wished to leap to Father's defense, but she knew better than to interfere when grown-ups were speaking. Father was just misunderstood. He had big dreams, like she did. He would come for her. It might not be right away, but one day she would live with him and his family. That's why it was important to show her grandparents how much she had changed, that she could contain her emotions in front of company.

Maud thanked her grandpa for his gifts and her father's letter, and after he left, she took her things upstairs and wept.

Thankfully, Maud didn't have much time to think about Father's troubles—not when there were preparations for Christmas exams and, even more important, the Christmas concert, which included dialogues and singing. She and Mollie had a scene to perform, and Annie and Clemmie were to sing. The concert was very successful and Maud got a standing ovation. Her grandparents came again to see her, but just as before, they didn't offer any praise.

Maud also finished her essay on the wreck of the *Marco Polo*, which she gave to Miss Gordon right before the break. She loved writing it, because no matter what was going on in the rest of her life, when Maud wrote, all her troubles faded away; it was her and her story of the great wreck.

Miss Gordon was very pleased with the essay and submitted it to the *Montreal Witness,* along with essays from Nate and a few other students. Maud was confident Nate was going to win. While his essay was a bit too flowery for her liking, it was truly good, and he had written on the railroad, a very popular topic.

Maud finally heard from Father at Christmas. He sent her a package that included a letter; a photo of him and his new wife, Mary Ann; and a picture of Katie, Maud's baby half-sister. He also included a pile of magazines because he knew "she enjoyed reading about the fashions and stories." But she couldn't quite bring herself to read them—they reminded her too much of what she missed not being with him—so the magazines were left unread on her bureau.

Still, Christmas was full of fun, with the evening church service and her grandmother's famous turkey and Christmas cake. Even her Uncle John Franklin was in a good humor when they opened presents on Christmas Day. It was difficult to arrange to see Nate outside of school, so they exchanged letters over the holidays, but Mollie and Pensie came by often to work on their sewing projects.

School started up again the first week of January, and they all settled into the new term while winter bore down on them. Maud loved the way the ice carved its way around the bare apple trees, and how the red roads crept up through the white snow, giving the land a pinkish hue. The evenings were warm and cozy in her grandparents' house, and Maud found herself enjoying the quiet. Maud worked on her crazy quilt or read, while her grandfather smoked his pipe and read the newspaper, and her grandmother sewed or knitted.

Often, Maud slept over at Mollie's or Pensie's house, staying up quite late, the girls huddled together to keep warm. Sometimes, Mollie "helped" Maud write by holding her inkbottle when she wrote in her journal. There were even times when Maud would read parts of it aloud. It was weird and wonderful to relive things that had only just happened, as though her journal had a story and life of its own. She remembered experiencing the events, but reading about them—even a few weeks later—made it feel as though they had happened so long ago, as though she were talking about a different person.

The first week of January also brought a series of prayer meetings that took over Cavendish. Bundled up in their scarves, wraps, and capes, Maud, Mollie, and Pensie marched their way through the crunchy snow to either the Presbyterian or Baptist church. All of the villagers (except Maud's grandparents, who claimed that it was much too cold and difficult to go) went to these prayer meetings, no matter what church they regularly attended.

Mostly, Pensie sat with Mary or Quill, leaving the Four Musketeers to band together. Maud wished that Pensie would sit with them, but she told them—very loudly—that that she was "too old to sit with children." The boys laughed her off, but Mollie glowered. Maud swallowed her tears. How was it that Maud was good enough to sleep over at Pensie's house, but not good enough when she had her school friends with her?

Being in the back pew was fun, and watching Nate and Jack joke together helped distract Maud from whatever Pensie was doing with Mary and Quill. During one of Reverend Archibald's speeches, Nate and Jack passed the girls notes, writing silly rhymes about those in attendance, which Mollie and Maud read with their heads together, desperately trying to contain their giggles, and ignoring poor George, who sat near them to get Mollie's attention. It was nearly impossible for Maud to be the proper girl Grandma expected her to be.

The more time Maud spent with Nate, the more she enjoyed it, and she forgot about the issue of their different religious backgrounds. She no longer felt nervous walking home with him, and they always found things to talk about. She didn't want to think about him going away next year, but there was time enough to worry about that.

But it all changed one night at Maud's Presbyterian church. Nate and Jack sat behind Mollie and Maud and, as always, tried to distract them by whispering in their ears, making jokes, and pulling on Maud's shawl, the same one she wore when Nate walked her home. When Maud spun around and told him to stop, Mrs. Simpson turned in her seat in front of Maud and said, "You are carrying on like little devils."

Maud tried to look apologetic while fighting to hold in laughter.

"Wait until your grandmother hears about this," Mrs. Simpson said. Maud's laugh caught in her throat. This was no idle threat. While they certainly weren't friends, Mrs. Simpson was Grandma's contemporary, and Maud knew she would definitely make a call—it was her duty, after all—and just in time for tea.

After the prayer meeting, Mrs. Simpson and Mrs. Clark were in line for some hot cider near where Maud and Mollie were helping Miss Gordon.

"It is no wonder that girl behaves the way she does," Mrs. Simpson said. "Her Grandma worries so."

"I want to pour cider on her head," Mollie said in a low voice to Maud.

"After all that trouble last year," Mrs. Clark said, as they passed. "It's no wonder."

"I heard the old teacher was kicked out of the house because of Mr. Macneill's temper. He's definitely what drove Clara into the arms of a man who was beneath her, perhaps not in station, but in temperament."

Maud gasped, and the ladle she was holding slipped back into the glass bowl, sending drops of cider spattering across the table. She couldn't move. The first part of Mrs. Simpson's gossip was true. Miss Robinson had left when she'd had enough of Grandfather, but the second . . .

Is that why no one ever talked about her parents?

The women continued as if they didn't notice Maud standing there.

"Well, he was much older than her. Imagine eloping in the middle of the night," Mrs. Simpson said. "And we all know why."

"He certainly pulled the wool over Clara's eyes," Mrs. Clark said. "Poor lamb." She gave Mrs. Simpson a knowing look. "That man sailed in and sailed out as quickly as he came. If his father were not a senator, there would be no value in him at all."

Beside her, Mollie picked up the ladle and continued with their duties, making a show of not listening to what was being said. Maud was aware of other people milling around—could they all hear them?

She swallowed hard. They were telling stories about her family, about people who weren't here to contradict them. Eloped! Grandma had never indicated anything of the kind. And no one had ever hinted at that, not even Aunt Annie or Pensie's mother. No wonder people thought so little of her. Tears betrayed her and she turned to the wall so no one would see.

Mollie put her hand on her friend's arm. "Come, let them get their own cider." Maud sniffed and, grabbing their capes and scarves, the girls abandoned their post and went outside. It had started to snow, covering the old dirty snow with a fresh, light coat.

"It is so frustrating." Maud dabbed her teary cheeks and shivered. "No one ever talks about Mother. Whenever I asked Father, he smiled and became sad and talked about what a wonderful woman she was." She stopped herself from saying anything else.

Mollie was a dear friend, but would she be able to keep this a secret? "Swear," Maud said. "Please swear that you'll not tell a soul."

"Of course, I will. It isn't right," Mollie declared, wrapping her scarf around her neck. "People should mind their own business."

"Who should mind their own business?"

The girls looked up to see Nate with his coat on, looking concerned. But the last thing Maud needed was for more people to hear about what her parents might have done—especially Nate. Besides, this was a private family matter and not for the ears of the Baptist minister's stepson.

"Nothing," Maud said, drying her eyes. "Just the cold."

"Really," he said, and his concerned look turned a little chillier. "I thought we were beyond secrets, Miss Montgomery."

Maud sighed. She knew he could never stand being left out of things.

"You know us girls are allowed to have our secrets," Maud said, trying to lighten the mood. "You don't need to know all of our business."

Nate scowled. "While that's true, there are things that a fellow can help with if he's given the chance."

Maud wished she could say something, but this was too personal, and a family matter. "Nate, this is really between Mollie and me."

He frowned. "I guess I thought we had gotten past this—"

"It's not—"

"No, Maud. I know when I'm not wanted." And he sulked off into the snow.

Mollie put her arm around Maud. "He'll come around. You know he can't be angry at you for long." Maud hoped Mollie was right.

Pensie came out of the hall dressed in her navy blue wool cape. "Maud, I saw you leave," she said. "Is everything all right?"

She'd already embarrassed them tonight by not sitting with them, and now there was the matter of her lie! "Why didn't you tell me?"

Pensie put her hand on Maud's arm, but Maud shook it off. "Tell you what?"

"Didn't you know? . . . About my parents?" Maud couldn't look at her.

"What about your parents?"

Maud put her head on Mollie's shoulder. Pensie glared at Mollie. "You finally did it, didn't you? Spread lies about me."

"I did no such thing," Mollie said, rubbing Maud's shoulders. "This has something to do with—" She stopped and shook her other hand as if to think.

Maud lifted her head. "This has nothing to do with Mollie," she said. "It has to do with you keeping something from me."

"I haven't kept anything from you," Pensie said, her eyes watering. "Maudie, I promise."

At the sight of Pensie's tears, Maud felt her chin tremble. What was she doing? Pensie wouldn't lie to her, keep things from her. "I'm sorry," Maud said, hugging her friends close.

"She has had a shock," Mollie said.

"My poor Maudie," Pensie said, as Maud pulled away. "Tell me. What happened?"

But just as Maud got up the courage, Quill emerged. "Are you ready to go, Pensie?"

Pensie took a long look at Maud. "I might have to stay for a little while longer."

"It is getting rather cold," Quill said. "I promised your parents I would have you home promptly after refreshments."

Of course he had, but it was enough to Maud that she had wanted to stay. "It's all right, Pensie. Mollie's here with me. I promise to tell you, but not tonight."

Pensie bundled herself deeper underneath her cape. "I shall hold you to that." She said good night and she and Quill walked down the hill.

"I'll go and let Jack know we are leaving," Mollie said. "Wait here."

Maud was grateful to be left alone. She was tired and cold and wished she could take a long walk through Lover's Lane to clear her head. But it was getting dark, and with all of the snow, the lane was precarious.

A few moments later, Mollie emerged with Jack and the three friends walked toward home. Maud tried to pretend that she was having fun, even though Mollie certainly knew the truth and covered for her, but she couldn't stop thinking about what those women had said. How was she ever going to find out the truth when no one was willing to talk to her about Mother?

# CHAPTER SIXTEEN

For the next week, Nate was like the Island weather: cold one moment and warm the next. Some days he would come to school and she would get the friendly Nate, inviting her to go sledding and sending her silly notes, including a poem about the night of the lecture when he had walked her home for the first time. But when she still wouldn't tell him why she had been so upset the night of the prayer meeting, he would pout.

Whatever worries she had about Mrs. Simpson telling Grandma about their behavior at the prayer meeting were forgotten. Instead, she focused on figuring out the truth about what she and Mollie had started calling their "secret discovery." She couldn't come out and ask her grandparents if her parents had eloped; they would most likely deny it, or tell her it wasn't her place to ask such questions. Worse, they might be too mortified to even respond. Her grandparents and Aunt Annie had never said anything, so why would they now? And Aunt Emily in Malpeque was so cold to Maud last time she was there, Maud was sure she couldn't talk with her.

One day after school, the older students went up to the Cavendish Hall to hear a lecture by the Reverend Archibald on a missionary effort under way in South America. Now that Maud had gone to a number of lectures without—as far as her grandparents knew—incident, they had been more lenient about letting her attend. Nate was in one of his better moods, and he joined Mollie, Maud, and Jack on the way up the hill. Clemmie, Nellie, and the others were right behind them.

"Are you girls ready to tell me that secret yet?" Nate asked in a tone that Maud decided was much too loud.

Mollie pulled Maud a step or two ahead and whispered, "Maybe you should tell him." Mollie hated what was happening between Maud and Nate because it was causing tension between the Four Musketeers, as Jack always stood by Nate.

"No," she said. She couldn't tell him. What might he think of her when he found out? She turned to face Nate. "Secrets are kept for a reason."

Not getting the answers he was looking for, Nate hung back and went home instead of going to the lecture.

"I guess he's in one of his moods," Maud said, pretending it didn't bother her.

"You do make it difficult," Mollie said.

"It isn't my fault he takes things so personally."

"You know he can't think straight when he's around you," Jack said.

Maud and Mollie stopped in surprise. "Jack Laird, you are always so quiet, but when you speak, sheer nonsense comes out," Maud said, immediately regretting it.

Jack's ears went a bit pink and he shuffled off ahead.

"Now you've done it," Mollie said. "I was hoping he'd sit with us."

"I'm sorry," Maud said. "This whole thing . . ."

"I know." She took Maud's hand. "Jack doesn't hold a grudge. I'm sure if we apologize, he will forgive us."

Maud had enough people displeased with her. They found Jack inside and sat beside him. Mollie was right: he forgave them instantly.

But that night after the lecture, Maud couldn't sleep. She desperately missed Nate. She felt heavier, grayer, as if she were trying to move after a dense dream. Sitting in the front parlor with her grandparents after supper, she had to redo the crazy quilt squares she was sewing three times because she kept making mistakes.

It rained all weekend, adding to her desperate loneliness and melancholy. She went over to Mollie's on Saturday, but her head ached and even her best friend couldn't make her feel better, so she returned home. Grandma gave Maud a cold compress and told her to go to bed.

But on Monday, Maud found a note slipped into a copy of *Shakespeare's Sonnets*:

*Dear Polly,*

*I have a great interest in who you shook hands with after counting nine stars for nine nights. As your good friend, I think it is important that I know whom your future husband is going to be. One has to be sure he is worthy of you.*

*I will gladly tell you my person if you would be open to divulging yours. That way we'll both be in the know.*

*Your chum,*
*Snip*

"This is why he was so upset with you?" Mollie asked, when Maud showed her Nate's note during math class later that afternoon.

"He thinks this is our secret?" Mollie laughed. "Boys really don't know anything, do they?"

"No." Maud stared at the note for a long while. She remembered the night of the literary in November, the way they had held hands after she had counted to nine stars, the way he had kissed her hand. "I didn't realize he was this serious."

"Of course he's serious." Mollie giggled. "He is like the proverbial cow, *moo*-ning over you."

"What do I do?"

"Write him back. You're both so much better at expressing your feelings on paper than you are in person."

Mollie was right; Maud and Nate had always found it easier to write letters. That night she read over Nate's letter and then wrote:

*Dear Snip,*

*I've considered your proposal, and while I don't think it was fair, I will consider telling you, but you will need to tell me who yours is first.*

*Yours,*
*Pollie—with an "ie"*
*(Since that is the only way to spell it.)*

The next day at lunch, Maud and Mollie sat down with Jack and Nate, who were in the corner playing cards. It was too cold outside, so Miss Gordon had allowed them to have recess indoors.

Grandma would have been so proud of Maud's composure, for even though her heart was pounding, she kept her feelings hidden. Mollie said later she looked as cool as lemonade on a summer's afternoon.

Nate picked up a card and placed it on the makeshift crate he and Jack were using as a table.

"Maybe this will clear some things up?" Maud said, and handed Nate her note. He took it, read it, and cleared his throat. Without a word, he slipped the note into his pocket and said, "Maud, we need to concentrate on this excellent game of cards. Right, Jack, let's not allow these girls to distract us." Jack said nothing, as usual, but smiled slightly and placed his card down.

Infuriated, Maud and Mollie went back to their desk and discussed the issue at great length. Then, after hours of excruciating waiting, and right before Miss Gordon called the end of day, Maud found a little piece of paper sticking out of her reader.

*Dear Polly—with a "y,"*

*I'm glad to see that you're willing. Your proposition is certainly interesting, and I am willing to take it under advisement—but with one caveat. You must do something else for me in return. I am the one taking all of the risk, telling you something before you tell me, and that carries more weight than whatever you might say.*

*So here is my position: you must answer fair and square, without any further evasion, the truth of your nine stars. Of course, as I am a gentleman, you can ask me a question and I pledge I will answer it—only after you tell me yours.*

*Your friend,*
*Snip*

After school, Maud quickly made her excuses to Mollie and ran home, going straight to her room to think. What was Nate going to ask next? The only way to resolve the issue was to agree to his demands. Sitting down at her desk, Maud carefully crafted a response, and then slipped it to him on their way to school the next day.

Before lunch, a note was tucked into the pocket of the sweater hanging on the back of her chair.

*Dear Polly—with a "y,"*

*After much consideration and folly here it is: you were the person I shook hands with after counting nine stars in nine nights. It was the night of Reverend Mr. Carruthers's lecture when Jack and I walked you and Mollie home and I took your hand for a moment—do you remember?*

*Now to my question about your nine stars, and a follow-up: Which of your boyfriends do you like best? And is he your nine stars?*

*Snip*

Maud almost tossed the note at Nate's head. The nerve! She had never dreamed Nate would be so bold. What was she going to do? Of course she liked Nate best. He was the most intelligent boy in the school, but to tell him so—in a letter? In words? That was something she wasn't sure she was prepared to do . . . or something she *could* do. She would ask him the same in return, and then he would let the whole thing drop.

*Dear Snip,*

*I will tell you that while it has been difficult for me to get to the nine stars, it appears the fates have aligned and—yes—it was you. As for your question, I will only answer it if you answer the same one in reverse: Which of your girlfriends do you like best?*

*Poll<u>ie</u>*

Maud gave Nate the note before school. He went off to read it, but soon came back all sheepish and said, "I think this is getting kind of out of hand, Maud, don't you think? Shall we let it all drop?"

"I don't know, Nate. You've certainly given me much to consider," Maud said.

Nate stuck his hands in his pockets and blew soft puffs of cool air. Maud wondered if she had taken it too far. "I only meant . . ." She stopped. She certainly wasn't going to apologize; he was the one who had put her in this situation. But she also didn't want him walking off either. She sighed. "All right, Nate. Yes, let's drop the whole thing."

"Excellent," he said. "Let's go in?"

It was a short reprieve. Later that afternoon, she found another letter in her history book, tucked between a passage about Sir Walter Raleigh and Queen Elizabeth.

*Dear Polly,*

*I have thought out this matter thoroughly and have reconsidered my decision. I will answer your question, but you must answer mine. It isn't fair for a body to back out of a bargain. It doesn't show good comradeship, and aren't we good comrades above all else?*

*Snip*

*Dear Snip,*

*Fine, but only if I see your note first.*

*Pollie*

*Dear Polly,*

*I'm not fond of this idea, but I shall cater to this one demand.*

*Snip*

That evening, Maud—after much pacing and some dark looks from Pensie, who had come over for their nightly walk and was annoyed when Maud wouldn't tell her what was wrong—sat down to write another note.

*Dear Nate,*

<u>*You*</u> *have a little more brains than the other Cavendish boys, and I like brains—so I suppose I like <u>you</u> best—though I don't see why after the trick you've played on <u>me</u>.*

*Maud*

She would give it to him only when Nate had given her his note. And as she blew out her lamp, she thought: *If he has another girl's name, I'll never forgive him.*

## CHAPTER SEVENTEEN

N ate gave her his note first, right before reading period. Maud got permission from Miss Gordon to go to the outhouse, and then threw on her wrap and scarf and ran down to the grove of maple trees in the Haunted Woods. It was one of those warmer days in February where faeries made mischief by tricking you into thinking spring was coming early.

Her hands shook as she read its contents. He had written it in red ink!

> *Well, Polly, it must be done. I at first intended to write quite a lengthy epistle, setting forth my poor opinion of myself, my very inferior <u>personal</u> endowments, my happiness, or rather ecstasy if your note proved favorable to my wishes etc. etc. etc. But I have altered my plan of arrangement and resolved to give you <u>hard</u>, <u>dry</u>, <u>plain</u>, facts, for they may possibly appear as such to you, but they are nevertheless as true as gospel. Here goes:—Of all my feminine friends the one whom I most admire—no I'm growing reckless—the one whom I <u>love</u> (if the authorities allow that word to come under the school boy's scholarship vocabulary)*

*is L.M. Montgomery, the girl I shook hands with, the girl after my own heart.*

*Yes, Polly, it is true. I always liked you better than any other girl and it has kept on increasing till it has obtained "prodigious" proportions. Oh, <u>wouldn't</u> I like to see you reading this. But I must conclude or you will say it is very lengthy after all. Remember I am waiting for you to fulfill your part of the transaction with ever-increasing impatience.*

*from*
*Nate*

*P.S. I suppose you'll say I'm very sentimental. Well, perhaps <u>rather</u>. However, it's not much difference. I was just laughing over the tenacity with which we cling to our diverse manner of spelling Polly! (Pollie). I'm going to cling to my manner <u>ad finem</u>, because it's right. I expect you'll prove stubborn, too.*
*N.J.L.*

In the unseasonably warm sun, Maud almost wept with joy. It surprised her how happy she was to receive the letter after so much uneasiness. But then she wondered if it was a good idea to encourage this now. She couldn't have such entanglements. It was too complicated. Even if Clemmie had calmed down, there were the rest of the Baptist and Presbyterian congregations to consider— not to mention her grandparents, who could never know about this. They would certainly be ashamed of her.

In addition, once Maud handed Nate her note it would be done. He would know she liked him, liked him best.

What was it Reverend Mr. Carruthers had said about being an example? How was this being an example? Pensie would tease her and say, "I told you so." She had been right; Nate had wanted more from Maud all along.

Icicles plunked against the snowbank.

He loved her. No one had ever told her that before. And she admired him. But was it love? She had made him a promise and she was going to have to give him her answer. Maud returned to school and avoided Nate for the rest of the morning.

At noon, Maud passed Nate the answer she had labored over the previous night in her French grammar book. The rest of the afternoon was one of the slowest Maud had ever experienced, even worse than when Nate hadn't been speaking to her. Every once in a while, she was sure she heard him whistling quietly over his sums.

Finally, the long afternoon was over and Maud scooped up her books and ran home. She was sorry for the whole sordid mess. And yet, there was something exquisite—triumphant—about having a boy fall in love with her. Maud had never believed anyone would think of her in that way. Now here it was—in red ink.

Going over to her bureau, she unlocked it and copied the letter into her journal, carefully locking it back in the drawer when she was done.

## CHAPTER EIGHTEEN

As the days passed, letters were found in schoolbooks and sheet music. Nate also carved her nickname in cipher above her school hook: *Ἴδλλυη*.

Maud found this letter after her organ lesson:

*Dear Polly,*

*I hereby solemnly swear to you I would never show interest in any other girl than you. Don't you know how I feel about you? Haven't I shown you with my interest in your words and our conversation? It might be easier for everyone if we were of the same traditions, but as we've discussed in the past, our core feelings about Him are similar. Let the dogmatists fight among themselves while we prove to them that none of it matters.*

*We can be our own—dare I say it—<u>Romeo and Juliet</u> story, save the dreadful ending.*

*Yours,*
*N.*

The next day, Nate discovered this under his French book:

*Dear Snip,*

*It is hard to swear upon things we cannot know of.*

*Sincerely,*
*Poll<u>ie</u>*

Nate then smuggled his last plea during geography class.

*Dear Poll<u>y</u>,*

*I know we don't believe in love at first sight, but I think of the first time I saw you and believe, maybe, that the poets know something we don't yet understand.*
    *There was also a certain way you turned your head that day at the prayer meeting, and I looked up from my hymnal and I became yours. Would you ever see me as anything other than a chum? You might even think this letter is too silly and you would be right. But, Polly . . . please, let me be yours.*

*N.*

Each time she received one of Nate's letters, Maud had a fluttery feeling she didn't know where to put. It started at her toes and traveled up her spine. She wanted to simultaneously run from and embrace it. There were nights she ached to be held by him, imagining him kissing her forehead, and then her lips, whispering how dear she was to him.

On Valentine's Day, Nate stuck a red paper heart inside her copy of Tennyson that said, *Be My Valentine. Meet me under our favorite tree.* The Tree Lovers, the one with two branches curved in on each other in a constant embrace, had become their special place. It was then that she finally admitted to herself that she was in love with Nate Lockhart and decided she would meet him.

As Maud turned down the path, she heard the familiar whistle.

He was waiting for her.

As she approached, Nate took off his glove and extended his hand for hers. In a daring move, she took off hers. They walked in silence. Now that she was alone with him, the giddiness had faded and was replaced with uncertainty over what would come next . . . what she wanted to come next.

"Did you submit your essay on the railroad for the *Montreal Witness*?" she said to fill the silence. It was a conversation they'd had many times.

"You know I did." He squeezed her hand.

She couldn't speak, then; she was too fascinated by how warm Nate's ungloved hand felt in hers. Maud had taken his hand before, but this was different. Back then she had believed—or pretended to believe—they were good friends, that they were teasing. Now she was aware of his fingers around hers. There was a steadiness in holding his hand she had never felt before, a knowing he would always stand by her. This thrilled and terrified her. She wanted to both let go and hold on.

He rubbed his thumb against the top of her hand. She shivered. Her ring felt cool against his warm skin.

Nate stopped and Maud turned to face him. He had turned his cap around so it was on backwards, just the way she liked it.

"May I kiss you?" he asked.

Maud could scarcely breathe. "Yes."

He leaned in, and their foreheads knocked together.

Their second attempt was more successful. This time she didn't move, allowing him to guide her. Her head tilted to the right, his lips tentatively met hers.

How sweet his kiss was. Her first kiss.

When they pulled apart, she was ready to tell him the truth about her parents—or at least, the truth that some believed. "I have something to tell you. My secret. My father," Maud said, and pulled away, but he took her hand again. Maud didn't speak. Her black boots cradled in the faded red snow.

"Maud, I don't care what people say about your family. We are not responsible for the actions of our parents."

With all of the stories Maud had heard, she wasn't sure she believed Nate. After all, we were a combination of our family's stories, were we not?

"You knew what people were saying about my parents?" she said. All this time, she had thought she was protecting him, protecting herself. "Why didn't you say anything?"

"Because I had hoped you would tell me." He pulled away. "Why wouldn't you trust me with this?"

"It's a family matter, Nate," Maud said, reaching out to touch his arm. Why did she have to ruin this perfect moment?

He turned to face her, and there was a softness in his expression. "Do you know about my father?" he asked.

"Just that he died on a ship before you were born."

"That's true." He took her hand and led her to a large rock near a small pool of water. "The truth is that my father went missing. He was a ship captain and the boat got lost somewhere near Argentina."

"How dreadful!"

"My mother tells me that for weeks they didn't know if he was alive or dead. But then a letter came from one of his officers confirming her worst fears."

"He was dead."

117

Nate sniffed. "There are still rumors that he was murdered, but we will never know for sure. It was one of the reasons why my mother came home to live with her parents and was grateful when my stepfather proposed."

Maud could see why. Being connected to someone who might have been murdered could truly damage a woman's reputation, even if she had nothing to do with it.

He put his other hand on top of hers and laid it gently on the rock between them. "So you see, Polly, my Polly, we have more in common than you realize. I heard this story from my mother only recently, because she wanted me to hear it from her. People will talk."

Yes. Yes they will.

"It is why I changed my name back to Lockhart. I wanted to show them that I was proud of my father. I believe it was an accident."

Maud blinked back tears. He did understand. He saw her without judgment. He was her knight and she, the girl who needed saving. She wanted to be loved, and he loved her.

"Thank you for trusting me with your story," she whispered.

"Don't you see, Polly?" He leaned in. He had the most marvelous freckles. "You could always trust me."

Her second kiss was even sweeter.

## CHAPTER NINETEEN

"You look flushed, Maud. Be careful not to get overheated," Grandma warned when she got home a few hours later. When Maud was younger she had burned her finger on a poker and got very sick, almost dying, and since then Grandma was always concerned when Maud looked "flushed."

But all Maud could think of were Nate's lips—he kissed as though he was writing in the margins of a book, with deep intensity. Sometimes he moaned, and she was equally flattered and uncomfortable. Heat bloomed up the back of her neck when she allowed herself to think about it.

She even dared to write about it in her journal, often rereading the entries that led up to their first kiss, including his love letter to her. How silly it all seemed now that they were together. And then one day, as she was locking her journal away, she saw a letter lying on top of her bureau near the pile of unread magazines. She froze when she saw her father's familiar handwriting.

It was now early March, and Maud hadn't heard from Father since she had received the package of magazines. Should she disturb her fragile joy with another disappointing letter? In the end, curiosity won.

Father apologized (again) for his long absence, but he had a good reason. After "settling some matters," he had finally returned to Prince Albert, to Eglintoune Villa. The next part made Maud hold her breath, rereading the sentence until she finally believed it might be true.

*I'm writing to my father to inquire if he still plans to come west at the end of the summer. I know he's been interested in inspecting the railroad expansion. Perhaps you can join him?*

Maud practically pranced down the stairs to show her grandparents the letter. Of course, they had seen it come through the post, but they didn't know the contents. Grandfather was sitting near the window. He watched as Grandma read the letter quickly and hand it back to Maud as if it was a soiled rag. "I'm glad he has the foresight to arrange travel plans for you, as it is indecent for a girl your age—or any woman, for that matter—to be traveling by train alone."

"Does he mean this to be permanent?" Grandfather said, clearing his throat.

"There are no specifics given," Grandma said.

"I see," he said. "Perhaps we need to give it some thought."

Why couldn't her grandparents see how this was a good thing? But she didn't want anything to ruin this chance, so she agreed to wait until they had a chance to talk it over.

But, the next day, while walking in the school woods at lunchtime, Maud couldn't hold it in. She told Nate about her father's letter.

Instead of being happy for her, Nate scowled. "You haven't thought this through," he said. "What happens when you leave? When would I see you? With me leaving for school next year, we would have even less time together."

Maud didn't have any answers, and was perturbed that he couldn't simply be supportive. "Do you expect me to wait around for you?"

Nate put his hands in his pockets and didn't meet her gaze. "I don't relish the idea of you being so far away."

Maud didn't relish the idea of being so far away from her friends—or him. "He's my father, Nate," she whispered.

Nate took both of her hands. "Of course. If I had the opportunity to see my father again, I would take it. It is that I would miss you." He gave her his adorable chin-dimpled grin and she forgave him.

"Things will work themselves out," she said, not even allowing herself to think the idea might not come to fruition.

When Pensie came by for the mail a few days later, she remarked that it was foolish for Maud to get her hopes up. Her father had to see if Grandpa Montgomery was going out West; there were still so many things to decide. Maud knew Pensie wasn't being cruel in being so practical; her friend cared about her, but that didn't mean she needed reminding of all of the times Father had hurt her. It also confirmed that Maud was right to not tell her about the rumors she had overheard about her parents. Pensie wouldn't understand. Maud needed compassion, not judgment.

But as winter faded into spring, so did Maud's hope. She heard nothing more from Father or Grandpa Montgomery.

Maud took her mind off of the disappointment by going to lectures at the Cavendish Hall with the Musketeers and preparing for exams. Miss Gordon had planned a concert in June, so after the April examinations were over, the entire class turned their attention to that. Maud and Mollie were going to do a rendition of "Mary Queen of Scots," and by then the winners of the *Montreal Witness* contest would be announced. Miss Gordon was hoping it would be one of her students. Each person had to practice reading their essay out loud.

Maud and Nate walked home regularly together after her organ lessons or school, or one of the many lectures. She was uncomfortable when he grew serious, talking about next year, when she had no idea when—or if—she would be going. Or if she would be coming back.

Still, with everything feeling so uncertain, it was nice to have the idea of a possible future, even if Maud knew somewhere within that her grandparents—if they ever found out about Nate—would forbid it. So she enjoyed her time with him.

Until everything fell apart.

CHAPTER TWENTY

Maud came home from organ practice one early May afternoon and found her grandparents sitting together on the sofa in the parlor. Waiting. Grandfather stared right through her.

"We know about Nathan Lockhart," Grandma Macneill said. "You're to end it now."

Maud held her shaking hands in front of her. "There's nothing going on between us . . . we're just friends."

"Really?" Grandma said. "Mrs. Macneill, Clemmie's mother, was here earlier today with the most fantastic story."

Maud balled her fists. Clemmie's mother. Not Mrs. Simpson! They'd found a way to get their revenge after all.

"Mrs. Macneill said that you and the Lockhart boy have been seen together after school—"

"That woman should pay more attention. She knows I take organ lessons with Mrs. Spurr," Maud said.

"Watch your tone!" Grandfather said.

"Sorry," Maud mumbled. She unclenched her fists and sat down on the chair near the window. A crow pecked at the red earth and flew away. "We are only friends," she said, but even to her this sounded false.

123

"Look at us when we are speaking to you!" Grandma said.

Sitting as tall as she could, Maud faced them. This was the hour of judgment.

Grandma glared at her over her spectacles.

"Gallivanting with boys—and a Baptist, no less," Grandfather said. "All of Cavendish is talking about it. I will not have our good name sullied by a girl who is more interested in boys than her reputation."

There was no need to stop the tears now flowing. Her grandparents were going to think what they wanted about her.

"Tears aren't going to help you now," Grandma said. "You need a steady hand—one we cannot give you." She sighed. "I cannot believe it has come to this, but perhaps finally being with your father will help to curb this attitude."

A long silence filled the room—a silence that stretched out until Maud's heart broke. She was as unwanted as an orphan. There was nothing more she could do that would disappoint them. It was time to find out the truth. Her heartbeat almost drowned out her words, "All of Cavendish already talk about Mother and Father . . . what's one more thing?"

Without a word, Grandfather stood up and left the room, banging the back door behind him.

"As if you haven't upset your grandfather enough." Grandma sank into herself. "Poor Clara has nothing to do with this."

"How would I know? You never talk about her!" Maud was weeping now. She didn't care that they knew about Nate. She was actually relieved.

Grandma rubbed her hands against her lap. "I will not discuss this." She cleared her throat. "Your grandfather and I are deeply disappointed with you. We thought you had learned your lesson when we sent you away last year. It is clear that we were wrong. Perhaps by leaving Cavendish, you will finally understand what happens when you allow your emotions to guide you instead of the rules."

Maud rubbed the cuff of her sleeve against her face and took a deep breath. It was no use. Grandma had judged Maud according to gossip and found her wanting. She had prioritized reputation over family. Again.

Grandma stood up. "It is settled. Your father wrote about you joining him, but I don't think he was truly serious. Now it is time he was."

How had her deepest wish suddenly become a punishment? Maud had always wanted to go to Prince Albert to live with Father, to have a real family. But now he was being forced into it. What would he think of her? Shame strangled her as tightly as one of her lace collars.

It would be best if she left.


That night Maud lay in bed, watching the sky, looking at how the cool moon shone on a dark sea of stars.

What was she going to do? How was she going to tell him? Part of her wished she could go back. Back to when counting nine stars for nine nights was only a game.

Nate was so in love with her that he would probably wait. He'd come back from Acadia University and she could return here and marry him. Nate would believe in their love because he thought he was a gallant knight and that was what one did.

Maud quietly slipped out of bed and walked over to her chest where she kept all of his letters, wrapped in two blue ribbons made from an old dress that no longer fit. She reread them, remembering his kisses, his touch, his whistle. Would she ever get that lilting tune out of her head?

Thank goodness her grandparents hadn't seen these.

Maud had so little power over nearly everything in her life; she hadn't ever experienced a thrill like the power she had over Nate's emotions. There was passion. Their stolen glances. Their first kiss. And he loved her and would wait to marry her, and she—she wanted to travel and write. She couldn't settle down. Not yet.

Nate had assumed she would always be here waiting for him, but deep down she knew that the future he had imagined for them wasn't possible. She didn't love him the same way he loved her. And her future plans? She wasn't sure how yet, but she was going to be a writer and attend school. It wasn't fair to him, for as much as she did love him—oh, and she did love him!—she didn't love him as deeply as he loved her.

As the cool moon caressed a gray cloud, Maud knew what she had to do. She had to let him go.

The following day her grandparents sent word to Grandpa Montgomery and Father, telling them about Nate. She was mortified, and worried that they would think ill of her. It took almost two weeks before her grandparents received a letter from Grandpa, who wrote that he was planning a trip to British Columbia on railroad business at the end of August and would bring Maud with him then. As Grandma read the letter out loud, there was none of Grandpa's usual warmth and humor. Instead it was business, factual, as if he were writing a letter to one of his fellow politicians in Ottawa.

Now that Maud was leaving, she wished she could go back to a time when she and Nate were just friends, when things hadn't gotten so complicated, when she could count nine stars without understanding the consequences.

One evening, Mollie suggested that they walk down to the Hole in the Wall. When they got to the shore, Maud told Mollie what had happened with her grandparents. Mollie was shocked that they knew, and sympathetic.

"As much as we don't care to admit it," Mollie said, putting her arm around Maud, "your different religions matter."

Maud rested her head on Mollie's shoulder. "I wish it didn't." And it was true.

They were quiet for a while, watching the icy water carve and crack itself around the Hole in the Wall.

"I'm going to miss this," Mollie said.

Maud kissed her friend's cheek. "I'm going to miss you." They embraced, and Maud was comforted by the strength of Mollie's arms around her. A consistent and constant friendship. When they pulled apart, she said, "You must promise me you will keep me informed of all the goings-on."

Mollie wiped a stray tear. "You have my solemn oath."

They walked and the conversation changed to other things, and Mollie asked Maud what she was writing. Even if she didn't always understand it, Mollie always told Maud her writing was "simply splendid."

"Do you promise not to laugh?"

"I would never laugh at you," Mollie said.

"I decided that when 'Cape LeForce' is ready I will submit it for publication."

"Ooo!" Mollie embraced her. "How thrilling!"

Maud appreciated how much her friend believed in her, even if she herself was so nervous about it. "I do enjoy writing about history. And you know that writing verse is my true calling."

"I'm so impressed, Pollie. I will never have a talent for such things. My talent will be finding a husband. One my mother will approve of."

Maud didn't want her friend to get married.

"We're not even sixteen yet," Maud said.

"True," Mollie said. "But Mother said that it was time I started to think about it. She was married at eighteen, you know."

"I think mine waited," Maud said, not thinking. "It was March." Then she remembered what Mrs. Simpson had said and her cheeks grew warm.

Mollie was quiet for a while, then said, as if she had been reading Maud's mind, "I'm sure it was not as those women suggested. You know they were trying to hurt your feelings."

While Maud was sure that was true, she was also certain there was some truth in what they had said. Why else would no one talk of her parents' courtship? But she didn't want to talk about it anymore, so instead she asked, "Do you have any suitors in mind?"

Mollie blushed. "I think you know."

"Jack."

Mollie nodded. "I keep hinting, as a girl is allowed, that I would be . . . open . . . to it. But he's not seeing me." Maud didn't want to discourage her friend, but Maud noticed that every time the Four Musketeers were together, Jack never walked close to Mollie or tried to take her hand, as Nate had when he'd first tried to show her how he felt. Maud wondered what would have happened if she had been in the same situation. Would she have been relieved, or as unhappy as Mollie was?

"Isn't that Jack and Nate coming over the dune?" Mollie said.

"Mollie Macneill, did you arrange a clandestine meeting?" Maud said, feigning shock.

Her friend shrugged. "It isn't my fault if the boys decided to take advantage of this early Island spring day and come down to the shore." She took Maud's hand. "You don't have to tell him today."

Her best friend was right. She needed more time.

"I know things seem dire, Pollie, and your grandparents are adamant about ending it, but please let's not ruin today. Let's keep things as they are before . . . before it all changes." Suddenly, Maud saw the sadness behind Mollie's summery disposition. With all that had transpired, Maud hadn't seen until now how this would affect her. Maud's relationship with Nate wouldn't be the only thing ending. With Jack and Nate going off to college, and Maud to Prince Albert, Mollie would be left here, alone.

The idea hit Maud like the icy waves of the Gulf, and she felt so sorry for Mollie that she forgot her own troubles. But even as she did, she realized that Mollie didn't want her pity right now; she just wanted one more day of fun, before reality set in.

So Maud greeted Nate and Jack as if it were any other day, and the four friends walked closer to the Hole in the Wall. The sun was low in the sky, mirrored in the water, and Maud thought how beautiful, how perfect her Island was even when her heart was aching.

"You seem quieter than usual today, Polly," Nate said as Mollie and Jack walked farther ahead. Mollie laughed really loudly at something Jack said.

"Just much to think about," Maud said.

"I suspect that's much of your predicament." He took her hand. "Thinking too much."

She laughed to cover up the tears in her throat. "Why do you think I write so much? My thoughts need somewhere to go." There was truth in this. Whenever things did get too much—too emotional—she would write in her journal.

"Come." He pulled her along, closer to the Hole in the Wall.

There was always a danger in crossing through, for if the tide came in, one could be swept up in it, but that was also part of the fun. They carefully stepped inside.

They didn't talk. The space was too small for sound. They leaned against the wall, still holding hands. A shiver of something that resembled repulsion or passion—she wasn't sure—caressed her spine. They kissed, and somehow she knew that this would be the last time she would allow him to do it, allow herself to feel him. After today she would have to tell herself to harden her heart. Tell herself that his kisses repulsed her. Tell herself she never really loved him at all.

## CHAPTER TWENTY-ONE

H er grandparents talked about sacrifice, but they would never
know—no one would ever know—what she had given up.

After that beautiful day at the Hole in the Wall, she had to
make it clear to Nate that she no longer loved him. If she told
him that her grandparents had discovered their secret, and about
their ultimatum, she was sure Nate would only see this as another
obstacle to cross. Nate was as romantic as she was, believing that
their love could weather any storm. So, she would have to show
him her feelings had changed. She would become detached. It
was the only way.

Even more challenging, she was still taking organ lessons.
Grandma didn't want to bring any attention, so she told Maud to
go, but to behave herself and come straight home. It was impossible to refuse Nate when he offered to walk her home. She made
him say goodbye to her before the cemetery. If his mother suspected anything, she didn't let on.

At school, it was worse. Maud avoided Nate, hoping that some
distance would ease the blow to come. So when Nate approached
her at lunch hour to go for one of their walks, Maud pulled Mollie
away as if she hadn't seen him, ignoring the profound hurt on his

face. It also made it difficult for Mollie to see Jack. Maud felt bad about this, but Mollie was her friend first. She just hoped Mollie understood.

Maud eventually told Pensie that she was leaving. She had looked so sad. She said she was sorry to have misjudged Maud's father, and promised to write long letters, full of all the news. Maud almost mentioned the elopement then, but something stopped her. Soon she would see Father and ask him about it herself.

But the longer Maud held off telling Nate—not only that she was leaving, but that they could no longer be together—the worse it became. No matter what she did, Nate would surely despise her, and the thought of him hating her was unbearable. It would be something she would have to live with forever.

A week after Grandpa's letter, Maud invited Nate for a walk through the Haunted Woods. They walked in silence for a long time. Knowing that this could be the last time they would have alone together, she found she couldn't quite let him go.

"I have something for you," he said, pulling out a letter.

She didn't take it. She knew the kinds of things it said, and she couldn't bring herself to read them. She couldn't bring herself to tell the truth.

"I'm going to Prince Albert in August," she said simply.

Nate crumpled the note. "So you decided it was better to ignore me rather than tell me the truth?"

She stared at the letter. If she had taken it, then at least she would have had one last note from him.

"I thought we were done keeping secrets." He touched her arm. She knew she should pull away, but she couldn't. She had a sudden desire to push his brown hair behind those irresistible ears.

"I didn't want to hurt you," she said instead.

"Your behavior hurts me," he said. "After all we've been through, don't you know how much I love you and will wait for you?"

Maud's chin shook from holding back her tears. It was true. His words echoed what she had always known. They were similar, so similar. For if she had loved him the way he loved her, she might have waited for him. Loving Nate meant not only defying her grandparents but also denying herself what she most desired—independence, a life of writing and education.

She had something that would cut deep into his heart, something that would make him stop pursuing her, fighting for her, fighting for them. She hadn't known until that moment if she would have to use it. But she did have to. She reached into her satchel and pulled out the book with the exquisite mermaid cover he had "lent" her all those months ago and held it out to him.

He gasped.

She turned away from Nate, focusing on Lover's Lane, their woods. Would she ever be able to be here without thinking of him? Then the words bubbled up, echoing something Pensie had told her so many months ago. Maud spun around, finding the kernel of emotion that made her believe what she was about to say was true. Forcing the book into his hand, she said, "I think we were fooling ourselves, Nate. We love the idea of Love. That is what this is. I wish you weren't so moony all of the time. It ruins things."

Nate's face went white. Would he actually weep? She couldn't bear it. "I believed that's what you loved about me," he stammered.

Romance was wonderful in books, but in real life, love was something altogether complicated, painful. It was time for the final blow.

"I think we can only be good friends," she said.

Nate took two steps, fumbling backwards, dropping *Undine* on the ground. She reached out to stop his fall, but he flung his arm out of the way. His casual demeanor was gone; his normally warm, gray eyes suddenly as cold as an Island storm.

"Don't you see, Maud," he said, picking up the book. "We never were."

## CHAPTER TWENTY-TWO

*W*e *never were.*

The words cut through her like shards of glass.

Maud tried to forget Nate and what he had said, but he was everywhere: school, concert practice, the Cavendish Hall. She'd see a boy on the road and think he was Nate. A final turn of the knife came when Nate sent Jack to return *Little Women* by way of Mollie. He couldn't even give it to Maud himself.

For a while she wasn't sure she would be able to look at or read it again, but a few days later she was in her room after dinner and picked it up from where she had left it on her bureau. She cried when she read about Jo reading *Undine*, but then she found herself back in Alcott's world. There was comfort in returning to a place where she knew what was going to happen. She communed with it, cutting out a picture from the *Young Ladies' Journal* of a young man with floppy hair and a clever smile who reminded her of Nate, and what she imagined Laurie to look like, and glued it to the title page. She underlined different sections this time, understanding Jo better now, and her ambition.

When Maud finished reading it, her heart still ached for Nate, but she felt more sure of her decision. She hoped one day he would forgive her. Things weren't always as clear in life as they were in books—and sometimes not even then. But she would never forget the first boy who loved her. Whom she had loved.

At the end of May, Miss Gordon announced the results of the *Montreal Witness* newspaper contest, with Nate coming in second and Maud third. Somehow, in all of the drama, Maud had completely forgotten about it.

It smarted when Miss Gordon reminded Nate and Maud that they would read their essays at the June concert, and Nate wouldn't even congratulate her. Not even when she wished him luck did he acknowledge her.

But Maud was learning to hide her emotions, and she read her essay, proud and strong, even when it broke her. And this time, there was no standing ovation.

Mollie was upset because, as Maud had foreseen, it was impossible for the Four Musketeers to remain as they were. More than once her best friend complained about this, and Maud wondered if Mollie blamed her. Eventually, they saw less and less of Jack, and Maud couldn't help but feel guilty about the rift she had caused.

School came to an end, which helped a bit, as Maud didn't have to see Nate and Jack every day. Maud enjoyed her summer the best she could by doing things with her friends: berry picking with Lu, going to lectures with Pensie and Mollie. Jack and Nate were there, but they sat on the other side of the hall. She wished Nate would forgive her. He would see her and pretend she wasn't even there. In a few weeks he was going off to college, and she would leave for Saskatchewan. She desperately wished to part as friends.

Now that travel plans had been settled, and it was clear to them that she had broken things off with Nate, her grandparents were much easier with her. Most of the summer was spent preparing for her trip, sewing clothes Maud would need. "We don't know what they've got out there in the Wild West, so we'd best make sure," Grandma said on their way to Hunter River, where they would be doing most of their shopping. It wasn't quite as big as Charlottetown, but it was only ten miles south of Cavendish and, being a main railway stop, had the materials they needed.

Aunt Annie came to Cavendish to help Maud with her travel suit because everyone knew she had the best needlework this side of the Island and those out in Saskatchewan could not outdo her. She even convinced Grandma that it was appropriate for Maud to wear a long skirt because she was almost sixteen.

Aunt Annie also showed Maud how to dress herself now that she had to wear a more severe corset instead of just a chemise. Drawers, chemise, corset, petticoat, corset cover, bustle, under-skirt, skirt, bodice, jacket, and a hat—there were so many pieces that Maud wondered how she would manage. Maud had seen Pensie dress before, of course, but now she understood why her best friend had initially complained at getting up a half hour ear-lier to get herself ready. Maud was going to have to get used to the weight of these new layers.

Toward the end of August, Maud was picking blueberries down by the school woods for a pie Grandma was going to bake, glad for the opportunity to take one last ramble before she left. She had allowed her hat to fall against her back, the sun stroking her skin. She was bent down, partaking of a few sweet berries, when she heard the familiar whistle.

She stopped mid-chew.

"Hello," he said.

She swallowed, placed her hat awkwardly back on her head, and stood up. "Oh, hello."

"Shall I walk you home as though it were old times, Polly?" he asked. "With a 'y.'"

She couldn't help but smile when she heard her old nickname. "Yes, Snip."

Nate took her basket, and then popped a few pieces of fruit into his mouth. When a smear of juice ran down his cheek, he blushed and wiped it away.

They were silent for a few steps and then he said, "So I'll be leaving for Acadia next week."

"Mollie told me," Maud said. "Father wrote me there is a high school in Prince Albert, so I'll continue my studies."

"Do you still want to teach?"

It felt so right to walk together and talk about the future, even if the future wasn't going to be as either one of them had imagined it.

"Miss Gordon advises it is a good profession for a woman," she said. "And then I can write too."

"Perhaps you'll become famous like Louisa May Alcott," he joked, but there was an edge to his teasing she hadn't heard before.

"I'll never be Alcott," she said, suddenly wishing they hadn't taken this walk.

When they reached the path to Maud's grandparents' house, he leaned against the old tree and, handing her the basket, crossed his arms over his chest. He looked at her like he had a year ago—like he could see through her. She ached for those days of friendship. Of love.

"When do you leave? I hate to think of Cavendish without you here," he said.

"This Sunday after church, I think. It depends on whether my Uncle Cuthbert can get away. I'll be staying with Grandpa Montgomery and then we'll be traveling west together."

"It sounds as though it could be quite an adventure," he said.

"I hope so," she said. "I need a change. I've disappointed—everyone."

Nate didn't contradict or defend her. Why would he?

He took a step forward.

"I will miss you, Maud," he said. "That day at the Hole in the Wall." He breathed out through his nose. "I've gone over what happened and it doesn't make any sense. It all seems so sudden."

"It was a wonderful afternoon," she smiled back, forgetting herself.

He reached out for her hand, but she pulled back. "I see," he said, letting his hand fall against his leg. "Can you at least tell me what happened to change your feelings? What I did?" He blinked and sniffed. If he cried now, she would let her guard down, and he would know how much she still adored him.

Why couldn't she have loved him enough?

"It was nothing you did," she said, finally. "But we come from different traditions and want different things. We are romantics, you and I." It would be so easy to take his hand. But he was staying east, she was going west. She had grand plans and—as much as it pained her—they didn't include a future with Nate Lockhart.

"Will you write to me?" she asked.

"Do you want me to?"

"I wouldn't have asked if I didn't want you to."

He smiled, sadly. "Letter writing was something we were always good at."

## CHAPTER TWENTY-THREE

There was one more thing Maud had to do before she left Cavendish.

The night before she was due to leave, Maud and Pensie took their last walk along the shore, and Maud finally told her about what had happened with Mrs. Simpson and Mrs. Clark, and what they had said about Maud's parents. Maud watched Pensie's expression change from shock to sadness and then to anger.

"How could you keep something so important from me?" Pensie said.

"I was ashamed," Maud said.

"Ashamed of your parents, or ashamed of what you thought I might say?"

Maud couldn't answer that. As usual, Pensie could see right through her.

"Pensie," Maud said, allowing her tears to come. "Please, forgive me. It has been such a challenging time."

"What about your precious Mollie?" The venom in Pensie's tone surprised Maud. She'd always suspected Pensie disliked Mollie, but she hadn't thought she hated her.

"What about her?" Maud said.

Pensie didn't say anything for a long while. She had turned toward the Gulf, her brown hair had come loose, and her crying mingled with the wind.

"Please," Maud said. "Say something."

Pensie turned around. "I know that I can be difficult. That I am bossy and always telling you what I think. But it is only because I love you, Maudie."

"I love you too, Pensie," Maud said. "But you were off with Quill, and Mary, acting as though you didn't need us—need me—anymore, as though our friendship didn't mean anything."

"That's not true!"

"It is true! Ever since the week of lectures in January you've been different. Sitting with Quill and Mary, saying that my friends and I were like children."

"Well, what about you and Mollie, and those boys? You had your own little group that didn't include me," Pensie said. "And if I have been different, it is because I've had things going on too."

"What things?" Maud asked.

Pensie sniffed. "Quill has asked me to marry him, and I have not refused him exactly, but I haven't accepted either."

"Why didn't you tell me?"

"Because I know what you think of him—oh, don't give me that look, Maudie. You think him dull, and one thing you cannot tolerate is someone who is dull."

Maud smiled then. She couldn't help it. Pensie knew her so well. Seeing Maud smile, Pensie did too.

"I guess we both have something to be sorry about," Pensie said.

"Do you forgive me then?" Maud said.

"Yes," Pensie said. "But it might take me a while to trust you."

The idea that Pensie didn't trust her clawed at Maud's heart, but she was learning that certain things needed time to heal.

———

The next day was Sunday, and after church, Maud took one last walk to the cemetery, alone. "It is all my fault," she said to her mother's stone as the warm August wind gently blew on her face. How disappointed her mother must be.

Afterwards, there was a little gathering of friends and family to say farewell to Maud. Pensie came, but she was quiet much of the time and only gave Maud a brief goodbye. Maud wanted to run after her, but after last night what more could be said? In time her friend would fully forgive her.

Even Grandma was silent most of the day. When she did speak, she told Maud to be respectful of her stepmother's rules, then later stuck some money into Maud's hand when no one was looking. Miss Gordon paid a call and gave Maud a small book of poems, *Sonnets from the Portuguese* by Elizabeth Barrett Browning.

"To me, this is some of the most truthful writing on love," Miss Gordon said.

Maud took the red-bound book and caressed its edges. Even now, after all that had happened between them, her first instinct was to tell Nate about the book—perhaps even find a poem to read together. But she couldn't now. Not today. They might have left things on a friendlier note, but it still hurt too much to see him.

Packing her trunk later that evening—the poems she had written, Aunt Annie's quilt, Nate's letters—everything seemed significant. She packed her beloved books: *Little Women*, *Jane Eyre*, *Wuthering Heights*, *Shakespeare's Sonnets*, *Pride and Prejudice*, and *The Last of the Mohicans*, which she planned to read on the train as it had good descriptions of Indians. Aunt Annie had suggested that Maud wear her hair up for the trip, and showed her how to do it. The first time Maud saw herself with her hair pinned up she realized she was no longer the scared young girl who had come back from Park Corner last summer.

Maud wrapped Nate's letters in the white shawl she'd worn that first night he walked her home and placed them delicately in the chest. She wasn't sure if she would be returning to the Island again, and she didn't want to think what Grandma would do if she ever saw them. She still thought of the old journal, the one she had burned not even a year before. So much had changed since then. It was probably just as well that she had burned it—it was as if it had been written by some other girl.

"Come in," Maud said, when she heard a soft knock at the door.

Grandma entered, holding something against her chest, and sat down on the bed beside a pile of clothes. Maud could see she was cradling a square item in her hand. Maud sat down beside her grandmother. The only sound was the waves of the Gulf lapping the shore.

"It is almost your mother's room again," Grandma said.

"I'm going to miss the sound of the water," Maud said. "Father says there is a river near his house, but I'm not convinced it will be the same thing."

Grandma gave a kind of strangled half laugh. "It won't be. You can be sure of that." Then she cleared her throat and sniffed. "I have been keeping something for you. I was considering giving it to you for your sixteenth birthday, but as you won't be here, I was thinking you could have it now." Grandma held on to the item for a long while and then passed it to Maud.

Maud took it from her as delicately as she could. It was wrapped in a worn piece of cotton, faded brown with flowers. It would make a lovely quilt square.

"Before you open it, there is a story I want to tell you. I suspect you'll be too distracted by the item once you unwrap it. You should know what it is, who it belonged to, and why you are getting it now."

Maud placed the package carefully upon her lap, suppressing the urge to open it.

"When your mother was nineteen years old, there was a popular notion among her friends to collect signatures and stories. Not unlike an autograph book, but it was called something different. Although I suspect that they are similar in nature."

Maud's heart thumped loudly.

"This belonged to your mother when she was a little older than you."

Everything went silent. Even the waves.

"I don't have anything that belonged to Mother."

Grandma took a deep, long breath. "You do now."

With shaking fingers, Maud delicately unwrapped the cloth, revealing a brown square book about the size of a prayer book. The spine was a little frayed but it was still in excellent condition. Leaning it over to the lamp, Maud could see the cover had the word *Scrap* written in gold across the middle with raised borders of fancy swirls, reminding her of royal carvings.

Maud's tears fell on the old worn cover.

"It is called a Commonplace Book," Grandma said.

"You've had this all this time?" Maud said. She was too surprised to be angry.

Her grandmother didn't respond. Maud tore herself away from the Commonplace Book in time to catch Grandma discreetly wiping her eyes.

"It was too painful," she said, after a while. "You know I don't enjoy talking about . . . her."

Because of what she did and the shame she caused? The question was on the tip of Maud's tongue. But if she asked, would Grandma take the book away? Would it ruin one of the few good moments she had had with Grandma since that awful day almost a year ago when her journal was discovered?

Maud placed her hand on top of the book, then carefully opened it and read the inscription on the flyleaf: *Miss Clara W. Macneill. Cavendish. April 11, 1872.*

Her mother's handwriting. Had she ever even seen it before? She opened the book and started to read through it.

There were poems: poems written by family members to her mother, and a few in what appeared to be Father's handwriting. Maud couldn't be sure.

"Your mother didn't know how clever you would be or foresee your talent for writing, which I suspect you get from my side of the family—although I'd deny it if you said anything," Grandma said. "Your grandfather is much too proud of the Macneill bloodline in that department."

Maud froze. There were blank pages. Blank pages she could fill with her own words!

"Thank you, Grandma," she whispered.

Grandma stood up, tapped Maud gently on her hand, and left.

Sitting in her mother's bedroom, Maud turned each page as if the book were a long lost relic.

Picking up her pencil, Maud wrote one sentence and then another and another. It felt as though she and her mother were having a secret conversation, one that reached back in time and brought her to a deep understanding of who her mother was: a woman in love with a man her parents didn't approve of.

As Maud crawled into bed that night, she thought of all that had happened in the last year, all that had changed. She realized that she would miss her grandparents, the constancy of them. She would miss the constancy of her friends nearby. The constancy of daily rituals and school days with Mollie and Jack and, yes, Nate. Would he write, as he'd promised?

And who would do the readings at next year's lecture, or perform at Miss Gordon's concerts? Would there be another Four Musketeers to take their place? Certainly the job could not be left to Clemmie and her ilk, but Mollie was still there. She would do her best to represent them.

And what of her favorite haunts? Would there be a Lover's Lane, a Haunted Woods, or a Hole in the Wall in Prince Albert?

Maud had learned that Saskatchewan was being christened "A New Eden," promising rich, fertile farmland, full of opportunity. Her father had also written about her going to high school. It was rare to have that opportunity—for a woman, anyway. It sounded as though it would be the perfect place to start over. Her grandparents wouldn't be there to judge her; there would be no whispers from the townspeople, from families who claimed superiority.

She was proud of being part of the Island's history; its forests and flowers were imprinted on her heart. And she was bringing with her Grandfather Macneill's stories, her journal, and Mother's Commonplace Book. They would connect her to a treasured past while she climbed to a bright new future.

# BOOK TWO

## *Maud of Prince Albert*

### 1890–1891

To be fully appreciated, Saskatchewan must be seen,
for no pen, however gifted or graphic, can describe with
anything like justice, the splendid natural resources,
the unequalled fertility, and the rare beauty of the
prairies of this Western Eden.

–L.M. Montgomery, "A Western Eden."

# CHAPTER ONE

As twilight descended upon the Saskatchewan prairie town of Prince Albert, exhaustion hung on Maud like the red caked dirt on her travel suit. She was in her new room in her father's home, Eglintoune Villa; she had immediately christened the room "Southview," as it looked south on the main road, which went uphill to the newly erected courthouse. It was all so different from her beloved Cavendish. She desperately missed the Tree Lovers, she missed the Gulf's dull roar, she missed the Island's red roads. Although she was a short walk from the North Saskatchewan River, and she thought the poplar trees here were beautiful, Maud hadn't realized how much of the Island's beauty she had taken for granted.

She had kept a record of the seven-day, three thousand–mile journey she had taken from Cavendish and had promised herself that she would copy it over into her regular journal when she arrived; she didn't want to forget anything.

Although happy to be reunited with Father the previous day, a part of her wished to be back in Grandpa Montgomery's grand house in Park Corner, where she had stayed for three days before they set out on their journey across the country. It had been a rainy and gray morning the day she and Grandpa left Park Corner.

Uncle Cuthbert drove them south to Kensington Station, where they'd picked up the train to Summerside to catch the ferry the following day.

At Kensington Station, when Grandpa came back with the tickets, he had exciting news. Prime Minister Sir John A. Macdonald and his wife were on their way to Summerside for a political rally via Charlottetown. Grandpa wired a telegram to them, arranging for them all to travel together. How thrilling! Her first train ride *and* she was to meet one of the most powerful men in Canada, one of the Fathers of Confederation.

When the special car came, Maud followed Grandpa on board, and suddenly, there she was, standing next to the great man himself. He was spry-looking, not handsome, but with a pleasant enough face. Lady Macdonald was fairly quiet and—despite her beautiful silvery hair and imposing stature—was dressed quite dowdily in her high, laced collar and black cap.

The prime minister and Grandpa discussed shipyard closures, but Maud was too busy looking at the Macdonalds and the elegant furniture of their train car to pay attention to the exact nature of what they were saying.

About half an hour later, they arrived in Summerside and, after saying goodbye to the Macdonalds, were greeted at the station by Grandpa's daughter, Maud's Aunt Nancy, and her husband, Uncle Dan Campbell, who took them back to the hotel they ran. The next morning, Maud and Grandpa took the ferry to Pointe-du-Chêne and then the train to St. John, New Brunswick. Even now, copying down the moment she had left the island for the first time, Maud's chin trembled as she remembered the boat floating away from the dock. As she stood on the deck, gripping the railing, tears whipping against her cheeks, she watched her beloved red earth fade from view.

From New Brunswick they boarded another train, traveling

through the wooded hills of Maine to Montreal, where Maud went out on her own along the Old Port, as her grandpa had stayed at the hotel to get some rest. She stayed close enough to the hotel so she wouldn't get lost, but she couldn't help feeling a spice of adventure in walking alone in such a big city where no one knew who she was.

They took a sleeping car that evening and Maud woke in a region that was all stumps and rocks in Northern Ontario and wrote in her travel journal as they entered the province of Manitoba. After a short stop in Winnipeg, which looked as though someone threw a handful of streets and houses down and forgot to sort them out, she and Grandpa finally arrived in Regina, Saskatchewan, at five o'clock in the morning. It was so cold and foggy that it was hard to see the city; she could only make out a series of gray buildings and matching gray sky. Grandpa checked them into the Windsor Hotel across the street from the train station, and Maud was so exhausted that she almost didn't make it up the stairs into bed before falling into a dreamless sleep.

A few hours later she was woken up by a knock at the door. She was expecting to see only Grandpa, so it took her a few moments to realize that the man standing beside him was her father. A few more lines to his face since the last time she'd seen him, but with the same brown hair and beard, and friendly cobalt-blue eyes that were exactly like hers. At the sight of her, he opened his arms and, without hesitating, she stepped into his big hug and breathed in his smell of summer sun, fresh-cut wheat, and tobacco.

"I'm so happy to finally have you here," he said, with his hands on her shoulders.

"I didn't expect to see you until we got to Prince Albert," she said, delighted.

"We didn't know if we would be able to arrange it." Grandpa slapped Father on the back and laughed. Maud had forgotten how they shared the same explosive laugh.

"I was able to come with a friend of mine who was traveling here on business," Father explained to Maud, "but we are going to have to be creative getting back to Prince Albert." Father unbuttoned the top of his jacket and sat down on one of the plush mauve chairs. "While the freight train now goes to Prince Albert, there's no passenger car. So we have to stop in Duck Lake first."

Maud had an absurd vision of them lugging their trunks through acres of wheat fields.

Her father laughed when he saw the dubious expression on her face. "At the end of every freight train, there's a little red wooden carriage called a caboose," he went on. "It's a three-hour journey, and it will be a little cramped, but nothing we can't handle, right, Maudie?"

Her father's enthusiasm was contagious and, even though her sense of adventure had left her in Winnipeg, she found herself smiling back at him.

"In the meantime, I was able to arrange a horse and buggy to tour Regina for the day so we can see the sights—what sights there are to be seen," he said. "How does that sound?"

Maud couldn't stop staring at her father. The whole trip out West, Maud had been worried that he would be ashamed of her, but, instead, he had planned something for them to do together. "Yes!" she said, when she could find her voice. "That sounds wonderful."

After Maud got herself dressed and had a quick breakfast of tea with toast and jam, they stepped out of the hotel onto Broad Street, where the horse and buggy were waiting. Around the train station, a new business district had formed, and as Father drove Grandpa and Maud through Regina, Maud watched people going about their everyday lives. She had never seen a North West Mounted

Police before and was struck by how many of them they were—and how handsome their uniforms were. She had seen police officers when she had visited Charlottetown with Grandma, but there wasn't much of a need of one in Cavendish. Regina was also so new-looking, compared to her home's older, more established houses and farms, whose founding families had come over one-hundred-and-fifty years before. The recently completed Government House, the official residence of the lieutenant-governor for the North-West Territories and Saskatchewan, was a grand two-storey imposing building made of stone and—according to Father—had running water and flushing toilets.

When Father detoured outside of Regina to show them the farms in the area, all Maud could see was dust and dirt; she prayed that Prince Albert would be better. She longed for Cavendish's rolling hills and deep green pastures and red shores.

All through the tour, her father and grandpa chatted, and while she appreciated the time to absorb her new surroundings, she also couldn't wait to be alone with her father so she could talk to him about Mother's Commonplace Book, and about Mother. She knew this wasn't the right time, though; if she were going to find out the truth, the timing would have to be perfect.

So she sat back and listened to Grandpa and Father discuss the "rough and tumble" Prince Albert politics.

"I'm glad that you got that matter settled with your supervisor," Grandpa said.

Father cleared his throat. "In addition to my duties as agent at the Confederation Life Insurance Company, there are a few ventures that look promising." When Grandpa didn't respond, Father went on. "You'll find that I'm quite well respected in Prince Albert, Father. People are happy I'm back, and there's talk of me running for local government."

"Following in the family business," Grandpa said. "About time."

When they finally boarded the caboose later that evening, Maud found herself shivering in the tiny car, which was lit by oil lamps and not much else. Her head hurt and she ached for a warm bed and some hot tea. A few hours later, they arrived at Duck Lake, a small town a few hours south of Prince Albert, where they stayed with one of Father's friends, Mr. Cameron. It was so late when they arrived that Maud just tumbled into the small bed in the spare bedroom and fell immediately into a deep sleep.

Maud woke refreshed the following morning and was relieved to find the world outside had changed from dusty brown to luscious green. There were even some poplar trees nestling in the distance.

After breakfast, Father's father-in-law, John McTaggart, arrived to take them on the last stage of the journey to Prince Albert. Mr. McTaggart was a local businessman and government land agent; his job was to convince people to move west—and to hear him talk, it was all he could do to keep people from coming. "Everyone wants to start fresh. Already Prince Albert can boast two thousand homesteaders who have come to work the land," Mr. McTaggart said as they drove away in his horse and buggy and started the journey north.

"It's a fool's notion," Father said. "I'm not going to rely on the land; I've seen too much of that back East. I make a good living as an auctioneer and, then—" He turned and winked at Maud. "Who knows."

"Yes," Grandpa Montgomery said, "who knows."

Father ignored his remark. "Things are about to move in our favor, Maudie. You'll see." Maud was quiet. Father appeared to be all set up in Prince Albert with a new family and new opportunities. Perhaps this "New Eden" would favor her as well.

The three men continued to talk about the expansion and the railroad while Maud took in her new surroundings. A warm sun guided them through rolling prairie hills blanketed in wild flowers and bluebells. Mr. McTaggart told Maud and Grandpa he had moved to Prince Albert with his second wife and children four years ago. Maud couldn't decide if she liked him or not—he certainly enjoyed hearing himself talk—but she was so tired she was happy to let him.

In the mid-afternoon, they arrived in Prince Albert. Mr. McTaggart pointed out his white-painted two-storey home on the top of the hill, just on the edge of the town. It appeared to be a friendly sort of place. "We call our home Riverview," Mr. McTaggart said, "because it has a lovely view of the Saskatchewan River from our front window. You can see all the way down the hill."

As they drove slowly down the hill on Central Avenue, she gasped in delight. Prince Albert was built on several natural terraces along the riverbank, with hills sloping back over the rolling prairies, peppered with groves of willow and poplar trees and tiny blue lakelets. It certainly didn't have Cavendish's traveled roads and ancient trees, but it did have a quaint, medieval quality.

As they traveled down Main Street, Father said, "And there it is, Eglintoune Villa." The house had two storeys, with a porch on the left-hand side, a white picket fence around it, and a tin dog perched upon the front gate. It was much newer than her grandparents' home, or most of the homes on the north shore. It faced the manse and Prince Albert's St. Paul's Presbyterian Church. According to Mr. McTaggart, the Presbyterian Church owned much of the property in Prince Albert, with the Hudson's Bay Company still trading on the land east toward Goschen. A number of people were congregating in front of Eglintoune Villa waiting to greet them.

"Welcome," her father said. As he helped Maud out of the cart, she made note of the small yellow house next door with a porch, which, much like everything else in town, faced the river.

Two young people and a woman around Aunt Annie's age sat looking out at their arrival.

"Next door is the Kennedy residence; they're related to the Pritchards," Father said, noticing where she was looking. "That's Laura Pritchard on the stoop with her brother, Will. They're about your age, Maudie. Their father, Richard Pritchard, was the one who drove me to Regina. He owns a homestead and ranch outside of town near Maiden Lake."

Following her father and grandpa to the house, Maud glanced over at the Pritchards, who stopped talking and raised their hands to greet her. Maud wasn't used to people living so close to one another, and her hands were full with her bag, so she gave them what she hoped was a friendly nod. In Cavendish, although it seemed so small, there were a few acres between farms. It seemed strange to see other people on their porches, so close together. She felt rather exposed.

As Maud followed her father through the gate, both siblings stared at her. Maud looked away and then, after a few moments, heard the girl laugh. She hoped that they weren't laughing at her. Maybe they had somehow heard what she had done in Cavendish and were judging her. Would Father have told his new wife all about it, who, in turn, told the neighbors? Father hadn't even mentioned Nate, or the real reason she was here. Who knew what he thought of her?

Father pushed the gate open and guided Maud toward the house. She turned away from the Pritchards and recognized her stepmother from the wedding picture. The little girl, who Maud assumed was her sister, Katie, hid in her mother's light green skirt. Maud's new stepmother was a few inches taller than Maud and stood so erect that it seemed as though she was waiting for judgment day. Father had written that her stepmother preferred to be called "Mamma." Maud felt a little old to be doing so, but she didn't want to get off on the wrong foot. Mamma didn't appear to be much older than Miss Gordon, about twenty-five or twenty-six, and wore a plain black chemise, which stretched slightly over her stomach, with pretty embroidery along the sleeves.

"You must be tired after your long trip, Maud," Mamma said, after giving her a light hug. "I remember being so exhausted when I arrived here, and that was just from Ontario. You have traveled so much farther."

"Maudie was a good traveler," Grandpa said, shaking Mamma's hand.

"I'm sure," Mamma said in a tone that indicated she wasn't convinced of any of Maud's talents. Maybe it was just nerves. It isn't every day one meets a stepdaughter. Katie extended her arms and called for Father. "This is Katie," Father said, lifting her up.

"Hello, Katie," Maud said. Katie had angel curls of the palest gold and the same cobalt-blue eyes as Father. The little girl hid her face in her father's chest, and then she threw back her head and laughed in sheer delight as he swung her around. Maud gazed at the river, ignoring a prickling feeling in her throat. Father used to twirl her around when she was small.

She focused on the wind and the river. She had never been anyone's older sister; she had never been anyone's sibling. In Cavendish, Maud had felt like she was always a visitor, some sort of distant relative. Even with the Campbells, who adored her, Maud felt like she was a guest: not really a member of the close-knit group of cousins.

"We'll be the best of friends." She tickled Katie's ankle and the little girl giggled.

Except for Mamma, who seemed a bit subdued, Maud's step-mother's family, the McTaggarts, were all cut from the same cloth, loud and opinionated, each talking over the other. It was all so removed from the quiet reserve of the Macneill clan; even the jovial Montgomerys weren't as overbearing. But she liked Mrs. Mary McTaggart—Mamma's mother—who made sure Maud had a place to sit and a nice piece of pie. "I remember how I felt when I first arrived here. Plain worn out."

The hired girl, whom Maud heard Mamma call Edith, helped with the serving, but as the room filled with conversation and references to people and places Maud didn't know, her head clouded over and it all became a maze of noise. It was clear the town had its own version of the clans: the McTaggarts and Pritchards, as well as one of the founding families, the Agnews, who ran a hardware store in town. Maud wasn't sure where she would fit in to this new community.

Finally, one by one, they all said good night and Father instructed Edith to take Maud upstairs.

"My name is Edith but you can call me Edie," she said. Edie had dark hair, almost black, tied up in a low bun, brown eyes, and an inviting smile. It was a little strange to Maud, as she wasn't used to living in a house with a hired girl. Grandfather and Grandma Macneill didn't have one; Grandpa Montgomery did, but the maids lived in a separate part of the house near the kitchen, so Maud didn't know them very well.

The upstairs had four bedrooms: there was the master bedroom facing the front of the house, a nursery beside it, and a "spare" one where Maud was sure she was staying. She stopped in front of it, and was surprised when Edie kept going to the end of the hallway. When they arrived at the south bedroom, Maud was immediately confused. There were two beds. Did Mamma expect her to push them together, or pick one?

"Which bed do you want?" Edie asked, leaning against the doorframe. "I have been sleeping on the one next to the door in case Mrs. Montgomery needs me."

Coolness swept over Maud, and she dropped the carpetbag

she was holding. Father hadn't said anything about her sharing a room. And with a complete stranger who was—no offense to Edie, who seemed nice enough—a hired girl!

Maud almost turned around and marched back downstairs to have a word with Father and Mamma, but she remembered how Grandma had told her to be respectful of her stepmother's rules. This was Mamma's house, and there must have been a valid reason why she wanted Maud to stay in this exact room. It did have a lovely view of the sloping prairies, covered with newly planted trees.

"How about I take the other one?" Maud said, sitting down on the bed. "I enjoy sleeping near an open window anyway."

"There is a lovely view from that window. Facing south."

Now, as she came to the end of the long entry, she wrote, *Southview. A place I can name.*

# CHAPTER TWO

I t was strange for Maud to be in a place where she didn't know every corner, where she wasn't part of its history. In Prince Albert she wasn't sure where she belonged, and she began to wonder if Mamma thought that it was in the kitchen with Edie.

After the first few days, Katie's shyness faded, and she quickly became Maud's little shadow, following her wherever she went. It reminded Maud a little bit of her Campbell cousin, Frede. When Frede was little, she would get upset when her parents sent her up for her nap because she wanted to "play with Maudie." But something told Maud she couldn't quite let her guard down around her new stepmother. Mamma was nice enough: polite and cordial, making sure Maud was comfortable in her new surroundings by having Edie place fresh-cut flowers in their room, and providing whatever else she needed. Mamma was also often exhausted, complaining that the late August heat wasn't good for her. Since Maud wanted to make a good impression, she often helped Edie with the dishes and meals. Mamma rewarded Maud for this good behavior by tasking her with the weekly dusting.

Maud missed her daily rituals: walking along the shore with Pensie, helping Grandma with supper, and her adventures with

Mollie and the other Musketeers—including Nate. She tried not to think of him, but she often found herself wondering what he was doing. He must have left for Nova Scotia by now. Was he enjoying Acadia? Did he miss her too?

Thinking about all of this made Maud homesick. She wished there had been letters waiting for her when she arrived, despite the fact that it was too soon for any mail.

During Maud's first week, Grandpa rested and prepared for his journey farther west. She had kept an eye out for the Pritchards, the ones she had seen her first day, but she overheard the neighbor, Mrs. Kennedy, tell Mamma that they had gone back to the ranch a few miles outside of town. A place called Laurel Hill.

One morning when she had been there for about a week, Maud asked Father if he might take her and Katie on a drive around Prince Albert so she could get better acquainted with the town. Mamma was tired and Grandpa was sending telegrams, so she finally had Father (mostly) to herself. She hoped she could show him Mother's book, and perhaps, if she could get the nerve, ask him what had happened all those years ago.

That afternoon, Father borrowed Mr. McTaggart's horse and buggy and drove Katie and Maud north toward the river, past the church, and then down the main street, which paralleled the North Saskatchewan River, where merchants were loading furs onto riverboats heading west. They also passed a cluster of Indian women in bright colors. Although they appeared tired and thin, they were industriously embroidering what appeared to be mittens, and one woman was working on a beautiful jacket. The way they were working reminded Maud of evenings in Cavendish with her grandmother. Father drove up the hill, past the McTaggarts' house and the almost completed courthouse, and out of town. Poplars stood tall against the baby-blue sky, and as they drove along the countryside, Father pointed to some farms down the way.

"That's where many people, such as the Pritchards, are making their claims. You'll meet them at church."

Maud was more interested in Father's life than in people she didn't know. "You've been a lot of places, haven't you, Father?" she asked, holding Katie, who was sleeping soundly against her chest.

"That's right. As you know, I was a young sea captain and traveled to England, the West Indies, and South America—"

"So thrilling," Maud said. "I wish I could do that."

"A merchant ship is no place for a woman," he said. "But it is a good way for a man to see the world . . . then I returned to the Island where I met your mother."

For a while, the only sound was the horse's hooves swishing in the grass and then Maud dared to ask, "And then what happened?"

Father cleared his throat and said, "I met your mother, and then you were coming along . . . so I had to make sure I had something closer to home."

One answer spiralled into more questions. How had he met her? Why did he stay home? What wasn't he telling her? But she was too slow to speak, and Father continued, "Afterwards, your uncle Duncan McIntyre, a drunk and a thief, I might add, ruined our general store and we parted ways. Then . . . after your mother died . . . it was time for me to make it better for you—for us—so I went back on the ship to Boston and worked in various trades there, which included my time as a clerk, and that has helped me run for office in Battleford. You never know where experience will create opportunity, Maud. Remember that."

Being here had certainly given her opportunities to travel and see parts of Canada. And her family.

"Father . . ." Maud looked down at sleeping Katie. It was so peaceful listening to the clicking of the wheels, the wind talking with the trees. Dare she destroy this peaceful moment with more questions?

"Yes?" Father put his arm around her and she leaned her head against his shoulder.

"Nothing."

Later that afternoon, when Edie was downstairs, Maud was alone in Southview rereading the love poem in Mother's Commonplace Book. She was suddenly overcome with the desire to know the truth about her parents' relationship. After her pleasant afternoon with Father, she knew he would be open to sharing this with her. He had to be.

She had made her way to the top of the steps when she heard Mamma say, "I think it is inappropriate for you to call a girl of almost sixteen 'Maudie.'"

"It is only a term of endearment, Mary Ann," Father said, keeping his voice low. "I don't know why this matters to you."

"I'm concerned for you—for us," she said. "People are paying attention to you, to see how you conduct yourself with your family, how your family behaves. It is important that we put forth a good impression."

Maud slid onto the top step, the book falling against her chest.

"I think Maudie behaves quite well for a girl her age," he said.

At least Father was defending her.

"Most girls her age don't put on airs like she does," Mamma said.

What did she mean, "airs"? Who was Mamma but a small-town Ontario girl?

"What were her grandparents teaching her out there on that island?" her stepmother went on. "Given why she's come to us, I think this is our opportunity to show her what is appropriate."

Opportunity. This time it felt as though the word was working against her. Here was yet another woman who wanted to tell her what to do.

Maud heard her Father kiss Mamma. "Please don't worry, particularly in your condition." He paused. "We don't want any complications."

Maud cradled the Commonplace Book in her lap, tears falling against the pages.

"Then allow me the latitude I need to handle her properly," Mamma said. "This is woman's work."

Handle her? Was she some horse Father had asked her new mother to break in?

Father sighed. "Very well, I will stop calling her 'Maudie.'"

Her heart felt stretched to the point of breaking. She had felt this way only once before, when her grandparents had found her journal. Mamma wanted to mold her, train her—into what Maud wasn't sure. Would she go through her things? Should she go west with Grandpa and then back to Cavendish? Would anyone take her in?

Maud held the book tight against her chest. Hearing Mamma—and Father's response—it was clear that Mother's Commonplace Book wasn't safe. Maud had to keep it hidden.

Outside the Southview window, thick gray clouds hung low, almost reaching the green fields. There was a crash of thunder, and a sudden pounding of rain splattered on the roof. It felt as if she was being battered, as if the rain was a punishment for her crimes against Nate, against her grandparents, and against her mother's memory.

Despite the fact that it was so many miles from the Island, Prince Albert was turning out to be much like Cavendish: no one was going to stand up for her here, not even her father could defend her against her stepmother. And in some ways, Prince Albert was worse. Maud was now in a place where she had no history, where no one cared if she was a Macneill or a Montgomery—although her Mamma obviously cared what others thought. Maud was dependent upon the whims of anyone who decided it was their duty to take her in.

Opening up her trunk, she buried her mother's book underneath her clothes, books, and pieces of the crazy quilt she had yet to sew. Only when it was safe would she finally ask Father her long-cherished questions.

In the meantime, Maud would make things right for Father and for herself. She wouldn't complain; she'd be the dutiful daughter and show that woman she was wrong about her, that she didn't "put on airs." And she would do so well in school that Father would pay for her to go to college. She would never be dependent upon the likes of Mamma.

No, she was not Maud's Mamma; her behavior certainly didn't deserve that title. Maud would be respectful and cordial to her stepmother in public—even call her Mamma—but she would be Mrs. Montgomery in Maud's private journal, as if she were a stranger who had no power over her. And she would keep a separate, more public journal. One that would only contain musings about the weather and silly anecdotes about school, when she started. Because the truth was more dreadful. Mary Ann McRae Montgomery was the supreme monarch of this little castle in the west, and Maud her subject. Maud had no more power here than she'd had in Cavendish.

## CHAPTER THREE

During those first two weeks in Prince Albert, Maud had such an attack of homesickness that she almost wrote her grandparents begging them to take her back. Every night she would check the table in the hall where Father left the mail, but there was nothing. It didn't help that they were having a particularly bad rainy season. It seemed to add to her despair.

She tried returning to the rhythm of writing in the morning. Her piece of verse, "On Cape LeForce," was almost ready to send to the *Charlottetown Patriot* and, while that prospect helped a little, it was still difficult to concentrate.

One evening, she and Edie went hazelnutting on the bluffs along the riverbank, which had a splendid view of the poplar trees and the water. Across the way, some of the Indian women and girls were picking Saskatoon berries, talking. Maud admired the soft, musical language they were speaking. Seeing them together reminded Maud of when she and her friends would pick berries together back home for pies. The thought of it reminded her of the last time she picked blueberries, and Nate.

Pushing the memory aside, she looked over at Edie, who seemed like a nice enough girl. Quiet, but good humored. And they did share a room. Perhaps they could be friends? Maud had never made friends with someone she hadn't known practically her whole life and didn't quite know where to start.

"Where do your people come from?" Maud asked.

Edie stopped picking hazelnuts and her shoulders tensed. "Why do you ask?"

Had she offended the girl? Maud had heard her grandmother ask such questions to people who were from away. This way, she said, one could gauge where in Scotland or England they came from.

"I'm sorry, Edie," she said in a voice she reserved for her elders. "I was only making conversation. Given that we are spending so much time together, I thought it would be good to get to know one another."

Edie's shoulders dropped. "I see." She tossed one of the hazelnuts into the basket. "My family lives in Battleford." Maud took note that Edie didn't go into a lot of detail about who her family was, or where they came from. She wanted to ask, but she thought it would be rude. She also knew what it was like to have a story you didn't wish to tell.

"Most of my family is back in Prince Edward Island," Maud said, searching for something else to say.

"Do you like it here?"

Maud gazed over the river. Two of the little girls were sitting close together, clearly telling secrets. Her mind wandered to the empty table in the hall. "I miss my friends. Pensie and Mollie, especially. They're my bosom friends." She also missed Nate, but she was certainly not going to mention him.

"I miss my family too," Edie said. "But working for your family is a good opportunity."

Maud had a hard time imagining working for Mrs. Montgomery as an opportunity, but she also knew that for some women it was the only option.

"My mother works as a maid for the wife of a North West Mounted Police officer," Edie went on. "That's how I got this position."

She had overheard Mamma talking to Mrs. McTaggart about how grateful she was that the "half-breed" had decided to come with them so that she didn't have to train someone else. Maud paused. Was it Edie they were talking about? Perhaps that was why she was so quiet?

One of the women across the river laughed.

If it was Edie they had been speaking about, perhaps she would know more about the women across the river. "Do you know what language those Indian women are speaking across the river?" Maud asked.

"They're speaking Cree. In their language they call themselves *Nehiyawak*, meaning 'the People.'" She moved over a bit and picked from another bush.

"It is quite beautiful."

"Yes." She picked up another hazelnut and stared at it for a long time. "My mother speaks Cree with the local women when they bring items to trade."

"Do you speak it?" Maud said. "I always thought it would be wonderful to speak another language. We learned Latin in school, but I think French would be wonderful. I heard some men speaking it in Montreal and I wished to know what they were saying."

Edie put the hazelnut in her basket and sat down sideways in the grass, her skirt covering her knees and ankles. "Actually . . . I speak a language that blends Cree and French, called Michif."

"How very exotic," Maud said, placing her basket down and getting comfortable.

Edie laughed. "I don't know if it is exotic, but it is the language of the Métis."

Maud returned her gaze to the river and listened to the sound of the wind through the poplar trees. If she closed her eyes she could almost imagine herself back on the island. "I love this," she said after they had picked more hazelnuts. "The river. The trees. Maybe I'll write a poem about it and send it home to Pensie."

"It is beautiful," Edie said. "Do you know that this river, the Saskatchewan, has a name that is Cree in origin? Perhaps you can use it in your poem."

Maud smiled. She knew there was a reason she liked Edie. "I adore hearing about the history of a place. Please tell me its spirit."

Edie smiled. "The Cree call this river Kisiskatchewani Sipi, which loosely translates to 'swift-flowing river.'"

Maud gazed out over the river. "I wonder . . . my teacher, Miss Gordon, told us one day while we were studying the history of Prince Edward Island that the Indians who live there, the Mi'kmaq, called it Abegweit, which means 'cradle on the waves.' Do you think it is connected somehow? Isn't that wonderful to imagine?"

"Yes." Edie smiled.

Maud smiled back. They picked hazelnuts silently for a while. It was nice being with someone who had such a pleasant disposition, unlike her stepmother. "Edie, may I ask . . . why do you think working for my stepmother is a good opportunity?" She didn't add anything about putting up with her sour nature. No opportunity could be worth that.

"One of the reasons I agreed to come to Prince Albert is because the high school allows Métis to attend. My sister only made it to sixth grade, but I want to be a teacher."

"Me too," Maud said.

"Do you!" Edie's brown eyes brightened. "There are convent schools out East that are willing to take Métis women. Being a teacher is one of the few professions, besides being a maid, that is acceptable."

It seemed she and Edie had more in common than Maud realized.

"Besides, with Mrs. Montgomery expecting, she'll need my help and possibly give a good recommendation to the convent school about how good I am with children."

Maud felt a creepy-crawly tickle down the back of her neck. "What do you mean 'expecting'?"

"Oh no!" Edie dropped her pail, hazelnuts scattering across the grass. "I didn't realize that Mrs. Montgomery hadn't told you. I know that it is a delicate matter, but I thought . . ." She bit her bottom lip. "I shouldn't have said anything. Please, don't tell her I told you."

Mrs. Montgomery. Pregnant.

"Why wouldn't Father tell me?" Maud leaned her head against a tree. "I know it isn't proper to discuss such things, but if I am going to have another brother or sister, I should know."

Edie stepped timidly toward her. "I only know because I help Mrs. Montgomery with her maternity corset. She started wearing it this week. But, if she finds out I told you, she might send me back to Battleford."

"Why didn't she want me to know?" Maud said. "It doesn't make sense. I am thrilled!" And Maud realized that despite how she'd found out, she was excited to have the opportunity to be a big sister again.

"I don't know," Edie said. "But I wouldn't be surprised if Mrs. Montgomery had plans for you."

Plans? What kind of plans? Didn't they know that she had plans of her own?

Maud closed her eyes. People talk of stillness, but for Maud the wind, the grass, the river, the trees were in motion.

After a while, Maud opened her eyes and promised Edie she would keep this to herself. Across the river, the Cree women and children still diligently worked. Maud would not let on that she knew Mrs. Montgomery's secret. In time her stepmother would confide in her. She would work with Mrs. Montgomery, show her she was dependable, a daughter who would help her family with whatever they needed no matter the sacrifice.

The following day, when Maud entered the dining room, Grandpa, Father, her stepmother, and Katie had already started eating breakfast. Maud tried to not think about Grandpa leaving at the end of the week. She had become quite fond of having him around; he was often a shield between her and her stepmother. This was never more apparent than that morning.

"Good morning," she smiled at everyone.

"Is it?" Mamma—no, Mrs. Montgomery—said as Maud sat down, trying to see if the corset betrayed her stepmother's secret. It didn't. "Practically afternoon, I think."

Maud toyed with her ring and checked the grandfather clock at the far end of the parlor. It was not yet 8 a.m.

"Maud is probably still tired from our travels, Mary Ann," Grandpa said, wiping his mouth. "We don't want her to be ill because she's so worn out. Remember how Agnes McKenzie traveled from Halifax, caught a chill, and died?"

Father laughed. "I don't see that happening with Maudie—Maud. She has a strong constitution."

"She's been here over a week," Mrs. Montgomery said.

Grandpa placed his hand on Maud's. "Even so, we don't wish her ill, do we?"

In that moment, Maud wanted to beg her grandpa to take her with him. But she knew it was impractical; he had work to do in British Columbia, and she would only be in the way. She quickly sat down, surveying what was left for breakfast. Maud was suddenly not hungry, but she didn't wish to worry her grandpa; he thought that if you didn't have an appetite, you must be dying.

"Tea?" Mrs. Montgomery motioned the pot to Father.

"I think we have time for one more cup before we visit some people at the Kinistino Lodge," Father said to Grandpa. "You know I helped to start it for Scottish expats when I first arrived in Prince Albert, and it's thriving."

Mrs. Montgomery poured Grandpa's tea, then Father's, and then her own before replacing the teapot on the table.

She ignored Maud's cup.

Maud opened her mouth to ask for tea, again, but then Grandpa asked Father, "Did you tell Maud your news?"

Was he going to tell her about the new baby? Had Father changed his mind? Did he want Maud to return to the Island with Grandpa? Maud wasn't sure if she was angry or relieved.

Father simultaneously winked and added some milk and sugar to his cup. "Your arrival was in the paper!"

"How exciting!" Maud clapped, finding she was, in fact, relieved to have been spared another journey—and the possibility of an awkward conversation about such delicate matters in front of her grandpa. Perhaps she was a bit hungry after all. She picked a piece of toast off the main plate and spread some butter over it.

"It was nice of the editor, J.D. Maveety, to mention it," Mrs. Montgomery said to her husband, slowly sipping her tea. "Shows how well respected you are in the community."

Maud eyed her own teacup. It must have been an oversight. Perhaps she didn't think Maud wanted tea. She would be brazen and ask for tea, that was all. Maud was getting up the nerve when Mrs. Montgomery turned to her with a cold expression. "What are you waiting for, girl? You were late for breakfast; the least you could do is eat your toast quickly so you can help with the dishes."

Maud had been used to Grandfather's attacks, but something in Mrs. Montgomery's tone pierced any last, faint hope Maud had of receiving a mother's love from her. She hated her for it.

Maud cleared her throat. "May I have some tea, please?"

Father and Grandpa exchanged a look. Mrs. Montgomery's face went pale. Without a word, she picked up the teapot and poured what appeared to be very strong tea.

"Thank you," Maud said.

Mrs. Montgomery slammed the teapot down.

"Toast!" Katie said.

"Here, Katie," Maud said, handing her little sister a piece of her toast, careful to avoid her stepmother's eye. "Have a little bit of mine."

What had she done in the brief time she'd been in Prince Albert to make Mrs. Montgomery behave so? She would rather have Grandma's constant nitpicking than this inexplicable hostility.

"You know, Maudie," Grandpa began, but he was interrupted by Mrs. Montgomery clicking her fork against her plate. Grandpa placed his napkin on the table. "if you miss Cavendish too much, you can always return with me when I come back this way in September."

"Maudie—Maud will have started school by that time," Father said.

Mrs. Montgomery started rattling the dishes together to clear them away. Maud stood up to help her, but she shook her head. "Don't bother," she grunted, and went into the kitchen. It was clear that Mrs. Montgomery, at least, would enjoy sending Maud home.

Soon the awkward breakfast came to an end, and Father went to tend to some business, leaving Maud and Grandpa alone.

"I meant what I said, Maudie," Grandpa said, leaning toward her. "You don't have to stay here."

Maud didn't know why she deserved her grandpa's kindness after what had happened with Nate in Cavendish.

"Thank you, Grandpa," she said. "But Father is right; high school starts next week. I'll stay."

## CHAPTER FOUR

A few days later, Father and Mrs. Montgomery took Grandpa to the train station in Duck Lake. Maud said goodbye to him on the porch, little Katie clinging to her leg. The parting was bittersweet. Although Maud knew that she would see him again in a few weeks, she couldn't shake the feeling that she was losing an ally.

As soon as they left, Katie complained that she was hungry. "How about a little tea party, just you and me?" Maud asked, remembering the tea parties she and Aunt Emily used to have when she was small, before things went sour between them.

Katie nodded her head excitedly.

Maud extended her hand and the little girl took it. "Come with me." And they toddled together to the kitchen. Maud put Katie in her chair and went to the pantry. She lifted the lock, but it wouldn't budge. She tried again, nothing. After turning the knob left and right and struggling with it for a few minutes, she looked over her shoulder at her sister and said, "It appears to be stuck."

"Stuck," her sister repeated.

"Edie!" she called, searching the kitchen drawers for a key. Why was the cupboard locked?

Edie, who had been upstairs cleaning, came down, broom in hand. "Yes, Maud."

"Do you know where the key to the pantry is? I wanted to have a little tea party with Katie, but it is locked."

Edie swung the broom from one hand to the next.

"Edie?"

"Yes." The broom swayed back and forth.

Maud strode over to the girl and stopped the broom. "The key?"

"She keeps it locked," Edie said.

"What?"

"She keeps the pantry locked up."

"Mrs.—Mamma locks the pantry?"

Edie nodded. "She says so she can keep track of things."

This was madness. Katie needed to eat. Even her grandparents wouldn't have done something so ridiculous.

"Is the cold box unlocked?" Maud asked.

Edie grinned. "Yes, there is no lock."

Maud wiped her hands against her apron. "Excellent." She went over to the cold box and found some cheese and milk. It would have to do.

She played with Katie most of the afternoon, crafting exactly what she would say to Father when he got home. But that night Father came in with letters from Mollie and Lu, and in her excitement to see them, Maud forgot all about it. Letters were exactly the elixir she needed.


The next day, Maud was outside in the back garden rereading the letter from Lu, which gave her the latest goings-on at school, when Mrs. Montgomery's stepsister, Annie, who was Maud's age, waltzed in. Maud reluctantly whispered a farewell to Lu and Cavendish, and put the letter in her pocket.

"Hello!" Annie said, making herself comfortable in the chair beside Maud. "Where are Mary Ann and your father?" Annie was wearing a stylish navy blue skirt and matching bodice and her hair was pulled back with clips. Maud found herself envying Annie's fringe bangs.

"They're at the lodge," she said.

"How are you finding things here?" Annie said, after a few moments of awkward silence.

"It is very different from Cavendish." Maud wasn't sure how much she could trust Annie.

"I'm sure." Annie leaned back against the chair. "It was quite a change for us to move from Ontario to this rough country. And the dirt!" She slapped at her skirt. "No matter how often I beat this skirt it never comes clean."

Despite herself, Maud laughed. "True." She wiped the dirt off her own light brown skirt. "But it is an adventure. Certainly bigger than Cavendish."

"Possibly." Annie picked an imaginary speck off her shirt. "But compared to Ontario, Prince Albert is a backwater. Mother says thank goodness for the church or there would be nothing but drunken men philandering about. And there's also the school, of course."

When Maud arrived, she had heard Mrs. McTaggart say something similar, but she would have never dreamed of repeating it! She was both impressed and surprised by Annie's candor.

"We have a new teacher this year, Mr. Mustard," Annie went on. "You know he's a friend of Mary Ann's—they went to school together—and is supposed to be well educated."

Maud got that familiar creepy-crawling feeling down her back; it tended to happen every time her stepmother was mentioned. What lies had her stepmother told Mr. Mustard? It wasn't an ideal situation in which to produce a good first impression.

"I'm hoping he'll be better than the last teacher, who couldn't control the boys at all," Annie went on.

"I miss my old teacher, Miss Gordon. She could control a room with one look."

"Our teachers in Ontario were the best-educated," Annie said. "So this Mr. Mustard has much to live up to."

Maud hid a smile. Annie did enjoy putting on airs.

"Do you want to walk over to school together?" Annie asked.

"Edie and I were planning on it," Maud said. Normally this might be considered improper, walking to school with the hired help. But given Maud's newfound friendship with Edie, she didn't see the harm. "I know where I'm going. Father showed it to me on our drive around town."

"That's perfect then!" Annie said. "I'll stop by early and we can all walk over together. I'm not sure how many girls are actually going to be there; some of them go to the convent school up the way, and others are home."

"Father told me the girl next door goes to the convent school."

"You mean Mrs. Kennedy's niece Laura? Yes, she goes to the convent school, although she's Presbyterian. Can you imagine? My parents would never allow that." So some things in Prince Albert were the same as in Cavendish. "Her brother, Will, has been helping on his father's ranch most of the summer, so I'm not sure he'll be in school."

He must be the redhead Maud had seen on the day she arrived.

"So, tomorrow?" Annie said, standing up. "I'll pick you and Edie up."

Maud wasn't sure about being friends with Annie, but if Mrs. Montgomery had asked her stepsister to spy, it might be best to keep her close. Besides, while Annie did put on airs, she knew a lot about the people in town.

"All right," Maud said. "I'll see you tomorrow morning."

––––––

That evening, after dinner, Father said he had some auctioneering business at Agnew's store. While Katie slept, he left Maud and her stepmother alone for the first time. Maud had hoped to hide up in Southview with her letters and journal. She also had to write some new material for the fake one she was leaving for Mrs. Montgomery.

But clearly, Mrs. Montgomery had decided this would be a good opportunity to impart some of that "guidance" she had mentioned to Father. Perhaps this was part of how her stepmother planned to "handle her"?

"We haven't had an opportunity to get to know one another, and I have something particular I would love to discuss with you, woman to woman," she said, patting the spot beside her.

Mrs. Montgomery's change in attitude surprised Maud, and she stopped in the doorway. Perhaps she was going to tell her that she was pregnant? So she sat down beside her stepmother on the burnt-yellow couch in the parlor.

"As your new mamma, I think it is important that we are able to discuss certain"—she paused—"delicate things."

That would be lovely," Maud said. Perhaps she had been wrong about her stepmother. Grandma was always saying one must never assume what is going on in a person's head.

Mrs. Montgomery put her hand on Maud's arm and stroked it briefly, but then—as if sparked by fire—pulled it away.

"Has anyone ever discussed your hair? Perhaps your grandmother?"

"My hair?" Maud's hand instinctively came up to the bun sitting on top of her head. What did her hair have to do with her stepmother's pregnancy?

"Yes, your hair." Mrs. Montgomery twisted her hands together, as though she were tying a knot. "You do know you're a little young to be wearing your hair up."

She was almost sixteen! But she didn't want to make an enemy of her stepmother, so she said, "Aunt Annie suggested I wear it up for traveling, and I got used to it being off my neck."

"Just as I suspected," Mrs. Montgomery said. "It isn't appropriate for a girl of not-yet-sixteen to be wearing her hair up. Even my step-sister Annie—who is your age—wears her hair down with a bow."

Maud wanted to say something to counter the argument, but it was true. Even in Cavendish, girls didn't wear their hair up until they were sixteen.

Mrs. Montgomery fiddled with her thumb and forefinger. "It is rather embarrassing, but the truth is . . . you are going to laugh at me, I'm sure. It is so silly. I know there are only a few years between us—"

"I will be sixteen in November," Maud said.

"Yes, but you see, I worry if people see you with your hair up, they'll think me older than I am. You understand."

Maud understood all too well. Mrs. Montgomery was a married woman in her twenties. And, even though she was hiding it right now, expecting! It would be hard to dismiss that statement of fact. The plain truth was that her stepmother didn't want Maud to wear her hair down, not because of fashion or morality, but because of her own vanity. Maud clasped her hands tightly in her lap. But, if it would resolve the friction between them, she would acquiesce. She unclasped them and stood up.

"I'll go and take care of it now."

Mrs. Montgomery stood up as well and—almost too energetically—hugged her.

Up in Southview, Maud slowly pulled out the hairpins, her heavy hair falling down her back one strand at a time. Then she took a pair of scissors, parted her hair, and, after some very deep, defiant breathing, cut her hair into fringe bangs.

## CHAPTER FIVE

"Where is that blasted ribbon?" she muttered the following morning. The last thing she needed was to be late for her first day of school.

Katie's cat, Pussy, must have knocked it down or taken it with him on one of his many nightly prowls. He was an aggressive little thing, but a good mouser who would often cuddle with Maud when she was writing. Pussy didn't have much use for humans, the only exceptions being Maud and Katie, even if the latter loved to pull on his long black tail.

Wherever it was, Maud's ribbon was not on her bureau, and she was running late. Edie had gone downstairs to help with breakfast, Annie was going to be there any minute, and it had already taken Maud too long to fix her corset.

What was she going to do? Given her recent conversation with Mrs. Montgomery, she had to wonder what would be worse: going back on her word to wear her hair down or being late for school? She suspected that not being able to find a ribbon for one's hair would be a sorry excuse for tardiness. Hopefully Mrs. Montgomery would understand.

Maud tied her hair in a bun, liking the effect. With her corset accentuating her waist, her ring against her shirt, and her new fringe bangs, she could almost pass for one of those drawings she admired in the *Young Ladies' Journal*.

When Maud came down to the kitchen, she noted how much more active it was compared to the reserve of her grandparents' home. Annie was talking with Mrs. Stovel, Mamma's niece, who had come by to discuss the forthcoming church dialogue. Maud had done them in Cavendish—it was like a play, only with a religious moral—and she thought it might be a good way to get to know people, and to get out from under what was quickly becoming Mrs. Montgomery's suffocating supervision. Mrs. Stovel was just recently married and very enthusiastic about the church and being involved. She had encouraged Maud to take part in the church's concert "as there was never enough young people."

Edie was serving breakfast while Maud's stepmother was doing her best to listen to Mrs. Stovel and help Katie, who was more interested in putting porridge in her hair than in her mouth. Father was absorbed with the paper, completely oblivious to the noise around him.

If Maud had hoped that all the activity would distract Mrs. Montgomery from the hair situation, she was deeply mistaken. Mrs. Montgomery did notice, and glared at Maud as though she had broken one of the Ten Commandments.

"I see you added your own flare to my advice," Mrs. Montgomery said.

"Nice fringe bangs, Maud," Annie said, linking arms with her. "You are now perfect."

Maud smiled in gratitude and said, "I was looking for my ribbon, but I think that it fell behind the bureau, or Pussy has taken it."

"That's her excuse? The cat ate it?" Mrs. Montgomery murmured. She picked up a dirty Katie and left the kitchen. While her stepmother's reaction came as no surprise, it bothered Maud that something so trivial upset her.

Saying goodbye to Father, the three girls headed out.

Only a year before, she had been nervous about what her old classmates (and a certain boy) were going to think about her. Now Maud was worried about what kind of first impression she was going to make on a new teacher in a new school in a new town with new schoolmates.

As the three girls walked down the street, they passed a few men huddled, shuffling, in Hudson's Bay blankets. One of them looked directly at Maud, his brown eyes seeing right through her. She looked away, but Edie didn't.

Maud turned back to see the Hudson's Bay blanket disappear around the corner and remembered something that Prime Minister Macdonald had said on the train, and had even appeared proud of: that he was keeping the Indians on the verge of starvation as a way to teach them a lesson. At the time, she hadn't quite understood what he meant, but, now, seeing these men, it troubled her.

"The high school was once a hotel," Annie said, quickly forgetting about the starving men. The girls stood in front of the building that currently housed the high school while the new one was being built. It was two storeys tall, brown, and bleak. "They haven't even considered taking down the sign," she went on, referring to the big rectangular wooden board that read "Royal Hotel."

"It's . . . quite something," Maud said.

"Don't be surprised if it appears the classrooms are being used for other things." Edie giggled.

"Other things?" Maud said.

"It's better if we show you." Annie smirked, pulling her toward the building.

It was certainly grander than the Cavendish school, or even the Cavendish Hall. There were a few boys playing outside, about twelve or thirteen—maybe fourteen—years old, roughly kicking a ball around. Normally, Maud wouldn't mind playing with the boys, but these ones were different. It was the way they played: deadly serious, as though the game wasn't just for sport.

"Are we the only girls?" Maud asked.

Edie and Annie exchanged a look.

"Some girls come and go," Annie said.

As they climbed up the wooden steps, Maud was impressed by the size of the building. On one side of the hall, they passed a room that was so dusty and full of cobwebs Maud wondered if anyone cleaned it at all.

"The Town Council room is upstairs." Annie pointed up and put her hand over her mouth so Maud and Edie had to lean in. "The back of the building contains patrol quarters where two or three Mounties guard jail cells."

"Jail cells!" If Grandma knew this, Maud was sure she would come out here and drag her home by her hair, or send her to the convent school—Papist institution or not.

"I've seen them drag drunken men through the town and lock them up until they're sober," Edie said.

"Will they be doing that during school?" Maud said.

"If they have to," Annie said.

"Unbelievable."

"Not what you expected, is it?" Edie asked.

Maud shook her head. Not what she had expected at all.

Maud was even more disappointed when she saw the state of the classroom. Unlike her old school—which always smelled of lemon water and fresh cedar—this one smelled of dust and sod.

"No one thought to dust," Maud said, taking a handkerchief to a chair near the window.

"Oh, aren't we a pretty little thing," one of the boys who had been playing outside said as he sat down. His face was filthy.

"Didn't anyone tell you that you should wipe your face for school, Tom Clark?" Annie said.

Tom Clark wiped more dirt across his face and grinned. If Miss Gordon were here, she would have sent him home.

Then another boy, about twelve years old, with blond hair and freckles, who Annie called Willie MacBeath, winked at them. At least he was a little cleaner.

"He prides himself on getting ladies with his charm." Edie giggled.

Maud didn't see any charm in him.

A few more rowdy boys burst in. There was Frank Robertson, Maud learned from Annie, a tall dark-haired boy of about sixteen, whose expression suggested that he was always looking for trouble, and two boys who were the reverend's sons, Bertie and Arthur Jardine. According to Annie, the "younger and stupider brother, Bertie," definitely meant to make mischief—but something about his older brother, Arthur, told Maud that she might have liked him if he hadn't been chumming around with those other boys. Thank goodness Edie and Annie were there.

"That's Joe MacDonald." Annie pointed to another boy. "And over there is Douglas Maveety. Mr. Mustard is going to have to keep those boys under control."

"Many of those boys are Métis," Edie whispered to Maud. "If they keep behaving that way, Mr. Mustard won't give them a chance."

"Now, how am I going to study with such beautiful brown hair in front of me?"

Maud froze, then Annie giggled. Maud slowly turned around to see the red-haired boy from the Kennedy place—the one she had seen on her first day. He had, she admitted, the most charming green eyes and the most agreeable smile. Still, after the ridiculous behavior these boys were exhibiting, she wasn't about to allow him to get away with teasing her. It was dangerous to let boys get away with things. She was probably blushing.

"I guess you'll have to manage," Maud said, turning around. Now she was definitely blushing.

"I didn't think your father would let you come to school so early, Will," Annie said.

"I'll certainly let my father know, Annie," he said.

Edie passed Maud a note on her slate: *That's Will Pritchard. His aunt lives next door.*

*I've seen him before*, Maud wrote back.

As Edie dutifully erased the messages, a tall, thin man with short brown hair ran in, out of breath. Some of the boys laughed, but he rapped his ruler and they stopped.

*That must be Mr. Mustard.* Maud scribbled on her slate, then erased it and sat up straight. She wanted to make a good first impression.

Mr. Mustard stood as though he had been told to always stand at attention in case Queen Victoria herself came for tea. His welcoming address was certainly not as inspiring as Miss Gordon's had been, and was as dull as he appeared to be. Worse, the textbook was new, from Ontario, and didn't resemble Maud's *Royal Reader*. She was used to finding the same poems she had read throughout her school life, and this textbook also contained mathematics—something she always despised. Bewildered, she had a hard time keeping up when Mr. Mustard put them to work right away, drilling them tediously through each math equation but never giving proper instructions.

When Maud raised her hand to ask for clarification, he sniffed, stuck one of his hands in his vest pocket and said, "Everything you require is in the textbook."

At lunch hour there was really nothing to do. The boys played ball outside, and Will joined them. Although he wasn't as rough as they were, he could hold his own. Maud, Annie, and Edie walked around the school and then stood on the balcony of the old hotel, watching people go by.

There were more men and women shuffling past, all of them very skinny. Maud wondered if she should help them in some way. Wasn't she supposed to help? Isn't that what they were always doing at church, sending money to the missions? Even last week at church, Reverend Jardine had asked everyone to put a little extra in the collection plate for the missionaries. She sighed. There was so much to understand in this New Eden.

As the week progressed, Maud completely lost faith in Mr. Mustard—and any hope of learning in such a forsaken place. One morning she even found a pink feather floating by her foot; Edie informed her that the upstairs was used as a ballroom, so the ladies used the classroom as a dressing room.

At the end of the second week, Douglas came in late from lunch break with dirt smudged across his cheeks, staring down at his scuffed shoes, and smelling like a rotting pig. Maud took her handkerchief, placed it over her mouth and coughed.

"Why is he even here?" Edie asked. "He smells as if he's been hit in the face with a skunk."

"I suspect he didn't want to be marked truant and face the whip," Annie said.

"Girls, quiet," Mr. Mustard said.

The boys were shifting in their seats, and there was a lot of coughing and a few chuckles. Mr. Mustard put the textbook down and stuck his index fingers in his vest pocket. "Douglas, what is that foul odor?"

Douglas's dirt-smudged cheeks went red. "I was helping the public school kids with a pesky skunk, sir."

"That skunk got the best of you," Bertie said, which brought the class into hysterics. Even Maud had trouble keeping a straight face.

Mr. Mustard cleared his throat and pointed at Douglas. "Go to the corner."

"I'm not sure that's going to help, sir," Willie MacBeath said. "He smells like my outhouse."

This sparked another round of laughter.

Douglas slowly went to the far corner of the room, while everyone else tried to focus on their lessons. Within the hour, the smell had sullied the whole room, and there was so much fidgeting and coughing that—finally—Mr. Mustard relented and sent Douglas home.

By the end of the week, it was clear to Maud that teaching was not Mr. Mustard's calling. During lessons, Maud often caught him gazing out the window with the grimmest expression.

This was no place to get a quality education. She had to come up with a new plan. But she had no idea what that plan might be.

## CHAPTER SIX

Homesickness clouded everything. Maud hadn't heard from Pensie or Nate, two people whom she loved but who were clearly irritated with her now. And there was nothing she could do. Maybe she needed to write and show them both how much they meant to her. With Nate, though, it was too dangerous; he would get the wrong idea. But she could show Pensie with words.

One day at school, while Mr. Mustard was again gazing somberly out the window, Maud, instead of doing another dreaded math equation, wrote a long poem to Pensie, illustrating all of the beautiful things she loved about her house in Cavendish. She called it "My Friend's Home," trying to portray in verse what she was feeling, emulating what she had observed in Tennyson and Browning.

> 'Tis not my home though almost 'tis as dear
> And next to home the fairest spot on earth
> That little cottage in a far-off land
> In that blue-circled isle that gave me birth.

She gave Pensie a queenly presence, evoking images of Cupid's bow like those in Tennyson's poems. She had to show her how much she loved her. She sent the poem in the post the following day.

When Father brought in a stack of letters a week later from Mollie, Grandma, Jack, and Pensie (which included some gum), Maud leaped for joy. She would submerge herself in these stories under Aunt Annie's quilt in Southview and forget everything. She didn't know if Pensie's letter was in response to her poem, since it was too soon for the poem to have reached the Island, but it did mean that her bosom friend had written to her! Pensie still loved her. She would save her letter for last.

Mollie's letter was full of school news:

*Dearest Pollie,*

*It is hard to imagine that once again when I enter school tomorrow you won't be there. Nothing is the same here since you've moved halfway across the world. Even Miss Gordon is bored without us Four Musketeers causing all sorts of fun. I suspect she will miss your help with the Christmas Examination Concert this year as she has to rely on Clemmie and Nellie, and there is Annie's claim to know everything.*

*Jack and I try where we can, of course, but with Nate gone, I'm not sure how effective we are. Jack is quiet at the best of times, so it falls to me and that is no fun. Speaking of Jack, did he tell you he was leaving? He is following in Nate's footsteps and going off to college. Can you imagine Jack a teacher? I suppose someone should tell him he is actually going to have to speak to his students . . .*

*I miss you dreadfully, Pollie! Oh, I know it isn't your fault everyone is leaving me behind. I am to be alone, forced to befriend Clemmie, Nellie, Mamie, and Annie. It helps to be among them, particularly when George Robertson comes to a literary or prayer meeting. It seems no amount of teasing from us will dissuade him from his intentions. If only Jack would make his move, then George might leave me alone! I might have to resort to some drastic measures to make my feelings known.*

*Besides, Mother and Father are talking about how my attentions should be on a suitable husband rather than college.*

*Have you heard from Nate? I haven't, but Jack says he's well.*

*Do tell me all of your news from out west. Have you seen a buffalo?*

*Love, Mollie*

Jack confirmed Mollie's news, his letter as brief as his speech:

*Dear Polly,*

*So funny to call you that. We are not those four anymore, are we? Although Molly certainly tries. I suppose she's told you I'll be off to Prince of Wales College next term. I certainly cannot allow Lockhart to get ahead of me. It will make his head swell more than it already has.*

*Will you be back in the summer? I'll be home before I head off to college. It would be nice to see you again.*

*Write soon and tell me about Prince Albert.*

*Sincerely,*
*Jack (a.k.a. Snap)*

Maud took a deep breath and, chewing some of the gum Pensie had sent, finally read her letter. As she read, her stomach twisted more and more. It was deeply disappointing: a series of facts about the weather and nothing about her cats, or anything else Maud had asked Pensie about in her previous letter . . . and, what's more, she asked about Nate in a way that appeared more than just mere curiosity: *Have you heard from Nate? I am sure the two of you are now writing secret love letters.*

Why would Pensie bring that up? Was she trying to upset her? Clearly, she was still angry. She knew about Maud's feelings. And maybe that was the point. Was this her revenge? Maud needed to convince her otherwise—and show her loyalty.

*Now see here Pen I am going to give you a little scolding,* she wrote, her hand shaking. She took a deep breath, steeling herself against what she knew she must write. *I think you are too awfully mean for anything to keep teasing me eternally about that detestable pig Nate Lockhart.*

*Detestable* was a good word. But was it strong enough? She took another breath.

*You know I hate him, and if you mention his name in your letters one more time, I'll never write to you again.*

A few week weeks later, Pensie finally wrote back and apologized for her comments, and while her letters continued to lack creativity, they at least came regularly.

Maud had been wrong when she'd believed she would be spending more time with Father. Between the Kinistino Lodge, his auctioneer business, and now running for counselor, he was frequently gone most of the day—and even when he was home, there were always people coming to see him.

Unless she was too tired, Mrs. Montgomery often insisted on accompanying her husband, which meant that most days after school, it was up to Maud to feed, play with, and put Katie to bed. Maud didn't mind so much, but as more of the household chores fell to her and Edie, there was less time to write.

Maud was also wrong when she had believed taking care of Katie would alleviate the tension with Mrs. Montgomery. While her stepmother was happy to see Maud "pulling her weight," she was never gracious, nor grateful. In fact, it was as though she had expected Maud to play nanny to her half-sister all along.

Spending so much time with Katie reminded Maud of something her Aunt Emily had said to her two years before, after the Izzie Robinson incident. When Maud arrived at the gray house in Malpeque, Aunt Emily had frowned and said, "Once again, you've been thrown at my door. Wasn't giving up eight years of my life enough for my mother?"

Before Aunt Emily had met Uncle John Malcolm, she had been like an attentive older sister. Maud had fond memories of Saturday picnics at the shore and lectures at Cavendish Hall. But as Maud grew older, Aunt Emily had grown cruel, often fighting with Grandma and Grandfather about wanting to go out with her friends. Maud blamed herself. Clearly, she had asked too many questions and had become, as Aunt Emily accused her, "entirely too childish and dreamy."

One Sunday at church, Aunt Emily abandoned Maud to be with her friends—that was when her aunt had met John Malcolm Montgomery. Later, when Aunt Emily returned home, Grandma and Grandfather chastised her for shirking her duty, but she fought back, and that was when John Malcolm properly started courting.

Sometimes Maud was told to accompany them, which only angered her aunt even more. And when Maud begged her aunt to take her when she got married, the answer was a resounding *no*. "You aren't my duty anymore," Aunt Emily had said on the morning of the wedding. "I've honored Clara's memory enough, and it's someone else's turn."

That was when Maud had turned to her favorite authors, finding solace in books and words. She kept her diary close and wrote about her loneliness, wondering what made her aunt hate her so much. Those few months at her aunt's two years ago had been no different. She still felt like a burden.

Now, as the prairie's stillness echoed the hollowness of Maud's heart, and the constant rain pounded into the center of her soul, she felt some compassion for her aunt. She loved Katie, but she also wanted to write and spend time with her new friends.

It was also increasingly clear that her stepmother had no respect for the things Maud cared about. When Maud had asked Father if she could have a copy of Longfellow's *Evangeline* for school, as there were not enough copies, her stepmother insisted they couldn't spend money on something as wasteful as a book. Maud was sure Father would defend her—the book was for school, after all—but he sighed and said that her stepmother was right, money needed to be specifically for essentials right now.

To Maud, books were essential; without them, she would have crumbled into despair. The fact that her father couldn't see this broke her heart. Perhaps it was because he didn't see her reading very much. Normally, Maud could lose herself in a story, but with all of her chores and schoolwork—what there was—much of her extra time was stolen for writing. Sometimes she would go back to old favorites, *Little Women* and *Jane Eyre*, and a few times she tried Cooper's *The Last of the Mohicans*, but her mind would wander. She couldn't focus.

School continued to be another disappointment. Maud had been right about Mr. Mustard. He did not have a calling for teaching, even making those subjects Maud would have enjoyed—such as studying Longfellow's *Evangeline*—tedious.

And it seemed that she couldn't even escape him after school; he had started calling in the evenings to visit Mrs. Montgomery, since they were old friends.

Sometimes Father was around, sometimes he wasn't. If it was Miss Gordon paying a call, Maud would have enjoyed having quality time with her teacher, but Mr. Mustard was as dreadfully dull outside of the classroom as he was inside.

Maud could think of only one way to make things better: the convent school. She resolved to ask her father about it, and at dinner one night, Maud waited for a lull in the conversation. "Father, things at school are horrible."

"Mustard needs to get control of those boys," Mrs. Montgomery said, cutting a piece of pork roast. "He's always been a little soft."

"Mustard comes highly recommended from Ontario," Father said.

"You should be paying attention to how I run this house," Mrs. Montgomery said to Maud, ignoring Father's comment. "You'll need to know more than whatever you are doing up in your room all of the time."

"Father, you know how much I love school." Maud gazed at her father, desperately hoping he'd understand and make the suggestion she wanted to hear. Mrs. Montgomery folded her arms across her stomach. They still hadn't told Maud about her pregnancy.

Father looked back at Maud and smiled. "Well, there is the convent school up the hill. Pritchard sends his oldest daughter, Laura, there; he was saying she is learning all sorts of things, such as art and music."

Maud clasped her hands together over her chest. It was amazing how Father could read her mind. "Father, that would be simply divine! I would adore learning art, and you know I already play the organ because I took lessons with Mrs. Spurr." She resolutely pushed aside the memory of Nate and continued. "I promise I will study hard and make you proud."

"You cannot be serious, Hugh!" Mrs. Montgomery exclaimed.

"No self-respecting Presbyterian family would send their daughter to that school. I've seen Laura Pritchard at church, and she acts as though she's better than us. I think she's picked up some of those Papist notions. They aren't only teaching the three *r*'s there, but the big *R*—religion—and not the right one, either."

"But, Mamma," Maud said, struggling to swallow the word. "That high school has so many boys; there are days when you make Edie stay home, and if Annie is sick, I'm the only girl."

"You can stay home with me and not study at all," she said.

Maud started to protest, but something in her stepmother's expression reminded Maud too much of Miss Robinson.

"I see your point, Mary Ann," Father said, and then turned to Maud. "Let me think about it."

Maud didn't say anything else, but she had a bad feeling about what her father's decision would be. This settled it. It was time to go home.

After helping Edie with the dishes, she wrote Pensie a long letter, telling her how much she hated it in Prince Albert and begging for news about Cavendish and her family: anything that would take Maud away from here and that woman. It had the desired effect. Writing to Pensie helped her believe that at least, maybe, someone was listening.

Later, Father knocked on the Southview door to tell Maud he had received a telegram from Grandpa, saying he would be coming through Prince Albert by week's end on his way back to the Island. Perhaps this was her chance. Grandpa had offered to take her with him to British Columbia; maybe he could take her home. But first she had to make sure she had a place to go.

After Father left, Maud put Pensie's letter aside and composed a new one to Grandma, begging her permission to come home. She wrote that she'd learned her lesson and promised to be obedient from now on.

She put Katie to bed and went downstairs with her speech all prepared. It would upset Father, but she suspected Mrs. Montgomery would cry with jubilation. They were sitting against the plush burnt-yellow couch in the living room, the evening light cascading over the family pictures on the wall.

"I'm glad you've come downstairs," Father said. "I've been thinking a lot about what you said."

For a second she wondered if he had changed his mind. She sat down on a chair adjacent to the couch, holding onto its wooden arms.

"I know it isn't proper to be speaking of such matters, but you are a young woman, sixteen in a few months, and we—Mary Ann and I—want to talk with you about the baby we're expecting in February."

"That's wonderful!" Maud said, hoping she sounded as if this was the first time she'd heard about this. "I'm thrilled about having a new brother or sister." She stood up and hugged her father and then went to embrace her stepmother, but something in Mrs. Montgomery's expression stopped her. "I'm pleased to hear this," Mrs. Montgomery said, "given that your priorities are apparently elsewhere."

Maud slowly sat back down and turned her gaze to the portraits. There was Katie as a baby, Father and Mrs. Montgomery's wedding picture, a few images of the McTaggarts—but none of her.

"My family is my priority, of course," she said. This was the truth. She wanted school more than anything. But if Father needed her, she would help him.

"We know you came here"—Father scratched his beard—"under certain circumstances. But we had hoped you might help us when the baby comes."

Maud didn't quite understand. "Of course."

"See, Mary Ann," Father said. "I told you she would help you."

"I don't think she understands," Mrs. Montgomery said.

"I would help you after school and on weekends, as I do with Katie," Maud said.

Mrs. Montgomery frowned.

Maud focused on the wedding photo.

"What about Edie?" Maud said.

"Edie won't be with us much longer," Mrs. Montgomery said. "As soon as we can arrange it, she'll be leaving."

Edie was right, Mrs. Montgomery had had a plan for Maud. And even though she suspected the answer, she asked, "But why?" Poor Edie! All she had wanted was to go to school. With no place for her to stay or employment, she would have to go back to Battleford. What about her plans to become a teacher? It wasn't fair!

Mrs. Montgomery and Father exchanged a look. "I'm surprised at your outburst," Mrs. Montgomery said. "Edie's services are no longer needed. That's all you need to concern yourself with."

Maud struggled to hold back her tears. She wouldn't give that woman the satisfaction of seeing her cry. Maud stood up, turning away from the family photos.

"You can continue with school until the baby is born," Father said. "But then you'll need to stay here." Although he appeared confident, his blue eyes pleaded for Maud to understand.

"Of course. Whatever you"—she focused on her father—"need."

Maud excused herself, slowly making her way to Southview. She was truly stuck here. Forever. No better than a hired maid.

This was why Father had agreed to have her come. The answer was clear now: she had been sent here to be a nanny. Even imagining herself as Jo in *Little Women* was no use. Unlike Jo March, who had taken the job willingly, Maud had had the job forced upon her.

Did Maud ever have a choice over anything?

Edie was getting ready for bed when Maud came upstairs. "So, you know," she said.

"I'm so sorry, Edie," Maud said, sitting down on her bed. "It seems we are both at her mercy."

"It's not your fault," Edie said, tucking her covers up to her chin. But Maud wondered if she could have somehow prevented all of this. Been better somehow. On the bed was her letter to Grandma. Maud ripped it up, letting each piece fall to the floor.

## CHAPTER SEVEN

Over the following weeks, Maud said goodbye first to Grandpa, who had arrived and stayed for about a week, and then, a few days later, to Edie. Their final day together, Grandpa and Maud took a walk down Main Street toward the river, and he expressed concern over leaving her with her stepmother, but Maud assured him that everything would be fine. She must not have convinced him, because that evening over dinner he suggested that maybe Maud could come and visit the Island next summer. And while the idea felt like sunshine to her soul, she doubted she was going anywhere, at least judging from Mrs. Montgomery's expression. Still, she was grateful to her grandpa for trying.

It was worse when Edie left. Maud had known she would be sad, but she hadn't expected the hollow ache in her heart. The night before Edie left, they sat up late in Southview talking, and Maud cursed her stepmother for making her friend go.

"What will you do about school now?" Maud said.

"I'll figure out something. After a few months in Battleford, I'll head south to Regina, or go east. My family has a long history of being uprooted, leaving everything we love behind." She frowned, but then shook it off and smiled. "Besides, Father Emmanuel wrote a letter on my behalf to the convent. Perhaps this, and my work in Prince Albert, will work in my favor."

"It is nice to have people looking out for you," Maud said. Why wasn't anyone doing that for her now?

"I'm a survivor, Maud. I'll find a way."

"You'll write and let me know how you're doing?" Maud said.

"I promise," Edie said.

The next evening, with Edie's bed now empty beside her and with Pussy at her feet, Maud wrote until her hand ached and ink was etched into her fingers. There was a certain satisfaction in this, as though through her pain she'd been cleansed. Maud placed her pen in the ink, her hands upon the written pages, and her chin on top of her hands. The sun was coming out over the horizon, showering the prairie in light.

As Mrs. Montgomery's pregnancy progressed, she did less and less. Maud did more of the cleaning and meals, taking over for Edie, as well as attending school each day. She begged Father for some help, but he said that they couldn't afford the expense. It was only a matter of time anyway, as the baby was due in February and she would be forced to give up school.

What was the purpose of dreaming of a happy family home when it was mere fantasy? She should have listened to Grandma long ago. Maud knew now that life with Father would never have lived up to her expectations, especially with Mrs. Montgomery there. He worked so hard, but nothing pleased her. Some nights Maud could hear them arguing over money—it was always over money. She complained that he was never around, when he was out running his business—for his family!

Every evening before dinner, Father and Mrs. Montgomery had the same conversation, and then would eat in a silence that rivaled the ones at Maud's grandparents' house. As Maud cleaned up, Mrs. Montgomery would complain that he was always leaving her alone with "his daughters." Father would argue how imperative it was for him to canvass for votes at the lodge, since the other local candidates were doing what they could to buy votes. She would say she missed him, and he would kiss her cheek and leave them to clean up. "It's only until January; it will be easier when the election is over," he'd say.

One night toward the end of October, Mrs. Montgomery was complaining about how much extra work she had to do now that Edie was gone and she had to entertain visitors on her own.

"If by 'visitors' you mean John Mustard," Father said, "you know he's more your friend than mine, and you always end up talking about old school days." Mr. Mustard was calling two or three times a week, and Maud and Mamma were the ones entertaining him. The few times he was home, Father looked so bored, Maud completely understood; the last thing she wanted to do was socialize with her teacher.

Her stepmother sighed. "Aren't you going to help us with the dinner plates, Maud?"

"I was about to," Maud said.

"Good." Mrs. Montgomery leaned against the chair. "I'm rather tired now." She slowly stood up and held her lower back, trying to look poised as she went upstairs.

"This too shall pass, Maud," her father said when Mrs. Montgomery was gone.

Maud doubted it, but she didn't want to upset Father. She stopped stacking and smiled brightly. "I understand completely." She put her hand on his arm. "Now, go to your meeting. I'll handle things here."

"You are such a responsible girl," he said, kissing her lightly on top of her head.

As Maud washed the dishes, she allowed her mind to drift to Cavendish and what her friends and family would be doing. Grandma continued to write faithfully each week about the farm and grandfather's health, and Lu had written Maud about a church social. Maud imagined she was there with Mollie and Lu and the boys, Nate smiling up at her while they sang "God Save the Queen." It was all such a lovely, faraway dream that Maud lost herself there until a knock—and the near-breakage of her stepmother's favorite serving dish—brought her back to reality.

The knock came again, in full force. She sighed and put the platter down.

"Mamma, someone is at the door," she shouted.

Silence.

"Mamma!"

Nothing.

Maud dried her hands and went to the front door. Mr. Mustard had returned. Didn't he have better things to do? She was almost embarrassed for him.

"Is your stepmother home?" Mr. Mustard asked, clearing his throat. "I had hoped to call upon her."

"He does realize that my stepmother is married," Maud mumbled to herself.

"Pardon me?" he said.

Maud told him to wait in the parlor while she got her stepmother. She was sure Mrs. Montgomery wasn't up for company, but since she had left Maud with the dishes, Maud figured she would retaliate by making her spend a few hours with boring Mr. Mustard.

Maud skipped upstairs and knocked noisily three times. No answer. Maud imagined her stepmother, upon hearing Mr. Mustard's voice, huddling under the covers, clothes and all, pretending to sleep.

"I'm sorry, Mr. Mustard," Maud said when she returned to the parlor. "My stepmother is not receiving visitors tonight."

Mr. Mustard clasped and unclasped his hands in front of him but continued to sit where he was—on her favorite spot on the couch.

Grandma would have been horrified to see someone not show such disregard for propriety. But it would be a mark on the Montgomery and Macneill names if Maud didn't at least offer Mr. Mustard some refreshments and play the good hostess. Perhaps Mrs. Montgomery didn't think that Maud could do it? Perhaps because she believed Maud had come from— what did her stepmother usually call Cavendish?—"a backwater small town"?

Maud put on her best smile and said, "Do you want some refreshments, Mr. Mustard? Mrs.—Mamma—and I made some delicious mock cherry pie this afternoon. It is quite delicious."

"No, thank you." He sniffed. "I don't believe in eating after seven o'clock, as it doesn't agree with one's digestion." Mr. Mustard spread his hands out so one sat on each leg.

"It is your loss; some say that Mamma's pie is the best in Prince Albert."

"High praise indeed," Mr. Mustard said. *Sniff.* "Perhaps next time I will come earlier, and then we can share in the delight together." *Sniff. Sniff.*

Maud sat at the farthest end of the yellow couch and the two stared at the floor for what felt like hours. In those precious minutes, Maud's mind spun for something to say, but the incessant sniffling coming from the man across the way was too distracting. She now agreed with her stepmother and wished Father had chosen to stay home. At least she would be free to go upstairs.

"Where's your father on this cold night?" Mr. Mustard finally asked.

"He's gone to the Kinistino Lodge to meet with the Sons of Scotland expatriates. I suspect there will be some revelry and possible card playing afterwards."

She admitted to herself she was egging the poor man on with that final sentence. Knowing Mr. Mustard's abhorrence of all things fun, Maud was not at all surprised when he said, "I don't approve of card playing; it is only one step removed from gambling, and gambling is a sin." *Sniff.*

"I also enjoy singing in choir," Maud said, glancing quickly over at the grandfather clock—nine o'clock. He should be leaving soon. "We are to give a recitation in a few weeks."

Oh, why did she tell him that? He would think she actually wanted to talk with him.

"I think I'm going to request that we move the classroom to the other side of the hallway," he said, suddenly changing the subject. "It is inappropriate to expose young people to the kind of gallivanting in the hall that goes on in the evenings." Maud was quite sure that Mr. Mustard would never be accused of gallivanting. "I can truthfully argue that it is a larger room with a better heater. It will be good for everyone." He leaned over in the direction she was sitting. "Don't you agree?" *Sniff.*

Maud elbowed herself more deeply into the couch's arm. Truth be told, she actually did agree; she didn't enjoy discovering stray feathers in her notebook when she got home, but she certainly wasn't going to tell him! So she said, "Oh, I don't know; I've heard those girls have all sorts of laughs."

This made her teacher turn the shade of Mrs. Montgomery's mock cherry pie.

The grandfather clock continued to witness the excruciatingly slow evening, and finally showed mercy by bonging at ten o'clock. Maud couldn't take it any longer and feigned a huge, indelicate yawn, which had the desired effect. Mr. Mustard stood up and announced that he should be going home.

Slamming the door behind him, Maud wondered why her teacher had decided to stay when it was clearly Mrs. Montgomery he had come to see. And for two of the longest hours of her life. She had listened to sermons that were more interesting than poor Mr. Mustard. And what could he possibly have to gain having a conversation with one of his students? Certainly he would prefer conversing with people his own age, wouldn't he?

Sitting down on the yellow couch, Maud gazed at the clock that had witnessed the evening's events as if it would solve the mystery. But it had no opinion to offer.

Then she recalled how he'd looked at her when he asked her opinion about the classroom, as though she might have all of the answers. A creepy-crawly feeling trickled down the back of her neck. No. It was ridiculous. Was it possible that the teacher had designs on her? She'd heard about such things, of course, and it wasn't necessarily frowned upon, as teachers had a valued place in the community. If this was what he was doing, Maud was going to have to stop it. Immediately.

# CHAPTER EIGHT

The following morning, Maud was careful to put her hair down the way Mrs. Montgomery liked it. While the family was finishing breakfast, she brought up Mr. Mustard's odd visit.

Mrs. Montgomery was helping Katie feed herself. "You are being overly dramatic, as usual," she said, wiping Katie's chin. "He's lonely."

Maud played with her porridge. "But he's your friend. Not mine."

"I'm sure it is harmless." Father gulped down the last of his tea. "Besides, he appears to be a nice fellow, if a little awkward."

An image of Mr. Mustard staring out the window in melancholy all day flashed into Maud's mind, followed by the memory of him with whip in hand. The violent contrast made her drop her spoon. Its clang against the china plate rattled everyone.

"Please be careful with our dishes, Maud," her stepmother said. "Or do I have to help feed you as though you were Katie?"

Maud delicately picked up the spoon and mumbled an apology. Father poured himself some more tea and opened the paper. There was an article about the election, reporting on the upcoming debate. Father had been preparing for it all week. Maud couldn't help but be proud.

"And you could do worse than Mr. Mustard," her stepmother went on. "A girl your age needs to be considering suitors."

She was tired of boys—men—all of it. "I have plans to do more than be someone's wife," Maud retorted.

Her stepmother stood up, scooped up Katie (who screamed that she was still hungry), and swept upstairs.

"That was uncalled for, Maud," Father said over his paper.

"I'm sorry."

Father sighed.

Maud started clearing the plates; Mrs. Montgomery's departure had left her alone with the chores.

"Did you do anything to encourage him?" Father asked, after a while.

Maud almost dropped the plates she was carrying, but saved them by carefully—shakily—placing them back on the table. She sat down before her legs could collapse under her. "I am his student," she said, as evenly as she could, although inside she was crying like Katie. Why was she under attack? First Pensie, and now Father: Why was she to blame for a man's actions? "I treat him the same as any other teacher."

Father stood up and put his coat on, his beard twitching into a slight smile. "You must have done something. A man doesn't usually go after a girl unless she's done something to attract his attention." He kissed Maud on top of her head.

"But why would he want to spend time after school with a girl of almost-sixteen?" Maud asked.

"You might be almost-sixteen"—Father fixed his collar—"but you are also intelligent, and I suspect an educated man such as Mr. Mustard might be attracted to someone with your interests."

As Maud cleared breakfast away, she wondered if perhaps Father was right. She needed to be more careful. Maud wasn't sure what she was going to do, but she had to turn Mr. Mustard off her. She had worked so hard to be a proper lady—the kind Grandma would be proud of—but perhaps that was why Mr. Mustard thought her older than her years. She was going to have to remind him that she was younger than him, practically still a child.

If she showed him her immaturity, by acting out, it would certainly turn his attentions elsewhere. But did she dare? It had certainly been a while since she had done anything of the sort, and she usually had Mollie to help her put any plan into action. This had to be all on her.

Her opportunity came that afternoon when Mr. Mustard was helping Willie MacBeath with his sums—all they ever did was sums—and Annie and Will Pritchard were quietly working beside her. Will had missed a few days helping his father on the family ranch in Laurel Hill, and Maud admitted to herself that she was glad Will was back where she could feel his quiet presence behind her. He was so different from the other boys in school: older and more responsible, not concerning himself with the mischief the others were always getting up to.

Maud didn't want to tell Annie or Will about her plan. Mr. Mustard might not whip a girl, but he would definitely whip a boy, and the last thing she wanted was to get Will into trouble. Besides, this was her fight and she was going to have to win it—as with most things in her life—on her own.

On a piece of paper, Maud penned a little Island folk song, imagining a lilting fiddle, and began to sing. Annie's eyes widened in surprise, and Maud tried to hide her smile. The song was about a teacher who had no control over his students and would do silly things to get their attention. It was entirely possible the "thin lad with a thin mustache" was Mr. Mustard, but she would neither confirm nor deny it.

After a few minutes, Annie began drumming a rhythm against her desk with her pencil and picked up the tune, humming in harmony to compliment Maud, and then—to Maud's utter surprise—Will hit the edge of his desk with his hand, joining in on the lower notes, their volume growing louder and louder, eventually adding in hand gestures and clapping.

Mr. Mustard lost his temper. "Why are you three singing? Stop this immediately!" he bellowed.

"I don't know what you mean," Maud said, as Will and Annie kept singing. Will reached over and passed the paper to Douglas, Frank, and Willie M. so they could join in.

"Oh, a thin man with a thin mustache, had a hard time holding his cash," they screeched.

"Silence, this instant!" As his ears grew redder, Mr. Mustard's thin mustache seemed to grow even thinner.

The younger boys stopped, as they had seen that expression before and didn't want to go another round with Mr. Mustard's whip.

Maud was surprised they had gone on as they had. Annie and Will should stop, as this had nothing to do with them, but she had underestimated their complete lack of respect for the man—and possibly their friendship for her.

"If you don't stop right now, you three will have to stay after school," Mr. Mustard shouted above the singing.

"A thin man, oh, he's a thin man," the three rebels sang.

"Enough! You three will stay after school and do one hundred sums each before you can go," Mr. Mustard said.

*Maud, we need to stop. Remember practice*, Annie chalked on her slate. Maud had forgotten their promise to Mrs. Stovel about helping out with the Christmas dialogue.

*Okay, one more round*, she wrote back.

The three gave the song one more resounding cry, which was met with grand applause by everyone but the tall, thin man standing at the front of the classroom.

After school, Mr. Mustard forced Maud, Annie, and Will to complete the one hundred sums. Annie and Will did them, but Maud was determined to not pick up her pencil.

"Miss Montgomery, you do realize I'll keep you here until you have completed your task," her teacher said.

"I do realize that, yes," Maud said, lighting a candle she had in her desk and taking out her book of Tennyson's poems.

"Please put that away," he said. "You can either do math problems or nothing at all."

Maud blew out the candle. "Then I'll do nothing at all." He could have kept her there until midnight and she wouldn't have budged.

"I'm done, Mr. Mustard," Will said, tossing the problems on the teacher's desk. "I'm expected at the church to help with the Christmas concert."

"I'm surprised he's going," Annie whispered. "I didn't think his father would let him out for a dialogue. He's always working his son so hard."

"It is a church function."

"Aren't you coming?" Will asked at the door.

"We are expected at the church," Maud said, facing her teacher. "You cannot keep us here against our will, Mr. Mustard. Especially when we are expected at the church to do *His* work."

"We are playing an important role in the church dialogue," Annie said.

Mr. Mustard pretended to be interested in a student's paper.

"I'll be sure to tell Mrs. Stovel that you'll be a bit late," Will said as he left the classroom.

"You are the oldest students in school and should be setting an example." Mr. Mustard said after Will had gone. "I expected more from you."

"If you don't treat us as if we are children," Annie said, "you might see something better from us."

"Watch your tone, Miss McTaggart. I tend not to whip girls, but if this wildly inappropriate behavior continues, you might see it."

Annie breathed hard through her nose. "I would hate for you to see what happens when I tell my parents how you spoke to me."

Mr. Mustard frowned. Maud couldn't believe it. Annie had stood up for her—which people rarely did. She was certainly walking a dangerous line. Maud had already seen firsthand how Father and Mrs. Montgomery would take her teacher's side, but for a new teacher, disciplining certain students could be a gamble. Annie's father, Mr. McTaggart, was an important man in town, and it wouldn't do for Mr. Mustard to get on the wrong side of him.

"Fine," Mr. Mustard said, waving his arm, defeated. "Go. But don't think we're done here."

As Maud scurried out, she hoped at least her performance would mean he was done with her.

## CHAPTER NINE

M aud was thankful that St. Paul's Presbyterian Church was only a few blocks away from the school—and right across the street from Eglintoune Villa—so she and Annie could quickly drop off their books at home and race over. They were still late, and as they burst into the room, Mrs. Stovel was already putting people in their positions for one of the tableaux, a drama technique where everyone stood still, as if they were standing for a photograph. Frank Robertson was in the back row with Will, who surprised Maud with a quick wink.

Pretending to ignore Will, Maud waved at two young women she knew from church, Lottie Steward, a lovely girl from Québec, and Alexena MacGregor. Maud was fond of Alexena, who had a kind smile. Both girls were already frozen in position but discreetly smiled in her direction.

"I'm so relieved you both could make it!" Mrs. Stovel said, throwing both hands up in the air. "Will mentioned you were detained, but he was able to make it on time."

Maud and Annie exchanged a look. "Getting us in trouble already, Will?" Maud called out to him. His green eyes were mischievous, but he didn't move . . . most likely because Mrs. Stovel was standing in front of him and he didn't want to incur her wrath.

Maud and Annie allowed themselves to be guided, and Mrs. Stovel fluttered around, trying to make everything "absolutely perfect."

When Mrs. Stovel gave them a ten-minute break, Maud went over to the stained glass window of an angel protecting Christ, where Will was standing beside his sister, Laura. She had the same wise nose and mischievous green eyes as her brother, but her face was rounder than Will's, and she had soft brown hair worn up in a bun.

Since that first day in Prince Albert, Maud had seen Laura a few times at church and was overcome by the feeling that she was a long-lost friend, a kindred spirit. She wanted to get to know her better, but Laura lived out of town on her parents' farm, only visiting her aunt next door occasionally—and since she went to the convent school up the hill, the only opportunity for Maud to talk with her was at church. Helping Mrs. Stovel with the Christmas concert was the perfect opportunity for Maud to become better acquainted with her—and to see Will away from Mr. Mustard's infernal lessons.

Over the next few nights, the dramatists practiced at the McTaggarts' and the Kennedys' as Mrs. Montgomery "wasn't up to rowdy guests." Maud was grateful to have an excuse to leave the house, and her stepmother seemed open to giving her time off from her housekeeping duties. Maud supposed this was because Mrs. Stovel was her niece, but it didn't matter why. She was just glad to have time to spend with her new friends.

Even though being in the play brought back bittersweet memories of her friends in Cavendish, it helped dull the heartache of homesickness. Laura made beautiful bunting from old dress scraps of green, red, and gold, and recruited Alexena, Lottie, and Maud to help her put it up in the church, making it look quite festive.

Once, as they practiced "Silent Night," Maud was certain she caught Will eyeing her in a way that reminded her of Nate. She truly liked Will and didn't want to cloud their friendship with romance, nor did she want to unwittingly encourage him. She'd had enough of that with Mr. Mustard.

Yet there was something about Will that made her forget Nate—or at least made her feel less guilty. It meant so much that he had stood up for her with Mr. Mustard; they had even started passing notes in class. It wasn't the same as with Nate—Will certainly didn't have Nate's romantic notions or love of verse—but he did have the knack of making her laugh. And she so badly needed to laugh.

But Mr. Mustard was persistent, coming by the house a few times a week. And no bad behavior deterred him. Maud never said anything to her father or Mrs. Montgomery, as it was clear that, unlike Miss Robinson, Mr. Mustard was not going to tell on her. Perhaps it was pride that kept him from doing it, not wanting to show his lack of control over the classroom.

Clearly, she was going to have to try another maneuver.

Her new friendship with Will offered an opportunity. Mr. Mustard certainly disliked how much fun she and Will—and Annie, who insisted on joining in—were having, and he constantly made them stay after school to "discuss their behavior." She didn't want to use Will, as he was the nicest boy in school, but she had to admit that she liked how flustered Mr. Mustard got when he caught them passing notes.

Sadly, this also meant that Mr. Mustard would find any excuse to keep Maud, Annie, and Will in detention. One afternoon, a few days after the "thin mustache" incident, Mr. Mustard announced that he was keeping Maud and Annie after school for "undignified conduct and slang."

"I'm not sure what you mean," Annie said, crossing her arms

over her chest. "Just because we come up with something on the fly doesn't mean anything."

"That is precisely what I'm talking about," Mr. Mustard said.

"I think you're being mad as hops," Maud protested, slapping her hand—with much gusto—against her desk. Beside her, Willie M. and Frank snickered.

Will coughed to stifle a laugh, pretending to read—although Maud knew he could not be studying; the class hadn't cracked a book open all day.

"You and Annie will remain after class," Mr. Mustard said.

Will raised his hand.

"Yes, Mr. Pritchard."

"Sir, don't you think this is kind of daft?"

Mr. Mustard breathed heavily through his nose. "You will also stay after school."

But when Will went to shut the door after the rest of the class had left, Frank burst through, panting. "Pritchard, you need to come with me now. There's an emergency," he said, leaning over to catch his breath. Will didn't even ask for permission; he just grabbed his things and left.

Mr. Mustard marched over to the door and called after them, "Yes, for emergencies you can leave, Mr. Pritchard."

Maud wondered what the possible emergency could be and hoped that it wasn't anything serious, or to do with Laura. But then Annie wrote on her slate that it was all a trick to get Will out of the classroom. She had overheard him ask Frank at recess to come and get him because he had to get to the ranch to help his father, and everyone knew that Mr. Pritchard was a man who hated for anyone to be late—even if that person was his son.

Mr. Mustard began to look haggard. "If you are silent for the next five minutes, I will let you go."

"Did you hear that, Maud?" Annie said. "He says if we stay quiet for five minutes we can go home. Isn't that kind of him?"

"Oh, so terribly kind, Annie," Maud replied. "He is certainly an upstanding pillar of our education system."

"You know he came from Ontario."

"Really? I hadn't heard."

"Yes."

"You don't say."

"Miss Montgomery! Miss McTaggart! If you don't desist, I shall insist on keeping you here," he said.

Maud and Annie continued to talk, and when they couldn't think of anything else to say, they whispered poetry. Maud was particularly fond of Tennyson.

Finally, when Maud was sure it was almost suppertime, she groaned, "Leave hope behind, all ye who enter here."

"Misquoting Dante shows me you are more intelligent than your behavior would suggest, Miss Montgomery," Mr. Mustard said. "I hope we shall see a better performance from you in the future. And from you too, Miss McTaggart."

As they ran to the church to practice their dialogue, the girls felt that they definitely—although painfully—had won another round.

## CHAPTER TEN

B y the end of November, Maud wasn't sure how she was going
to manage her responsibilities at home, church, and school.
She tried to look forward to her sixteenth birthday on the thirti-
eth, but she started getting headaches: a low, dull, persistent ache
on the back of her head, as though she was being choked from
behind. She refused to give in to them, but the struggle drained
her energy away.

Mrs. Montgomery was now seven months along and spent
much of her time in bed, which meant that Maud had to do even
more work around the house. Father was often out working or at
the club. This left Maud alone with Katie, who clung to her from
the moment she got home, following her all over the house and
"helping" where she could. Maud found herself telling Katie the
stories her grandparents had once told her, hoping to pass on to
her sister the spirit of the stories she herself had loved.

She had also finally submitted "On Cape LeForce" to the
*Charlottetown Patriot*, and was sure that when she opened the
next edition she would see it. But as the weeks passed, she began
to dread the arrival of the paper; it marked rejection. One more
dream unrealized.

But that didn't stop her. Writing saved her when she woke up in the middle of the night and couldn't get back to sleep. It saved her when Mrs. Montgomery was particularly cruel. It saved her from those moments when homesickness completely overwhelmed her.

Laura and Will saved Maud too. They were living next door for the winter, since it was easier to stay in town than to drive the hour back and forth to Laurel Hill in inclement weather. Maud loved their Aunt Kennedy, who reminded her of Aunt Annie, as she was so kind and patient. She insisted that Maud call her Aunt Kennedy as well. Aunt Kennedy didn't have any children of her own and so doted on Laura and Will—and Maud too.

As demanding as Mrs. Montgomery was, she didn't keep Maud locked up at home. She allowed her to go next door, or somewhere close by, "in case she needed her."

Returning home one evening after shortbread and dark tea at Aunt Kennedy's, Maud found a number of letters from Cavendish on her bed. Pussy had followed Maud to her room, pouncing upon the pile of letters Father had left and hissing when Maud shooed him off. Maud spread the letters across the bed, touching each one, wondering which to read first.

Pussy jumped back on the bed and made himself comfortable on the edge, his deep purrs singing. She absently scratched behind his ear as she leaned back against the headboard.

There was the weekly letter from Grandma, of course. Maud could read between the lines, though; what Grandma really wanted to know was if her granddaughter had failed to live up to her expectations here. Maud refused to let her know how difficult things were. She would probably blame it on Maud anyway.

Lu's letter was light and full of fun, giving Maud all of the school and church gossip. Now that Jack Laird was planning on leaving for college, Mollie was rather moody, Lu reported, and Maud felt a stab of sadness for her friend, who would be there on her own.

There was a lovely long letter from Miss Gordon, giving Maud an inspiring list of books and a bit of much-needed encouragement:

*I would not be the educator I am without first asking how your studies are going. I only know Mr. Mustard by repu-tation, and I hear he is quite knowledgeable, so I hope you'll take advantage of this opportunity. Not a lot of girls have been able to get to high school, myself included . . . although I am proud of my accomplishments as one of the first women to enter the teaching certificate class at Prince of Wales College.*

If Miss Gordon knew the truth about Mr. Mustard, Maud wondered if she would have the same opinion.

Among the pile was an envelope marked with postage from Nova Scotia. She froze. She knew that handwriting all too well. Maud placed the other letters in her chest, leaving the one marked from Acadia College on her bed.

They hadn't written to each other all fall. She picked up Nate's letter and, in a rush of sentimentality, gave it a sniff—thinking it might hold a trace of his soap; it smelled only of dust and paper—and then promptly giggled. She had spent so much time sealing thoughts of him away; she simply mustn't give in to these roman-tic notions.

Pussy raised his head. "Don't judge me," she told him.

Pussy simply laid his head across an outstretched paw, leaving one eye open.

She carefully chiseled at the letter with the opener. For months she had been wondering what he had been thinking about her. When he hadn't written, it was easy to imagine he hated her. Now, here was news.

*Dear Polly,*

*It is hard to imagine that a few months ago you and I were picking berries and now I am sitting in my cold dorm room at college and you are halfway across the country. I know I should have written sooner—as I had promised—but I haven't heard from you, either, and wonder if you really meant it when you asked me to write. But I couldn't wait any longer; there is so much I want to tell you about the college and my life here.*

*You would enjoy my history class. The professor's specialty is British history, and I think he and Miss Gordon would have quite a lot to talk about. While there are many good teachers, she would definitely teach circles around some of the professors here. I think I'm taking the lead in all my courses, naturally. There is a fellow who is vying for the top of the class, but you know I'll surpass him. And there are some girls, too, but it isn't as much fun as competing with you.*

There was certainly no one vying for the top of the class in Mr. Mustard's classroom. She would give anything for one of Nate's notes slipped into her French book. She envied those girls who had been allowed to go to college, who somehow found the financial support they needed to go. How was it that these girls could go to college, but Maud couldn't even get her father to buy a copy of *Evangeline*!

Nate went on to discuss the many athletic pursuits and classical studies he had undertaken, including theology. He didn't want to be a minister, but since Acadia was a Baptist college, all students were required to take it.

Pussy sat up and arched his back, and she absently stroked his fur.

"I am going to write him a long letter and tell him about all of the things I am learning," she said to Pussy, who hopped off the bed and left her to her correspondence. "I will not be left behind."

## CHAPTER ELEVEN

With a renewed sense of ambition, Maud returned to her daily reading and writing schedule, even though it meant less sleep, as she had to get up early in the morning with Katie. She focused on that far-off goal, that alpine path. Her headaches subsided.

If Mrs. Montgomery's sniping or Mr. Mustard's attention got too much, Maud would open the old notebook where she had copied the poem in the front and read it. It reminded her that she had come here with expectations, and while she had been disappointed, the only way she was going to succeed was relying on herself. But focusing on education meant getting more serious in the classroom again, and she didn't want to give Mr. Mustard the wrong idea by suddenly applying herself to her studies. Her sights were definitely not set upon him!

Maud was a little cheered by the fact that she had finally turned sixteen and was able to wear her hair up again. Father had tried to make Maud's birthday a grand event, inviting the McTaggarts and some people from the church to the house to celebrate, but at the last minute, Mrs. Montgomery decided not to appear, pleading a bad headache. This turned out to be the perfect gift for Maud: celebrating without having to worry about her stepmother's negativity.

Laura and Will came and gave her a card and some candies from Andrew Agnew's father's store. Andrew was a tall man in his twenties with glossy black hair, dark eyes, and serious intelligence—and he was completely smitten with Laura. He had also served during the Riel Rebellion, helping the women and children to the safe house. And he smoked, which Maud thought was completely scandalous, but Laura found intriguing. There were also gifts from Cavendish: lace and gum from Pensie, and a luscious long letter from Mollie. Afterwards, Maud went to Southview and dug out Mother's Commonplace Book, reading over the pages she had written the night before she left Cavendish.

A week after her birthday, Maud went downstairs for breakfast before church, though she would have preferred to stay in bed, given the damp drafts of December. Mr. Mustard had shown up the previous evening for another visit and she had been forced to entertain him on her own, since Father and Mrs. Montgomery were out.

Maud was exhausted, but it was Sunday, and woe betide the girl who didn't go to Sunday School.

Mrs. Montgomery was preparing breakfast while Katie was on the floor chasing Pussy. Father came in with the previous night's mail, carrying a few copies of the *Charlottetown Patriot*. Over the past few weeks, she had continued to check for her poem, getting more and more disappointed, but with her newfound resolve, Maud had to take the chance. She seized the paper and, with a beating heart and trembling fingers, opened it.

"My goodness, aren't we anxious?" Mrs. Montgomery said. But Maud ignored her, scanning and crumpling each page.

"Are you all right?" Father asked.

The letters danced dizzily. There it was, in one of the columns. Her poem!

*On Cape Le Force.*
*[A legend of the early days of Prince Edward Island]*
*Lucy Maud Montgomery*

The whole room pulsed with light. After a grueling month of endless rain, perhaps the sun was finally coming out.

Her name in print. She'd never seen such a lovely sight.

"Maud, what is in the paper? You look like Pussy when he's caught a mouse," Father said.

Still shaking, Maud handed him the paper. Would he be proud of her? Maud didn't know what Father thought of women writers. Maybe he would think her too daring.

Father frowned, reading quickly. Slowly he began to smile, and then let out a wild "Hurrah!" He grabbed Maud and swung her around, kissing both cheeks. "Well done, Maudie!" Mrs. Montgomery cleared her throat, looking quite appalled at her husband's exuberant behavior, but he waved her off. "How incredible! My Maudie—Maud—in the paper."

Maud laughed, holding back the tears she was sure would come. Her Father was proud of her. "I didn't want anyone to know in case it wasn't published," she managed to say.

"I would say this is a cause for celebration. Don't you think so, Mary Ann?"

"It is certainly . . . something," Mrs. Montgomery said. "But you don't want to be late for Sunday School, Maud."

Father rubbed his hand through his hair. "No, that's true. We'll celebrate this evening!"

Not even Mrs. Montgomery could ruin this moment for her. Grabbing her Bible and the newspaper, Maud floated to church.

The moment Maud arrived, however, Mrs. Rochester, the new reverend's wife, pulled her aside. She was a stout woman who always had a cheery disposition, but today she looked worried.

"Oh, Maud. Kate McGregor didn't show up to teach the girls' Sunday School," she said. "Would you please take her class?"

Maud was surprised she was even being asked, and she felt a bit cheated, too; she had so wanted to share her good news with her friends—and with Will. She suppressed a smile as she remembered she would soon see him since Will worked in the church library, which was in the same room that was used for the girls' Sunday School classroom. She turned her attention back to Mrs. Rochester. "I've never taught before," she said.

"It's easy." Mrs. Rochester squeezed Maud's arm. "This week's lesson is Noah's ark."

Although Maud certainly knew the story, that didn't mean she could teach it. But Mrs. Rochester looked so desperate, and Maud knew what her grandmother would say: "A good Presbyterian doesn't shrink from her duty."

"All right," Maud said.

After many exclamations of gratitude, Mrs. Rochester introduced Maud to the group of little girls dressed in their Sunday best and then left her alone.

Six pairs of eyes gazed up at her. Maud told them to open their Sunday School readers and asked them a series of questions she herself had been asked a hundred times about the Lord telling Noah to build an ark that would save only his family and each and every animal, two by two. But none of the girls had done their homework, and instead of answering her questions, they had a few confounding ones of their own:

"Was Jesus on the ark?"

"Did everyone go to heaven or hell?"

"How did Noah know the voice came from God and not Satan?"

She was saved when Will entered with a pile of books. "Noah knew that it was God because Satan's voice is deeper," he said, placing the books on the shelf.

The girls listened, entranced, as he began a long explanation as to how Noah would know the difference, and then they peppered him with questions. Eventually, Mrs. Rochester came to take them to their parents, and Maud and Will were left alone in the room.

Maud leaned against the wall and started laughing with deep relief. Thank goodness that was over.

"Got caught today?" he said, shelving a book.

"Yes," Maud said, collecting the readers. "I've found myself transformed from pupil to teacher."

He took the books from her and placed them on the shelf. "Did you enjoy it?"

"I enjoyed it well enough. One thing I can say is that I'm certainly better at it than Mr. Mustard."

Will laughed.

"Thank you for your help," she said. "They definitely know how to put someone on the spot."

"And you wouldn't know anything about that," he said in a way that made her cheeks warm. She turned her face to the picture window so he wouldn't see.

"How about being the librarian here?" she said, after she regained her composure. "I mean, do you enjoy your time here?"

"Yes," he said.

"That's good, if I'm going to be a teacher."

"Me being a librarian?" He chuckled.

Maud laughed nervously, and she helped him put away the rest of the books. "Actually," she said, "I have some interesting news today."

"Really?" he said. "A teacher and a holder of secrets?"

She handed him the *Charlottetown Patriot*, and he smiled widely when he saw her name. He had the most agreeable smile. "Congratulations! I know you always have a pen in your hand, but I had no idea you had real aspirations. This is excellent, Maud. We'll have to find a way to celebrate your good fortune."

"Father said the same thing," Maud said. "But nothing is as wonderful as seeing one's name in print." She breathed deeply. "Will, this proves to me that my greatest dream will come true. I am going to be a writer."

"It is good to know who you really are," he said. They stared at each other for a few moments, and Maud found herself suddenly anxious to fill the silence with words. But before she could do so, Annie burst into the room.

"Those boys are such terrors!" Annie taught the third-grade boys.

"They need you to show them the way, Annie," Maud said, turning toward her.

Annie placed the books on the table next to Will. "Hello, Will."

"Hello, Annie," he said, picking up the pile. "I'd better finish this so I can get to my aunt's in time for lunch. My mother, father, and all of my brothers and sisters are coming too, and it promises to be quite a feast."

Maud pictured Will and Laura gathered around a table with their family, and then remembered the tension and arguments that awaited her at home. She felt a sudden stab of jealousy.

"Goodbye, Will," Maud said.

"Goodbye, Maud," he said in a way that made her feel as though he was saying "hello."

# CHAPTER TWELVE

After weeks of preparation and rehearsal, the day of the Christmas concert arrived. Mid-December brought with it terribly cold weather, with the kitchen thermometer reading forty below.

"Could the Lord have picked a colder day?" Mrs. Montgomery said, wrapping a red wool scarf around Katie's head. She glared at Maud as though she had somehow conspired with the Almighty to inconvenience her stepmother with the inclement weather.

"Maud and her friends have worked so diligently on the Christmas concert," Father said, straightening his gloves. "Besides, your niece Mrs. Stovel has directed it, so you might want to show your support."

"At least it is only across the street." She flounced out, leaving Maud to carry Katie—and part of her costume.

When they got to the church, Maud handed Katie to Father and went to the makeshift dressing room, which was much too tiny for anyone to get around in. No one could find their costumes, Alexena kept tripping on her skirt, and Lottie was sure she'd forgotten "everything she'd ever learned."

But once on stage, the performers played with near perfection.

Only one of the tableaux was a complete disaster: when Lottie almost fell into Alexena because Frank accidentally stepped on the sheet she was wearing as a cape. But Maud's recitation of "The Child Martyr" was so excellent, she received a standing ovation. The audience even demanded an encore, so she recited part of her own work about Cape LeForce and spun it as well as her grandfather had.

The ladies had baked their finest for the tea that followed the performances, and the room smelled of sugar and pine. Many people came up to Maud to congratulate her.

"I knew you were scribbling something," Mrs. McTaggart said, "but I had no idea you were such a talent."

"I was so impressed by your elocution." Aunt Kennedy hugged her. "Laura told me she helped you practice and knew you would be a success."

Mrs. Rochester invited Maud to the Bible Study that was beginning in the manse in the New Year. "We need someone with your talents," she said.

After waiting patiently for everyone to leave, Will came up to Maud and asked if she was going with them to the train station. Now that the train was coming through Prince Albert, a popular evening activity among the young people was watching it come in. Because of her duties at home, Maud had yet to be allowed to go.

"I'll have to ask my father," Maud said. She hadn't been able to get to him because people kept stopping her to talk and offer congratulations.

"Will!" A tall man who was an older version of her friend called to him.

"My father," Will said to Maud, before turning to face him.

"How do you do, Mr. Pritchard?" she said.

"Will," he puffed. "Didn't you hear me calling you?"

"Yes, Father," Will said. "I was finishing up my conversation with Maud. Didn't she perform her reading wonderfully?"

Without acknowledging her in the slightest, Mr. Pritchard looked over Maud's head and said to Will, "When I call you, you must come. Your mother was looking for you. I believe she wants you to drive her and your brother and sisters home."

Will and Laura's five other siblings lived at Laurel Hill with their parents. "Aren't you going home, Father?"

"I have people to speak with," he said. "Be sure to take her and your siblings home."

And then he was gone.

Maud realized she was deeply disappointed that Will wouldn't be at the train station—not that Father would let her go anyway.

"I guess I'd better go," he mumbled and walked away.

Maud had drifted across the room, moving closer to her own father, when Laura came up and kissed her. "Will has to take Mother and the brood home, but you'll come, won't you?"

"Go where?" Mrs. Montgomery said. "You have to put Katie to bed tonight."

Katie was looking rather tired; the little blue bow Maud had fought so hard to tie earlier in the day was halfway out of her hair. "I guess I have responsibilities," Maud said to Laura.

"There you are, Maudie—Maud." Father hugged her. "I'm so proud of you."

For the first time in a while, Maud saw that old spark in his cobalt-blue eyes. The fact that she had caused it was all Maud needed to make it the perfect night.

"I was telling Maud that Katie needed to go home," Mrs. Montgomery said.

Katie yawned widely and laid her head against Maud's skirt, pulling it a little. Maud lifted her sister up and let her rest her head on her shoulder.

"You might have told me, Hugh, that you had such a talented daughter," Mr. McTaggart said. "People are asking about her."

"Really," Father said, and exchanged a glance with his father-in-law. "Yes, she is quite a marvel, isn't she?"

Maud shifted Katie. Mrs. Montgomery had crossed her arms, as if refusing to take her own daughter.

"Mr. Montgomery," Laura piped in. "Perhaps Maud would be allowed to join us at the train station after she puts Katie to bed? On a night such as this, we wanted to celebrate."

What was her friend doing? Couldn't she see that Mrs. Montgomery was not going to allow Maud to go out? Her role in this family was quite clear.

But then Father did the most extraordinary thing. "Laura, you are right. Maud can go with you." He extended his arm to his daughter. "After I introduce her to some of my friends, that is."

"What about Katie?" Maud said.

Father didn't say anything as Mrs. Montgomery continued to stand with her arms crossed.

"Mary Ann," Mr. McTaggart said. "You can see how important it is for Maud to say something to your husband's possible voters."

"It's much too cold for either of us to be out," she said, but there was no longer any power in it, and she took Katie from Maud. She didn't even wish anyone good night as she left.

If she hadn't so enjoyed being taken around on Father's arm, Maud might have felt sorry for her.

## CHAPTER THIRTEEN

Finally, they all left the church. It had started to snow, warming up the early evening air enough so that being outside was tolerable. As the group of performers walked up the hill toward the train station, reliving their successes and tragedies, Maud felt as though she might be able to make Prince Albert her home after all. With Laura and Annie, Alexena and Lottie—even Frank—it felt as though she was becoming part of a crowd again.

Maud was sorry that Will was missing it. He was as much part of the success as anyone else.

"Will he stay at Laurel Hill tonight?" Maud asked Laura as they rounded the corner.

"Most probably," Laura said. "It will be too dark to come back."

"It is too bad he couldn't stay," Maud said.

Laura was silent for a moment. "Mother needs help. She has so much to take care of on the ranch and with all of us. With me away, I know it is harder for her, but she wanted me to finish school this year."

"She cares about your education," Maud said.

"She was a teacher before she got married," Laura said. "If it were up to Father, I would have left school last year. Particularly after my sister died. Mother was sick for a while."

"I'm so sorry, Laura," Maud said. "I didn't know."

Laura stopped walking and gazed out to the frozen river. "It was right before you got here. We don't talk about it much."

They were quiet for a few moments.

"Mother said she wanted me to enjoy my freedom while I could," Laura said, after a while. "I'm so grateful I get to study art at the convent."

"You are very talented," Maud said. "I enjoyed those sketches you showed me when I was last at your aunt's."

"We're going to have a show in June; you must come."

June seemed so far away. By then her little brother or sister would have been born, and Maud would no longer be in school herself. "I hope to be there."

Laura took her arm and the two walked on.

When the group arrived at the station, people began to pair off. While one of Laura's suitors, George Weir, wanted her attention, it was Andrew Agnew who won out, taking her to a quiet corner near the ticket window. Frank was trying to get Alexena's attention, but she would have none of it.

For once, Maud was happy to be watching without anyone really noticing her.

"Now, how come you are alone?" Maud jumped at the unexpected sound of Will's low voice.

"I thought you were staying at Laurel Hill tonight?" she said, hoping her voice didn't betray how excited she was to see him.

"Once I got everyone home, Mother said I had done such a fine job tonight that she wanted me to celebrate with my friends. Besides"—he grinned—"I'm used to traveling in the dark."

"You must have ridden quickly," Maud said.

He didn't say anything, but his grin made it impossible not to blush.

"Will, you came after all," Laura said, rushing over. "I was telling Maud that you probably wouldn't be."

"So you were talking about me," Will said.

Maud opened her mouth, and then shut it.

"We were amusing ourselves," Laura said, slapping her brother's arm. "The station manager tells me that a train should be coming through in about ten minutes. Shall we go get a good view?"

The cold wind hit them the moment they stepped out onto the platform. Maud pulled her wool scarf over her mouth. Will went to the edge where the tracks started, picked up some snow and packed it into a ball, and then threw it into the dark. Maud followed him.

"I'm sorry about my father," he said. "He can be so focused that he forgets his manners."

"What is he so focused on?"

The wind blew open the door and it banged against the wall, letting out the warmth and the conversation of those who'd had the wisdom to stay indoors.

"He trusted our neighbor to watch out for our farm a few years ago when he went to help fight in the rebellion. Many of the men went—"

"Yes, my father did," Maud said.

Will concentrated on the train tracks. "I was too young."

Laura and Andrew walked up ahead.

Will extended his arm and, despite her nervousness, she took it. The train's wheels chugged in the distance.

"So what happened?" she asked.

"When you make a homestead claim, you must stay on the land to prove to the government that you are farming it. But being gone for those six months meant that he wasn't."

"But you were," she said.

"Yes," Will said, and didn't speak for a few moments. Maud squeezed his arm to encourage him to go on. "The claim isn't in my name. And as my father is so fond of reminding me, I wasn't a man yet."

Maud understood how it felt to disappoint someone you love.

"Mr. Coombs has always wanted our land, so he told the homestead office. Father has been successful so far explaining the matter, but this Inspector Coon won't relent. Father has had to prove his claim twice. It's no excuse, but . . ." He let go of her arm and turned to face her. "Maud, I hope we are friends," he said. "I wish to get to know you better." She could see his breath in the snow-haloed lantern lights of the station.

"Don't you already? My grandma says I wear my heart on my sleeve." She walked away from him and heard his soft steps shuffle the snow.

"Your grandma doesn't know you."

Maud laughed and turned around. "No, but she thinks she does." She blew on her hands.

"My father thinks he knows me," he said, throwing another snowball into the dark.

"I'm sure he thinks he does," Maud said, wondering how much her own father really knew her. "In his way."

"Perhaps." He breathed puffs of white air. "He wants me to take over the farm when he's gone. I like farming, particularly working with the horses," he said. "But I also like learning, and I think I would enjoy going to college, but it would mean going back East, and he can't spare me."

"I often feel as though I'm stuck."

"Something else we have in common," he said. Their eyes met, and as he opened his mouth to say something more, a shrill whistle blew twice, forcing them both to look away.

In the distance, Maud could see a red light coming toward them. It would have been so much easier if her cross-country trip had taken her directly to Prince Albert.

Will grabbed more snow and tossed it onto the track. Then he rolled another snowball and handed it to Maud. "Here," he said. "I find that sometimes taking action in one small way helps keep a person heading in the right direction."

"Such as?" She took it.

"Such as getting lost in someone's brown hair." His green eyes shone in the dark, and she shivered.

"Toss it," he whispered.

Maud held the snowball in her hand and remembered all of the dreams she had lost since coming here. Maybe Will was right; it was the doing of one small action that helped a person move forward. She threw the snowball into the dark.

After Christmas, the election was held. Father earned a seat on the town council, winning by fifty-two votes. He was also appointed to the Board of Works. That night, everyone celebrated at the Kinistino Lodge until the early hours of the morning. Maud had never seen her father so happy.

But the following morning was the first day of school after Christmas Break and, tired from the previous evening's festivities, Maud slept in. It was only when Annie had come around banging on the door that Maud realized with a horrible start that she had slept in. Why hadn't anyone woken her up?

Maud leaped out of bed and quickly got dressed, wrapping herself up in a wool petticoat. As she ran downstairs, she noticed that her Father's coat was missing; most likely, he had already started at his new job. When she came into the kitchen, her stepmother was sitting at the kitchen table feeding Katie. "I wondered if you were going to join us today," she said.

Maud wondered if Mrs. Montgomery had purposely made her late for school.

In retrospect, the girls should have turned around the moment they walked out the door and saw the swirling snow, which was so dangerous on the prairie. But they were determined, and made their way ever so slowly to the high school.

Finally, the girls burst through the doors, hair wet from the snow and eyes bright from the wind.

"You're late, Miss Montgomery and Miss McTaggart," Mr. Mustard said. "Is this the way you two wish to start off the new year?"

"I'm sorry, Mr. Mustard," Maud said. "We had such a time getting through the snow."

"Really?" he said. "Everyone else was able to make it here without trouble."

"We've never been late before," Maud said, her hands clenched in frustration.

"With the heavy snow, this morning was different," Annie said. "I prevail upon your good judgment and ask you to allow us to take our seats."

Maud was pretty sure Mr. Mustard's good judgment—if he'd had any to begin with—had left him long ago.

"Please stand against the wall for the rest of the morning."

"Excuse me?" Annie said.

"I said stand against the wall or leave." Mr. Mustard stuck his index finger in his vest. "It is up to you."

"If I leave now," Annie said, with a determination Maud had never heard from her before, "you will not be seeing me in your classroom again."

"What about your teaching certificate, Miss McTaggart?" he said.

"I'll make other arrangements."

Annie marched out. And if she wasn't staying, neither was Maud. She gave Will a sympathetic glance and followed her friend.

With their heads once again down, the girls fought their way home through the swirling snow. Maud urged Annie to reconsider, but her decision was final.

"I will speak to my father," she said. "I overheard him mention there was a new school in Lindsay that needed a teacher."

"I'm going to miss walking to school with you," Maud said, surprised at her own words. Annie might put on airs, but she always stuck by Maud.

"Oh, you won't get rid of me that easily," Annie said with a smile.

"I'm not going to let Mr. Mustard get away with this," Maud said. "I just need to figure out how to get back at him."

When Maud got home, no one was there, and she remembered hearing Mrs. Montgomery say something about visiting Mrs. McTaggart.

What was she going to do? She certainly didn't want her imprisonment to start so soon—and for something that was entirely her fault. She had been both late and impertinent. Father would almost certainly take Mr. Mustard's side; after all, her teacher was Mrs. Montgomery's old friend and an adult. Even if things hadn't quite gone as she'd planned, she desperately needed to finish the school year.

Maud paced in Southview the whole blustery morning, only coming downstairs to answer a knock at the door around lunchtime. The caller turned out to be a certain red-haired young man with a distracting smile. "I hope you'll consider coming back to school, Maud," Will said. "It will be no fun without you."

Feeling quite daring being alone with him, Maud invited Will inside. "Would you like some tea?" she asked.

Will rubbed his hands. "I can't stay very long. I need to be back at school."

"Of course," she said. "But I'd feel as though I were betraying Annie if I went back."

"I can't imagine you enjoying spending your day"—he stretched his arms out—"here."

"I was just thinking that," she said, bringing him into the parlor. "The thought of being cooped up here all day. But how can I show my face after what happened? What shall I do about Mr. Mustard?"

"I'll stand by you."

Surprised, Maud sat down on the sofa. She didn't say anything for a few minutes. How incredible that her own father couldn't say these words, but this young man—this stranger, really—was willing to help her. He was like a knight in a novel.

"I can't let you do that!" Maud stood up abruptly. "It will get you in trouble."

He smiled, and she found herself smiling back. "What is life without a bit of trouble? Come back with me, Maud."

That afternoon, Maud and Will returned to school together. A smug-yet-frowning Mr. Mustard made them both stay after school because they were supposedly late.

Maud didn't say a word for the rest of the day, which aggravated her teacher even more. No matter what Mr. Mustard did, she would nod or shake her head, making sure she was extra friendly with everyone else—even Frank and Willie M.—and was extra, extra friendly with Will, who had no trouble returning her sentiments in kind.

It had the desired effect. Mr. Mustard became angrier and angrier.

The next day when the end of day bell rang, Mr. Mustard asked Maud to stay behind. Maud listened to her classmates gathering their things.

"Miss Montgomery." Mr. Mustard stood up from his desk and walked over to hers. She had the urge to stand up so he wouldn't have the advantage of towering over her. "I don't understand your behavior. I thought we had an understanding." Maud clenched her lips together. She would not speak.

She heard the door open and close as her classmates left, one by one.

He inched closer, his nasal breath warm against her cheek. "Why won't you speak?"

She pushed herself as far back against the wooden chair as she could. She stared at a crack in a floorboard, urging it to break open and swallow him whole.

"I'm as upset as you are that Miss McTaggart is no longer with us," he went on. "I certainly don't think she's ready to teach, particularly when she acts as though she were still a child."

There was some shuffling in the hallway, and Maud wished that one of the officers were bringing someone to the jail to, as Annie once whispered, "sleep it off."

"You know the only reason that I keep you after school is out of my sincerest concern for your well-being." He sat down at the adjoining desk—Annie's desk—and leaned over to her. Maud pressed against the chair. She would not move.

"You may go, but I hope to see your manners much improved tomorrow."

Maud couldn't get out of the room fast enough, and when she entered the hallway, she found—to her surprise—Will leaning against the wall, arms crossed against his chest.

"Are you all right?" he whispered.

"Hello, Will," Maud said, a little louder than was probably ladylike. It sounded even louder to her because she hadn't spoken all afternoon.

"Hello, Maud," he said, much louder than his previous whisper. "Shall I accompany you home?"

"That would be most kind," she said, and mouthed, "Thank you."

Mr. Mustard lurked in the doorway, scowling. Will approached Maud and took her books, laying them on the bench in front of their hooks. Maud's attempt at getting her arm in her coat sleeve was in vain.

"Here," Will said, and helped her on with her coat, his hands pausing for a moment on her shoulders before he slowly slid them down her back and away. Maud didn't dare steal a glimpse at Mr. Mustard's face.

A few minutes later, Will and Maud were safely away from the school, crunching through the snow.

"That man needs a good whipping," Will said, his gloved hand grazing Maud's sleeve as he took her books.

"I don't know what I'm going to do." Her boots made somber-looking impressions in the snow. "He is not a good teacher. He is moody and intolerant and doesn't know what he's doing. He whips those boys, keeps us after school for no reason"—Will lifted an eyebrow—"Well, all right; we aren't helping matters, but he's intolerable. No one will do anything because he's the teacher and his rule is law. It is a wonder I've learned anything at all in his class."

"I think you'll make an excellent teacher, though," Will said, and cleared his throat.

She turned to the frozen river. "I would be a better teacher if I'd had better instruction."

"I promise to do what I can to help you in school," Will said as they approached her front door.

"What about Mr. Mustard?"

"We'll carry on much like we did today." He leaned a little closer. "As though we are good friends."

Were they good friends? She kept her gaze steady. "My friend Nate and I used to use a cipher code to send notes."

Will's expression darkened. "I'm not about to repeat things you had with another boy."

Of course he wouldn't. She breathed ice. "That isn't what I meant."

Will rubbed his hands.

"It is really something that would drive him—Mr. Mustard—mad," she said. "And in the meantime, I'll freeze him out. I'll only speak to him when absolutely necessary."

At least their plan might keep him away.


Over the next couple of weeks, Maud stayed completely silent in school, speaking to Mr. Mustard only when necessary. Will and Maud started sending notes, keeping their activity expertly hidden from the teacher, who begged her to break her silence. Her silence was her answer.

After that first day back at school, Mr. Mustard had not called on her, which was a blessing—and an incentive to continue. The silence was worth it if it meant he would stay away.

But it was getting harder and harder to keep it up. One day toward the end of January, Mr. Mustard asked Maud about Tennyson, and she simply couldn't stay quiet. It was a grave error, because that evening, Mr. Mustard was back at Eglintoune Villa.

"Are you going to let me in, Miss Montgomery?" he asked, smiling as though nothing had transpired between them.

Maud wished that Mrs. Montgomery would at least make an appearance, but she had gone upstairs right after dinner, refusing to come down.

It was as though her father and stepmother wanted this tedious, pedantic man to court her. She wouldn't put it past Mrs. Montgomery, but Father? No. Surely not. In the end, there was nothing Maud could do but let the man inside.

## CHAPTER FIFTEEN

The prairie blizzards of January settled into the heart of winter and Maud no longer slept through the night; her mind spun with memories and lost dreams. Her headaches were back, more painful than before. Sometimes it was all she could do to get out of bed.

One night in late January Maud woke from a nightmare that left her feeling cold and abandoned. And then it all came back to her: what had happened earlier that evening, after coming home from visiting Will and Laura.

Father had called Maud as she was climbing the stairs and she sat down beside him on the burnt-yellow sofa in the parlor. He looked tired and old.

Maud tucked her shawl under her chin. "What's wrong?"

He heaved an aching sigh. "I have something difficult to tell you." He put his hands on hers. "I hate asking, but . . . in case . . . Katie . . ." He let go, cradling his head in his hands.

Maud placed her hand on Father's shoulder. "What happened?"

Father rubbed his hair and gazed up at her. "I need you to tell Katie that Pussy ran away."

"Did he?" Maud had seen the rascal this morning; he had been batting a mouse in the kitchen. "It is so cold out, he won't last the night."

His eyes reminded her of the frozen Saskatchewan River. Maud shivered. "What did you do?"

"I had to, Maudie. She was worried he would hurt the baby."

What had Mrs. Montgomery made him do?

"I drowned him."

Drowned him! Maud swallowed the tears coming up the back of her throat. Pussy had been a mean old thing but a good companion.

"The cat was taking too many fits," he said.

Such things could be trained from a cat, if you knew how to deal with them. Clearly, Mrs. Montgomery wasn't willing—and neither was Father.

"You understand, don't you?" he said.

"Yes," she mumbled and ran upstairs so quickly, she almost stepped on it.

At the foot of the Southview door was a dead mouse.

Her skin prickled and she held in a scream. Pussy must have left it for her sometime between this morning and . . .

Her chin trembled.

Like when her journal had been discovered by her grandparents, it was as if she were watching herself from above. Slowly, she pulled at the handkerchief tucked in her sleeve, and, swallowing bile, placed the dead mouse in the cloth, tying it tightly. In silence, she walked through to the back porch and buried it in the snow.

Now, an overwhelming sense of being lost crawled into her heart and stayed so long that she couldn't breathe. She opened the window a tiny crack, allowing the frigid air to cut through her. She went to her bureau and took out her journal, pen, and ink.

Maud hadn't been writing very much. The burst of energy she had months before had faded, and in its place was fatigue and a desire to sleep. There was the poem she'd written for Pensie, her journal, and letters to home, but Maud hadn't allowed herself to revel in imagination.

Maud went over to the frosty window. In the dark morning she wrote about the frozen river, and how the ghostly poplar trees hugged it. She wrote out her spinning thoughts about Pussy and Mr. Mustard's unwanted visits, about how everything felt so out of control.

Then she wrote about some of the good things. She remembered her first Bible Study earlier that week and wrote about that. Maud had been skeptical at first, worried that it would be much like Sunday School, that it would be more like being told what to believe than a time for discussion and reflection. Growing up in her grandparents' home, she'd been discouraged from questioning. But she soon realized it was actually an opportunity for theological and intellectual discussion.

The new minister, Reverend Rochester, explored a different chapter or psalm each week, but he also encouraged his students to lead discussions. Maud's turn was in two weeks. The idea both thrilled and terrified her. Grandma would say a girl of sixteen discussing theology was blasphemy.

Listening to the reverend, Maud had imagined the hand of God weaving and writing the world. When she wrote, she felt as though she was doing something similar, although she would never dream of falling prey to the hubris of comparing herself to Him. But creating a world of characters who spoke to her, sharing the stories she knew and loved, this was her calling. Most of the time, she didn't feel she had control over anything but her words.

The Bible Study had closed with a hymn: "Lead, Kindly Light." She had sung it before, of course, but that night it was as though she was hearing it for the first time. As so often happened when she reread her favorite books and poems, she discovered something new. "The night is dark, and I am far from home." She was so far away from all she loved . . . and she'd had such plans before she came here: to be with Father and go to school, to perhaps have an education, to go to college. None of it was how she'd believed it would be. She could almost hear Grandma say, "It is all in the hands of Providence."

Maud had stood between Will and Laura as they sang. Mrs. Rochester played the small pipe organ, her voice ringing above everyone else's. There were moments in Maud's life when she could feel the power of prayer, where word and song enveloped her soul. This had been one of them. When they all sang, "And with the morn those angel faces smile," both Will and Laura turned to Maud and grinned. She returned the smile, and it was as if they were sharing a hidden truth. A knowing.

Now, here in the dark, Maud wished for some moment of clarity—something to reassure her that she wouldn't be forever in the dark, forever caught between what she wished and what was expected of her.

Tracing the hymn in her mind, she felt that shiver of knowing: "With the morn those angel faces smile / Which I have loved long since, and lost awhile."

She'd experienced that moment when she first saw Laura at church, the feeling that they were twin souls reunited.

Perhaps it wasn't what she'd originally believed would happen, but she would never have dreamed of Laura and Will's friendship. And, yet, here they were.

"Lead on," she said to the dark night and the moon and the stars. "Lead on."

## CHAPTER SIXTEEN

One morning toward the end of January, they had an unexpected visitor. The leader of the federal Liberal party came to visit and the men spent a number of hours in Father's study. When they emerged, Father's eyes had that look of adventure in them, and he pronounced that he was entering federal politics, running on the Liberal ticket.

"Are you sure this is wise, Hugh?" Mrs. Montgomery said. "You've always been a staunch Conservative supporter, even helping with Mr. MacDowall's campaign. Now he's going to be your opponent. People are going to think you are being opportunistic."

"Trust me, Mary Ann," Hugh said. "They'll vote the man, not the party."

Maud could see her father was excited by this new opportunity, but she wasn't sure what to think. Her whole life her father and grandpa had been Conservatives, and hadn't Father's positions been given to him because of Prime Minister Macdonald and his party? He must know what he was doing.

But before her father could begin campaigning, the arrival of her baby brother took over the household. Her father looked so proud when Mrs. McTaggart brought a sleeping baby Bruce into the parlor, all pink, swaddled in the blanket Maud had knitted during all those long nights she had been forced to listen to Mr. Mustard.

In those first few weeks after Bruce arrived, Mrs. Montgomery was happy too. She smiled and was even kind to Maud, thanking her for all that she had done. Perhaps her stepmother's boorish behavior had been because she was tired from her pregnancy?

Father talked cheerfully of a bright future, his business, and the election. He didn't discuss how the paper was calling him "a renegade," or how people were criticizing him for "crossing the floor," as her stepmother had warned that they would.

Maud didn't attend school, nor did she see her friends for those first few weeks. She would snuggle with her two siblings on the bed in Southview. She couldn't get enough of Bruce's little, darling toes and nose. Katie would cuddle up beside them, reaching her arms out to hold him as if he were one of her dolls. "Mine!" she'd say.

"He's ours," Maud would say, letting her little sister pet him.

In those quiet moments, Maud almost believed a peaceful home was possible.

Unfortunately, Mrs. Montgomery's predictions were right, and in the first week of March, the news came out. Father had lost.

Her father had been so light of heart and full of fun since Bruce's birth, but now he lost his joy. It worried her. What would this mean for them? Would his auctioneer business be enough to sustain them?

As the weeks progressed, Father and Mrs. Montgomery fought more and more. They fought about going back to Ontario, with Father in favor but Mrs. Montgomery staunchly opposed. They fought about money, particularly about "extra people in the house who didn't pull their own."

It was too much—not to mention unfair. Now that she had stopped going to school, and was helping with Katie and the baby full-time, she felt busier than she'd ever imagined, preparing meals, doing the laundry, and cleaning the house. Maud loved her siblings, but this was not how she saw her future. She took advantage of the fact that Father had hired a quiet Métis girl named Fannie and asked if she could go back to school, at least to finish the year. While Mrs. Montgomery complained that she didn't want to be left alone in the house with just the children and the "help" for company, Father allowed Maud to return.

"At least you can say you've finished what you've started," he said. Maud leaped up and hugged her father.

But time away had romanticized Maud's memories of high school. As soon as she got there and saw Mr. Mustard and his thin mustache, she realized nothing had changed.

Her first day back went downhill fast. First, Will slipped her a note, inviting her to go tobogganing that night at the barracks, but this time Mr. Mustard saw it and forced her to show him, telling her she was "wasting her time" and giving them both detention.

Then Douglas came in dripping wet from being pushed in the snow, and Mr. Mustard made him go stand in the corner for being tardy.

When the students were working not-so-diligently on their geography, Maud caught her teacher staring forlornly out the window, as was his wont . . . but there was a new darkness in his expression that frightened her.

Frank and Willie M. behaved as they normally did, roughhousing and teasing when they should have been studying—but then again, no one was really studying. Perhaps it was because Frank had already been warned that his "outbursts" would have "dire consequences," or maybe it was because Mr. Mustard had been staring out the window longer than usual, but when Willie M. shoved Frank one time too many, Mr. Mustard marched over to them, grabbed Frank by the collar, and shoved him against the wall. Frank clutched the teacher's arms, pulling them off him, and swung—

Maud turned away. She couldn't watch. Burying her head in between her arms and her desk, she stared at the crack in the floorboards as she heard a slap and then another and then a grunt. Someone—Willie M.?—cheered, but then there was the slap of a ruler against skin and it grew silent.

A few minutes later, Mr. Mustard dismissed them.

It was over. Maud slowly lifted her head to see Frank doubled over in pain, and Willie M. rubbing his palm against his leg. The floor creaked as Frank fell to his knees.

She felt sick—she had never seen such violence in the classroom before. But then she felt a familiar hand on her shoulder.

"Maud," Will said. "Are you okay?"

"Will, I—"

Her head felt as though it was mired in mud.

"Frank got the worst of it, getting punched in the stomach," Will said, helping her stand. "But he did get in a few blows. I don't think Mr. Mustard will be hitting him again."

She looked over at her teacher, who was now back to staring out the window, arms crossed against his chest, a slight bruise forming on his chin.

"I heard—" She swallowed. She couldn't even describe what she had heard.

"Come." He guided her out. "I'll walk you home."

Three days later, Fannie quit without notice or reason, leaving Maud once again in charge of Bruce. After six months of fighting, Maud resigned herself to her fate. She did not return to high school.

## CHAPTER SEVENTEEN

There were few people in her life Maud had truly hated. She used to think she hated Clemmie, but her feelings toward Mr. Mustard were altogether something new. Bile would rise in Maud's throat when she saw him. After the brutal incident in school, she never felt safe with him. She wished to never see him again. But now that she was no longer his student, he seemed even more inclined to come over almost every night, staying sometimes until eleven o'clock. Even with the election over, Father still found excuses to go out, and often Mrs. Montgomery would follow, leaving Maud to tend to Bruce and Katie alone.

In her journal, Maud tried to overcome her loathing by making her former teacher into a figure of comedy. It was easy to do, as he was so awkward, having no idea how to read social cues.

What was worse—if one could get any worse than being a deplorable human being—was that Mr. Mustard was intolerably boring. Every night it was the same conversation, rehashing the same stories Maud had heard now at least a thousand times. If it wasn't about the new Presbyterian church being built, it was about how much he detested card playing and dancing. The conversation would eventually lead to his school days and then to ancestry and nomenclature.

Even worse, people at church were starting to talk about their supposed connection. At Bible Study, Mrs. Stovel and Mrs. Rochester both asked Maud if things were serious with Mr. Mustard.

She had to talk to Father.

A few weeks after she had left school, Maud found her father looking over some auctioneering papers in his study.

"Father, I know you are busy, but I desperately need to talk with you," she said.

Father put his papers down with a tired smile. "Well, I need a distraction from these bills. How can I help?"

Maud took her time explaining the full business of Mr. Mustard's dreary, dogged courtship, being sure to keep her tone even. She didn't want it to sound as though her detestation for the man was coloring her words.

"Mr. Mustard is a teacher, Maud," Father said. "He will probably make a good husband."

"Husband!" Maud said. She was only sixteen! "That man is a bore."

Father chuckled. "Don't be unkind, Maud. I know that Mustard is a bit, shall we say, awkward, but your stepmother can vouch for his good character."

Given her stepmother's own character, Maud had doubts about that endorsement. She had to try another tactic. "Grandma would never let me be alone in a room with a man."

Father hated being compared to Grandma, and the dig at his wife was unmistakable. Her father picked up his pen and then placed it in the ink. "Perhaps. I trust you, Maud. You've grown up in the past few months, taking on more responsibility." He gave her a long look. "Preparing yourself for a life as mother and wife."

Even if her stepmother wanted her to be strapped to Mr. Mustard, Maud couldn't imagine that Father—no. He disliked Mr. Mustard, didn't he?

"I don't feel that way about him," she said, barely choking the words out.

"If you are not interested, you need to tell him. It isn't proper to lead a man on. People will talk if a woman gives a man the wrong idea." He picked up his pen again.

But she had done everything in her power to deter Mr. Mustard. She had been rude to him both inside and outside of school. There was also Will. "I'm not sure what else I can do," she said. It wasn't as though she could tell him directly. That would be too mortifying for both of them.

"You are an intelligent young woman," he said. "Now, I need to get back to this."

Maud left her father to his papers and went to the backyard.

Everything was so out of sorts. Sitting on a large piece of chopped wood, Maud wrapped her shawl around herself and allowed a few quiet tears to come. She'd been doing that a lot lately—crying. Too much crying. Each time, she knew what Grandma would say: she was being too sensitive.

"Are you all right?"

Maud looked up to see Laura standing there, wrapped snugly in her warmest shawl.

"It is too cold to be outside," Maud said.

"I could say the same thing to you." Laura picked up a large round log, sat down, and kissed her cheek. "What's wrong?"

"Nothing for you to worry about."

"Nothing for me to worry about!" Laura put her arm around Maud. "My friend is crying in the cold, and there's nothing for me to worry about."

Despite herself, Maud laughed. "I truly don't want to burden you."

"Please," Laura said. "Burden me. Weren't you the one who said we are twin souls finding each other? If you cannot tell your twin soul, who can you tell?"

Maud traced the frozen mud with her boot. There was always so much mud in Prince Albert. She was tired of that too.

"Is it your stepmother? Is she working you too hard?"

"That is my lot here," Maud said, with a wry smile. "But no, this is something else."

Laura was quiet. They listened to the last of the ice cracking on the river.

"Father says it would be a good match." She buried her head in Laura's shawl. "Perhaps I'm wrong?"

"Who? Your old school teacher?"

Maud raised her head.

"I see him here most nights. He's persistent." Laura gave Maud a mischievous grin. "Will isn't happy." She placed her hand against Maud's cheek. Maud buried herself back in the soft shawl. "But I know you, and I suspect if it's gotten you this upset, there is nothing you did wrong."

"I honestly don't know what I'm going to do." She sniffed. "I've feigned disinterest, was rude to him in school, and, well, even Will helped to give the impression we were—you know." The ball of her foot cracked the frozen mud.

"I don't think you and Will were acting at all." Laura nudged her. Maud lifted her head up and giggled. "And I suspect that has upset Mr. Mustard and made him more persistent."

"But how can I stop him? No matter what I do, he keeps coming."

"Is your father going to sit with him?"

"He's rarely here now." Maud realized that her Father had never really been around.

"Maybe you can get permission to come over to our house?"

"One never knows with Mrs. Montgomery."

"I'll help you," Laura declared. Her smile reminded Maud of the look Will got when he was up to something.

"What are you planning?"

"What is the thing the good teacher is most uncomfortable with?"

"Will and I passing notes," Maud said, remembering.

"Besides that."

Maud sat up straight, and for the first time in a while, she believed she could actually control this situation. "Anything interesting."

"Right!" Laura said. "We are going to make his time here more . . . interesting."

Maud giggled, but quickly sobered. "The problem is, there's no rhyme or reason to his visits. How on Earth will we plan something if we don't know when he's coming?"

"There must be a pattern," Laura said.

Maud thought for a moment. "Well, he does tend to come on Mondays when Father and Mrs. Montgomery go out to the lodge," Maud said.

"So he is a bit conniving, isn't he?"

"I swear . . . my stepmother is behind this." Maud had suspected it, long suppressed it, but now, saying it out loud made it truth.

"She would stoop that low, wouldn't she? And she probably thinks he is a good match."

Maud laughed. "How did you know?"

"Because it is the sort of thing Mrs. Montgomery might say."

"Even the congregation knows. And last night Father couldn't ask me for the mustard without chuckling!" Maud sighed. "It is mortifying. I hate that man so much. No one is on my side."

Laura clasped Maud's hands and kissed them. "I'm always on your side."

Over the next few evenings, Laura made sure she was nearby in case Mr. Mustard dropped by. The first night, Laura instructed Maud to move the clock in the parlor a half hour ahead so he thought it was 10:30 p.m. when it was actually 10 p.m.

The following evening, Father and Mrs. Montgomery went to visit the McTaggarts, and Laura arrived just as Maud was putting the baby and Katie to bed. When Mr. Mustard showed up at 9 p.m., they moved the conversation into a heated debate on theology and the doctrine of predestination. Mustard upheld it, Maud opposed, and Laura played devil's advocate on both sides, even though she was a deep believer.

But the very next evening, Laura was sent home to help her mother take care of her siblings, so Maud was left to endure the miserable visit on her own.

Between caring for her siblings and Mr. Mustard's visits, Maud was not getting any rest—let alone finding time for writing or reading. Rundown and exhausted, she picked up a nagging cough that no amount of tea could quell.

Every time she even picked up a book, Bruce would cry, or Mrs. Montgomery would call her for something. They had finally hired a woman to do the laundry, but all of the other chores were left up to Maud—with no gratitude from her stepmother.

One morning, she woke up with coughing spasms, as if knives were plunging into her chest, making it almost impossible to breathe. Maud complained to her stepmother, who promptly said Maud was exaggerating. There was no respite from the round of daily chores. Even the indefatigable Mr. Mustard didn't notice, staying until after eleven o'clock that evening.

The following day, Maud woke up sweating and cold, the cough threatening to tear her chest apart. Through a dazzling haze of fever, she thought she heard her father say, "You have whooping cough."

Mrs. Montgomery and the children stayed at her family's house so they wouldn't catch it. Aunt Kennedy came by to help the doctor and Father take care of Maud. It was a double blessing; Mr. Mustard kept his distance and she did not have to contend with her stepmother.

Sometimes Father sat with her and told some of the old Montgomery clan stories. She felt like she was back in Cavendish around her grandparents' table or in Park Corner with Aunt Annie. Maud almost asked him about the Commonplace Book, and about Mother, but she didn't want to disturb the new peace in the house. She never wanted it to end.

After a quiet, heavenly three weeks of only her and Father in the house, Maud was well enough to come downstairs. Sadly, it also meant that it was time for Mrs. Montgomery to come home, and Mr. Mustard's visits would most likely begin again.

Still a bit weak, Maud entered the parlor to greet her stepmother. Mrs. Montgomery was cuddling Bruce while Katie was taking her nap, and Father was reading the paper.

"It's nice to be able to come downstairs," Maud said.

"I'm sure you enjoyed your little holiday," Mrs. Montgomery said.

"Being sick isn't a holiday," Maud said.

"What about all of the things that fell on my shoulders while you were upstairs sleeping?" Mrs. Montgomery said. "I think you might have been sick at first, but afterwards, you simply wanted an excuse to do nothing."

"That's enough, Mary Ann!" Father yelled. He never yelled. Maud almost leaped into his arms. He had finally stood up for Maud—against *her*.

Mrs. Montgomery glowered and bounced the baby.

"I truly don't know what you're upset about," he said, more evenly.

Mrs. Montgomery stood up and put Bruce in his bassinet; he immediately started crying. Maud went over to pick him up, but her stepmother stopped her.

"I'll do it. He's my child, after all." She picked up the wailing baby. "You coddle her, Hugh. She was sent here to take care of me and the children, not go tobogganing or take part in Bible Studies or even go to school."

Maud slid into a nearby chair. She was almost too weak to be angry. "I came to be with my new family and go to school," she said.

"You silly girl." Mrs. Montgomery flounced over to her with a sniveling Bruce in her arms. "Is that what you think? Your old-fashioned grandparents sent you here from that little nothing of a village because you shamed them with your behavior. And from what I can see by the way you walk around with that Pritchard boy, nothing much has changed. I had hoped you might finally see what a good match Mr. Mustard is, but you don't know when something good is presented to you. Yes, that's right. Do you think with your Father's meager salary at the auction house and his recent political setback that we can afford to keep you? We planned you might find a good match so you would be provided for."

"Mary Ann—"

"No, Hugh. I've had all I can tolerate from this girl."

Father rubbed his hands through his hair.

Maud's whole body, weakened from her recent illness, was shaking like a birch tree in a winter storm. This must be what true wrath and indignation felt like.

"I don't think I can live here anymore, Father," Maud said. Even as her body shook, her voice was solid and sure. "I'll write to Grandma and see if she would be willing to take me back."

"Maud . . . I . . ." He gazed down at his hands, lying open upon his knees, as if in surrender. "Perhaps that would be best."

## CHAPTER EIGHTEEN

The next day was miserable. Father spent the whole day working on his auctioneer business and Mrs. Montgomery locked
herself in her room. But that evening, Maud escaped and asked
Laura and Will to walk along River Street. When she told them
what had happened and that she would be leaving Laura burst
into tears and Will mumbled something Maud couldn't quite
make out and he ran toward the river.

"I don't know when I'll be going. It all depends upon Grandma
and Grandfather Macneill." She paused. "What they'll say. If . . .
if they'll take me back."

Laura hugged Maud tightly and kissed her on the cheek.
"They love you," she said. "I'm sure after you told them—"

"Maybe." It felt right to have her head on her bosom friend's
shoulder, listening to the quiet breaking of the ice. How had it all
gone so wrong?

After a few moments, Laura and Maud broke apart. Drying
her eyes, her friend said, "We have you right now, so we are
going to make the most of it and spend as much time together
as possible."

Maud smiled. Laura always knew the perfect thing to say.

But as the two friends gazed out into the mirrored reflection of the prairie twilight, watching Will walk along the river, Maud couldn't help but notice how the crimson light accentuated Will's auburn hair. He definitely had a way about him that intrigued and intimidated her. That made her want to know him better. That made her want to march over to him and run her hands through his auburn hair.

"I think Will allowed himself to get too close to you," Laura said after a while. "Now you are leaving with no clue when—or if—you'll return."

"You could come and visit me . . ." But even as Maud said this, she realized the possibility would be as remote as Mrs. Montgomery's acceptance.

Laura echoed her thoughts. "All we have is now. Until Providence shows us otherwise." A stray piece of Laura's hair stuck out under her hat and fluttered in the wind.

"I'll miss you." Maud hugged her, again, enjoying the comfort of her friend's touch. "The idea of not seeing you every day makes my heart ache."

They stayed that way for a long time. Holding one another as Will stood apart, deep in his own thoughts.

"I've done it again," Maud said when they pulled apart and held hands.

"Done what?"

Maud didn't answer. She hadn't the strength right now to talk about Nate—bringing him up wasn't right for the here and now. He was the boy of the past, a sorrow she could not undo. But here she had the opportunity to do things differently. Will wasn't Nate. Will was . . . Will. He had kept Mr. Mustard away during school, putting himself at the risk of the whip, and had done more for her than—even if she didn't want to admit it—her own father had.

As if hearing her thoughts, Will came slowly back to her. Laura let go of her hand and walked ahead; like the pieces of breaking ice on the river, the siblings changed places.

Maud felt the soft wind wash away the orange in the sky, along with whatever reservations either of them had. For a moment it was as though she was standing on the bluffs of Cavendish Shore, with Will breathing beside her.

Will took Maud's hand. It happened so swiftly; if she'd had a second to think about it, she might have pulled away in fear. His hands were cool from the spring air and slightly coarse from fieldwork.

He whispered, "If I'm going to have the pleasure of your company for only a few more months, then I'll be darned if I'm going to let this hand out of my sight."

Her breath caught the wind.

"Maud, will you go riding with me this Saturday?"

The setting sun sparkled against the ice as she turned to face him. Once again she had to stop herself from running her hand through his auburn hair. "If I can get away," she managed to say, "and Father can spare me."

And when the twilight rose from the sun's final bow, Laura came back to them and took Maud's other hand and the three swayed with the river in silence.


That Saturday, much to Mrs. Montgomery's dismay, Father gave Maud permission to go driving with Will. While Maud knew Grandma would never have allowed her to go out with a young man unchaperoned, after all of those nights alone with Mr. Mustard, there was little for her father to say against it. Plus, the Pritchards were a respected family in the community.

Will picked Maud up after dinner wearing a freshly pressed, blue button-down shirt (which accentuated his auburn hair), brown pants, his spring coat, and Sunday hat. Maud had put on her favorite brown-and-red tartan summer skirt and white waist with lace collar. She completed the look with a light brown hat she accentuated with some prairie flowers. His buggy was pulled by a new horse named Plato with a lush, dark mane and a skittish attitude.

"Where shall we go?" Will asked, clicking the reins.

Maud pondered the road ahead. "Must we have a destination?"

Will grinned. "I have an idea." They drove by the river toward Goschen, the Hudson's Bay trading post east of town. When they got past it, Will handed Maud the reins.

"I've never driven before."

Will smirked. "I'm surprised that would stop you."

She took them and held on tightly. It felt powerful and scary to have her life essentially in this horse's hands. One false move and she could drive them into a slough.

"It is a balance." Will held his hands over hers, and she loosened her grip. "Let the horse lead you, but you need to also be in control."

"Easy enough," she muttered, and was a bit sorry when Will let go. Still, she enjoyed driving, and after a while found herself allowing the horse to take them down the road.

It was a beautiful day: the sky was a crisp blue, and the poplars swayed in the gentle breeze. They turned up a road toward Maiden Lake, a park four miles away from Prince Albert.

"When the weather gets warmer, there are some nice trails to walk," Will said, pointing in the direction of the park. "And last year there were a number of picnics, so perhaps we'll have more."

Would she still be in Prince Albert to have a picnic? "Sounds lovely."

They rode south toward the park in silence.

"It is difficult to talk and drive," Maud said at one point, thinking she wasn't being a good companion.

"It will get easier," Will said. "Once you trust yourself. And Plato."

But Maud gave Will the reins. "If you don't mind, I would rather watch this view as we talk. We were always told on the Island that the prairies were so flat, but not here. There are such handsome bluffs and hills."

"It is pretty, isn't it?" he said, and she was sure he was looking at her. They passed a few more trees. "I don't know if I should ask you this, if it is prying, but I wondered how things were with your father."

"They are what they are," she said.

"You wish to remain mysterious?"

Did she? In some ways, she didn't want to keep anything from this young man. But that would also mean no longer keeping things from herself.

"A few years ago, about four I suppose, I was staying at my Grandpa Montgomery's home in Park Corner and I overhead my uncles talking about Father." Will's eyes remained on her, as if encouraging her to go on. "Why am I telling you this?"

"We're friends." Will said. "And you can trust me."

She knew that to be true. "Father traveled for a number of years, and I always believed he would come for me, but my uncles said that Father was irresponsible." She remembered how she had wanted to march into the dining room and defend her father, but remained hidden in the kitchen. "I think that's why Grandpa Montgomery was so pleased to see him follow in his footsteps in politics. But now that he's lost the election, things aren't quite the same . . ." She let her voice trail off.

"We are taught to honor our parents," Will said. "It isn't always easy."

"Your father?"

He nodded. "I actually got it into my head to ask him about going to medical school, and you know what he told me?"

Maud could imagine, but she shook her head.

"He said that there was no money for the extravagance, that my duty was to him and Laurel Hill." Maud had a sudden urge to take his hand, but she clenched her knees instead.

"I'm so sorry, Will."

He shrugged. "At least I can work with horses, like Plato here. See, he's done well today." He clicked the reins. "I hope we can take him out again sometime."

"I would enjoy that very much."

## CHAPTER NINETEEN

While Maud waited to hear back from Cavendish and continued to help Mrs. Montgomery, taking care of her siblings and doing her chores, she also planned to make the rest of her time in Prince Albert mean something — something that Mrs. Montgomery could complain about.

Maud continued to go to the Reverend and Mrs. Rochester's bi-weekly Bible Study at the manse and teach Sunday School. Being with Will and Laura was such a welcome contrast to the thick tension of Eglintoune Villa and Mr. Mustard's persistent visits. And more than once, Will took Maud (and sometimes Laura) out with Plato on Sunday afternoons after church. Maud couldn't wait for those evenings where she could safely escape and enjoy a reprieve from the continual crying and shouting.

Father and Mrs. Montgomery didn't go out as much as they had before. The other night, Maud overheard Mrs. Montgomery say she wished she'd known the truth about Father; she never would have married him, she said, and gotten herself stuck in this "godforsaken town." Even though Maud herself was disappointed in her father, she couldn't help but bristle at her stepmother's words. Couldn't she see that Father was trying so hard, looking for work and focusing more of his attention on the auction business? None of it was good enough for her.

Maud, Laura, and Will made the most of the spring that turned the prairie from brown to green. Sometimes Andrew joined them. One Saturday, the four of them walked along the river toward Goschen, as far as Strachan's photo gallery. Will and Maud were admiring the photos while Laura and Andrew walked down to the river.

"You should get your photo taken before you go," Will whispered.

"That would be rather extravagant," Maud said. "I doubt my father would pay for it."

Their faces mirrored in the glass reminded Maud of a portrait of her grandparents hanging at home, and she was suddenly desperately sad that she and Will would never have one taken together.

"Would you get one taken?" she said. "For me?"

In the window's reflection, Will said, "When I've saved enough money, it will be the first thing I do." He grazed his pinky against the palm of her hand and the intensity of his words, his touch, his stare was too much. She turned toward the river.

Laura and Andrew were deep in conversation.

"Maud?"

She slowly turned to face him. "The next picture I take is for you."

When Laura and Andrew returned, the four walked back to the Kennedys', where Andrew said goodbye, as he had to help his father at the store.

Maud took in the amber sun diving into fire over the prairie. It had been a perfect afternoon.

Gazing up at the sky, she was suddenly overcome with the desire to count nine stars. But she let it go. That belonged in the past, with another girl. She realized how many different types of girls she was, how many different types of girls she could be.

Laura and Maud rested on the Kennedys' top porch step while Will sat down close behind them, leaning against the side banister.

"Don't you need to get back?" Maud asked. Will had finally returned to living on the farm in order to help his father with Courtney, the family's newest horse.

"It's not yet nine o'clock," Will said. "I have a bit of time."

"I wish you could come and stay at Laurel Hill," Laura said.

"I'd love to come and see Laurel Hill." Maud leaned on Laura. "Hopefully Mrs. Montgomery won't cause trouble."

"I've got plans for us to go riding," Will said. Maud rested her head on Laura's shoulder, keenly aware of Will's breathing behind her. She stretched her arm out to the side, lightly grazing the porch with her right hand. The air smelled of prairie flowers.

"When you come to the farm, we'll take Courtney out and dress up as though we are placing a real house call," Laura said. "Won't that be fun, Maud?"

The tips of Will's fingers gently touched Maud's right hand. "Yes," she said, not sure if she was agreeing with Laura or allowing Will to take her hand, but she didn't argue when he caressed his index finger across each of hers.

"I don't know if Courtney is ready for you ladies." Will's breath whispered against Maud's ear.

She closed her eyes.

"Well, I say by the time Maud comes—and you will come— she'll be ready."

Maud heard Aunt Kennedy puttering around in the kitchen. Will didn't stop. The idea that their aunt could catch Will sitting so close to her thrilled Maud more than she dared to admit.

Will's finger fell upon her index finger, the one where she wore the ring Aunt Annie had given her.

"And we'll pick wild strawberries and lie in the grass all afternoon," Laura said.

And with his index finger and thumb, Will quickly drew the ring off Maud's finger.

Practically knocking Laura over, Maud stood up and tried grabbing the ring back from him. "What are you doing?" she demanded, hands on her hips, trying not to break into a smile.

Will placed her ring on his pinky—it was snug but it fit—and chuckled. "I was admiring it."

Her finger felt naked after wearing it for so many years.

"Will, don't tease," Laura said, looking a bit annoyed that their moment of dreaming had been interrupted.

Maud knew she should be angry. She should be furious. But she wasn't.

"How long do you wish to admire it?" Maud said.

"That depends"—Will brought the gold ring right up close— "on you."

Maud went to grab his hand, and he flung it out of the way.

Aunt Kennedy called from the house. "Laura, time to come inside."

"Coming," Laura said.

"Will, you too," Aunt Kennedy said. "Say good night before you drive back to the farm. I don't like the idea of you traipsing alone in the dark."

"Yes, Aunt Kennedy," Will said. "I promise, after I make sure Maud gets home safe."

There was a pause and shuffling from the house. "Very well. But be quick!"

"I won't be long," he said to Laura.

"I doubt that," she muttered, and then hugged and kissed Maud. "I'll see you tomorrow."

Taking Maud's arm, Will led her the ten steps or so between the houses. Pausing at the gate, he stood in front of her. The sunset's glow washed against Father's gate.

"I wish we were a little older and settled. Maybe then things would be different."

"It is a nice dream," Maud said, knowing, deep down, that her future involved education and writing, something altogether different than what Will was imagining. But she loved his version too. Why wasn't there a way she could have both?

"I've been thinking," he began, then broke off. He smiled sadly and took both her hands, tracing her palm with his index finger; she shivered in the warm air and stared at the golden earth. "How much I've enjoyed our drives together and how much I loathe them to end."

She loved the feeling of their hands together, the poet and the farmer.

"We can't do anything about that right now," she said.

"That's true," he said. "So I will have to keep you . . . close."

"You must promise me something first," she said.

"Anything." His hand caressed her chin, lifting her face up.

She almost couldn't speak. He was so beautiful. She took his hand away from her face, but didn't let it go. "I've told you about Nate."

She expected his expression to darken, as it had when she'd mentioned the cipher, but all Will did was silently watch her.

"We were friends, and things—well—fell apart, and they've never been the same," she said. "I believed I loved him, but I think it was that I was so happy to have someone love me, I dreamed myself into believing it."

"And with me?" He stepped forward.

"With you." She swallowed. "With you, everything is different."

"Maud . . . I . . . "

She took a deep breath. "Promise me we'll never despise each other."

"I could never despise you, Maud."

"Promise me."

"I promise that I will never despise you. Besides"—he smiled—"I don't think my sister would allow it."

She giggled.

"I think I'm going to need to inspect this ring a little more," he said, raising his finger.

Maud couldn't look away from the ring—her ring!—around his finger. "Again, I ask: How long do you expect to need it?"

He leaned in. "As long as you'll let me."

It was different from kissing Nate. Will's kisses were tender, but more confident. He kissed her once, softly, and then again and again. She leaned into him, his arms wrapped around her shoulders. She shivered. It scared her, but being here with him was like coming home, and she allowed him to kiss her neck, her cheek, her throat, her lips.

She leaned her head against his chest. They fit together so well.

Will rubbed her back, and she dared to look up at him and looped her arms around his neck. "Take good care of my ring," she said.

## CHAPTER TWENTY

M aud and Will were as discreet as possible. And, as Laura would say, Providence provided many opportunities for them to meet. There was Bible Study at the manse and, as Will predicted, now that the weather was getting warmer, there were picnics almost every weekend. Maud still hadn't heard from Grandma, so she decided that she might as well enjoy what time she had left. And what better way than with people she adored.

One of the trustees, Mr. McArthur, held a special picnic on his ranch to celebrate Queen Victoria's birthday. The ranch was twelve miles out of town, and Maud drove out with Lottie, Alexena, and Dr. and Mrs. Stovel over a beautiful trail. Mrs. Montgomery had one of her headaches, so Father stayed home with her.

"Have you been working on your writing, Maud?" Dr. Stovel asked from the front seat. Since her publication in the *Charlottetown Patriot*, he was always asking what she was writing.

"I have been reworking a poem I started in Cavendish called 'June,'" Maud said.

"Marvelous," he said.

"I don't know how you do it, Maud," Lottie said. "Words don't come to me easily. I sometimes have a hard time writing a letter."

"Maybe it is who you are writing it to," Alexena said. "I know there are people whom I don't care to write to and my letters to them are dull. But then there are others . . ."

"Such as Frank?" Lottie teased.

"Perhaps," Alexena said, picking an imaginary piece of dirt off her sleeve. "But that is not who I meant."

"Ladies," Mrs. Stovel said. "It isn't appropriate to talk about these matters, particularly around Dr. Stovel."

Alexena was about to open her mouth in retort when Maud interjected. "I think the poem on June is almost ready to send for publication."

"I would love to read it," Dr. Stovel said.

"Dr. Stovel scribbles a bit himself," Mrs. Stovel said.

"My wife is much too kind," he said. "I dabble in what some might call writing, but I have no aspirations."

"I'm sure that isn't so," Maud said. "Truthfully, I rarely share anything with anyone before I think it is ready." It was rare she could find someone to discuss writing with anyway.

When they arrived, Maud, Lottie, and Alexena helped Mrs. Stovel set up her basket, and then Maud went looking for Laura and Will. She found them helping their mother set up her basket, with a number of their siblings running around. Mrs. Pritchard had the same kind eyes as Laura, and had given Will her sturdy chin; she appeared exhausted, but she had a pleasant smile.

Maud helped the siblings finish unpacking the last of the luncheon. She and Will had decided to take a long walk when Dr. Stovel came over, insisting they join in on a baseball game. Maud hadn't played sports in a long time and she was rusty and winded quickly, but it felt good to run and focus on winning a simple game of ball, rather than wondering about what would happen to her if Grandma and Grandfather Macneill wouldn't take her. Would she have to rely on one of her other cousins?

Depend on their charity? It was so frustrating to wait, but there was little else she could do.

After the game, Maud was on her way to find refreshments with Will, Laura, and Dr. Stovel when J.D. Maveety, the editor of the *Prince Albert Times*, approached them. The three friends saw this as a good opportunity to go off on their own, but the editor stopped Maud and said, "I was thoroughly impressed with the way you conducted yourself at the Reverend's manse on Sunday, Miss Montgomery." Maud smiled. She had led the Bible Study the previous week for the second time, choosing Timothy 4:12, the same verse that had inspired her last year at the Reverend Mr. Carruthers's lecture.

"Thank you," she said.

"I also read your essay on the *Marco Polo*," Mr. Maveety said. "Actually, Stovel and I here were talking about it, and we wondered if you would be willing to write a piece for us on your perspective on our town."

Maud wasn't sure she'd heard him correctly. "You want me to write for you?"

Mr. Maveety laughed. "Yes! You heard correctly."

She felt lightheaded as she heard herself agreeing.

The rest of the day was a haze. Maud kept thinking about the kind of article she would write about Prince Albert. Mr. Maveety was looking for a piece that would show how much she loved Prince Albert. She certainly couldn't write about the disappointment she'd experienced here. She thought she would find a loving family, the promise of a fine future. Not what happened at school. Not what happened to Edie. Not—thinking about what Prime Minister Macdonald had said on the train about his plans for the Indians—those poor, hungry men shuffling under blankets.

She remembered how the Cree and Métis women had told stories and secrets while they picked berries that day across the river, and how hard they worked to create those beautiful beaded clothes for trade. She had read how one day they will all be gone.

And suddenly, she understood.

All that she had imagined about coming to Prince Albert—about her father's house, even about what she'd thought the Indians would be like, something out of Cooper's *The Last of the Mohicans*—had been a lie.

She was so focused on these musings that she agreed to Will's offer of a ride home without a second thought, forgetting what people might say about seeing them together. Indeed, for once she didn't care. She would be leaving soon anyway.

"Isn't this out of your way?" Maud said, noticing this only when they were halfway home. He didn't answer, and Maud realized that he hadn't said anything for a while.

"Are you all right?" she asked, retracing the afternoon in her mind. She really had been hazy! Perhaps Will had felt ignored?

"Yes," he said. "I'm trying to think about how to tell you something."

Maud wrapped her shawl around herself.

"I'm sorry," she said. "I sometimes get lost in my head."

Will stopped the buggy on the side of the road under a few trees.

"Why are you apologizing?" he said, taking her hand. She stroked her ring on his finger. It was somehow comforting seeing it there.

"I feel dreadful about this, but my father wants to send me to Battleford for a few days on business. I told him I didn't want to go." He paused. "But when he pressed me for a reason why, I couldn't tell him. Forgive me, Maud; I knew Father wouldn't understand me not wanting to leave you. I would have to explain to him who—what—we are to each other."

What could she say? Here was a boy who didn't want to leave her, even for only a few days. Couldn't she stay in Prince Albert for

276

him? Maybe things between them really could be as they dreamed: her writing, him farming. She had never really considered marrying a farmer, but there was something about being with Will that made her imagine it could be possible. He encouraged her writing and certainly wouldn't stop her from doing it, but when she imagined a life with no more education, something hollow swept up inside her.

She held his hand. "I'll be here when you get back."

"At least"—he kissed one cheek and then the other—"we are here now."

Will left the first week in June. And despite herself, Maud missed him dreadfully. "It's only a few days," she had told him. "You won't be gone long enough for us to miss each other."

But she found herself looking for him in the library when she was teaching Sunday School, wishing he was sitting beside her in Bible Study. She realized she had become used to him being on one side of her, while Laura was on the other.

Father had finally hired a new maid, so Mrs. Montgomery stopped complaining about not having help because her stepdaughter was out "gallivanting with that Pritchard boy."

Having a writing project made it easier. Maud worked on the piece for the *Times*, and read other articles in the paper to become familiar with its style. She focused on every detail, making sure she didn't forget to mention the characteristics of the town and its people, but she struggled with the balance of honestly showing the things she'd seen while delivering what she knew people were expecting to read. Mr. Maveety was expecting an essay describing how Prince Albert and Saskatchewan were an important part of the Dominion. But she knew that it wasn't the whole story. Nor was it one that people were ready to hear. At least not directly. Mr. Maveety was giving her a chance and she couldn't waste it. Still, there were things here she couldn't ignore. And she wrote and rewrote whole passages about the Cree people. But it felt false.

Maud would never have believed it, but the solution ultimately came in the form of one bashful and horribly awkward suitor.

Oblivious to Maud's complete disregard of him, Mr. Mustard continued to call in the evenings when she wasn't at Bible Study or out with Will and Laura. One night, he called with flowers and they went for a walk. She couldn't think of an excuse not to go. Bruce and Katie were in the care of the new nanny, and there was nothing she could do but go with him.

Another night, when Father and Mrs. Montgomery had left her alone with the children, Mr. Mustard arrived, his thin mustache looking thinner than usual.

"I've been thinking, Miss Montgomery, of making a change," he said, when they sat down in their usual spot in the parlor, with Maud holding her sleepy baby brother. "I don't believe my calling is teaching."

Maud heartily agreed, but held her tongue and let him continue.

"But I'm not sure what the Almighty wishes of me." He frowned. "What do you think I should do?"

Maud said, as seriously as she could, "I couldn't ever tell you what you should do."

"I've been considering going back East, perhaps attending Knox College in Toronto to be a minister."

"I see." Maud tried to keep her composure by rocking Bruce.

"Yes, a minister." He smoothed his mustache with his index finger and thumb. "What do you think, Miss Montgomery?"

Maud cleared her throat to stop the laughter bubbling up. The idea! This man, who couldn't even command a classroom, providing theological and spiritual insight to a congregation.

"He should follow the road out the door and into the lake," Maud said, when she recounted the story to Laura the next day. They were sitting on Aunt Kennedy's porch.

"I pity the woman who marries him," Laura said.

"I have a sinking suspicion he wants me to have that honor," Maud said.

"My mother and Mrs. Stovel mentioned they saw you two walking together the other night."

"Oh, Laura!" Maud grabbed her arm. "I had no way of refusing him. For once my parents were home, so I had no excuse."

"You could refuse," Laura said.

Maud supposed Laura was right, but she had no idea how, not when Mr. Mustard was apparently oblivious to ordinary social decorum.

"He came by and asked if we could go for a walk. And, Laura, he had flowers! As though he was trying to be a romantic hero."

"Flowers." Laura laughed. "Oh, dear. That does sound serious."

"There was no way I wanted anyone to see us, but we bumped into Aunt Kennedy and Mrs. Stovel, who nodded to me as if she knew of Mr. Mustard's intentions. You know how she does that. Laura, don't laugh. It was terrible. You would think that my spending the whole walk ripping one flower petal after the other would offend him, but it hasn't deterred him in the slightest."

"Maud, for such a dreadful situation, you do have a talent for finding the humor in it," Laura said, laughing. "I'm sorry, my darling, but it is true. You are quite funny."

Later that night, Maud was thinking about what Laura had said as she reread some of her writing and passages in her journal. There were indeed some amusing moments and anecdotes, particularly when the pathetic Mr. Mustard was involved. It had been fun writing him as a fool; Maud felt that it gave him less power over her. She remembered something Miss Gordon had said about humor when they'd been writing their compositions, about how certain writers used satire as a way for us to laugh at ourselves, but also to show the truth.

Perhaps Laura was right. The power lay in the laugh itself. If she could use humor to persuade the *Prince Albert Times*'s readers to laugh at how they believed things to be, at their own preconceived notions, perhaps she could at least show some of the hidden truths.


Maud worked hard on the piece for the next few days, grateful to have something to distract her from thinking about how much she missed Will. When he returned home the following week, he accompanied Maud to the convent school to see Laura's art show. Maud had seen Laura's art before, but viewing it hanging on the wall among her classmates' work, she understood how good her friend really was. When Maud suggested that Laura continue her artistic studies, she reached up and touched the edge of her painting and said that her father had decided it was time for her to stay home and help her mother.

"It was never a real choice for me," Laura dropped her head to the side as if to surrender. "I will probably marry Andrew, or someone similar. I'll have children and be content. I don't have the same ambition as you, Maud."

Maud was deeply disappointed that her friend wouldn't fight for her art, but she also understood. She remembered Miss Gordon's words about the difficult road that lay ahead for any woman who wanted a career. It took a special kind of determination, one that she knew she had.

## CHAPTER TWENTY-ONE

On July 1, Dominion Day, Maud watched men lay down the cornerstone of the new Presbyterian Church and wondered if a person could be homesick for the future. It was odd to think that she wouldn't be here to see the church completed. It was warm, but not too humid, with a lovely breeze floating off the river. Everyone stood around in a semicircle, the sky was clear blue, and the world glowed green. There was a ceremony marking the laying of the first stone of the new church in the morning, and in the afternoon, there would be Dominion Day activities at the fairgrounds up the hill nearby that included horse racing.

Grandma had finally replied to her letter the week before, giving Maud permission to come home. Maud scarcely dared to dream about seeing her dear friends and Cavendish again. Maybe even returning to school. But the idea that she might never see Laura and Will again, and having to leave Father, made her feel cold. When she told Laura and Will about Grandma's letter, Laura made her promise to ask Father for permission to go to Laurel Hill—as there was no time to lose.

The question now was when would she leave Prince Albert. Grandpa Montgomery wasn't sure when he could leave Ottawa;

Prime Minister Macdonald had just died, throwing the Parliament into chaos. It was strange to think how Maud had been traveling with him less than a year ago and now he was dead.

Maud pushed these thoughts away and focused on the present. The stone was laid, and now the townspeople all stood together, as Mr. Maveety had hired a photographer to commemorate the event. Maud stood between Laura and Alexena, with all of the townspeople around them. She was here, among these good people, to see something begin, and she thought how strange that there was joy and sadness in beginnings, as with endings.

After the stone ceremony, Maud waited until Father was alone to ask him if she could go to Laurel Hill for a few days. Father placed his hand on her arm and kissed her forehead, whispering, "I think we can spare you. We're going to have to soon enough."

She knew Father wasn't trying to be harsh, but the words still burned. Why could they spare her? Why couldn't they need her more? Why couldn't they love her?

When Maud returned home after the day's festivities, Mrs. Montgomery and Father departed quickly, as they were meeting the McTaggarts at the lodge, leaving her behind with the babies—and also, as she learned later, with her fate.

There was a knock at the door, and Maud knew exactly who it was. She hadn't seen him at the fairgrounds; he was probably too proper for such frivolities. As she had been trained, Maud brought the man into her parlor and offered him tea—which he, as usual, declined.

Maud sat down on the farthest corner of the yellow couch, rocking a snoozing Bruce and focusing on his perfect eyelashes. Mr. Mustard perched himself at attention on the other end. A tiny piece of yellow yarn from a booty Maud had been knitting had fallen on the carpet. She stared at it, noting the way it twisted in on itself.

Save for Mr. Mustard's sniffing, the silence between them was awkward, giving Maud a familiar creepy-crawly feeling.

Mr. Mustard cleared his throat and sniffed. "Miss Montgomery, I have"—*sniff*—"immeasurably enjoyed our time together." *Sniff, sniff*. "Do you think, Miss Montgomery, that our acquaintance could ever become something"—*sniff*—"deeper?"

That creepy-crawly feeling fluttered across the back of her neck and she shivered. He had finally mustered the courage. She had to give him that.

Staring at the twisted yellow string, Maud said in the most normal voice she could manage, "Mr. Mustard, you flatter me with your attentions, but I really don't see what else can develop."

"You don't?" He actually appeared surprised. Sad.

Just then the front gate banged, and Mrs. McTaggart rushed in, searching for Maud's parents.

"They were supposed to go with us to the river. Have they left yet?" she asked.

"I'm sorry, they left quite some time ago," Maud said, ignoring how much Mr. Mustard was sweating.

"All right, dear, I'll go see if I can catch them." And she fluttered away.

Then there was silence. Dreadful silence. Even Bruce's tiny snores failed to shatter the ghastly hush.

Finally, after another interminable stretch of speechlessness, Mr. Mustard said, "Miss Montgomery, I know that sometimes young women are told to deny a man's attentions so they don't appear"—*sniff*—"forward."

Maud stood up, rocking Bruce so her former teacher wouldn't see her shaking. "I assure you, Mr. Mustard, that is not what is happening here." She regained her composure and sat back down, at the far end of the couch. Shifting Bruce to the other shoulder, she took the opportunity to sit as tall as she could. "I'm completely sincere in my refusal of your proposal. I thank you and wish you a good evening."

Perhaps finally understanding that he had lost, Mr. Mustard stood up, straightened his jacket, sniffed, and stretched out his hand. As Maud literally had her hands full with the baby, he retracted it. "I . . . truly . . . hope . . . you aren't . . . offended by my question, Miss Montgomery. I certainly don't wish to have any . . . misunderstandings between us."

"Of course not, Mr. Mustard." Maud put on her most winning smile, walking him to the door. Soon this excruciating evening would be over.

"Good night, then," he said.

"Good night," she said, practically slamming the door behind him. She cooed to Bruce, "Here's to that being the last of him."


That Sunday, there was another church picnic at Maiden Lake. Will gave Maud a bag of penny candies and they walked quietly through the asters, bluebells, and daisies. He picked a bouquet of flowers and pinned them to her dress. They then found a quiet place under a grove of trees and, with their backs against a poplar, leaned comfortably into each other. It felt so right to be together, and Maud found herself wishing he would propose to her because then she might say yes and stay with him. But with only this summer to be together, she wanted to enjoy her time with him without the talk of marriage complicating things.

At first she had wanted to tell Will about Mr. Mustard's proposal, but she hadn't the nerve. She thought if she didn't talk about it, perhaps that meant it never happened. But she hated to keep things from Will. She had seen what happened when she hid things from those she loved, so she gave him the full account of what Mr. Mustard had said and how she responded. Even now she couldn't get that piece of yellow yarn out of her mind.

"Has he called again?" Will asked when she was done.

"No," she said. "Thank goodness."

Will held her hand. "I swear to you, Maud, if he tries to do this to you again, I will whip him myself."

"Will—" Maud laughed, she was so surprised. "That won't be necessary."

He let go of her hand. "I am sorry. I don't mean to be this—" He broke off. "I suppose I'm a little jealous. If anyone was going to propose to you, it was going to be me." Maud's heartbeat quickened, and for once, she couldn't find any words at all.

She was aware of his warm breath against her skin, and as she turned her head, he took her face in his hands. He slowly kissed her cheek, her mouth. She returned his kiss. They had kissed before, but this was different. A passion that scared her so much she had to pull away. Her body was hot, and she took a moment to catch her breath.

"I'm sorry," he said and took her hand, and Maud resisted the urge to pull him back into a kiss. They stood up and continued walking.

"What you said . . . if things were different . . ."

His sigh was different now. "Maybe we should take a page from Laura's book and believe in Providence. Who knows what He has planned?" Will kissed her hand, and she caressed his cheek.

Hope was something Maud had practically forgotten about, but when she returned home that night, she pressed the bouquet Will had given her into her scrapbook.

## CHAPTER TWENTY-TWO

A week later, Maud was all ready to go to Laurel Hill. As promised, Will would drive her and had planned a surprise stop along the way. No manner of pressing would persuade him to tell her what it was.

After leaving Sunday School, Will and Maud headed for Eglintoune Villa, and as they got closer, they noticed someone sitting on a porch chair. She stiffened.

It was Mr. Mustard.

Will offered his arm and she took it. "Don't get any ideas, Will," she whispered, remembering his threat at Maiden Lake.

"Only if he doesn't," Will muttered.

As they strode over to their old teacher, Maud caught the outline of her stepmother's shadow through the upstairs window. No doubt she was behind this, putting him—and her—through this one last ordeal.

Mr. Mustard stood. "I came to say goodbye, Miss Montgomery. I'm leaving tomorrow."

"Maud," Will stressed her first name, making it clear to the teacher who her suitor was, "is doubtless grateful for your consideration."

"Indeed I am. Thank you, Mr. Mustard," she said. "I wish you luck in Ontario. Now, Mr. Pritchard and I have a journey of our own ahead of us, so if you will excuse us."

After a dreadfully long silence, in which Maud was keenly aware of some rustling behind the upstairs curtains, Mr. Mustard fumbled with his hat, and mumbled some excuse of his own she didn't quite hear—nor did she care to!—and shuffled away.

From inside the house, Maud heard a door slam shut. That was one fence that would probably never be mended, she thought.

After Maud got her bag, Will drove her out of town and she forgot all about disappointed relatives and bumbling suitors and focused on the bluffs and the poplar trees. They rode in silence, content in the quiet of being together. Maud took the opportunity of being so close to Will to memorize his profile, fixing it firmly in her memory so she would still have it in her mind's eye in a few months. The long eyelashes over those keen green eyes, his lips, the way his hands grasped the reins. Even though the buggy was covered, she felt quite warm. When she looked back over at Will, he quickly turned away, as if she had caught him staring at her.

"Are you going to tell me your surprise?" she asked.

He put his finger to his lips. A little farther on, they stopped at the grove of trees near Maiden Lake where the church picnic had been the week before. He came around to her side of the buggy and helped her down. His hand was warm, and Maud kept a hold of it as they walked. When they came to a muddy patch, Will helped her across, stepping around it and guiding her through. They came to a spot where four trees bent and curved back on each other. Will undid his jacket and laid it out for her so she could sit down.

"Why are we here?" she asked.

"I was thinking about last week and how we"—he cleared his throat—"walked here." Maud grew warmer at the memory.

"You have your gift of words," he said, removing a small knife from his jacket pocket. "I have my own talents."

The leaves whispered as she watched his arm move in deep swift curves, the little knife scraping softly against the ancient bark. He was carving their initials into the tree, starting with the *L* and moving swiftly to the *M*.

How was it that the idea of carving one's initials in a tree was overly romantic—ridiculous, even—but now, watching his arm dance with the tree, it obviously went deeper than some fancy romantic notion? It reminded her of an old tale.

"Do you know the story of Sir Walter Raleigh and Queen Elizabeth?" she asked as his arm swung smoothly, finishing the *M*. He blew on the tree and flakes of bark fell.

"I know he was one of her suitors and a loyal soldier," he said, wiping the knife off and adding an ampersand.

"She had given him a diamond ring as a reward for placing his cloak at her feet—"

"That is quite a reward," he said, finishing the *W* and moving swiftly to *P*.

"Yes, yes it was," she said. He was chiseling a heart around their initials now, and she flushed.

With the inscription complete, he sat down. "So, what happened?" She wasn't sure what he was asking; she was fixated on his jaw, the way his lips curved. "With Raleigh . . ."

"Oh." She knew he would know her cheeks weren't red from the heat. She cleared her throat and turned her gaze to the tree. "Raleigh was deeply in love with Elizabeth and wanted to show her how much she meant to him, so he went to her bedroom and carved a quote into the windowpane with the diamond from the ring."

"What was it?"

She dared to look at him. He had stretched out and was leaning on his elbows. She held back her desire to kiss him.

"Fain would I climb, yet fear I to fall."

"Was he afraid of falling in love?" Will said, turning on his left side, crossing one ankle over the other, and letting his right hand fall, softly, on her forearm.

"She knew how afraid she was of falling in love, but it was worse not to," she said. "Queen Elizabeth saw the carving and responded using her own diamond ring." His hand was now on her shoulder.

"What did she carve?" he prompted.

What were the words? She knew this, but there were hands on her back, and the sun against her neck. When did her hat fall away? And, as he drew her into a kiss, Maud found them: "If thy heart fails thee, climb not at all."

## CHAPTER TWENTY-THREE

Despite their detour, Maud and Will arrived at Laurel Hill just in time for dinner.

Mrs. Pritchard had made a pork roast with potatoes and carrots, enlisting Laura to bake fresh bread and Laura's sisters to help with dessert. She had wanted Maud's first night with them to "be special," and Maud assured her hostess that the meal was delicious, and that being on a farm with sloping emerald hills and charming baby poplars was special enough.

During the meal, Mr. Pritchard took the opportunity to admonish Will, "I'm disappointed in you. You misled me when you asked permission to get Maud."

Will's knife scraped his plate.

"You took the whole day, and I needed you here."

"Things sometimes happen that are beyond even your control, Father," Will said.

"Mr. Pritchard, it was my fault," Maud said, using the voice she reserved for people like Mrs. Simpson. "My father and stepmother needed my help with the children before we left."

"I'm sure," Mr. Pritchard said in a tone that showed he wasn't convinced.

Laura's suitors were also in fine form. Both Andrew and George Weir had arrived in the afternoon and Laura hadn't had the heart to send them away, so both stayed. After supper, they all went into the parlor and Maud showed her skills at the organ by playing the hymns from Isaac Watts's *Psalms, Hymns, and Spiritual Songs*. Will stood near her, turning the pages. With the memory of their afternoon fresh in her mind, she had a difficult time concentrating.

Later, as Laura played and Andrew and George fought over who was going to help her with the music, Maud and Will sat on opposite ends of the couch, but somehow, by the last hymn, the space between them had narrowed. She wanted to show Will how much she felt about him, to return his gallant gesture.

It came like one of her flashes of insight when she was writing: a daring idea.

"Will," she said. "Will you give my ring back?"

"Oh." He frowned. His thumb skated off his pinkie finger, but he didn't remove it. "Why?"

"Just for the night," she assured him.

Reluctantly, he pulled the ring off and placed it in her palm.

"What are you up to?" he said.

"You'll see soon enough," Maud said, standing up. "Laura, I'm going up to do a bit of"—she turned to Will—"writing."

"All right," Laura said. "I'll be up as soon as I bid these two fellows good night."

Carrying a candle, Maud went upstairs and walked down the hall to the back bedroom, which she knew Will's to be. Easing his door open, she quickly ducked inside and went over to the window. Her heart thumped as, with the edge of her ring, she started carving.

———

About an hour later, Laura found Maud safely tucked in for the night, writing in her journal.

"Who do you think we'll be?" Laura said, when she had finished getting ready and crawled in beside Maud.

"When?" Maud asked, putting her journal, pen, and ink on the bedside table.

"When we grow up?"

"Many would say we are already grown up."

Laura's laugh mingled with the night wind. "It is true. If those two boys downstairs have any ideas, we'll be an old married couple soon." Laura grew serious. "But I meant ten years from now."

Maud didn't know how to answer the question. "All I've ever wanted to be is a writer," she said. Before her bittersweet Prince Albert journey, Maud had had so many dreams; writing the piece for the *Prince Albert Times* and having her poem published had rekindled something in her that she thought had been burned out.

"Of course you will be writing." Laura turned over and lay on her front, kicking her heels in the air. "But I wonder what else we shall be doing. Will you come back here so that we can be sisters for real? Will we have a brood of children at our feet?"

"That would be a wonderful dream." Maud didn't know which would be more perfect, being Laura's sister-in-law—which would be splendid—or being Will's wife. "I wonder if it will come to anything—your brother and I."

"If my brother has his way, it will."

"We'll probably end up being good friends." She played with the ring.

"Be hopeful, Maud," Laura said. "If the Lord wishes it, you'll return and marry Will."

Maud wasn't sure. There were so many things she wanted to accomplish before she got married.

"We could write ten-year letters to one another," Maud said, changing the subject. "Miss Gordon told me about them. We write them, seal them, and then don't open them until a decade has passed. It's as though we are writing to our future selves."

Laura kicked her heels in the air again, clapping her hands. "That would be fun!"

"Yes," Maud said. "I had such plans when I came here." Her mind flickered to the first journal, burned long ago now. She was glad she would never have to read that little girl's diary again. But this would be different.

Laurel Hill was lovely, the perfect cure after months of servitude cooped up in a house with a woman who was always thinking the worst and locking up the food. Maud was relieved to be in a home with dear friends who cherished her as much as she them. It could be another forty years before she came west again, and by then she and Laura and Will would be too old and too mature to relax and have fun.

The three of them lay out blithely together in the meadow, until Andrew called on Laura, asking her—rather nervously—if she wished to go for a drive. She agreed and left Will and Maud alone.

"I think someone was making mischief last night on my window," Will said. "Someone English? Perhaps Sir Walter Raleigh and Queen Elizabeth?"

"I have no idea what you mean, Mr. Pritchard," she said with a British air.

"Do I get my ring back now?" he asked.

"Your ring?" Maud slipped it into his hand.

"I have a confession to make," Will said, putting it back on his pinky. "I talked with Andrew last night and asked him to come and take Laura out so we could be alone."

Maud pretended to be cross, but then laughed. "I'm sure Laura will be absolutely furious."

"I don't know," Will said. "I believe my sister enjoys her time with Andrew more than she says."

"She'll get to see Andrew after I'm gone; I only have her for a few short weeks more."

"She told me about the ten-year letters you are writing," he said, leaning on his side.

"Yes. It should be interesting to read them."

"I wondered." He picked at a blade of prairie grass. "If perhaps we could do the same?"

"A ten-year letter?"

"I think it would be—as you said—fun. And who knows? Maybe you'll be beside me when we open them together."

She thought of those initials carved in the tree, the permanence of them.

"Yes," she said.

## CHAPTER TWENTY-FOUR

Maud returned to Eglintoune Villa from Laurel Hill three days later. She was putting away some of her things when her Father knocked on her door.

Father rarely came into her bedroom. He always joked that Southview was Maud's tower and he would never wish to disturb her. Father could never have disturbed her. She relished any moment they had together, there or otherwise.

How was it that in a year she could count their time alone together in just a few precious moments? Those three weeks she had been ill and a few private buggy rides were all they had had. It was that woman's fault; Maud was sure of it. She would never forgive Mary Ann Montgomery for ruining her relationship with Father. Never.

Father sat down on the chair near the window, the curtain waving delicately behind him. He smiled, but Maud recognized the shadow behind the blue sparkle.

"I have heard from Grandpa Montgomery." He handed her a letter. She took it, scanning without quite reading it. "You are to leave with Eddie Jardine at the end of August—"

"Eddie Jardine!" Maud had met him at church. The man was all arms and legs, stammering each time he tried to engage in basic formalities and then swiftly falling silent.

"Yes. I wish I could take you myself, but your stepmother needs me here." No, Mrs. Montgomery certainly wouldn't let him go for something as frivolous as seeing his daughter home.

"End of August. That's only six weeks away!" After her beautiful time in Laurel Hill, Maud had almost allowed herself to forget she was leaving. But, as with most truths, there was no more hiding. "Is Eddie Jardine going all the way to the Island? I recall Mrs. McTaggart saying something about him going to school in Toronto."

Father laughed. "Good thing we have my mother-in-law or one would never know what was going on in town."

Maud feigned a small smile.

"Eddie's going to school in Toronto, so you can go with him as far as the city. Then you'll have to travel alone until Ottawa, where my father will meet you."

A woman traveling alone was unheard of. People would think she was someone lower class, or worse. And it was dangerous. "You're letting me travel alone?"

He sighed. "I don't have a choice, Maud. But I know you'll be careful and responsible." She couldn't believe it. It was scandalous.

But as with so often the case, she didn't have a choice.

He then smiled that winning smile, the one Maud realized she had also learned to feign. "We thought you could try the other route and travel through Northern Ontario by Lake Superior this time around. It's supposed to be quite breathtaking, and that way you'll see another view of our great country. Doesn't that sound exciting?"

Although it broke her heart, she responded with her own winning smile. "Yes, Father. Yes, it does."

"Things will be better for you in Cavendish," he said. "You belong there among the beauty. This is rough and tumble country."

The curtain rose and fell behind Father's head. "You're right," she said, hoping her tone didn't betray the rawness scratching at her throat. "Cavendish has always been my home."

It dawned on her that this might be the only time—the last time—she would have Father to herself. Was she to live with half-truths for the rest of her life? She needed to know. She hadn't come so far and endured so much to return home without an answer to this one question. Maud went over to her chest, carefully lifting the quilt and the woolen clothes she had packed away for the summer, and picked up her mother's Commonplace Book.

"Have you seen this before?" She brought it over and he reached out, slowly and gently taking it from her hand—as if he were holding Bruce.

The curtain suddenly blew round like a balloon.

"I had no idea you had this." His eyes filled with tears, making Maud's do the same. She hadn't seen him cry since Mother's funeral. "Who gave it to you? I . . . I thought it had been . . . lost."

"Grandma gave it to me before I left."

"It was how I met her, you see." He turned the book over in the palm of his hand, as if it would wind them back in time. "We were at a Literary Society meeting in French River. She was visiting her sister—your Aunt Annie—and was having a few people sign it. Mostly enjoying showing off her poetry—"

The curtain sucked against the window.

"She wrote poetry?"

"Not quite like you." He squeezed Maud's hand. "She mostly imitated other people's poems, but she also enjoyed collecting them, having people write down their own favorites. I was back from one of my trips abroad. I knew of her through the Campbells, of course, as they lived across the road from your grandpa. She was such a sweet young thing, your mother. Barely twenty when we met, and so beautiful. She loved hearing about my adventures and I loved telling her about them. I wasn't planning on staying; I had lined up another job, but—things happened as they do—and I stayed."

"You fell in love."

Father was quiet for a while. "Things changed and I had to adjust." He gave the book back.

"What happened?"

Father tapped his knee. There was something he wasn't saying. Wouldn't say. "Your grandparents didn't approve of me. So we did what we had to."

The prairie wind puffed the curtain away, revealing low gray clouds caressing the sky.

Mrs. Simpson was right: her parents had eloped.

Maud had so many more questions. Why did they have to marry so quickly? Why didn't he ever take her with him? Why wouldn't he fight for her now? But Father quickly stood up and kissed the top of her head. And then he was gone.

But she had gotten her answer, hadn't she? Sometimes it's what isn't said in the story that gives the most answers. Mother must have truly loved Father to marry him against her parents' wishes.

She was the daughter of people who had taken risks for love and happiness; she could live with that, even if others could not.

## CHAPTER TWENTY-FIVE

The end of August came. Maud had spent a busy few weeks preparing to leave, but she'd also had another writing opportunity. Mr. Maveety had been so impressed by Maud's essay about Prince Albert, "A Western Eden," that he agreed to publish one of her poems, "Farewell." She had written it during one of her "2 a.m. moments" in the middle of July, when it was so hot that she couldn't sleep. That day, she'd walked with Will and Laura down the river toward Goschen, as was their ritual. While nothing significant had been discussed, there was the mingled pleasure and sadness of a perfect moment combined with the knowledge that at this time next summer, she would be back in Cavendish.

She wrote:

*Farewell, dear friends, your kindness,—*
  *I will cherish*
  *Among all memories sweet*
*Long years may pass ere once again*
*I'll greet you,*
  *Yet oft in thought we'll meet.*

She would see them again in memory, but she also knew that in memory things changed, and what she had now would never be the same.

And now here she was, finally packing up the last of her things, preparing to say goodbye to Southview. It had been a good room for her, a refuge from the rest of the house.

She had to say goodbye to Laura. She had to say goodbye to Father and Katie and Bruce. She had to say goodbye to Will. And unlike her parting from Cavendish, where a small part of her always believed she would return, she couldn't imagine ever coming back to Prince Albert.

During the last week at Bible Study when they all stood up and sang, "God Be with You Till We Meet Again," Maud almost couldn't finish for the tears lodged in her throat.

Afterwards, she and Will exchanged their ten-year letters. Maud was tempted to read hers, but she quickly placed it in her trunk, out of view. Some things were better left in the unknown future.

Dr. Stovel gave her Washington Irving's *The Sketch Book* and a copy of Emerson's *Essays*. "Promise me you'll keep up the writing," he said. "I hope to buy one of your books someday."

But an additional sadness hung over this final morning. Laura had told Maud that Mr. Pritchard had to go to Battleford, leaving Will in charge of Laurel Hill; he didn't know if he could get away. The last time they'd seen one another was at Bible Study, and they had promised a final goodbye. Maud couldn't bear the idea of not seeing him one last time. She finished packing slowly, hoping that perhaps if she prolonged the process, he might make it after all.

In the afternoon, Father and Mrs. Montgomery went to visit the McTaggarts, so Maud had some time alone with Laura. Alexena, Annie (who was home from teaching for the summer), and Lottie had also promised to call and say goodbye.

Laura and Maud washed up the tea dishes—for even in Maud's

final moments, Mrs. Montgomery found a way to get her to do chores—and then went to the garden and picked bouquets of mignonette, petunias, and sweet peas. They were quiet as they did this. A solemn vow of friendship was made as Laura placed her bouquet in Maud's arms and kissed her on either cheek. Then, Maud did the same.

"You have changed me, Laura Pritchard," Maud said. "I will never have a friend like you again."

They hugged each other tightly, careful not to crush their precious bouquets. The comfort of Laura's arms around her made her feel not so afraid of what lay ahead, but she desperately didn't want to leave her dear friend behind. Maud caressed Laura's tear-stained cheek with her thumb and kissed her softly on the lips for the last time.

In the evening, when the sun had set so it was only a faint red glow over the prairie, they sat out on Eglintoune Villa's porch. "This will be my last prairie sunset," she said, adding silently: *I won't get to share it with Will.*

As if reading her thoughts, Laura said, "I have a letter from him. I'm supposed to give it to you in case he couldn't come."

Maud's chin trembled and she swallowed. She was about to allow herself to cry when she saw him coming around the corner with a determined stride.

Maud leaped up. "Is that him?" She held herself steady.

"Do you want me to keep the letter?" Laura asked when Will breathlessly sat down beside them.

"No," he said, taking it back. "But I don't have much time."

"Are you going to tell me what's in it?" Maud said. She couldn't believe that this would be the last time she would see him. She needed more time to say a proper farewell.

Will opened his mouth, but just then, Reverend and Mrs. Rochester came through the gate. "Hello!" the reverend said. "We wanted to make sure that we gave you a proper goodbye."

Maud hugged them both. "It was good of you to come."

"Of course, dear," Mrs. Rochester said. "You were such a wonderful addition to the Bible Study. Be sure to continue your studies in Cavendish."

"I promise," Maud said, as she caught Will checking the angle of the sun.

But as they left, Alexena and Lottie came with Frank. She would never forget how Frank and Mr. Mustard had come to blows. They all tried to stay positive, teasing Maud about going back to the quiet of Prince Edward Island after life as a pioneer. Will tapped his fingers impatiently against his worn brown pants. The sun had almost disappeared. He would have to leave soon.

Finally, everyone but Laura—who stood an appropriate distance away—left.

Will pulled out the letter.

"I wasn't sure if I was going to make it, what with Father away—"

"Laura told me."

He pressed the letter into her hand. "Something to entertain you on the train."

Maud traced the ring on his finger. Her ring.

"Maud."

"Don't say any more. Not now," she said.

And his lips were on hers. She grabbed his auburn hair and caressed his back, memorizing the way his strong but gentle fingers felt against her neck, the way his kisses tasted like home.

After a while, he reluctantly pulled back. "I have to go," he said, kissing her forehead.

She took his hand.

Laura emerged from the dark and the three walked silently to the gate. On the other side, they let go of each other's hands.

Laura said goodbye, as she had promised her aunt she would

help with dinner, telling Maud she would see her later that evening at the train station.

Maud stopped at the corner where Eglintoune Villa stood. The stars were just starting to shine in the clear August sky. She wanted to memorize everything she loved about Prince Albert in this moment. The way the prairie wind touched her cheek. The sloping hills and the sparkling river. She wanted to stand there with Will forever.

"Well," Will said, his voice shaking. "Goodbye." He held out his hand, and she took it. "Don't . . . forget . . . me—us."

How well their hands intertwined, the poet and the farmer, with her gold ring always connecting them. She was glad to be leaving it behind, with him.

"I'll never forget you," she said.

One last kiss. Couldn't she? Dare she?

"Goodbye," she said.

Their hands fell apart.

"Goodbye, Maud," he said.

Will Pritchard walked away.

Maud was numb, her mind silent. Her heart screamed to run after him, call his name. Something.

But she stood there instead, watching him disappear up the hill.

# BOOK THREE

## *Maud of the Island*

### 1891–1892

…our long journey is over at last and our destination
reached. And as our feet press the dear red soil once
more we exclaim, with heart-felt delight:-
'This is my own, my native land.'

–L.M. Montgomery, "From Prince Albert to P.E. Island"

## CHAPTER ONE

Maud's thumb rubbed against her naked index finger as she waited, her back pressed firmly against the wall of Kensington Station. She was oddly grateful that the bustle had gone out of fashion again so she could sit with ease.

Grandpa Montgomery hadn't specified who was coming to get her; she had assumed it would be one of her uncles. But she'd been sitting at the station for two hours now, and no one had arrived or sent a message, and she was beginning to wonder if anyone was coming.

Her new dark mauve travel suit, purchased at Andrew's store (while Laura flirted with him), was dusty from the long trip, and the adventurous spirit Maud had tried invoking when she left Prince Albert had completely abandoned her.

Maud had believed she understood loss, even what it meant to have one's heart disappointed in love. But as she sat in Kensington Station, the cool afternoon air brushing against her skin and the sun splitting shadows in the red earth, Maud realized she had not known true pain until now.

The long, dreadful farewell. The memory of Will fading away up that hill.

Why hadn't she called after him?

It had been so different from the other warm, tearful farewells she had experienced upon leaving Prince Albert.

Thankfully, Mrs. Montgomery had decided to stay behind at Eglintoune Villa. Maud had nothing more to say, and couldn't even feign sorrow at parting. Purely for Father's sake, Maud went to the kitchen to say goodbye. Mrs. Montgomery was having tea, blankly staring out the window into the yard.

Maud cleared her throat. "I'm leaving now," she said. She knew her grandmother would have expected her to show gratitude for the room and board, but Maud couldn't will the words. Mrs. Montgomery sipped her tea and said nothing. She didn't even turn around. Without another word, Maud left that woman behind.

Maud then went upstairs to kiss a sleeping Bruce good night; she wondered if he would remember his big sister. Katie, however, had refused to go to bed, and made such a fuss Father brought her to the train station where all of Maud's friends had come for one final goodbye.

When it was time to go, Maud picked up Katie, who was getting a bit too big for such things, and brought her over to one of the benches.

"It's going to be all right, Katie," she said, lying to them both. "We'll see each other again."

"Promise."

Maud didn't promise, as she knew the importance of not making vows one couldn't keep, but she kissed her sister's forehead and promised that she would write soon.

After the ordeal, she said goodbye to Father, who hugged her tightly. There was regret in his tone as he wished her "a safe journey."

And although she knew better, Maud couldn't help but keep looking for Will. Laura, knowing, as she always did, gave Maud a sympathetic hug and kiss that was "from both of them." A last-minute miracle was not to be. Will's father needed him, and the patriarch's word was law.

Maud might as well have been traveling on her own. When she and Eddie arrived in Fort William, Ontario, five excruciatingly long days later, and were forced to wait overnight, Maud had asked Eddie what they should do, but he simply stood there, saying nothing.

Maud refused to, as Mollie would say, "stand around like cattle waiting to be wrangled," and took control. She had already met another Islander onboard, Mr. Porter, and so she asked him if there was anywhere she could stay for the night. With an apologetic smile, he suggested that the Avenue Hotel was the least dreadful option.

The least dreadful option. If the Avenue Hotel was the most decent place to stay, then Fort William had much work to do. Although with the mountains and groves it was rather pretty, the town was still developing. The streets were littered with tree stumps, and Maud came upon more than a few pigs. However, sometimes one had to make sacrifices, so Maud thanked Mr. Porter, and she and Eddie went to the Avenue Hotel.

Maud almost wept when she saw it. The place was dark, dilapidated, and overcrowded.

"We have a room at the top of the stairs, Miss Montgomery," said a worn-out woman who desperately needed a bath. "And, you, Sir, can share with one of the men."

If Eddie had an issue with this, he didn't say, as it would require speaking, but Maud resolved to make the best of it and took the room. It was wretched, the size of Aunt Annie's pantry. There was nothing in it but a bed, a cracked basin, and a pitcher for washing. The floor needed washing as much as the woman who had served her did.

After an uncomfortable night, Maud was more than relieved to be back on the train to Toronto, where she said good riddance to Eddie three days later. The train to Ottawa wasn't due to leave until 8:30 p.m., so she went with Eddie to visit with his cousins and then was dropped off at the station that evening.

There was some confusion in Ottawa. Grandpa had forgotten her arrival time, so she took a cab on her own to the Windsor Hotel, where she knew he was staying. When he finally arrived, he apologized and tried to make up for it by showing her the Parliament buildings and the library. The joyful reunion was short-lived; Grandpa informed her that he would not be traveling with her back to the Island. Instead, he had arranged for a young couple from Charlottetown, the Hoopers, to be her chaperones.

Maud was thoroughly disappointed. She had enjoyed traveling with Grandpa and didn't know the Hoopers at all! Mrs. Hooper was nice enough, but Mr. Hooper was never satisfied with the service, the food, or the weather. It had been a relief to leave them behind in Kensington Station . . . where she now found herself wondering what she was going to do.

She wasn't ready to go to Cavendish. Her grandparents would be so disappointed in her; they would blame her for everything. Could she have done more? Been better? Grandma would certainly say that when they reunited, and then Grandfather would undoubtedly remark cruelly about Father. No. Not yet.

Maud assumed Grandpa had sent a telegram to one of her uncles in Park Corner, but he had been forgetful lately . . .

It was now 4 p.m.; she couldn't stay at the station all night. She was like an orphan, a stranger in a strange land she had once known but where she was now no longer sure she belonged.

Much of the trip home had seen her taking control and managing on her own. Hadn't she been the one to find that wretched room in Fort William? Hadn't she navigated around two cities that were much larger than Charlottetown or Prince Albert? There was only one place where she knew she would be accepted as she was right now: with her Campbell cousins.

Standing up, Maud headed across the street to call a coach. She was going to have to finish this trip—on her own.

## CHAPTER TWO

By the time the carriage stopped in front of the Campbells' house in Park Corner, it was late in the afternoon, and Maud had spun herself into such a fit that she worried she would be turned away. While she had called often when she stayed at Grandpa's house across the road, Maud had never shown up at her aunt's house tired, worn, and with her entire life packed in her dear old trunk. Would Aunt Annie notice the ring was missing and ask if she'd lost it?

Maud was grateful it was her eight-year-old cousin Frede who opened the door. "Mamma! Cousin Maudie is here!" She grinned her impish grin.

And with those words, Maud felt some of her nervous shakes begin to ebb away. It had been so long since anyone had called her Maudie without fear of retribution. The Campbell cousins all ran down to the kitchen and clung to her, chattering all at once. It was almost too much to be the reason for so much excitement.

"I hardly recognize you," Aunt Annie said, once Maud's cousins had been detached from her. "You've grown up."

"No longer the girl we saw drive away last year!" Uncle John joked.

Frede grasped Maud's hand and whispered, "Promise me you will never leave us again."

"One should not make a promise one cannot keep, Frede," Aunt Annie said, and gave Maud a sympathetic smile. "But we are so glad to have you home."

"How did you get here?" Uncle John asked. He had a mustache that was as jovial as his manner, but there was a serious undertone to his question.

"I took a cab from the Commercial House in Kensington," Maud said.

"Didn't anyone pick you up?" fourteen-year-old Clara said, turning to her mother. "Mamma, didn't you say a woman must never travel alone?"

Aunt Annie and Uncle John exchanged a quick look.

"There must have been a mix-up," Maud said, trying to cover up the awkwardness. "Grandpa is so busy with things in Parliament since Prime Minister Macdonald's passing, perhaps he thought he had already sent word to my uncles."

"Come," Aunt Annie quickly said. "You must be hungry." Maud gratefully nodded. "Let's get you fed." She put her arm around Maud's shoulders and squeezed. The kind gesture almost made Maud cry, but she had much practice now at hiding her emotions.

After a rousing dinner—where her cousins Frede, Stella, George, and Clara did much of the talking—Maud followed them upstairs, smiling at the screw stuck in the wall where she used to measure herself when she was young, and got ready for bed in her old room at top of the stairs where she had stayed two summers ago. Her cousins fought about who was going to sleep with her, and it was decided that because she was the oldest, tonight would be Clara's turn.

"Is Saskatchewan really like the Wild West?" Clara asked, when they had said good night to the others and gotten into bed.

"It certainly isn't as lush as the Island, but the town is growing, with a new church being built across the street from Father." Maud kept her voice steady, swallowing the lump in her throat when she spoke his name.

Sensing it anyway, Clara squeezed Maud's hand. "Don't worry, we'll have such fun while you're here. Mamma says that you, Stella, and I can go over to French River this Wednesday. They're having literaries there practically every night."

Maud kissed her cousin on the forehead. "Mollie and I performed in those concerts back in Cavendish—they were so much fun."

"I don't know if I could do that." She picked at the covers. "I think I'm too shy."

Maud laughed. "Clara, you're anything but shy. But it does take a certain amount of confidence and practice to stand up in front of others and recite. They're teaching that in school, aren't they?"

They talked for a little while longer, until Clara fell asleep, but Maud could not, despite the fact that she was so fatigued from her journey. She stared out the window at the half moon, wondering what was to come next. It was confusing to feel both lonesome for Laura, Father, her siblings, and, yes, Will, but to be so grateful to be in her cousins' loving embrace. The small clock beside the bed said 11 p.m. Normally, she would have gotten up and gone over to the window of her room to write, but with Clara sleeping, Maud quietly slipped out of bed, brought her pen, ink, and journal down to kitchen, and proceeded to make herself some warm milk.

There was a rustle in the doorway. It was her aunt, dressed in her white nightgown with a single long braid down her back. "Can't sleep?"

"Too much excitement, I suspect," Maud said, stirring the milk on the stove. "I hope I didn't wake you."

"Sit," she said, removing Maud's hand from the spoon and starting to stir. "With all these children in the house, a mother always sleeps lightly."

Maud sat down at the table. She loved this warm kitchen with its yellow wallpaper, raftered ceilings used to hang hams and cured meats, and the blue chest against the wall containing its own mysteries. When her cousin Eliza Montgomery had been left at the altar twenty years before in Park Corner, she put all of her things in it, commanding that it be locked up before she went to live in Montreal. Maud thought it had the makings of a wonderful story.

Aunt Annie poured the milk, putting two teaspoons of honey in each cup, and placed them on the table. They sat in silence. The honeyed drink and her aunt's warm presence were the magic elixir she needed. She desperately wished she could stay, but she knew her grandparents were expecting her.

"It's so good to see you again, Maud," Aunt Annie said with a kind smile. And at those kind words, Maud's eyes filled with tears; this time, she didn't bother to hide them. Aunt Annie placed her hand over Maud's. "You know, I'm a fine listener." She went to the counter and took out an old tin. "Also, there's nothing a little shortbread can't fix."

Maud laughed lightly through her tears. "I've missed your shortbread," she said. "There's no one who makes it better."

"Don't tell Mother." Annie bit into one, chewed, and swallowed. "I'd never hear the end of it."

When she was ready, Maud told her aunt the whole story: from the moment she had arrived in Prince Albert and Mrs. Montgomery's terrible treatment of her, to the unruly boys in school, and on through Mr. Mustard's tortuous courtship. She talked about Will and Laura, hoping she wouldn't show her true feelings, but her aunt smiled in a way that told Maud she hadn't been successful in hiding her emotions for one particular Pritchard sibling.

When Maud described her trip home, Aunt Annie gasped. "Maud!" she said. "Don't let my mother hear this story; she'll never forgive your father for letting you travel on your own."

"I wasn't on my own the whole time, only from Toronto to Ottawa—although as I've said, the companion he left with me wasn't much of one."

Maud then told her what had happened in Ottawa.

"So you're saying that your grandpa got too busy and forgot to get someone to pick you up?" Aunt Annie said. "And then he did the same thing here?"

Maud shrugged. She knew how much Grandpa loved her; it was inconceivable that he would have completely forgotten about her.

"Grandpa complimented me on the essay I wrote for the *Prince Albert Times*," she said, as a way to defend him. "He talked to a friend of his who writes for the *Charlottetown Patriot,* and he said that a piece on my travels from Prince Albert to Prince Edward Island would be just the thing the paper wanted."

"We were quite impressed by the essay in the paper," Aunt Annie said. "You described Saskatchewan so well, I feel as though I've been there. And it was funny."

Maud beamed. It was wonderful to be complimented about her writing. "I took notes in my travel journal on my way back," she continued. "Strangely enough, I was inspired by the geography book we read in Prince Albert. I'm going to write it as if I am taking the reader on a journey."

Maud sipped her milk. It had gone cold, but was still delicious. She realized she was truly excited about this new project.

Aunt Annie was quiet for a few minutes and then said, "You will always have a home here at Park Corner. You can stay here as long as you need." She put her hand on Maud's arm. "But I know my parents are expecting you in Cavendish."

"A few days, then?"

"Yes. I'll send a letter tomorrow so that Mother and Father won't worry. And then your Uncle John will drive you home." She squeezed Maud's hand lightly. "Now, finish up your milk and then it's time for bed."

## CHAPTER THREE

M aud had been in Park Corner for almost a week before she allowed herself to read Will's letter. She would be returning to Cavendish the next day, and something in her knew she had to let this final piece of Prince Albert go before she could begin again.

Sitting on the bank, she gazed out onto the pond's shining waters. Breathing deeply, she finally opened his letter.

*Wednesday, August 26, 1891*

*Dear Maud,*

*My hand is shaking so badly I can hardly hold this pen. You know I have more talent with horses than I do with words so I'm taking the same loving but firm approach with myself. Still I'll defer to you the poet and beg you don't judge this letter too harshly . . .*

*I don't know if I'll see you today so I'm writing this letter and trusted it with my sister (as with all things) to bring it* ~~to you~~*. I'm doing everything in my power to make sure we get one last goodbye* ~~at least for now~~*. And as you know Maud,*

*I always keep my promises. But Father's law comes first even before the Almighty if he had his way and so I have to tend to Laurel Hill while he goes to Battleford on business. It is good that he trusts me enough to tend to things but I ~~wished~~ wish it wasn't on our final day together.*

*I have always been honest with you. Knowing you the past few months has been extraordinary. Had things been different, I ~~think~~ know we ~~could~~ would have had many ~~more good times~~ years together. Perhaps you're laughing now, but you know we ~~had~~ have something special, something I've never had with any girl and I don't think I ever will again.*

*I shall wear your ring, and ~~one day~~ will put it back on your finger. Until then, ~~we~~ I will be contented with carvings on a windowpane and a poplar tree.*

*I need to show you the depth of my feelings for you and the true extent of how much I adore you. But I think these words fail me.*

*Love,*
*Will*

*P.S. ~~p~~ Please forgive the mistakes. I wish you were standing here. I am always better speaking, but will strive to become better as it is our only way of correspondence . . . for now.*

Maud folded up Will's letter. For now. The image of him walking up the hill still haunted her. It was lovely to dream that one day they might be together, but right now they were nearly three thousand miles apart. It appeared impossible for them to ever be together again.

Maud lingered near on her Lake of Shining Waters. Next to Lover's Lane, this was one of her favorite places on the Island. The more time she spent at Park Corner, the more she felt the fragile parts of herself mending. She was relieved to be back in a place where she could have a bit of anonymity, and if Aunt Annie had noticed a certain ring was missing, she never said. What's more, Maud had no idea what awaited her in Cavendish.

Maud loved the bedroom she slept in at the top of the stairs. There was a lovely desk on the far wall where she would spend her evenings writing, and a double bed on the east side with a direct view of the window. The lush forest trees were like dark ghosts dancing with each other.

Clara, Stella, George, and Frede were always so full of joy that it was easy to get caught up in their adventures. After the first two nights, Maud went with Stella and Clara to French River for a Literary Society evening, where people debated the latest political theories, discussed literature, sang, or—as Maud herself had done in Cavendish and Prince Albert—performed poetry or a dialogue. There she was reintroduced to Lu's shy cousin, Lem McLeod, and one of the Simpsons, Edwin, who had an air of appearing as if he would be above Queen Victoria herself if she entered the room.

Maud adored being among the loving Campbell family. Clara and Stella, who were only a few years younger than Maud, often peppered her with questions about boys and fashion. She wasn't used to this. One evening, while they were all in bed, Clara asked Maud when she could wear her hair up. It reminded Maud of how she used to look up to Pensie, and she vowed that her cousins would always be dear to her.

"Are you writing one of your stories, Maudie?" A voice interrupted her daydreams, and Maud shielded her eyes with her hands to look up at her young cousin.

"No, just thinking, Frede." She patted the earth. "Come, sit by me."

Frede was wearing a blue printed calico dress and seemed to have lost her shoes; one of her braids had come loose. "I wanted to tell you about this beautiful butterfly that I found, but it flew away." She frowned.

"That is what butterflies are supposed to do." Maud put her arm around her cousin. "But you can tell me about it now."

Frede described it for her and, after sitting quietly for a few moments she asked, eventually, a question: "What happens when you go and I have things to tell you?"

"Why don't you write me a letter?" Maud said. "I'm actually a very good letter writer, and I love having faithful correspondents."

Frede cuddled up beside her. "You're my favorite cousin, Maudie."

Maud kissed the top of her cousin's head. "You're mine too. But that will be our secret, Frede."

## CHAPTER FOUR

Maud had been back in Cavendish a little over a week, and it was now almost the end of September. School had already started and it would be impossible for her to catch up, or so she told herself. Everything was different.

At first, it felt as though she'd never left. When Uncle John Campbell had dropped Maud off at the homestead, both of her grandparents were there to greet her. Grandma had hugged her stiffly and told her that they had left things in her room as they were, while Grandfather reported that they'd a good apple crop.

And after Maud had climbed the familiar stairs to her old room, she saw that Grandma was right. The pictures Maud had pasted on the wall the previous year were still there, and a fresh, clean summer quilt had been laid out for her. "The nights are getting cool now; you'll need that," Grandma said.

After Maud had unpacked, she went down to call on Pensie, but then wasn't sure what to do when she saw Quill on the porch. Pensie, however, stood up, ran over and embraced Maud for a few minutes. She looked exactly the same, but her auburn hair done up in a tight bun accentuated her thin chin, making her seem more severe. Afterwards, the two friends stared at each other for a full awkward minute before Pensie spoke. "So you've returned at last. You must find Cavendish simply provincial after your travels."

"There's no place like Cavendish," Maud said. "You know that."

Pensie laughed in a high-pitched way that made Maud wonder if it was more for Quill's benefit than hers. "So you say," she said.

The rest of the conversation was similarly awkward, and Maud left soon after, hoping that her reunion with Mollie would be better. They had exchanged so many letters while she'd been away, and Mollie had written to say she couldn't wait to see Maud again.

But when Mollie came over for the mail, she was quieter than usual. And when Maud asked her what was wrong, Mollie actually snapped at her. Mollie had never snapped at her before.

To cover up the hurt, Maud asked if her friend had heard from Jack or Nate; Maud hadn't heard from Nate all summer. This had the desired effect, as Mollie always enjoyed talking about things other people didn't know.

"Nate was here in the summer," she said, sitting down at the kitchen table. "You just missed him! And Jack took me to a bonfire Clemmie Macneill was having. I know what you're going to say, but she was actually quite delightful." Mollie tucked a stray curl back underneath her hat and sat up a bit straighter. "We had fun, but I think Jack and I are only going to be good friends."

Maud suddenly understood why Mollie was so sad and snappish. "I'm so sorry, Mollie."

"I'm fine, Maudie," she said, looking out the window.

"No, you aren't fine," Maud said. "I know that expression all too well. Out with it."

Mollie sighed and tapped the letter she was holding on the table. "Well, I heard Jack ask Nate if things were really over between the two of you and . . . and if he would mind if Jack gave it a go."

Maud shivered, and it wasn't from the early fall breeze. Why did boys have to ruin everything! "Maybe you misheard?" Maud said. "It is ridiculous. We have all only been friends." Maud searched her memory for any moment when she might have made Jack think they were anything other than friends.

"There's nothing ridiculous about it," Mollie said. "You are genuinely more beautiful and intelligent than I am. A published author. Why wouldn't he want you?"

Maud reached across the table and held her friend's cool hand. "He's ridiculous to not see what a fine person you are. You are joyful, Mollie. I hope you'll keep that throughout your life. It is a gift."

"Perhaps." Mollie pulled her hand away. "But I want to marry for love."

Maud wanted to take Mollie's hand again, comfort her and tell her how they were still young, that things would work out for both of them, but it was clear that nothing she could say was going to help.

The two friends didn't say anything more about it, and Maud was relieved when Jack went off to school soon after she arrived.

Between the awkward reunions and the many whispers when she entered the church, Maud found her first Sunday trying. She hadn't expected much, but she had thought that people might have been a little impressed by her publications. Instead, they asked if there had been any beaux, forcing Maud to lie and say that there wasn't anyone. After the service, she overheard Mrs. Simpson mutter under her breath to her husband that Maud was definitely "giving herself airs," being away and wearing her hair up as they did in 'town.

She tried not to let it bother her very much, but there was a part of her that now understood how truly small Cavendish was. Ancient history was like yesterday, and memories were longer than most Sunday sermons, and no matter what she did, she would always be the overly emotional daughter of Clara and Hugh Montgomery.

Still, it didn't mean she couldn't try to be something different than what they expected.

After the service, when Reverend Archibald was available, she asked about the possibility of teaching Sunday School. It turned out that one of the teachers had left for Charlottetown and he was in need of one. He asked Maud if she could start the following weekend.

Then, Maud walked the familiar path to the cemetery, her thumb rubbing against her finger. As she did, she wondered if Will was doing the same thing, thinking of her.

She stopped in front of Mother's grave. Maud felt as though she understood her mother more; she was a young woman who had adored poetry and married for love. The question that still troubled Maud was, why the rush? Her parents hadn't been married very long before she came along. Was that why? It was too scandalous to consider, and she put it out of her mind by closing her eyes and concentrating on the feeling of the wind against her skin.

Maud opened her eyes and the ache of another unanswered question settled in her soul. What was she going to do? She felt rudderless, adrift. She needed a plan. Her grandparents had started to give her more responsibility at the post office, but she needed to get back to school—she just wasn't sure how to bring it up.

"Is that you, Maud?" A familiar voice interrupted her thoughts.

Miss Gordon! Here was a person who could help her figure out what that plan might be.

"Miss Gordon, how are you?" Maud exclaimed, and Miss Gordon enveloped her in a hug. She looked as stylish as ever in a brown Bedford cord lady's jacket. Maud had seen something similar in the copy of *Harper's Bazaar* she had bought in Toronto.

"You've really grown up, Maud," Miss Gordon said when they broke apart. "I almost didn't recognize you."

"I suspect it is the hair," Maud said.

"Yes, that must be it." She smiled. "I was just on my way to the Lairds' for Sunday dinner, but I knew when I saw you, I had to stop." She frowned. "You haven't been to see me."

"I've been settling in."

"I'm sure," Miss Gordon said. "But I had hoped you would come back to school."

"It's too late."

"It's never too late, Maud," she said.

"I don't know about that," Maud said.

"Your letters indicated that your experience in Prince Albert wasn't"—she clasped her hands—"quite what you hoped it would be."

Maud had finally told Miss Gordon the truth about school and Mr. Mustard in a letter last spring. "It was definitely disappointing."

"I was sorry to hear it. I had the impression the authorities out West were getting the best-educated teachers from Ontario."

"Perhaps, but a good education doesn't always mean a good teacher." Maud surprised herself with this answer. She opened her mouth as if to apologize, but Miss Gordon stopped her.

"No, you're quite right, Maud. Not everyone is meant to teach."

Maud watched the Gulf below. "I-I'm not sure what my grandfather will say about my returning, but I know I need to finish my year and study to prepare for the entrance exams if I'm going to get into college."

"You know, I was so impressed to see those essays and your poem in the paper," Miss Gordon said. "Wouldn't your grandfather have a similar attitude?"

"Perhaps, but he's never said." That would mean praising her.

"That doesn't mean he's not proud of you."

"Perhaps."

"Try again. Then come and see me and we'll settle on a course of study so you can catch up and be ready for the Prince of

Wales College examination in Charlottetown next summer. It isn't Acadia, I know, but it is a good school and not too far from Cavendish. The cost is seven dollars a term, plus room and board. And they are accepting women."

"Prince of Wales College?"

"Yes? Isn't that what you want?"

Maud took a deep breath. "Yes. It's exactly what I want."

Maud didn't think Grandfather was any closer to changing his opinion about the appropriateness of higher education for girls. Grandpa Montgomery might have even paid for college if she had been a boy! If she was going to get to college, she was going to have to convince Grandfather she was worthy of it first.

Sunday was not a day to ask Grandfather anything, so Maud waited until dinner the following evening to discuss it with him. She was as nervous as the time when she had asked to attend Reverend Mr. Carruthers's lecture two years ago. How important it had seemed at the time.

When Grandfather had finished his first helping of scallops and potatoes and was waiting for Grandma to serve him some more, Maud put her fork down and, in her most professional voice, said, "Grandfather, there is something I wish to speak with you about."

Grandma gazed at Maud over the top of her spectacles as if to say, "What is it now?" Then she scooped a serving of potatoes onto her husband's plate.

"What is it?" he said.

"Well . . . it's . . ." Why was it, when he looked at her like she was sent from faerieland, all the words she had ever known fell away?

"You know what I say, 'Speak your mind because no one else is going to speak it for you.'" Grandfather scooped some potatoes into his mouth.

"I saw Miss Gordon yesterday," she said.

"Ah, Miss Gordon. She is doing much better than that last one. Certainly able to handle the classroom," he said.

"I think so." He'd complimented Miss Gordon, which was promising. "She said I could return to school this year and prepare for the entrance exams to Prince of Wales College."

Grandfather stopped chewing for a moment, and then swallowed. "It isn't too late to sit the exams?"

"No. Not too late. If I study this year, I can take the exams in June."

He put his fork down, wiped his chin with his napkin, and scrunched it in his left hand on the table. "Maud, you know we've always thought it was important that you received a good education. You even had an extra year of high school."

Maud opened her mouth to say something, but a look from her grandmother encouraged her to close it.

"You've had enough school, more than most girls. I don't see why you need to bother yourself with more."

"It wouldn't be a bother," she said. "I hope to get my teaching certificate."

"You do, do you?" He scoffed. "You know what I think about educating women. It is fine to learn to read and write, but getting one of those BAs or certificates will muddle your mind. You remember that confounded woman who lived with us. That is what comes of higher education for girls!"

But Miss Gordon was respected in Cavendish; why couldn't he see that? She pushed on. "Grandfather, you know I've been published in the newspaper. Going to school will give me the credentials I need to make a go of it."

"As a teacher, you would be no better than a nanny," he said. "No granddaughter of mine will lower herself."

Having played nanny, Maud knew they were quite different. One more go. "If I try for a scholarship, can I go?"

Grandfather stood up. The discussion was over. "You've heard my decision, Maud. You can do that scribbling of yours, but your duty is here, not in some college in the city."

Maud couldn't breathe. It was as though she had been turned to stone. There was no justice here. Grandfather had brought down his judgment and his decision was final. Why did she think she could convince him? She was powerless.

Slowly, Maud helped Grandma clear the dishes. Why couldn't she support her granddaughter for once?

As Maud washed the old china, she had an image of herself doing the same thing, washing the same dishes, day after day for the next ten years, twenty. She would be opening Laura's and Will's ten-year letters in this same kitchen.

Nothing would have changed.

## CHAPTER SIX

What had changed was Mollie and Pensie, who no longer even tried to hide their dislike for one another, making it very difficult for Maud. She often felt like she was betraying Pensie if she decided to go left to Mollie's house, and Mollie if she turned right to Pensie's.

Neither girl was interested in leaving Cavendish, and while they still listened to Maud talk about Prince Albert or college, it was clear that—now they had both finished school—they would rather talk about finding a husband. Mollie was additionally distressed because she had been tasked with helping her mother care for her often-ill father. Mollie didn't want to let on, but Grandma had told Maud that his moods were getting worse.

It was odd, then, walking to school the following day with Lu, who had grown tall this past year. Now fourteen, Lu had confided to Maud that she had started counting her nine stars—and who she hoped her husband might be.

Had it only been two years since Maud had walked with Nate, since he'd been her nine stars?

The schoolhouse was exactly the same, even the cipher Nate had carved over Maud's hook was still there. But everyone else was either gone or moving forward, while she was stuck here in Cavendish, forced to be dependent upon her family's generosity.

When Maud told Miss Gordon what her grandfather had said, her teacher crossed her arms and began to pace in front of the blackboard that held the day's British history assignment. Maud would have given anything to sit at her old desk and study British history.

Miss Gordon faced the blackboard, her two index fingers tapping against her lips. "You know," she eventually said, "I'm going to need a lot of help this year. I have a much bigger class."

"Yes, but—"

"It would be so helpful for me, Maud. And you must also assist me with the Christmas concert. You've always had such a flair for these things." Miss Gordon paused. "It is your duty, after all."

"My duty," Maud said.

"Yes." Miss Gordon smiled. "Your duty."

Maud began to understand. Her grandparents couldn't object if she was performing Christian charity by helping her teacher. What would the community say if she said no?

Miss Gordon was right. Grandma certainly didn't mind Maud "doing her duty" by helping the teacher. Maud started the following day. And while her grandfather didn't want her to "fill her head with more foolishness," he also wouldn't stop a woman from performing her Christian duty.

It was comforting returning to the dependability of school every day, which still smelled of pine, chalk, and the lemon polish Miss Gordon had the students use to clean the desks. But, there were also those whom she had gone to school with before, junior students now in the upper levels, like Austin Laird. Always the joker, Austin tended to make trouble by teasing the girls, and more than once Miss Gordon had to send him to the corner for misconduct. Maud knew that if she were still a student, she would have laughed along with the class, but being in a position of authority, she kept her feelings hidden. Luckily, Maud didn't have to deal with discipline, as Miss Gordon tasked her with handing out papers or teaching the young ones to read.

One afternoon, when Maud had been helping Miss Gordon for a few weeks, the teacher handed her a stack of papers and books. There were a number of small assignments on different subjects, such as math and history, but the overall material was much more advanced than what Miss Gordon was teaching.

"Read through these lessons and come see me about them later this week."

"There's so much! How will I do this on my own?" Maud said. And to what end?

"You're not on your own. I'm here, and if anyone asks, you are helping me," she said. "Now, go and ring the bell."

Maud took the assignments home and, after sorting mail for Grandma in the post office, looked them over again. Miss Gordon had laid out a list of readings and lessons in all of the subjects Maud would need to prepare for the college entrance examination. Maud steadied her hands so they would stop shaking. If her grandparents discovered how Miss Gordon was secretly helping her to prepare for the forbidden examination, she would not be allowed back in that schoolhouse, Christian duty notwithstanding. But what did it matter if she couldn't really go to college? Why should she get her hopes up? It wasn't as though her grandparents were going to change their minds. She promptly put the pile on her bureau and pretended to forget about it.

Over the next few weeks, whenever Miss Gordon asked Maud about the assignments, she changed the subject, ignoring the teacher's disappointed expression.

While she continued to help Miss Gordon, Maud spent her weekends in October visiting her father's family in Park Corner and attending Uncle Cuthbert's wedding. It was lovely connecting with her Montgomery cousins. While she was there, Grandpa

Montgomery had reminded her about her travel essay. Maud had worked on it some, but when she returned to Cavendish, she finished it and was feeling quite jubilant over sending "From Prince Albert to P.E. Island" to the *Charlottetown Patriot*. She felt that it was rather good, with lush descriptions of the Canadian landscape.

Then, halfway through October, Mrs. Spurr caught Maud on the way out of the Cavendish Hall. Her organ teacher still looked the same, with her gray eyes that reminded Maud too much of Nate's. After exchanging formal greetings, Mrs. Spurr asked Maud to come for tea. On one hand, there was no way she could have politely declined, and on the other, she was very curious about what her old teacher could possibly have to say to her.

It was a golden November morning when Maud took the familiar path through the Haunted Woods for her visit to Mrs. Spurr. Maud stopped at the road, looking back over the well-traveled path behind her. It felt so familiar cutting through Lover's Lane to Cavendish Road, up the steep hill to the Baptist minister's gray-bricked manse, which—despite her bittersweet parting from Nate—welcomed her.

Mrs. Spurr brought Maud into the familiar parlor, where she half expected to find Nate sitting in his favorite chair reading a book and waiting to walk her home. Mrs. Spurr was wearing a dark woven skirt and a lace blouse with very fine stitching along the neck and wrists. Most Baptist minister's wives were dowdy in comparison to her old organ teacher, who always added a bit of tasteful finery to what she wore.

As Mrs. Spurr gracefully moved around pouring the tea, she asked Maud all the typical questions about her year in Prince Albert. By now, Maud had well-rehearsed answers, often referring to her essay about Saskatchewan, "A Western Eden." She carefully avoided mentioning Mr. Mustard or Will because this often led to questions about romance. That was the last thing she needed. Not when she was trying to prove to Grandfather how serious she was about school.

When Maud and Mrs. Spurr had settled themselves in front of a warm, friendly fire and had drunk enough tea, Mrs. Spurr began to talk about Nate and how well his studies were going at Acadia: he was top of his class and president of the sophomore class. The chair dug into Maud's back. And it was difficult balancing the saucer in one hand, and the teacup in the other. Placing them carefully down on the dark wooden table, she picked up a ginger snap, delicately chewing each bite.

When Maud was through her third ginger snap, Mrs. Spurr went over to the mantel, picked up a photograph, and brought it over. "He had this photograph done in Halifax this past spring." She handed it to Maud. "Isn't it well-taken?"

Maud stared at the image of the first boy who had told her he loved her. His haircut made his ears stick out, something she still found endearing; the memory made her smile. He wasn't smiling, though. There was an air of confidence she didn't like one bit.

"Yes, it is well-taken," Maud lied, and placed it on the table beside them.

"It's so important for a boy to get a good education," Mrs. Spurr said. "It sets him out into the world on the right foot."

It was important for a woman to get one too, Maud thought to herself.

"I think if a person can prepare himself through education and good service, he will make a good show of it," Mrs. Spurr continued, and then took a sip of tea. "I couldn't ask better for Nate. My husband has indeed been generous."

Maud couldn't help thinking that Mrs. Montgomery could have taken a lesson or two from Reverend Spurr.

"He's very fortunate," Maud said.

"Weren't you continuing your studies in Prince Albert?" Mrs. Spurr said. "You were one of the top scholars here in Cavendish."

"That's kind of you to say. I was merely adequate—especially at the organ," Maud said.

Mrs. Spurr laughed. "In truth, you were more than adequate— if I could get you to focus. Oh, don't give me that horrified look. I was a young girl too, once." She took a sip of tea. "Never tell my son this, but I think you were good for Nate."

Maud would never admit it, but he had been good for her too.

"You inspired him to take his studies a little more seriously. And you also got him interested in my brother-in-law Pastor Felix, the writer."

"I do admire his work," Maud said, and took another bite of ginger snap.

"Do you?" Mrs. Spurr leaned back in her chair. "Would you perhaps be interested in speaking with him? I shall write him on your behalf."

"Oh, that isn't necessary, Mrs. Spurr." What if he never wrote back? "I'm sure he is very busy."

"Ridiculous. He's family and will certainly respond if I ask him to." The gesture was so kind, so genuine. Maud turned to the fire in an effort to stop her eyes prickling. When she composed herself, she said, "I must ask: Why are you being so kind, after—"

"After things went a bit sour between you and my son?"

Maud was mortified. Of course Mrs. Spurr would have at least suspected what happened.

"When Nate's father died, I didn't have money of my own. As you know, he was lost at sea." Mrs. Spurr's somber expression told Maud how much her old organ teacher had loved Nate's father. "It was certainly respectable for me to live with my parents, but after Nathaniel's death, I needed to become more resourceful."

"Is that when you started teaching?"

"I had been teaching before, but needed more work, so I asked Reverend Spurr to recommend me as a teacher for lessons. Little did I know He"—she pointed up—"had other plans." She poured herself some more tea. "Do you mind if I give you a bit of unsolicited advice?"

"Of course not," Maud said.

"If you reapplied yourself to learning the organ, I think you could be an organ teacher yourself."

"Really?" It was something she had never considered.

"Yes," Mrs. Spurr said. "You can make a nice living for yourself—as I did—until such time as you find a husband."

While the tea tasted bitter at the mention of a husband, Maud knew that, unlike many of the women who had given her advice about marriage, Mrs. Spurr was being both kind and practical.

"It is a fine idea, Mrs. Spurr." Maud remembered Grandfather's thoughts on teaching. "But you know some people don't hold the same philosophy about women teachers."

"Think on it," Mrs. Spurr said. "Just because people don't share one's philosophy doesn't mean they cannot find some common ground." She smiled. "Look at you and me."

When the tea was done, Maud thanked Mrs. Spurr and took the long way home through Lover's Lane, pondering what the minister's wife had said.

Things were always clearer on Lover's Lane, where she felt close to the spirit of the woods. Since she had returned to Cavendish, Maud had walked it many times. The woods had cradled her again as she wept for the boy she had left behind, and the disappointments of life in the West. But now, among the embrace of yellow birches and the feathery leafy arches, anything seemed possible.

Maud walked over to the small pond and sat down on a nearby rock, watching a lone crimson leaf calmly floating on the pond's mirrored surface. Could she do it? Was it even possible?

The leaf dipped toward Maud and she picked it up. Its brilliant red color was so bold. Staring at it, Maud knew she had to be as well. If it was a chance to make money, to become independent, then she should take it and not waste this opportunity.

When Maud arrived home, she went directly to her room and placed the leaf in her scrapbook. She then began sorting through the papers and books Miss Gordon had given her. Yes, she could do this. She would make it work.

Later, when Maud came downstairs to help with supper, Grandma asked, "How was your visit with Mrs. Spurr?"

"Very pleasant." Maud picked up a potato and a knife and started peeling.

"What did she say?"

Maud watched Grandma peel the potato skin in one long piece. "She mentioned how well Nate was doing in school." The peel looped itself into a lovely swirl. "And we discussed other things."

"Oh?"

"We spoke about her life in Halifax and the organ."

"Are you thinking of taking lessons again?" Grandma asked. "Because I don't think I can pay for more."

"No." Her latest decision made Maud feel brave. "Actually." She put the potato in a wooden bowl and picked up another. "Mrs. Spurr suggested I could do something she did."

"Marry a minister?" Had her grandmother actually chuckled? "I don't think you have the temperament."

The notion made Maud burst into laughter and drop the potato, and her grandmother shook her head, but then smiled.

"She suggested that I teach organ."

Grandma peered over her glasses. "Really?"

"Yes," Maud said. "She said one could make a nice living at teaching the organ, until one marries." This last line Maud added for her grandmother's benefit, since she still had no intention of marrying anyone.

"Hmmm. Well, you won't be doing anything unless we get this dinner on," Grandma said. "Peel faster."

"Yes, Grandma." Maud knew now when to stop pushing and allow the idea to bud in her grandmother's mind, so she continued peeling, watching the red skin spin in lovely strips onto the table.

# CHAPTER SEVEN

As November grew colder, and her seventeenth birthday approached, Maud continued to study diligently, writing short stories and verse, as well as helping her grandmother organize the daily mail in the post office, practicing organ, and helping Miss Gordon. Maud tried to hold onto the small hope that if she studied hard, she could return to school and prepare for the entrance examination.

Some things were encouraging. "From Prince Albert to P.E. Island" had been accepted by the editor of the *Charlottetown Patriot* and then reprinted in the *Prince Albert Times*. And what was more, the editor at the *Patriot* had asked her for more pieces! Mrs. Spurr had also written to Pastor Felix, who had sent her a reply requesting some of Maud's poems. Maud was quite daunted by having to choose which ones to send.

One evening, Maud returned to writing Laura a letter she had started earlier that day. Writing always helped to clear her mind.

*Tonight I stayed home to write and study; such a change from last year, when I was constantly looking for ways to escape Mrs. Montgomery's tyrannical gaze. Of course having you and your brother around helped. You saved me, Laura. Have I ever thanked you for that? If not, let me thank you now.*

*I wish you could convince your father to continue with art school. You have such a wonderful talent. I remember when*

*Will and I went to see your show at St. Anne's. That landscape you had painted of Laurel Hill perfectly captured the spirit of your home. What I hope to do in words, you do in art. Just think: we could run off together, and you could paint and I could write! And, yes, Will could come along too and study medicine. All three of us would be free. Free to dream!*

*Deepest love,*
*Maud*

*P.S. Thank Will for the notebook and pencils, and tell him I'll thank him myself as soon as I'm able.*

Maud put the pencil Will had given her down, willed herself to go to her chest, and picked up one of her old school notebooks. Opening it to the front cover, she traced the poem "The Alpine Path" she had pasted there almost two years earlier with her index finger.

And she had succeeded, hadn't she? She'd been published four times now. But if she was going to make her living writing, she would have to learn about the markets she was writing for. Already she'd been studying the Sunday School magazines, such as the *Boys' and Girls' Companion*, and reading the *Young Ladies' Journal* to see the stories they were publishing. She wanted to find the right home for a short story she was working on about the blue chest.

There were a few good pieces. Maybe. Somehow, sending Pastor Felix some of her work felt different than sending it to a magazine or newspaper. He was a published author. If she was going to climb the Alpine Path, she was going to have to take the journey—and herself—seriously. With renewed determination, Maud found "June" and started copying it down to send to him.

———

Maud received a letter from Pastor Felix a week before Christmas. She was delighted to learn that he had been very impressed with her submissions. And he had even offered her some advice on how she could get published in more magazines. Things worked in her favor as, after Christmas, one of the worst winters on record hit the Island. Biting cold and snow set a stranglehold on the roads, and people stayed close to home, only going out when necessary. School was closed so Maud was happy to focus on her studies and stories, without the guilt of having to take time out for social events with her friends.

Around Valentine's Day, the weather calmed down and the mail could finally get through. Maud received a parcel from Will, which included a box of the candies she loved, the same ones he had given at the Maiden Lake picnic, and a letter. She avidly read the letter near the fire, enjoying one of the candies as her grandmother sewed. Her grandfather had already gone to bed. Thankfully, Maud got so many letters and parcels from her friends in Prince Albert that her grandparents didn't question the contents anymore. It had bothered her at first that she didn't get as many from Father, but he did send her news every now and then.

*January 29, 1892*

*Dearest Maud,*

*Happy Valentine's Day!*

*We miss you. If you were here, I would take you for a long drive with Plato under warm blankets and then return to my Aunt Kennedy's for hot chocolate. Too cold for a picnic right now but there would be candies. (Hopefully these will make up for it.)*

*As part of your Valentine's gift, I am finally fulfilling a promise I made to you last summer. I saved up enough to get my photograph done. It was taken this past Christmas in Goschen. When you look at it, know that I was thinking of you. Laura came with and we put on our "Sunday Best" and paraded into the photographer's studio. What do you think? I'm not sure it looks like me. As you know I'm much more comfortable in my work clothes. But, I can't have you remembering me in dirty trousers and a cowboy hat or perhaps you'd prefer that?*

*This is in exchange for the photograph you took when you were last in Charlottetown. I've placed it near my bedside table, inches away from a certain carving.*

*I keep thinking of ways to come and visit you. I thought of getting extra work in town, but when I broached the idea with Father, he said if I had enough time to work for others, then I must have more hours in the day to work for him. So he's put me in charge of breaking in two new colts. They are pretty wild things, but as you know, I like to keep a little of their nature intact—respecting their nature is how to win their hearts.*

*All my love,*
*Will*

*P.S. Note, not one mistake this time. Laura has been helping me and my hands aren't so shaky anymore. They just miss touching you.*

While it was pleasant sitting by the fire reading his letter and munching on candies, she would have preferred the writer more than his gifts. She pressed the photo close to her chest and closed her eyes, remembering how good it felt to be held and kissed by him that day near Maiden Lake. She was still haunted by their final painful farewell . . . but this picture made it seem almost as if he were with her. She had been given a frame for Christmas and had been waiting for the perfect picture to put inside. She also knew where she would put it: on her bookshelf next to her bureau so he would be close by when she worked.

"Are you in one of your dream worlds, Maud? I've called your name three times now," her grandmother said.

Maud placed the photo safely back in the letter. "Sorry, Grandma, what is it?"

"I have already spoken with your grandfather about this. I am planning a short trip to Park Corner while the weather holds."

Maud hadn't seen Aunt Annie since she had stayed at Park Corner last fall. "Oh, how lovely. May I come?"

Grandma put down her embroidery and shook her head. "I need you here to take care of your grandfather. He shouldn't be here on his own."

"But he hates the way I do things."

"He's particular, true," Grandma said, and started stitching again. "But I've spoken to him, and I'll be sure to talk with him again before I leave. He'll agree."

Maud was sure that no manner of talking would change Grandfather's attitude, but she promised her grandmother she would do her best.


"So, I have some interesting news," Grandma said to Grandfather three nights after her return from Park Corner. "Annie and I had a long talk about the girls. You know Stella and Clara are getting older, only a couple of years younger than Maud, and they haven't had much in the way of a musical education." She took a sip of water. "They need a music teacher, and I suggested Maud would do nicely."

Maud almost choked on her chicken pie. She'd thought that her grandmother had completely forgotten their conversation in November.

"Isn't that what Mrs. Spurr had said to you?" She turned to Maud. "That you had sufficient schooling to teach?"

"You know how I feel about women teaching—" Grandfather began.

"Yes, I am well acquainted with your feelings." Grandma scooped up some peas and put them on his plate. "But this isn't regular teaching in a school. Maud could go and stay with her cousins for a few months and show them what she knows."

Grandfather forked some peas into his mouth.

"Maud will be paid a small sum," Grandma went on. "We paid Mrs. Spurr fourteen dollars per one term of lessons and so, given this is your first time, Annie suggested ten dollars. This would include your room and board."

Maud was stunned into silence.

"I cannot believe you went behind my back and arranged this without consulting me," Grandfather said.

Maud couldn't either. But it would pay for a term at Prince of Wales College. And if she sold a story or two . . . Maybe . . .

But how could her cousins afford it with such a large family?

"Calm down. I certainly didn't agree to anything yet. If you don't agree, I'll write Annie this evening and tell her to find another teacher."

"Mrs. Spurr is the Baptist minister's wife, and she's still a respectable woman." Grandfather was speaking more to himself now than to them.

Grandma continued to eat.

"It would certainly mean all of that money spent on Maud's lessons wouldn't have gone to waste," Grandfather mused.

Maud's hand was shaking so badly that it made eating her peas difficult. She put her fork down. The idea was interesting. How would she work college preparation into this scheme? Maybe this was Grandma's way of refocusing her attention away from school? If Grandfather agreed, they were going to ship her off no matter how she felt about it. Unless Grandfather said no—but from the way he was talking, it was as good as done. At least it was Park Corner and not with Aunt Emily in Malpeque.

"Very well," Grandfather finally said. "Better Annie pay Maud than some stranger."

"Wonderful," Grandma said. "I'm glad you agree." She turned to Maud. "I'll send word to Annie that you will come within the next two weeks."

"What about my work with Miss Gordon?" Maud said.

"School has been closed because of the weather," Grandma said. "Besides, she wouldn't want to stand in the way of this opportunity."

"No," Maud said. "I suspect she wouldn't." And she picked up her fork and finished her chicken pie.

## CHAPTER EIGHT

Maud arrived at Park Corner on a snowy Saturday afternoon in March. At first, she hadn't been sure where to begin. Mrs. Spurr had given Maud some books and tips, but she knew that whatever followed would involve improvisation. As they continued, Maud discovered that Frede actually showed quite an affinity for music; the hours she spent teaching her cousin were some of the most pleasurable she had spent in a long time.

Being across the street from Grandpa Montgomery's house also provided opportunities for Maud to get to know her Montgomery relatives better, and it was as if she was learning about them for the first time. She was older now, and they began to tell her many more family stories.

Maud was also in a flurry of creative activity, spending many evenings in her bedroom writing and studying. She was doing something that Pastor Felix called "spade work," outlining stories and characters. Sometimes her characters emerged fully formed; other times, she didn't know where they belonged. She had long abandoned the stories about dying queens and had turned to ones based on her own experiences.

After "From Prince Albert to P.E. Island" was published, things had become clearer for Maud. Upon rereading it, she recognized how pieces of her memory were woven into it. She had been so focused on writing a good essay that she hadn't noticed how some of the descriptions, such as "to kiss the dew from the grasses and coquette with the waters of the blue Saskatchewan," reminded her strongly of Will's kisses. The way she described the rhythm of the train as they passed the "ripe Manitoban wheat fields and snug farmhouses" and the word *snug* reminded Maud of those nights cozying up with Laura on Laurel Hill.

It had made her somewhat embarrassed. Writing a piece of non-fiction was one thing, but to display one's soul on the page for the world to see was something Maud had never considered. As a sort of test, she asked in her next letters to Will and Laura what they thought about the essay, but neither one spotted what she had unwittingly done.

*It is high time you are recognized for your gift*, Will had written, and Laura sent along some bluebells as a memento, which Maud later pasted into her scrapbook. Maud was relieved. It would require a crack team of Sherlock Holmes-esque investigators to ferret out the truth hidden among the flowery lines of prose.

Throughout the early spring, Maud continued to observe what magazines were publishing, and started a rough version of her short story about the sealed blue chest in Aunt Annie's kitchen. If she was going to make a living from her words, she was going to have to understand how to do it—but once she did, nothing would stop her from taking that next step along the path.

Maud also made time for fun with her cousins. Sometimes it was joking and telling stories while they all sewed; Maud had finished her crazy quilt and was now working on one for her sister Katie.

On other nights they would go to the literaries in French

River, after which she sometimes allowed Lem McLeod or Edwin Simpson to walk her home. While Edwin seemed to lose interest quickly (which Maud decided to not let bother her too much), she suspected that Lem had more serious notions than she did. She tried to keep it light and friendly, saving a distance between them when they drove home together in his buggy, but she wondered if it only encouraged him more. After all this time, she still didn't know why she couldn't be friends with young men. Maybe the only way was through letters?

But the rhythm of Maud's time in Park Corner was interrupted when a letter arrived from the last person she would ever have expected: Aunt Emily, inviting her and her cousins to Malpeque for Easter.

## CHAPTER NINE

When Maud had arrived at Aunt Emily and Uncle John Malcolm Montgomery's doorstep in Malpeque three years before, after the Miss Robinson incident, the welcome hadn't been friendly. Clouds had hung low over the two-storey stormy-gray house that stood proudly against the strong winds on a cliff that backed out to the Gulf.

Now, the way the house loomed over the cliff reminded Maud of the bleak moors in *Wuthering Heights.* Many things had changed since she'd been there; Maud had taken a lesson from Grandma's book and had learned to hide her nervousness, so her cousins only saw a laughing girl who was excited to embark on a small adventure through the dreary late-winter afternoon.

Maud wasn't sure why Aunt Emily and Uncle John Malcolm had invited her and the cousins up for the weekend. She had not heard from her aunt in months; most of the time, news came through other family members. But after a long talk with her Aunt Annie, she'd agreed to attend. Perhaps this was Aunt Emily's way of making peace?

Since her time in Prince Albert, Maud had started writing to her aunt, but was never quite sure where to begin. Was she supposed to apologize for Mother dying and being put in Aunt Emily's care? What could she possibly say to make it better?

Now, Aunt Emily and Uncle John Malcolm stood on the porch, the wind whipping her aunt's dark skirt. Maud gingerly climbed down from the cutter in the midst of her cousins' excited chatter, trying to ignore the gnarled root twisting in her stomach. She was shocked to see that her aunt had gained considerable weight. And the way she held onto her back reminded Maud of how her stepmother had held herself at the end of her pregnancy.

In addition to her four children—Charlotte, Annie, John, and Edith—Aunt Emily was expecting another baby. Was this why her aunt had brought her here, as a ruse to repay her by asking her to play nanny to her children? Is this all she was to her family?

"We were beginning to wonder if you would all make it," cheerful Uncle John Malcolm said, hugging Maud.

"Yes, you are at least two hours late," Aunt Emily said, looking Maud up and down in a way that made her want to go right back to Aunt Annie's house.

"We had such a time getting here, Aunt Emily," George said. "We got lost and went down the wrong road. It was terrible."

"I don't doubt it," Uncle John Malcolm said. "This has been one of the worst Island winters." He patted George's shoulder. "Let's get you all inside."

As everyone walked to the house, Maud tried to get Aunt Emily's attention, but she refused to look directly at her. Why had she invited her if she wasn't even going to look at her?

The rest of the afternoon passed quite nicely; Maud had forgotten how funny her uncle was, and he kept everyone light and laughing. After dinner, Uncle John Malcolm went with the boys to tidy up the sleigh for the ride home, and Clara and Stella played with Aunt Emily's daughters, Charlotte, Annie, and three-year-old

Edith, so Maud went into the kitchen. She found her aunt preparing the bread for tomorrow's breakfast.

"Thank you for inviting us, Aunt Emily," Maud said. Why was it that after all she'd been through, Maud felt as if she were still a little girl in her aunt's kitchen?

Her aunt placed a light cloth over the bread. "This was your uncle's idea. He was saying we hadn't seen you since you'd stayed here several years ago, and it was time we did."

Maud swallowed the momentary pang of sadness—and tears. She stayed tall and strong. "Uncle John is a good man."

Aunt Emily wiped her hands and sat down. She looked tired and sad.

"Are you well, Aunt Emily?" Maud said.

"You need not concern yourself about me. I will always make do."

"You are my aunt. Of course I concern myself about you." She sat down beside her, but Aunt Emily immediately stood up and went over to the sink. Laughter from the parlor crackled through the walls. Maud observed the old kitchen. The dark green paper, the window over the sink with its green pump, and the stove in the corner. What could she possibly say to make it better?

"Aunt Emily, I played nanny to my brother and sister in Prince Albert." Her aunt didn't move from the window. "And while I love them deeply, there were many times I couldn't be with my friends or even go to school because of my responsibilities at home." Her aunt half-turned from the sink, her face hidden in shadow. "I don't pretend to know what you had to give up to take care of me, but I know a little."

Maud waited to see if her aunt's demeanor would change. She imagined Aunt Emily running over, embracing Maud, and apologizing for being so ill-humored. But her aunt didn't show any sign of forgiveness. Maybe this had always been her style, and Maud had been too young to notice.

"You're right, Maud," her aunt said. "You cannot pretend to know me." She sat back down heavily at the kitchen table. "But there was no one else to take care of you." She paused. "My parents asked me to step in while they took care of the arrangements. Lord knows, your father was useless."

Feeling defensive, Maud remembered Father's sadness when they had both looked down at her beautiful mother in her coffin. "He had lost his wife."

"I suppose so," Aunt Emily said. "There were things going on then, Maud. Things you don't understand. It was my Christian duty to take care of my sister's child. But I watched my friends get husbands, and I didn't want to end up alone."

"I remember," Maud said.

"I'm not you, Maud." Her hand shook. "I didn't have any talents to fall back on. And they weren't too keen on lady teachers then—not that my father would have let me."

"His opinion hasn't changed," Maud said dryly.

Aunt Emily leaned against the back of the chair and placed her hands on her stomach. They didn't speak for a long time, allowing the gaiety next door to carry the silence. Maud didn't know what more could be said. Her aunt had invited her out of a sense of duty, not because she actually cared about her. Maud did her best to make peace with things that had been, and continued to be, outside her control.

"We all do the best we can," Maud said, after a while.

Her aunt, finally, met her gaze. "Don't lose heart, Maud. Perhaps Providence will find a way to make your dreams come true. Just as He did mine." She slowly pushed herself up. "Come, help me with the tea."

## CHAPTER TEN

B ack in Park Corner, Maud sat on the Campbells' porch, facing the field. She was writing in her journal, recalling the past few months there, taking in the fresh beauty of spring. It was June, her favorite month. In a few weeks the lupines would pepper pink and purple petals across the green pastoral fields and the red earth, and (on a good day) with a clear blue sky, turn the Island into a rainbow of color. A warm wind danced across the shining pond. The long winter was finally over, and, after months of teaching organ and preparing for the college examinations, she would be leaving for Cavendish tomorrow. Frede was playing with her dolls in the front yard, talking to herself and making up stories.

The squeaky front door pulled Maud from her writing, and she smiled up at her aunt in silent greeting.

"Can I sit with you awhile?"

Maud nodded and shifted over so her aunt could sit down. Together, they watched Frede pick up a doll with dark hair and go dancing over the grass as if she were a flittering ladybug.

Aunt Annie leaned back on her palms, and the stance made her appear younger than her years. Until that moment, Maud had never considered how old her aunt actually was.

"Maud, there is something I've been wanting to ask you." Aunt Annie glanced quickly down at Maud's hand. "But I wasn't sure if there was a delicate way of putting it."

"The ring?" Maud asked, feeling heat rise to her cheeks.

"Yes. Your ring," Aunt Annie said. "I wondered if you needed it resized?"

Maud laughed. Aunt Annie had thought the indelicacy was related to her figure. "No."

"You lost it?"

"Not quite," Maud said. How could she explain it? If she did, it might sound more inappropriate than any change in her figure. But she didn't want to lie to her aunt either. "I gave it to a dear friend of mine to remember me by. It was the most precious thing I had. Who knows if we will ever see one another again——" At the thought, Maud choked and almost started to cry, but she held it in.

Aunt Annie placed her hand over Maud's. "It was your ring to do with as you wanted. I'm happy it is in a safe place. But, you're so young."

"There's so much pressure," Maud said. "All of my friends are looking for husbands."

"There were certainly some men in French River who expressed interest," Aunt Annie said.

"Yes, Lem and Edwin were vying for my attention at first, but it isn't . . ." Maud sighed. "Why can't we be friends?"

Aunt Annie laughed. "Men and women are not supposed to be friends; that is the role of the women in your life. And if you find the right ones, they can be your lifelong, dearest companions."

Maud thought of Laura, Mollie, and Pensie—even Annie and Edie—and how each were so dear to her, how much, even after all that had transpired between them, she adored them. But they were taking another path; she was climbing something altogether different.

Maud glanced down at her journal. Had she traveled so far and seen so much to leave the most important question unanswered? She had learned part of the story from Father, but she still had questions, and maybe Aunt Annie would be willing to answer them.

"Why don't we ever talk about Mother? There are so many things I want to know. About her. I thought when Grandma finally gave me Mother's Commonplace Book—"

"Ah, I wondered what Mother had done with it," Aunt Annie said. "I'm glad you have it."

Maud closed her journal and leaned her head against the post. "That's what Father said."

"Clara was so young." Annie focused her gaze on Frede playing. "And she died so terribly quickly." She rubbed her shoulders as if she was hugging herself.

"Father hinted at an elopement, but he wouldn't go into much more." The words had tumbled out, words Maud hadn't even dared to think out loud.

Annie pulled her gaze away from Frede and placed her hand on Maud's knee. "Is this what you thought?" When Maud didn't respond, Annie embraced her. Then, suddenly, another little hand was on her shoulder.

"Don't cry, Maudie," Frede said. "Mamma can fix it. She can fix anything."

Annie and Maud pulled apart and quietly laughed. "I don't know if I can fix this, dear one," Aunt Annie said. "But I am happy that you think I can."

Frede sat down between the two women.

"I'm not sure this is a story for young ears," Annie said, twisting Frede's braid with her index finger.

"I'm not young. I'm eight years old." Frede held up four fingers on each hand.

Maud hugged her. "You definitely have an old soul, dear Frede."

356

Perhaps because there were young ears present, old soul or not, Annie took her time answering. "They were caught together, alone. He had taken her on a buggy ride, and my brother John Franklin found them driving back. You know how people talk—"

Maud knew all too well.

"Being alone with someone—particularly someone my father, your grandfather, didn't approve of—well, it was decided that they should marry quickly to save your mother's reputation, and before Father could say anything in protest."

"So they did elope."

"Where did you hear that?"

"Two years ago." Maud caressed Frede's cheek. "Mollie and I heard Mrs. Simpson say something at one of the prayer meetings."

"Gossip in church." Annie frowned. "But there was talk . . . and Clara would never confirm to me if she had allowed things to get out of hand."

Everything went still. Was it possible? Somehow she knew. If she took a moment and counted back from the month of her birth, November, to the month her parents married, March, it was indeed possible. Mother would have had to have been pregnant almost immediately. Such things were possible, but . . .

"Maud," Aunt Annie said. "It was never clear what happened. Your mother loved your father very much, and they loved you very much."

Maud knew Aunt Annie was trying to take back what she hadn't said, what no one ever said.

Aunt Annie breathed deeply. She was in her own story now. "When Clara died, your grandmother became quite ill. A complication because of influenza. It almost killed her."

Maud had a hard time imagining her strong, stoic grandma ill.

"One night she actually lost consciousness, and we believed she had died."

"Why haven't I heard this before?"

"It's hard to talk about these things, Maud. The past is the past."

"But our family is always telling stories of the past. It is what we do."

"True." Annie laughed. "But there are stories of the past everyone wishes to bury, or allow to fade away like the edges of the Island."

Like what had happened with her parents.

"How did she get better?"

"I don't quite know. I suspect that one day she decided to. Emily was perhaps eighteen or nineteen and she was taking care of you. Maybe a part of my mother knew she had things to do."

"I don't think Grandma loves me." Maud thought of what Aunt Emily had said. "I'm only a duty to her."

"Lucy Maud Montgomery, don't you ever speak such nonsense again!" Aunt Annie said, tearing up. "My mother . . ." She took a deep breath. "My mother loves you. It is hard for her to see Clara's eyes staring back at her—"

"I have my father's eyes," Maud interrupted.

"You might have your father's shape, but the coloring is all hers, your complexion. I know it is hard for you to imagine, but you are so similar—all romantic and emotional. Clara enjoyed poetry too. I don't think Grandma even knows this consciously, but I truly believe you are the reason she decided to get better. That is how much she loves you."

Cradled by her aunt, with Frede snuggled in between them, Maud wept for all the lies she had believed, and the truths she had never known.

## CHAPTER ELEVEN

"I am a part of all that I have met," Maud read Tennyson's "Ulysses" aloud. On this beautiful June day, with the soft wind mingling with the sea air and the lupines in full bloom, cradling the Island in a rainbow of color, it was easy to feel a part of the land. Back in Cavendish, Maud was minding the post office for her grandparents, who had gone next door to conduct some business with Uncle John Franklin.

Truthfully, as much as Maud loved the laughter and lightness of Park Corner, she was happy to be home. Cavendish called to her, across miles of prairie, arboreal hills, and vast oceans. It was as much a part of her as her family's history and her favorite books.

After a few days back, Maud had found her rhythm. She was happy to reunite with her friends. She knew that their friendship would never again be as it was when they were young, but she was grateful that they could still do things together. Pensie had told Maud that she'd finally given Quill her answer and—to Maud's surprise—had refused him. She said she wanted someone who could know his own mind, whose self-doubts didn't make him petty. One day she would find someone, and only then would she cross that threshold.

Other things were changing too. When Maud had gone by the schoolhouse on her first day back, Miss Gordon told her she would be leaving Cavendish at the end of the summer to move to Oregon with family. The idea of it was almost too much to bear. No one had ever supported and cared about her ambitions more than Miss Gordon.

Maud's grandparents were also giving her more responsibility in the post office. This meant that Maud could keep watch for rejection letters—and, sadly, there were ever so many. The short story based on the blue chest had been rejected, but she would keep going. It was her calling.

Letters from Prince Albert continued to arrive every few weeks. She even heard from Father, who included a picture Katie had drawn for her. She wished that Katie could read; then Maud would write her sister her own special letter, without having to worry about others reading it. Maud could send it to Father, but she wasn't sure if Mrs. Montgomery would see it. Father wrote that he and Mrs. Montgomery were now working as wardens in the local jails—and that she had another brother. "You'll have to come and meet him," he wrote. But Maud knew that it would be years—if ever—until they met.

Maud ached with such a primal, deep urge to see Laura and Will. But the only way would be to marry Will or live with Father, and neither felt right. Marrying him would have made things so easy, but she wanted more.

Maud was turning the page when she heard the familiar whistle—like an old, half-forgotten song. She couldn't control the involuntary feeling of warmth that washed over her, from the back of her neck all the way down her spine. Slowly, she lifted her head and watched as he walked toward the door with the same swagger he'd always had.

Nate. He was taller, but otherwise, except for a more defined chin and mustache, he looked the same. She dropped her head and pretended to read, praying there was no stamp ink on her face or clothes, nervously closing her book and then reopening it. She wouldn't give Nate the satisfaction of seeing how much he'd flustered her. She hadn't heard from him in months and had thought their friendship finished, a long-ago pleasant memory. She focused on Tennyson.

"Reading love sonnets?"

She slowly lifted her head up over the book. "You know what I think about those, Nate Lockhart."

"I know what you would wish people to believe, Maud Montgomery."

How was it that he could still charm her with that grin?

"I wondered if we could go for a walk?"

"You're not here for the mail?"

"Yes, but it would be nice to reconnect with you, Polly."

The nickname rekindled an old spark that was as familiar as a hymn on Sunday morning.

"I'll check to see if there is any mail." She thought she had overcome the way she used to feel when he looked at her, but perhaps one never quite recovers from one's first love. There were two envelopes, which she brought back and handed to him.

"Give me a few moments to put these things away," she said, while he inspected his mail.

About twenty minutes later, Maud and Nate were rambling through Lover's Lane, the boughs and arches protecting them, giving them a place to walk unnoticed.

Nate talked of poetry and the law, and how he hoped to eventually set up a practice. As he spoke he grabbed hold of a branch, breaking off a leaf, snapping it in half.

They stopped and leaned against the broken fence.

"Will you be coming back here?" she asked.

"To visit. But if I plan to go to Dalhousie in Halifax, I think Nove Scotia is my home now. It is where I was originally from, after all," he said. "How about you?"

Maud took a few steps toward the brook, leaning into the leafy embrace of her favorite tree. "After traveling across Canada, things are different; they're smaller here than they once were." She turned around and faced him. "I would love to go to college in Halifax."

"A college education is certainly tougher than what we did back in our school days," he teased.

"Excuse me." Maud pushed off the tree trunk and marched right up to him. "I think I could still study circles around you."

Nate put his two hands up as if to surrender. "You definitely could." The familiarity of their banter was like coming home to something she had forgotten she missed.

"How long do you expect to be in Cavendish?" she asked.

"A few weeks."

"It will be nice to have you here to talk over old times. You, me, Mollie, and Jack."

"Yes, it will be nice." His smile hid his crooked teeth. "This is nice, now."

He was right. It was. She would never admit it to him, but there was, and always would be, something between them.

Nate was the first boy who had told her he loved her. He would always hold a place in her heart.

They stood there, under the arc of trees on Lover's Lane, in that in-between place where they had first kissed . . . and she wanted to kiss him now. It would be so simple to go back. But it wouldn't be fair to him, or to the boy she still loved in Prince Albert—or to her.

"Come," she said, extending her hand. "Walk me home."

# CHAPTER TWELVE

As Maud returned to the homestead, she briefly stopped at the turn that led up to the path past the schoolhouse. She admired the evening sun hovering over the Gulf and the small cemetery central to the whole village, watching over the people who still lived on this side of the veil. She whispered "good night" to her mother and turned toward home. Her grandparents were sitting outside, cool in the shade of Grandfather's nearby apple trees, which had started to sprout white flowers. The trees were calm tonight; there were only a few bugs and a little wind, and from a distance she could hear the Gulf murmuring. It was a truly perfect Island summer evening.

"How was Uncle John Franklin?" Maud asked, sitting down in an empty chair.

"He is well," Grandfather said.

"Lu was asking after you," Grandma said. "Perhaps you can go see her after supper. There are some raspberries over the hill and we can make a nice pie."

"A splendid idea, Grandma," Maud said and stood up. "Should I get supper on?"

"Just wait a moment, Maud." Grandfather said. "Please sit down."

That familiar creepy-crawly feeling tickled Maud's neck. Were they sending her away again? Had they discovered her journal? And if they had, would she burn it? It was one thing to condemn it to the flames when it had only been full of the trivialities of a girl who mostly described the weather, but it was entirely another to burn away the hard work of the last three years.

"Don't be so concerned, Maud," Grandma said, but she didn't say it unkindly. "One can always see what you're thinking." Grandma paused. "Like your mother."

Maud sat down, staring at her index finger where her ring had been.

"She does have that way about her," Grandfather said.

Grandma turned to Grandfather. "Much like you."

Maud stared, amazed. Had Grandma just teased Grandfather?

"Maud, your Grandma and I have been talking," Grandfather said. "We have been watching you these past few weeks, and we think you're wasting your talents."

"My talents?" Maud rubbed the back of her neck. "I-I didn't think you noticed."

Grandfather harrumphed.

"Just because we're old doesn't mean we don't see," Grandma said. "You've been working hard at the post office, but if we paid you a compliment it would give you airs, and people talk enough. But, we aren't getting any younger."

Maud's heart thrummed. What were they saying? Were they forcing her to move again?

And then Grandma said it: "Your grandfather and I have decided you can go back to school this year to prepare for the college entrance exam."

The Island grew quiet.

"While I still don't think it's appropriate for girls to teach," Grandfather said, "it's true we aren't getting any younger."

Maud was speechless.

"You already have some money saved up from your teaching this winter," Grandfather went on, "but you will have to manage the rest on your own. Perhaps one of those scholarships you wanted so badly."

She glanced at her grandmother, who was hiding the tiniest smile, and a suspicion quickly formed in Maud's mind. The organ teaching. Had this been Grandma's plan all along? She hadn't sent Maud away for being queer; she had orchestrated a way for Maud to make money. Maud had to admit that she'd wondered how her Campbell cousins, with all of those mouths to feed, could afford to pay for her room and board and salary each week. Now she understood where the money had come from. Grandma had devised a way for Maud to make money without Grandfather finding out. She was the one who had paid for Maud's months in Park Corner. If she weren't rooted to the spot—and if it wouldn't have shocked her grandparents—Maud would have leaped into their arms.

Grandfather stood up and absently patted Maud's arm. "Going to tend to the horses."

"Grandma. I . . . *thank you*, Grandma," Maud finally said, after he walked away.

"Close your mouth, girl, you look like a gutted fish." Grandma held Maud's gaze for a moment, still with that faint trace of a smile. "And you can thank us by studying hard and not falling prey to your emotions." She stood up. "Now, I need to go and get supper on. I'm sure you want to tell your friends the good news, but don't be long." As she watched her grandmother walk down the winding road to the house, Maud remembered what Aunt Annie had said about how much her grandmother really loved her.

A rush of wind and a crow's cry carried the silence into song and Maud ran down to the shore, the sun low and lapping against the Gulf. She undid her bun, the wind freeing her hair, carrying it up to the sky. Maud stood, gazing out past the Hole in the Wall to the far-off shore, tracing the place where her ring once was and knowing that one day it would be back on her finger.

Grandma was usually right about most things, but tonight she had been wrong: Maud didn't want to see her friends right now. There would be enough time to tell them the news, and Miss Gordon, before she left. Maud would write to Will and Laura, and even tell Nate when the Four Musketeers reunited over the summer.

For now, she welcomed the solitude of the moment between her and the land she loved.

Grandma was wrong about something else too. She had always tried to instil in Maud the idea that there was no place for her sensitive nature in this world, but that wasn't true. Maud could anchor herself in story.

She would write about girls who dreamed of words, art, music, and love—girls who were embraced by their communities and families, even if they were considered queer. She would create stories that came from the dark corners of her soul, giving voice to her rainbow valleys, shining waters, and disappointed houses. She would find a home for herself within them, living in the in-between.

# REFERENCES

p. 1, 76: Montgomery, L.M. *The Alpine Path: The Story of My Career*. Markham, ON: Fitzhenry and Whiteside, 1997.

pp. 111-112: Montgomery, L.M. L.M. Montgomery Journals. L.M. Montgomery Collection, University of Guelph Archives.

Rubio, Mary, and Elizabeth Waterson. *The Complete Journals of L.M. Montgomery: The PEI Years, 1889–1900*. Toronto: Oxford University Press, 2012.

p. 188, 191: Bolger, Francis W.P. *The Years Before* Anne: *The Early Career of Lucy Maud Montgomery, Author of* Anne of Green Gables. Halifax: Nimbus Publishing, 1991.

L.M. Montgomery to Pensie MacNeill, 1886–1894, L.M. Montgomery Institute Collection, Robertson Library, University Archives and Special Collections, University of Prince Edward Island.

p. 147, 299, 305: Bolger, Francis W.P. *The Years Before* Anne: *The Early Career of Lucy Maud Montgomery, Author of* Anne of Green Gables. Halifax: Nimbus Publishing, 1991.

p. vii: Bolger, Francis W.P. ed. *My Dear Mr. M: Letters to G.B. MacMillan from L.M. Montgomery*. Toronto: Oxford University Press, 1992.

p. 40: Motte Fouqué, Friedrich de La. *Undine*. London: Chapman and Hall, 1888.

This story is not a biography. While the plot, characters, and places are based on many primary and secondary sources, this is first and foremost a work of historical fiction.

After I was given this opportunity to write a fictional account about one of my favorite authors—a person whose novel *Anne of Green Gables* is so embedded in Canadian culture that people travel from all over the world to Prince Edward Island looking for Anne Shirley's grave—I remembered the biggest question I had while completing my first MA in history: What is the role of the historical fiction writer in creating a truth about who their subject really was, and how does that role influence our understanding of that subject? L.M. Montgomery is beloved by so many people, and I was cognizant of this, but in the end, I needed to listen to the heart of my story—who Maud without an *e* really is to me. My Maud had to be inspired by history, but she also had to be authentic. I needed to make her my own.

When Maud was fourteen, she burned the journal she had kept since she was nine and started a new one, but this one she vowed she would keep "locked up." I had to wonder: What was in it she didn't want people to see? And why?

This is where my story begins.

Maud left behind journals, scrapbooks, and other personal items (including her library), which are now mostly housed in the archives at the University of Guelph, in Ontario, Canada, and at the L.M. Montgomery Institute at the University of Prince Edward Island in Charlottetown. Although all of these items provide so many details about her life, Maud was very specific about what she wanted us to know about her. As she got older, Maud was focused on how her readers might think about her, so she created an image of a good minister's wife and mother, who was somehow able to balance both family and a prolific and prosperous writing career.

When she was in her forties, Maud sat down and decided to copy out her old journals into new, uniform ledgers, destroying the originals. These ten volumes can be found in Guelph and contain pictures that she took of her home, places she traveled, and the people she loved. And while Maud says that she copied her journals "word for word," there are sections that are so heavily edited (such as the mock trial scene that appears in this novel) they read like fiction. Also, some entries were sliced out, and then new ones, like Nate's love letter, were inserted. Maud's journal—normally a private document—was edited and revised into a version of her life she wished for us to see.

Another example of this is when Maud published her autobiography, "The Alpine Path," in *Everywoman's Magazine* in 1919, which focused on all of the things that influenced her writing career. Her editor had asked her to write about her old boyfriends, but she refused. Instead, she wrote about them in her journal. However, she had left specific instructions to her son Stuart that one day he could publish her journals. So, she wrote about something that she says she didn't want anyone to see with the full knowledge that her journals would one day be published!

Two people, Mary Rubio and Elizabeth Waterston, were asked by Stuart to edit the journals when the time was right, and they did. Most of the material that I used came from the original journals at Guelph, but also the ones that Rubio and Waterston edited: *The Complete Journals of L.M. Montgomery: The PEI Years,*

*1889–1900; The Complete Journals of L.M. Montgomery: The PEI Years, 1901–1911;* and the *Selected Volumes III, IV,* and *V.*

Maud wouldn't have known that her pen pals, G.B. Macmillan and Ephraim Webber, and friends, like Pensie, would keep her letters, giving us more information about their friendships and Maud's time in Prince Albert. I looked to these as well.

Some timelines were changed for the purpose of plot and pace. For example, the situation with Miss Izzie Robinson occurred in 1887 or 1888, when Maud was twelve or thirteen; Will doesn't appear in the journals until December 1891, and Laura appears a few weeks before that. I brought the time forward to strengthen the development of these relationships.

And, while most characters in the novel are based on people mentioned in Maud's journals and sources, my interpretation and creation of them is entirely fictional. A list of characters appears at the beginning of the novel. Certain friends and family members, such Mary Ann McRae Montgomery's half-siblings, and Mollie's and Pensie's siblings and others, were omitted to avoid reader confusion. This also meant that certain scenes, like the school trial, may have not included everyone: in the journal Clemmie, Nellie, Annie, Mamie, and others were there. As well, the character Mary Woodside's real name is Maud Wakefield, and Mrs. Elvira Simpson and Mrs. Matilda Clark are composites of some of the people Maud might have encountered.

The province of Saskatchewan was part of the North-West Territories and didn't officially become a province until 1905. In her letters to Pensie, Maud uses Prince Albert, N.W.T., as an address marker, but her journal says Prince Albert, Saskatchewan. This is most likely because the area was called the District of Saskatchewan in the North-West Territories. To avoid reader confusion, and because the area she was living in is Saskatchewan, I decided to simply refer to the province as we know it today. As well, Regina didn't officially become a city until 1903, but Maud mentions it by name in her journals.

It was also important for me to show what was happening with the Métis and Cree Nation peoples (*Nehiyawak*, specifically) while also being authentic to Maud's story. From her essay "A Western Eden," another essay she wrote in college, and a short story, "Tannis of the Flats," it is clear Maud was affected by what was happening to the Indigenous peoples.

"A Western Eden" and her journals have language and opinions that are offensive to us today, and some of this was replicated to show the times. Middle-class, Euro-Canadians like Maud believed that there was a big difference between themselves and Indigenous people. Maud would have felt compassion for the plight of the Métis and Cree Nation (*Nehiyawak*), but she would have seen them as less than her.

During the late nineteenth century, Indigenous people referred to themselves as either "Indian" or "Native." When Indigenous people called themselves "Indian," they didn't realize they were accepting an identity defined and controlled by the government. As Indigenous people's awareness grew, they began to insist on different terms. At first it was "Native", but this would also be rejected. More recently, people have preferred to use language or cultural names, such as *Nehiyawak*. The idea of identifying as a Nation is also relatively new.

As well, marriages between Indigenous and French settlers, which were forbidden by the Roman Catholic Church and Hudson's Bay Company, created a new people, identified as Métis by the French, who spoke Michif, a combination of French and Cree. These people established their own communities and cultural traditions. The term "Métis" was not used during this period by English people, who would have called them "Half-Breeds." Only the Métis would have identified themselves as Métis.

Maud did share a room with the maid, Edith (Edie) Skelton, but it isn't clear that she was Métis. It was common for people to hire Métis as maids, and given Maud's connection to this character, I decided to give Edie this identity. This also provided a personal reason for Maud's decision to write about the Métis and Cree Nation in "A Western Eden." I worked closely with Gloria Lee, a Cree–Métis from Chitek Lake, Saskatchewan, to help give Edie a voice. I'm indebted to her counsel for this part of the novel and for answering my questions on the Métis and Cree Nation in Saskatchewan. Every attempt was made for authenticity and accuracy; any errors are my own.

During the late nineteenth century, women in Canada didn't have many choices. While it is difficult for us to imagine, it was also not unusual for male teachers to show interest in a younger female student. Young women had little recourse in these situations, as teachers were considered symbols of authority in the community. If a man was seen courting a woman, like Mr. Mustard was, then it was also believed she must have done something to encourage him. It would also be one of the reasons why Maud's father might think that his daughter led her teacher on. Maud doesn't indicate if she ever went to her father for help, but does mention how he had joked about "passing the mustard" during dinner. Laura did conspire with Maud to make some of her evenings with Mustard challenging. And, although Will and Maud did pass notes in school and their friendship was troubling for Mustard, the amount of help Will provided was fictionalized.

Maud's use of humor in "A Western Eden" would be offensive to us today, but it does show, as I've explored in this novel, a young writer learning her craft. Maud would often use satire to highlight serious situations in her fiction, such as when Anne's teacher Mr. Philips in *Anne of Green Gables,* is shown to be a bad educator, not only because of his lack of skill, but also because of his flirtation with one of his students, Prissy Andrews. This was also most likely inspired by her experience with Mr. Mustard.

This novel takes place while Maud is just discovering what it means to be a writer and a woman. During a period where women's education (let alone being a writer) was considered inappropriate, Maud's passion, ambition, and dream for education set her apart. She didn't have the luxury that many women in the Western world have today, of being allowed to choose between ambition and career or love and marriage—or all of the above. Maud eventually would marry, in 1911 at the age of 37, and had three sons with Reverend Ewan Macdonald: Chester, Hugh (who died), and Stuart. By then she had worked for the *Daily Echo*, had a number of short stories and poems published, and was the bestselling author of 1908's *Anne of Green Gables*. Maud and her family lived in Leaskdale, Norval, and Toronto, Ontario, returning to the Island for visits in the summer.

Sadly, throughout her life, Maud suffered from depression. Her husband, Ewan, also had a condition called Religious Melancholia. Both took many different kinds of pills that were supposed to help them, but ended up doing them more harm than good. On April 24, 1942, after dropping off what would be her final manuscript, *The Blythes Are Quoted*, Maud died in her home, Journey's End, in Toronto.

Throughout her life, Maud wrote over five hundred short stories, twenty-one novels (one posthumously published), hundreds of poems, and a number of essays. She was a bestselling author who achieved financial success, as well as acclaim from her contemporaries, including Mark Twain. She became an Officer of the Order of the British Empire (OBE) in 1935, worked tirelessly for the Toronto chapter of the Canadian Authors Association, and mentored young writers, providing the guidance that she never really had as a teen writer.

My hope is that you will find something in my Maud to inspire you to ask questions, read her fiction, and discover your own ideas, your own truth, about who you think she is. And, perhaps, find a story of your own.

Melanie J. Fishbane, 2016

# WHAT HAPPENED TO MAUD'S FRIENDS

**NATHAN (SNIP) JOSEPH LOCKHART, JR. (1875–1954):** Nate completed his BA from Acadia College in 1895 and an MA in 1896. He and Maud continued to write letters and saw each other when he would visit his family, but eventually their correspondence trickled out. When the Spurrs left Cavendish in 1896, he stayed in Nova Scotia to teach, eventually entering Dalhousie University in Halifax and receiving his law degree in 1902. When Maud and Nate bumped into one another in 1901 at Dalhousie, she hoped he would contact her, but he didn't. They never saw one another again. Nate practiced law in Sydney, Nova Scotia, and married Mabel Celeste Saunders in 1906. That year, the Lockharts moved to Estevan, Saskatchewan, where he set up a law practice, and they had two sons. Nate had a very successful practice, eventually becoming a judge. After retiring to St. Petersburg, Florida, Nate died in 1954. He was seventy-nine. Some believe that Nate was the partial inspiration for Gilbert Blythe in the *Anne of Green Gables* series.

**AMANDA (MOLLIE) JANE MACNEILL (1874–1949):** After her mother died and her father (who suffered from depression) committed suicide, Mollie married George Henry Robertson (1875–1965), from Mayfield, a community part of the North Shore settlements, which included Cavendish. According to Maud, Mollie married George in July 1909 as a last resort, because she didn't want to end up an old maid. Mollie moved to Mayfield with George, where she lived for the rest of her life. They had no children. Maud and Mollie continued to correspond faithfully, but Maud often complained in her journals that Mollie had lost her youthful exuberance because she was unhappy in her marriage to a man she didn't love, growing old, sick, and bitter. Mollie's childhood home later fell into disrepair and was torn down when the government decided to build Green Gables park for the tourists who were coming to the Island to see where *Anne of Green Gables* took place. Hammie's Lane and the place where Mollie's house stood is now a golf course. Maud wished it had been turned into a historical site instead. Mollie died in 1949 at the age of seventy-five.

**PENSIE MARIA MACNEILL (1872–1906):** Pensie married William B. Bulman (1871–1947) and moved to his North Shore settlement, New Glasgow, in 1898. They had one son, Chester. Pensie and Maud maintained a friendship, but they were never as close as they had been when they were young, and Maud wasn't invited to Pensie's wedding, which hurt her quite deeply. Maud writes in her journal about how worried she was about Pensie's health and that she was working herself too hard. Maud's fears were well-founded; Pensie died of tuberculosis at the age of thirty-four, just when Maud was completing a draft of what would become *Anne of Green Gables*. Seventy years after Pensie died, Chester found Maud's letters to her childhood friend from her time in Prince Albert. These letters show how close these two women were when they were young, and how much their friendship meant to Pensie.

**LAURA PRITCHARD AGNEW (1874–1932):** Maud and Laura corresponded for over thirty-nine years, with a pause around the First World War, and Maud kept a picture of Laura on her bookshelf. After Maud left Prince Albert, Laura continued to court many beaux, including Andrew Agnew, who had to wait six years before she agreed to marry him on June 3, 1896, in Laurel Hill; he was thirty and she was twenty-two years old, and Will served as the best man. They had five children. Throughout her life, Laura volunteered for causes that were close to her heart, such as the Temperance movement, and played organ for prisoners at the local jail. In 1930, Maud contacted Laura as she was coming out West for a visit, and they had a joyous reunion, visiting Laurel Hill and reminiscing about her time in Prince Albert. Laura died unexpectedly two years later in 1932 at the age of fifty-seven. Many people believe that Laura inspired the character Diana from the *Anne of Green Gables* series. Maud's 1917 novel, *Anne's House of Dreams*, is dedicated to her.

**WILL GUNN PRITCHARD (1872–1897):** Will never went to university, working instead for his father on his ranch, but Will and Maud continued to correspond until his death of influenza in April 1897, at the age of twenty-five. When Maud found out, she read his ten-year letter and wrote, "It was a letter of love, and oh, how it hurt poor lonely me to read it!" Will is said to be another inspiration for the character of Gilbert Blythe in *Anne of Green Gables*. His photo sat on Maud's bedroom bookshelf, and when Laura sent the ring back, Maud wore it until she died, dedicating her final novel published during her lifetime, *Anne of Ingleside*, to "W.G.P."

# FURTHER READING

I'm grateful for the tremendous resources available through the L.M. Montgomery community. Below are some of the research and sources used to craft this novel.

## MONTGOMERY-RELATED WEBSITES

L.M. (Lucy Maud) Montgomery Literary Society http://lmmontgomery literarysociety.weebly.com

L.M. Montgomery Online http://lmmonline.org

L.M. Montgomery Institute http://www.lmmontgomery.ca

## ARCHIVES AND HISTORICAL SOCIETIES

Island Newspapers, UPEI, Robertson Library http://www.islandnewspapers.ca

Letters from L.M. Montgomery to Pensie Macneill, circa 1886–1894, University of Prince Edward Island, Robertson Library. University Archives and Special Collections. L.M. Montgomery Institute Collection.

The L.M. Montgomery Collection Archives and Special Collection, University of Guelph Archives http://www.lib.uoguelph.ca/find/find-type-resource/archival-special-collections/lm-montgomery

*Prince Albert Times*, Peel's Prairie Provinces, University of Alberta Libraries http://peel.library.ualberta.ca/newspapers/PAT/

Prince Albert Historical Society http://www.historypa.com

Provincial Archives of Saskatchewan http://www.saskarchives.com

University Archives and Special Collections, University of Saskatchewan http://library.usask.ca/archives/

Public Archives and Records Office, Prince Edward Island http://www.gov.
pe.ca/archives/

## MATERIALS ON MONTGOMERY

Bolger, Francis W.P. (1974) *The Years Before* Anne: *The Early Career of Lucy
Maud Montgomery, Author of* Anne of Green Gables. Halifax: Nimbus
Publishing, 1991.

Epperly, Elizabeth Rollins. *The Fragrance of Sweet-Grass: L.M. Montgomery's
Heroines and the Pursuit of Romance.* Toronto: University of Toronto
Press, 2014.

_____. *Through Lover's Lane: L.M. Montgomery's Photography and Visual
Imagination.* Toronto: University of Toronto Press, 2007.

_____. *Imagining Anne: The Island Scrapbooks of L.M. Montgomery.*
Toronto: Penguin Random House of Canada, 2008.

Gammel, Irene and Elizabeth Epperly, ed. *L.M. Montgomery and Canadian
Culture.* Toronto: University of Toronto Press, 1999.

Lefebvre, Benjamin, ed. *The L.M. Montgomery Reader. Volume One: A Life in
Print.* Toronto: University of Toronto Press, 2013.

McCabe, Kevin, comp. *The Lucy Maud Montgomery Album*, edited by
Alexandra Heilbron. Toronto: Fitzhenry and Whiteside, 1999.

Montgomery, L.M. *The Alpine Path.* Markham, ON: Fitzhenry and Whiteside,
1997.

Rubio, Mary Henley. *Lucy Maud Montgomery: The Gift of Wings.* Toronto:
Doubleday Canada, 2008.

Rubio, Mary Henley and Elizabeth Hillman Waterston, ed. *The Complete
Journals of L.M. Montgomery: The PEI Years, 1889 to 1910.* Don Mills, ON:
Oxford University Press, 2012.

_____. *The Selected Journals of L.M. Montgomery.* 5 vols. Don Mills, ON:
Oxford University Press, 1985.

Waterston, Elizabeth. *Magic Island: The Fictions of L.M. Montgomery.* Don
Mills, ON: Oxford University Press, 2008.

There are *many* different editions of Maud's novels. Here are some of the more recent ones.

Montgomery, L.M. *Anne of Green Gables*. (1908) Toronto: Tundra Books, 2014.

_____. *Anne of Avonlea*. (1909) Toronto: Tundra Books, 2014.

_____. *Anne of the Island*. (1915) Toronto: Tundra Books, 2014.

_____. *Anne's House of Dreams*. (1917) Toronto: Tundra Books, 2014.

_____. *Anne of Windy Poplars*. (1936) Toronto: Tundra Books, 2014.

_____. *Anne of Ingleside*. (1939) Toronto: Tundra Books, 2014.

_____. *The Story Girl*. (1911) Toronto: Doubleday Canada, 1987.

_____. *Emily of New Moon*. (1923) Toronto: Tundra Books, 2014.

_____. *Emily Climbs* (1925) Toronto: Tundra Books, 2014.

_____. *Emily's Quest* (1927) Toronto: Tundra Books, 2014.

_____. "Tannis of the Flats" in *Further Chronicles of Avonlea*. (1920) Toronto: Doubleday Canada, 1987.

## SOURCES ON HISTORY AND THE TIMES

Abrams, Gary. *Prince Albert: The First Century: 1866–1966*. Saskatoon: Modern Press, 1976.

Baldwin, Douglas. *Prince Edward Island: An Illustrated History*. Halifax: Nimbus Publishing, 2009.

Carter, Sarah. *Lost Harvests: Prairie Indian Reserve Farmers and Government Policy*. Montreal: McGill–Queens University Press, 1990.

Conrad, Margaret. *A Concise History of Canada*. New York: Cambridge University Press, 2012.

Lamontagne, Manon, et al., ed. *The Voice of the People: Reminiscences of Prince Albert Settlement's Early Citizens 1866–1895*. Prince Albert, SK: Prince Albert Historical Society, 1985.

Meacham, J.H. *Illustrated Historical Atlas of Prince Edward Island*. J.H. Meacham & Co. 1880: Compact Edition. Charlottetown: PEI Museum and Heritage Foundation, 2013.

Porter, Jene M., ed. *Perspectives of Saskatchewan*. Winnipeg: University of Manitoba Press, 2009.

Waiser, Bill. *Saskatchewan: A New History*. Allston, MA: Fitzhenry and Whiteside, 2006.

# IN GRATITUDE

If you are reading this in 2017, it has been roughly five years since I began working on this novel. I'm deeply grateful to the many communities of authors, scholars, historians, archivists, religious leaders, bloggers, and friends who took the time out to talk with me about horse-and-buggy math (Silvio Spina and Dad), late nineteenth century fashion (Lissa Fonseca and Jason Dixon), and other random questions (Facebook, my blogger friends, and Twitter peeps, I'm looking at you).

For being an "Editor of Awesome," Lynne Missen. You changed everything. Thank you for believing I could do this.

For additional feedback, copy, and editorial suggestions: Shana Hayes, Brittany Lavery, Peter Phillips, and Helen Smith.

For tea, scones, and being the Queen of Publicity: Vikki Vansickle.

For connections to Montgomery that are no accident: Liza Morrison.

And to the rest of the Penguin Random House of Canada team who worked on this novel, thank you for all of your efforts in helping to make this book the best it could be.

For believing in this project and support: Kate Macdonald Butler and Sally Keefe-Cohen.

For telling stories and driving with me around Cavendish: Jennie and John Macneill.

For telling stories and the mysteries of Park Corner: George, Maureen, and Pamela Campbell.

For telling stories and allowing us to prowl around Ingleside: Robert Montgomery.

To the entire L.M. Montgomery community and Islanders for providing insight and information— sometimes at a moment's notice: L.M. Montgomery Society of Ontario, the L.M. Montgomery Heritage Society, L.M. Montgomery Literary Society, and the L.M. Montgomery Institute at the University of Prince Edward Island. You are also: Balaka Basu, Linda Boutilier, Rita Bode, Vanessa Brown, Mary Beth Cavert, Lesley Clement, Carolyn Strom Collins, Elizabeth DeBlois, Elizabeth Epperly, Irene Gammel, Kathy Gastle, Linda and Jack Hutton, Vappu Kannas, Yuka Kajihara, Caroline E. Jones, Benjamin Lefebvre, Jennifer Lister, Simon Lloyd, Andrea McKenzie, Tara K. Parmiter, E. Holly Pike, K.L. Poe, Laura Robinson, Mary Henley Rubio, Philip Smith, Kate Sutherland, Åsa Warnqvist, Elizabeth Waterston, Kathy Wasylenky, Melanie Whitfield, and Emily Woster.

Christy Woster died suddenly before the completion of the novel. Her generosity in sharing her research on Maud's schoolbooks and hymnals was essential to Book One. I dedicate this section to her.

For giving me a place to stay, road tripping through northern Saskatchewan, and finding Laurel Hill: Wendy Roy and Garth Cantrill.

For gathering books, photos, journals, and other artefacts for me at the L.M. Montgomery Collection at the University of Guelph Archives: Jan Brett, Bev Buckie, Kathryn Harvey, Melissa McAfee, Ashley Shifflett McBrayne, and Darlene Wiltsie.

For giving me leads: the archivists who helped me at the Public Archives and Records Office of Prince Edward Island, the Presbyterian Church of Canada, and the Library Archives of Canada.

For telling stories and driving us around Prince Albert—and the map making: Ken Guedo.

For sending photos and documents, and verifying all of the little details: the Prince Albert Historical Society, and its archivist,

Michelle Taylor, as well as Jamie Benson, Norman Hill, and Glenda Goertzen.

For letting us explore the land that was Laurel Hill: Johannes and Emily Van der Laan.

For providing history and context at the Prince Albert Cemetery: Derek Zbaraschuz.

For showing me Summerside, nineteenth-century style: Archivist/Collections Coordinator at the MacNaught History Centre & Archives, Fred Horne.

To the staff at the Oakwood Village Branch at the Toronto Public Library, thank you for tracking down all of those books and being so supportive of this project.

To the many Canadian and American Indigenous writers, artists, and educators who took the time to speak with me, particularly Prince Albert Métis Women's Association, Wordcraft Circle, Indigenous Knowledge Systems Educator in Moose Jaw, Barb Frazer, and Gloria Lee, a Cree–Métis from Chitek Lake, Saskatchewan.

For the impromptu late-nineteenth-century history lesson and providing me with the cultural framework for this novel: Professor Gavin Taylor from Concordia University.

For providing me with insight into Presbyterianism and growing up Christian: Vanessa Brown, Andrea Hibrant-Raines, Julie Kraut, Andrea Lindsay, Rachel McMillan, and Blake Walker.

For explaining the organ: Edwin Brownell, Jacob Letkemann, and Mimi Mok.

For explaining horses: Felicia Quon.

A number of people also courageously read in part or in full many drafts. Thank you: Kathi Appelt, Mark Karlins, and the Vermont College of Fine Arts (VCFA) group who workshopped the first fifteen pages of a very early draft; Jen Bailey, Kelly Barston, Amy Rose Capetta, Beth Dranoff, Jessica Denhart, Betsy Epperly, Peter Langella, Benjamin Lefebvre, Meghan Matherne, Kekla

Magoon, Katharine MacDonald, Rebecca Maizel, Cori McCarthy, Mary Pleiss, Tristan Poehlmann, Simon Lloyd, Ingrid Sundberg; and those who attended the VCFA writers' June 2015 retreat: Katie Bayerl, Caroline Carlson, Mary E. Cronin, Erin Hagar, Jim Hill, Maggie Lehrman, Lori Goe Perez, Barb Roberts, Adi Rule, and Nicole Valentine.

To the faculty and community of the Vermont College of Fine Arts Writing for Children and Young Adults program, and the voices inside my head, my advisors: Sharon Darrow, Sarah Ellis, Mary Quattlebaum, and Rita Williams-García. As well as Alan Cumyn, who saw something in my writing before I did.

And, to the rest of my VCFA class, the Dystropians: Shayda Bakshi, Stephen Bramucci, Laura Cook, Rachel Cook, Heidi Landry Phelps, Winter Quisgard, Sheryl Scarborough, Jeff Schill, Heather Strickland, and Ariel Woodruff. We survive.

To the vivacious Canadian author communities of IBBY, CANSCAIP (and the very helpful listserv) and TORkidLit; as well as Karleen Bradford, Stephen Geigen-Miller, Linda Granfield, Claire Humphrey, Karen Krossing, Sharon McKay, Debbie Ridpath Ohi, Gillian O'Reilly, Marsha Forchuk Skrypuch, Arthur Slade, Kevin Sylvester, Frieda Wishinsky, and Nicole Winters.

For covering me while I worked on an early draft of the novel: members of Indigo's Online Merch team, especially Michael Bacal, Josh Fehrens, Michael Gallagher, Anne Lee, Meg Mathur, and Eva Quan.

For your continual support and encouragement: the faculty and administration of the School of Liberal Arts and Science at Humber College, including Trevor Arkell, Vera Beletzan, Eufemia Fantetti, Kelly Harness, and Matthew Harris.

For being there at the beginning, the middle, and the end: Sarah Cooper, Alex Gershon, Terry Gould, Holly Kent, Stephen Graham King, Caroline Nevin, Luis Latour, Alex MacFadyen,

Rachel McMillan, Kate Newman, Laird Orr, James Roy, Rosemarie Schade, and Tamar Spina.

To my parents for building a home that nurtured creativity.

To my brother for your bravery.

To my grandmother, who reminds me to "continue what it is that I'm doing."

And to Raff, for all of the things.

Thank you . . .